THE DEAD OF WINTER

Something tugged at the leg of his thermal suit.

Vito shook his foot reflexively. It was a moment before the thought hit him: nothing out here should tug at him. There was no animal life, no vegetation. As he swung the flashlight beam down to look, something ripped through the thermal suit, through the flesh of his leg, and scraped the bone below his knee. Not until he fell and saw the bright red arterial blood pumping out onto the snow did Vito slap at his communicator panel and open his mouth to scream for help. It was too late.

Claws ripped away his face plate and tore out his tongue...

—from *The Ice Children*

Other Avon Books by
Tim Sullivan

DESTINY'S END
THE MARTIAN VIKING
THE PARASITE WAR

**And Don't Miss This Other Horrific Anthology
Edited by Tim Sullivan**

TROPICAL CHILLS

Avon Books are available at special quantity discounts for bulk purchases for sales promotions, premiums, fund raising or educational use. Special books, or book excerpts, can also be created to fit specific needs.

For details write or telephone the office of the Director of Special Markets, Avon Books, Dept. FP, 1350 Avenue of the Americas, New York, New York 10019, 212-261-6800.

COLD SHOCKS

Edited by
TIM SULLIVAN

AVON BOOKS • NEW YORK

If you purchased this book without a cover, you should be aware that this book is stolen property. It was reported as "unsold and destroyed" to the publisher, and neither the author nor the publisher has received any payment for this "stripped book."

Additional copyright notices appear on the acknowledgments pages, which serve as an extension of this copyright page.

COLD SHOCKS is an original publication of Avon Books. This work has never before appeared in book form. This is a work of fiction. Any similarity to actual persons or events is purely coincidental.

AVON BOOKS
A division of
The Hearst Corporation
1350 Avenue of the Americas
New York, New York 10019

Copyright © 1991 by Timothy R. Sullivan
Cover art by Robert Goldstrom
Published by arrangement with the editor
Library of Congress Catalog Card Number: 91-91781
ISBN: 0-380-76160-2

All rights reserved, which includes the right to reproduce this book or portions thereof in any form whatsoever except as provided by the U.S. Copyright Law. For information address Valerie Smith, Literary Agent, R.D. Box 160, Modena, New York 12548.

First Avon Books Printing: August 1991

AVON TRADEMARK REG. U.S. PAT. OFF. AND IN OTHER COUNTRIES, MARCA REGISTRADA, HECHO EN U.S.A.

Printed in the U.S.A.

RA 10 9 8 7 6 5 4 3 2 1

ACKNOWLEDGMENTS

"The Ice Children" by Gary Brandner. Copyright © 1991 by Gary Brandner. An original story used by arrangement with the author.

"First Kill" by Chet Williamson. Copyright © 1991 by Chet Williamson. An original story used by arrangement with the author and the author's agents, the Scott Meredith Literary Agency, Inc.

"Colder Than Hell" by Edward Bryant. Copyright © 1991 by Edward Bryant. An original story used by arrangement with the author.

"The Kikituk" by Michael Armstrong. Copyright © 1991 by Michael Armstrong. An original story used by arrangement with the author and the author's agents, Curtis Brown, Ltd.

"The Christmas Escape" by Dean Wesley Smith. Copyright © 1991 by Dean Wesley Smith. An original story used by arrangement with the author.

"A Winter Memory" by Michael D. Toman. Copyright © 1991 by Michael D. Toman. An original story used by arrangement with the author.

"The Sixth Man" by Graham Masterton. Copyright © 1991 by Graham Masterton. An original story used by arrangement with the author.

Acknowledgments

"The Ice Downstream" by Melanie Tem. Copyright © 1991 by Melanie Tem. An original story used by arrangement with the author.

"Morning Light" by Barry N. Malzberg. Copyright © 1991 by Barry N. Malzberg. An original story used by arrangement with the author.

"Bring Me the Head of Timothy Leary" by Nancy Holder. Copyright © 1991 by Nancy Holder. An original story used by arrangement with the author.

"The Bus" by Gregory Frost. Copyright © 1991 by Gregory Frost. An original story used by arrangement with the author.

"Adleparmeun" by Steve Rasnic Tem. Copyright © 1991 by Steve Rasnic Tem. An original story used by arrangement with the author.

"Close to the Earth" by Gregory Nicoll. Copyright © 1991 by Gregory Nicoll. An original story used by arrangement with the author.

"Snowbanks" by Tim Sullivan. Copyright © 1991 by Timothy R. Sullivan. An original story used by arrangement with the author.

"St. Jackaclaws" by A.R. Morlan. Copyright © 1991 by A.R. Morlan. An original story used by arrangement with the author.

"The Pavilion of Frozen Women" by S.P. Somtow. Copyright © 1991 by Somtow Sucharitkul. An original story used by arrangement with the author.

CONTENTS

Introduction
  Tim Sullivan — 1

The Ice Children
  Gary Brandner — 7

First Kill
  Chet Williamson — 25

Colder Than Hell
  Edward Bryant — 37

The Kikituk
  Michael Armstrong — 53

The Christmas Escape
  Dean Wesley Smith — 89

A Winter Memory
  Michael D. Toman — 97

The Sixth Man
  Graham Masterton — 121

The Ice Downstream
  Melanie Tem — 141

Morning Light
  Barry N. Malzberg — 155

Bring Me the Head of Timothy Leary
  Nancy Holder — 163

Contents

The Bus
    Gregory Frost   *177*

Adleparmeun
    Steve Rasnic Tem   *193*

Close to the Earth
    Gregory Nicoll   *207*

Snowbanks
    Tim Sullivan   *223*

St. Jackaclaws
    A.R. Morlan   *251*

The Pavilion of Frozen Women
    S.P. Somtow   *265*

Introduction

by Tim Sullivan

What is it that chills us when we are afraid? Is it physiological? Biochemical? Or something less tangible? Even today, tribal cultures in the polar regions attribute much human and meteorological behavior to animism, just as they did thousands of years ago. Nor did the ancients separate internal sensations from external causes, as modern, psychologically oriented man tends to do. In fact, the forces of nature have been the province of the divine since prehistory, fostering beliefs that have mutated with the coming of civilization, but which have never entirely vanished. The spring sun is the kiss of the gods, and the gentle breeze their breath—or so the Greeks believed. The movements of the tides were due to the regularity of Poseidon's habits, and storms at sea to his rages. Even the movements of the stars were determined by Skyfather Zeus and his fellow denizens of Olympus. The Romans superimposed these humanoid gods upon the strange deities of Etruria, and later adopted such Eastern gods as the Persian Mithras and the Egyptian Isis to account for the mysteries of the seasons as well as the soul.

But these humanized gods were not worshiped north of the Mediterranean. Lug and other monstrous Celtic deities demanded human sacrifice, and their worshipers dutifully burned fellow human beings to death in baskets (this charming ritual was graphically depicted in the 1973 film *The Wicker Man*), or drowned them in the misty marshes of France, Switzerland, Belgium, and the British Isles.

Still farther north lurked the Scandinavian monster Grendel and his hideous mother, not to mention the gods and monsters of the *Völsunga Saga*—in which the murderer Sigi turns into a wolf in the opening stanzas—and later the German *Nibelungenlied*. Siegfried would not have been half the hero he was if he hadn't faced such terrors as a dragon and a twisted dwarf king, the latter wearing the cloak of Aesir, which rendered him invisible (wonderfully evoked by the great director Fritz Lang in the silent German epic *Siegfried*, 1922). William Morris's translation of the *Völsunga Saga* was a landmark of the pre-Raphaelite movement in nineteenth-century British literature, reawakening interest in the myths and superstitions of the ancient Norse, pagan beliefs that had seemingly vanished after the advent of Christianity.

One imagines these legends originally evolving around a fire as a wind coming off the fjord howls through the creaking beams of the mead hall. Fenris's shadow covers the land, and the gods of Asgard offer no succor to men and women raised in such a harsh and dreary place. Few crops grow in this inhospitable climate, so the men sail off to warmer shores and sing their berserker songs to Odin as they chop down their opponents and take booty where they may find it. Perhaps the modern mind cannot envision how terrible the Viking gods were, preternatural beings feared by these wild warriors more than death itself. Even at home, the Norsemen were not averse to violence in the name of their bloodthirsty deities. Missionaries were routinely slaughtered in Iceland until a volcano erupted, convincing the locals that the Christians labored in the service of a powerful god indeed.

Despite the ultimate encroachment and triumph of civilization, however, the darkness of the northern coun-

INTRODUCTION

tries has retained its angst-ridden mystique through the centuries. Poe's claim that the terror he spoke of was "not of Germany but of the soul," refers to his resistance to the popularity of Teutonic settings in the mid-nineteenth-century tale of terror. Even so, Poe succumbed to the temptation at least once, in the early short story "Metzengerstein." And any student of American literature cannot fail to recall that Poe himself died of exposure after lying in a Baltimore alley on a cold November night in 1849, a factual horror story that has been treated fictionally a number of times, notably by Angela Carter in "The Cabinet of Edgar Allan Poe" (1982) and by Fritz Leiber in "Richmond, Late September" (1969).

Desolate cold, land turned lifeless with ice and snow, naked trees whose jagged branches resemble skeletal hands in the moonlight . . . Is it any wonder that such wintry scenes evoke fear? Anyone who has read T.H. White's superb "The Troll," written in 1933, or "Silent Snow, Secret Snow" by Conrad Aiken (1934), can appreciate how effective such barren landscapes can be. Algernon Blackwood's 1910 tale of an evil Canadian Indian spirit, "The Wendigo" is undeniably a classic of horror. In the post war era, there is Howard Hawks's arctic-bound *The Thing* (1951), one of the scariest movies ever made (based on a 1938 science fiction story by John W. Campbell, "Who Goes There," remade by John Carpenter in 1982) and Stephen King's powerful evocation of the unrelenting bleakness of New England winter falling in *Salem's Lot*, for my money one of the creepiest passages in the entire canon of modern horror.

Which brings us to the original works at hand. Graham Masterton contributes a tale of polar exploration with bite, "The Sixth Man," displaying this popular British writer's aptitude for history as well as horror. Gary Brandner's fast-paced "The Ice Children" brings to life an ancient Eskimo superstition with chilling directness, showing the best-selling author of *The Howling* in fine form, while another werewolf novelist, S.P. Somtow (*Moon Dance*), takes us to a snow festival in Sapporo, Japan, for some cross-cultural terror in "The Pavilion of Frozen Women," an exceptionally beautiful title for an extraordinary novella. Edward Bryant shows his usual deft hand in "Colder Than Hell," and Michael Toman provides us with a subtle and effective parable, "A Winter Memory," concerning a time when the sun no longer seems to shine. A new sort of monster is created for the holidays by A.R. Morlan, in her highly original "St. Jackaclaws." The dangers of alcoholism in the Alaskan winter are explored in horrific fashion by Michael A. Armstrong in "The Kikituk," and the dread of aging and death is touched upon by Dean Wesley Smith in "The Christmas Escape." A freezing blast from the past is provided by Nancy Holder in "Bring Me the Head of Timothy Leary," a story as rambunctiously radical as its title suggests. In "Adleparmeun," Steve Rasnic Tem's tortured antagonist wanders the snow-swept streets of Denver, dreaming waking nightmare visions of an ancient tribal religion. Melanie Tem, who is married to Steve (can this be the first horror anthology containing separate stories by two life partners?), contributes a low-key piece that stays with you in "The Ice Downstream." "Morning Light" is Barry N. Malzberg's exquisitely turned meditation on the chilling torments of great artists. Gregory Nicoll's traveler stops into the wrong roadside diner on a particularly unseasonable night in "Close to the Earth," while Tim Sullivan tells of a little boy in New England who digs a little too deeply into some unusual "Snowbanks." Gregory Frost's "The Bus" mercilessly evokes a winter's day for a homeless person in a big American city. Finally, Chet Williamson does an expert job of disturbing the reader with his tale of two hunters in "First Kill."

So make yourself a cup of hot tea, toss some logs on

the fire, turn on the electric blanket, and settle back to enjoy sixteen *Cold Shocks*. Even if it's the hottest day in August, these stories are guaranteed to chill you to the bone.

The Ice Children

by Gary Brandner

Gary Brandner is a humorous, down-to-earth guy who hero-worships the late John Wayne. In fact, Gary does a pretty passable Duke impression. He was born in Sault Sainte Marie, Michigan, but grew up mainly in the Pacific Northwest, graduating from the University of Washington with a B.A. in Journalism. His early jobs included survey crew member, loan company investigator, television scriptwriter, advertising copywriter, and aerospace technical writer. He became a full-time free-lance writer in 1969.

His hobbies are pool, "old" radio, horse playing, beer drinking, and tennis. Besides John Wayne, his personal heroes are Hammett, Hemingway, Mickey Spillane, and Captain Marvel. Gary has published some twenty-nine books, sixty-eight short stories, and five screenplays.

The helicopter settled like a fat orange bug onto a smooth patch of glacial ice half the size of a tennis court. Powder snow whipped into clouds under the rotor. The blades slowed and stopped. The hatch opened, and four climbed out one at a time. They were clad in Day-Glo thermal suits of red, blue, green, and yellow for visibility and identification purposes in the frozen landscape of white and shadow.

Like the well-drilled team they were, the quartet performed their practiced tasks in covering the helicopter with thermal-reflective Mylar. This done, they came together in a huddle.

Colonel Mason Bettiger peered into the eyes of each of his teammates, trying to read the expressions behind the transparent face plates.

Vito Calli, slim and athletic in the blue thermal suit, raised a gloved hand in salute and grinned at him. Calli, a navy pilot, was the youngest member of the group. Each of them was checked out to operate the copter in an emergency, but Vito Calli had the confidence and experience necessary for flying into the icy unknown.

The dark, blunt-featured face of John Savitch, the geologist, betrayed no emotion. This land of ice and killing cold was his heritage, yet he alone of the four had to be persuaded to join the expedition. He smoothed the front of his green thermal suit and looked away.

Allison Denny, the photojournalist, could not disguise her trim figure, encased though it was by the bright yellow suit. Her calm intelligent gaze met Bettiger's, and it was he who blinked first.

"We're about, what, two hundred yards from the location shown in the satellite pictures?" His voice came clear and bloodless, filtered through the headphones built into each of the compact helmets.

Vito Calli touched his speaker button. "That's about right. This was as close as I could put down with all the broken ice in this area. This stuff is constantly shifting and throwing up jagged edges."

Allison Denny held up the winter-proofed videocam. "All right if I go on ahead? I want to get some shots of the site before anything's disturbed."

"We all go together," Bettiger said. "Maintain visual and voice contact at all times. Our first job is to set up camp. Then we proceed to the site. Together." He reminded himself that this was not a military mission, and his rank carried little weight with the two civilians in the party. He tried to soften his tone. "You'll have time for all the pictures you want."

"Two days max," said John Savitch. "That was the plan."

"That's still the plan," said Bettiger. "It's all the time we should need to identify whatever it was the satellite spotted. And for Miss Denny to get her pictures."

He could not resist throwing in the *Miss*. It rankled him that the mission was being bankrolled not by the economy-bound Defense Department, but by Allison Denny's employer, Transworld Media.

The four people moved efficiently, removing the materials in pre-sorted order from the helicopter. In forty-five minutes they had erected a sturdy, lightweight shelter a short distance from the copter. The shelter contained the necessities for their short stay, and provided protection from the deep sub-zero temperature outside.

When the shelter interior had warmed to about zero, Vito Calli popped open his faceplate, puffed out a cloud of steam, and stretched out on an inflatable chair. "No place like home."

"Save it, Vito, we've got a lot to accomplish before dark."

"Aye, aye, Skipper." The navy pilot winked, letting Bettiger know that he was well aware of who was paying for the show.

They checked their thermal suits and left the shelter single file, Vito first, then Bettiger and Allison.

John Savitch hesitated.

Bettiger punched the green button of his communicator panel, cutting the others out of the transmission. "Something bothering you, John?"

"This is a bad place."

" 'Bad place'? What does that mean?"

"There are legends."

"John, you're a scientist. You're not going to tell me you're worried about some Indian superstition."

"Eskimo, Colonel. My heritage is Eskimo. That's the reason I was sent on this exercise. There are plenty of geologists."

"All right, Eskimo then. What's the problem?"

"As I said, this is a bad place. I can feel it. We should not have come."

Bettiger controlled his impatience. "Well, we're here now, so we might as well do what we came to do—identify what showed up in those satellite pictures. Two days and we're out of here. Okay?"

"I hope so." Savitch clapped his faceplate shut and left the shelter.

Bettiger hesitated a moment before he followed. The last thing he needed was a geologist with an attitude. They had a forty-eight-hour window to accomplish their mission, and there was no slack for disagreements among the party. He mentally reviewed their mission. Photographs taken a month before by a U.S. reconnaissance satellite showed signs of human habitation high on the Greenland side of the Kennedy Channel, across from Ellesmere Island. That caught their attention in Washington, since nothing was supposed to live within 200 miles of the area. Not surprising, considering that the ambient temperature ranged from minus fifty degrees Fahrenheit downward.

The craggy, constantly shifting slabs of glacier ice made it slow going from the camp to the site of the photographs. As the four people topped the final ridge they stood motionless for a moment looking at what lay just below them.

As the satellite photos had shown, there was a dark rectangular patch on the ice, roughly twenty feet by forty. Clearly, it was the relic of a man-made structure, but not a recent one, as had been surmised by some at the Pentagon. This was what remained of a camp long abandoned.

"Looks like we can't blame the Russians for this one," Calli said.

"Vito, don't you know the Cold War is over?" Allison said.

"Oh, excuse me. I haven't read the morning update on who are the good guys and who are bad."

Allison ignored him. She balanced the videocam on her shoulder and began shooting.

"Let's go down and check it out," Bettiger said. "Watch your steps. We don't want any casualties."

The colonel and the pilot made their way cautiously down the icy slope to the remains of the structure. Allison followed, filming their progress. John Savitch remained above them on the ridge for a moment. He looked off to the white horizon, rubbed his upper arms as though the cold could seep through the green thermal fabric, and finally followed the others.

After forty minutes they had determined that the rectangle was indeed the remains of a camp structure. Vito Calli, chipping away an oddly shaped clump of ice called out, "Hey, Skipper, I think I've got something."

The others gathered around as Bettiger used his de-icer to uncover an electronic black box of a design not used in thirty years. A plate affixed to the box bore the initials H.L.K., and a series of code numbers.

Bettiger studied the inscription, then looked up. "It's the Kellogg expedition. The navy mission that never came back. That was what? Nineteen fifty-four?"

Allison lowered the camera as she looked at Bettiger. "But weren't they northeast of here a couple of hundred miles?"

Bettiger looked at her. "You've done your homework. That was where they were headed, but in all these years the ice shift could have carried their camp down here."

"How come the satellite pictures never showed it before?" Vito wondered.

Bettiger jerked a gloved thumb toward the blue-white sky. "Weather conditions. This area is under an almost constant storm. The most recent one lasted nine months. It was probably those winds that uncovered what we have here."

John Savitch was looking off to the horizon again. "This calm won't last long."

"All we need is today and tomorrow," Bettiger said. "Let's get as much done as we can before dark."

"*Oh my God!*"

The three men looked up from their tasks at the sound of Allison's startled voice in their headphones. They converged on her as she stood, camera hanging at her side, staring at a patch of upthrust ice she had rubbed clear.

"Sorry," she said in a controlled voice. "That wasn't very professional"—she pointed with the camera—"but is that what I think it is?"

Bettiger knelt and brought his face close to the smooth patch of ice. He rubbed it with the heel of his glove. Frozen inside, distorted by the refraction, but unmistakable, was a man's hand.

Bettiger rose and nodded to Calli. "Cut it out of there and let's get it back to the base. Be careful not to damage it."

An hour later the three men and the woman sat in their shelter around a microwave heating unit the size of a football helmet. Inside, thawed, and with the excess moisture evaporated, lay the hand. The flesh was bloodless and dead white, but otherwise in good condition. The nails were pared short, the palm uncallused. On the third finger was a class ring.

"Annapolis," Calli said.

"Commander Kellogg," Allison added.

"So it appears," said Bettiger. He rotated the turntable

THE ICE CHILDREN

of the heating unit to expose the wrist end of the hand. The pale flesh there was ragged, the bones splintered. Tendons protruded from the bloodless meat like stiff yellow worms.

Vito Calli spoke for all of them. "What the hell tore the man's hand off like that? And where's the rest of him?"

"And the others?" Allison said. "There were six in the party."

"No point in us speculating," Bettiger said. "We'll let the lab people in Washington answer the questions."

John Savitch touched his sleeve and beckoned him away. They walked over to stand by the thermal hatch and adjusted their communicators to exclude the others.

"We have to get out of here," said Savitch.

"The mission was planned for two days. We have one day left."

"The weather's going to turn tonight. And that's not the worst."

"What is this, Indian—pardon me, Eskimo—intuition?"

"This is a bad place."

"So you told me." Bettiger softened his tone. "John, believe me, I respect your instincts. That's one of the reasons you were chosen. But I can't abort the mission because you have bad vibrations."

"Then do this for me, post a guard outside tonight."

"To guard against what?"

Savitch gave him a tight smile. "Eskimo intuition."

Bettiger's expression remained grim. He nodded, opened his communicator to the others and called them together.

"Tomorrow at first light we'll resume at the Kellogg campsite. We have eight hours of darkness tonight. Each of us will take a two-hour watch outside while the others sleep. Allison, you take the first watch, then John, Vito, and I'll take the last."

Allison and Calli looked at him curiously, but Bettiger's expression discouraged questions.

He unholstered a .45 caliber Colt semi-automatic pistol. "This is the only weapon we have among us. I want whoever is on guard to carry it."

Vito watched as Allison accepted the pistol. "Colonel, it's too cold for anything animal or vegetable to survive out there. What are we going to shoot at?"

"Just carry the gun, okay?"

Vito shrugged. Allison tucked the pistol into her utility belt, took one of the powerful flashlights, and left the shelter.

Bettiger did not sleep during Allison's watch. Periodically the flashlight beam swept over the shelter's window panel. John Savitch stirred in his mummy bag, and Bettiger knew the Eskimo was wakeful, too. When Allison returned after her two hours he relaxed. He told himself he had been unduly influenced by the Eskimo's somber mood.

"Everything quiet outside?" he asked, making it casual.

"Why wouldn't it be?" Allison said. "The wind's picking up. End of report. What was I supposed to be watching for, anyway?"

"Just watching." Bettiger was feeling a little foolish. "Get some sleep."

Allison turned the pistol and flashlight over to John Savitch and zipped herself into the yellow mummy bag.

Savitch paused at the hatch and looked back at Bettiger. He gave the colonel a casual salute and went out into the frigid night.

Bettiger jerked awake from an uneasy sleep two hours later when Savitch returned.

"Everything okay?"

"Ice storm's going to hit by morning."

"We're equipped to handle it."

THE ICE CHILDREN

"Maybe."

Bettiger shook Vito by the shoulder. The pilot awoke grumbling, took the .45 from Savitch, gave his suit the routine check, and went out the thermal-lock hatch.

It was, Vito decided once he was outside, going to be a long two hours. The suit protected him against the killing cold, but the rising wind made it difficult to stay upright. He swung the powerful flashlight in an arc. Blowing ice crystals slanted across the beam. Blue-black shadows danced across the broken white surface.

He wished, not for the first time, that he had not been talked into giving up cigarettes. One would sure taste good right now. Not that he could smoke it here. The image of him lighting up inside the thermal helmet brought a wry smile. His head would explode like an egg in a flame.

The smile faded. The image of the ripped off hand pushed into his consciousness. The class ring from Annapolis somehow made it worse. Vito Calli, for one, would be damned glad to get out of this deep freeze tomorrow night and back to a climate where a man could take off his shirt without crystallizing.

What was that?

Something moved over by the shrouded helicopter.

Or was it a trick played by the shadows on his wandering mind? Vito swept the light across the machine's protective cover and over the ice clumps that surrounded the small landing area.

Nothing.

Still, it wouldn't hurt to take a walk up there and look around. It would give him something to do and make the time pass more quickly.

The powder snow swirled in little eddies around his boots as Vito clumped toward the blanketed helicopter. He leaned forward into the wind, fighting it. Overhead a cloud cover had extinguished the stars. John Savitch must have been right about the change in the weather. Calli didn't wish Bettiger any bad luck, but he hoped the storm would hold off until his own watch was ended.

Something tugged at the leg of his thermal suit.

Vito shook his foot reflexively. It was a moment before the thought hit him: Nothing out here should tug at him. No animal life, no vegetation. As he swung the flashlight beam down to look, something ripped through tough thermal suit, through the flesh of his leg, and scraped the leg bone below his knee. He knew a flash of blinding pain before the sudden paralyzing cold deadened his leg. Not until he fell and saw the bright red arterial blood pumping out of his leg onto the snow did Vito slap at his communicator panel and open his mouth to scream for help. It was too late. Claws ripped away his faceplate and tore out his tongue.

The glowing numbers on Bettiger's wristwatch told him Vito Calli was five minutes overdue. It was not like the pilot to overstay the end of his watch. Bettiger peeled away the mummy bag, secured his thermal suit, and left the shelter.

The wind hit him like a fist, knocking him momentarily off balance. Ice crystals spattered against his faceplate. The beam of Vito's flashlight was muted against the ice near the helicopter. Something lay there, still and dark. Bettiger plodded toward it, sweeping the ghostly landscape with his own light as he went.

There was not much that was recognizable of Lieutenant Vito Calli. Shattered bones, brittle bits of flesh, clumps of frozen intestine. All around him the ice was a slick blood red. The Colt .45 lay unfired beside the mess.

Bettiger fought down the impulse to gag and breathed deeply of the heated oxygen that was pumped into his helmet. He pulled the pistol free of the frozen surface,

THE ICE CHILDREN

turned stiffly from Vito's remains, and stumped back toward the shelter.

"But what was it?" Allison Denny said for the third or fourth time. "*What* could have done that to him? There's nothing up here." Her voice rose dangerously. "*Nothing!*"

"I don't know what did it!" Bettiger snapped. "We can worry about that later. Right now what's important is getting the rest of us out of here."

The shelter, space-age engineered to withstand the most extreme conditions, shivered under the blast of the wind outside.

"We can't go anywhere till this lets up," Allison said. She looked over at John Savitch, who sat at the communications console, manipulating electronic dials and switches. "The damn radio won't even work. These ice storms can last for days, isn't that right, John?"

The Eskimo did not look up. "Weeks, sometimes."

"Wonderful," Allison said bitterly. "What the hell happened to our weather window? The Bureau promised us a minimum of two days clear and calm."

"They screwed up," Bettiger said.

Allison looked toward the transparent panel in the shelter. Outside, the wind-driven ice crystals turned the scene into a milky blur in the filtered sunlight. "What's out there?" she said.

John Savitch abandoned the radio and looked at her. "You don't want to know," he said.

Allison stared at him. "Are you saying *you* know?"

He glanced over at Bettiger. "I know."

The colonel nodded wearily. "All right, John. I'll admit I have no explanation for what happened to Vito. I'm ready to listen to anything. Even your Eskimo legend."

John Savitch stood silently for a long time regarding Bettiger and Allison Denny. Finally he made a decision, nodded to himself, and began to speak in careful, measured sentences.

"In the time before the white man came to the New World, life for the North People was cruel. Winter was forever and the hunting season was short. There was never enough food to go around, even among the few who lived in this cruel land. Only the strong and the brave could survive. There was no hope for the old, the infirm, or the sick. When a child was born deformed or feeble or otherwise handicapped, its chances of surviving were zero. And if somehow it did live, another, healthier child would suffer. The North People dealt with this in a way we would find harsh today, but was then inevitable. The flawed child would be carried into the wilderness, its mouth stuffed with snow, and there left to die a swift and relatively painless death. They were called the ice children."

Bettiger and Allison listened without comment. When Savitch fell silent, Allison spoke.

"Those people just . . . left the babies out in the snow to die?"

"They had no choice."

Allison started to say more, but bit her lip and looked away.

Bettiger said, "That's a grisly story, John, but I don't see how it relates to our situation."

The Eskimo continued: "What I just told you is fact. Here begins the legend. The babies taken out into the snow could have no names. Once a child was given a name, it had a soul. If then it was left to die, it became an *angiak*. One of the living dead."

"You're saying these babies did not die?" Bettiger said.

"Their flesh decayed and their bones crumbled, but their spirits, as deformed as their little bodies, lived on. They lived for one purpose—revenge. Revenge against

THE ICE CHILDREN 19

those who abandoned them, and against anyone whose life had been spared."

"But, John, that kind of thing, if it was done at all, was hundreds of years ago."

"It *was* done," said Savitch. "Historical records exist. And what difference does it make how long ago? The spirit of the *angiak* does not die. Nothing can destroy them. They are as real and deadly today as they were in my ancestors' time." He nodded toward the plastic tub that contained the preserved hand. "They were real in 1954 when they found Henry Kellogg and his party. They were real last night when they caught Vito."

For a long minute the only sound in the shelter was the crackle of ice crystals blown against the flexible walls. The three people inside stood motionless.

Finally Bettiger spoke. "John, that's pure bullshit."

"Fine. You come up with a better explanation of what ripped Vito to pieces." Savitch clapped his faceplate into place, secured his suit and thrust himself out through the thermal hatch into the ice storm.

"That wasn't very diplomatic, Colonel," Allison said.

"I never said I was a diplomat."

"You could at least have listened to what John had to say."

"I *did* listen, for Christ sake. Babies in the snow. Deformed spirits of the dead. You want me to put that in a report? You want to sell that to your corporate boss? Maybe *National Enquirer* would go for it, but Transworld Media? They'd stick you back in the mail room."

Allison had stopped listening. She was staring out the transparent panel. "You shouldn't have let John go out there."

"Hell, he's better suited for the cold than the either of *us*. It's in his blood." Bettiger looked over her shoulder. "Anyway, I think it's letting up a little." He fastened his suit and reached for the faceplate. "I'll go out and see if he's through sulking."

Something hit the outer safety seal of the thermal hatch and the entire portal burst inward with an explosive *bang*. Ice crystals swirled into the shelter on a blast of numbing cold. Bettiger and Allison fumbled with gloved hands to secure their thermal suits and faceplates before the killing blast solidified their flesh.

John Savitch stood swaying before them. His face was unprotected. His lips were dark blue, his flesh glazed the color of ivory.

Bettiger snatched up the emergency kit and whirled back to Savitch just as the Eskimo fell silently and stiffly forward. He hit the composition floor of the shelter with a crunch as his frozen nose shattered into fragments. Allison's hands went to her faceplate. Bettiger stopped where he was. The entire back of the Eskimo's thermal suit was gone. So was the flesh and most of the meat of his back and buttocks. The spine and ribcage jutted from the raw red muscle like the skeleton of a derelict ship.

Bettiger snatched up a mummy bag and spread it over the ruined body. He spoke sharply to Allison who stood transfixed.

"Time to go. Your suit secure?"

Allison came to life. "Secure. Right. What about the equipment?"

"Leave it. Leave everything you can't carry out to the bird in one trip."

Together they looked toward the transparent panel. Ice crystals sizzled against the plexiglass.

"Can we take off in this?"

Bettiger looked down on the covered corpse of John Savitch. "We have to."

He gathered up his notes and the box from the Kellogg expedition. Allison quickly packed her photo-

THE ICE CHILDREN

graphic equipment, and they started for the shattered hatch.

"Holy shit!" Bettiger's voice crackled through Allison's headphones.

Down on all fours in the open hatch was a naked, humanlike creature. It had no lips. Naked yellow teeth glistened in bloodless gums. The creature's tiny eyes were sunk into darkened flesh. It crawled nimbly into the shelter, snarling in a grating, high-pitched voice.

"*Angiak!*" Allison whispered.

Behind the crawling thing came a bloated form with short flippers for arms and a head too small for the body. It was followed by a twisted creature with the face of a demented cherub and patches of coarse black hair on its body.

The first one, the little lipless one, jumped forward suddenly, froglike, and fastened its teeth on Bettiger's boot. The sharp pain was instantly followed by a numbing cold before the thermal suit sensed the damage and isolated the torn section. Bettiger fumbled the pistol out of his belt, pointed it at the hairless top of the thing's head, and fired. The impact of the bullet knocked the creature off his leg and put a dime-sized hole in its skull. The face looked up at him with a ghastly lipless smile. It started for his leg again.

Allison moved swiftly and planted a powerful kick on the crawling thing, sending it tumbling across the floor. But now the other two were inside. And more were coming. A babble of voices without words could be heard over the wind and crackling ice.

Bettiger leveled the pistol and fired. The first of the creatures, the one with the flippers, fell back momentarily. He shot another of them. And another. They showed no sign of pain at the shock of the bullets, but the impact knocked them off balance momentarily.

"Go!" he barked.

Allison hesitated, looking at him.

"Move, dammit! I'm right behind you."

With her photo equipment clutched against her body, Allison lunged through the broken hatch. Outside, misshapen nightmare creatures converged on the shelter. They were all sizes from infant to full adult, some with limbs missing, some with obscene growths on their bodies, still others more animal than human. The faces, cruelly deformed, mirrored a speechless rage. Allison lowered her head and ran through them toward the covered helicopter. She felt them clutch at her as she passed, one pierced her suit with a claw and ripped a gash in her arm. Behind her she heard the muffled booming of Bettiger's automatic.

She snatched at the quick-release loop of the protective shroud and it fell away from the helicopter. A gangly male form reached for her. Part of its brain bulged wetly through the skull. Allison swung the camera case by its strap, mashing the exposed brain. The creature fell to the ice, but immediately started to rise again.

"Bettiger!" she cried.

Turning, she saw him fighting his way through a swarming mass of deformed flesh. His voice came breathlessly through her headphones: "Get that thing started. I'm coming."

Allison scrambled into the helicopter. The interior, protected by the thermal cover, was warm in comparison to the subzero temperature outside. The wound in her arm began to throb, but she ignored it. She closed her eyes for a second, mentally calling up the checklist for takeoff. No time for the routine safety procedures. No time, either, for warm-up. Had to get the bird off the ground and pray it would stay aloft. She set the rotor pitch control, hit the ignition switch, and goosed the throttle.

Nothing happened.

Allison ground her teeth, swore, breathed a prayer,

THE ICE CHILDREN

and tried again. With a wheeze and a cough the big overhead rotor ground to life. The anti-torque tail rotor registered operative on the instrument panel.

While the flat rotor blades stirred the air with a rhythmic *fwup-fwup-fwup*, Allison leaned toward the door.

"*Bettiger!*" she shouted into her helmet mike, knowing as she did so that shouting was foolish.

She could see him plowing toward her, fighting off the freaky *angiaks*, kicking, swinging his arms, firing the pistol. His bright red thermal suit had larger patches of a darker crimson. The pistol shots sounded like cottony thumps through her helmet. Then the shots stopped. Bettiger threw the gun at one of the freaks. He lashed out at them with his fists. The creatures closed in on him. They chattered and screeched and tore at his suit. Bettiger stumbled to his knees.

Instinctively, Allison moved toward the door.

"*No!*" Bettiger's voice rasped in her headphones. "Shut that door. Get the fuck out of here."

"But—"

"Go, Denny! There isn't any—"

Bettiger's transmission broke off as the gibbering *angiaks* bore him to the ice. Allison could see nothing but the squirming pile of their malformed bodies. Then one of them came up waving a chunk of red uniform. Bettiger's arm was still in it.

Allison reached up numbly and pulled down the gullwing door. It closed with a solid thump, and she hit the latch-lock. Yank the throttle to full, adjust rotor pitch for ahead and up. The helicopter shuddered, gathered itself and left the ice, leaning into the icy wind.

Allison fought the wheel as it started to dip and roll to the left. Something was pulling her down. She looked out the side window and saw two clawed pale hands clinging to the skid. A face came into view. The eyes were small, red, and filled with hate. The nose was more of a snout with quivering hairy nostrils. The canine teeth were curved tusks.

"*Get off, you sonofabitch!*"

She yanked the controls violently, sending the helicopter into a series of gyrations as the icy ground rushed toward her. A wailing scream sounded over the thump of the rotor, and the claws lost their grip. The snouted thing fell tumbling back to earth, its ropy arms flapping like useless wings.

When at last she had righted the machine and gained altitude to where the wind was not so strong, Allison allowed herself a long, deep breath. She willed her hands to relax on the controls as she turned south toward Thule and safety.

As the interior temperature stabilized Allison leaned back and unlatched her faceplate. She drew in a grateful breath, and only then did she hear the piglike grunt. Something moved in the seat behind her.

Allison turned . . .

First Kill

by Chet Williamson

This ironic and powerful little story is the latest of more than fifty short stories, novelettes, and novellas that Chet Williamson has published in such magazines and anthologies as The New Yorker, Playboy, The Magazine of Fantasy and Science Fiction, Twilight Zone, Razored Saddles, Night Visions 7, *and many others. Chet's latest novel is* Reign *(Dark Harvest). His other novels include* Dreamthorp, Ash Wednesday, Lowland Rider, Soul-storm, *and* McKain's Dilemma. *He has been a finalist for the Mystery Writers of America Edgar Allan Poe Award, and he has received four Bram Stoker Award nominations from the Horror Writers of America. He lives in Elizabethtown, Pennsylvania, with his wife Laurie and son Colin.*

For days now, the hunter had thought about widows and orphaned children, and decided that he would try and see if the man wore a wedding ring. With his 4x Weaver scope, he thought he should be able to catch a glint of gold on the left hand.

However, the Monday after Thanksgiving was often cold in the woods of northern Pennsylvania. Odds were that blaze orange mittens would cover most hands, to be slipped warily off only at the sound of hooves rustling dead leaves. Even then, most men fired rifles with their right hands. A wedding ring would still be covered. Still, he would try to avoid a father, making an effort to show the mercy the earth he loved did not have.

But if he could not see the hand, he would accept whatever target was offered.

Peter Keats awoke an hour before dawn, pushed in the button of the wind-up alarm clock, and shivered with excitement and the cold. The fire he and his two cabin mates had set the night before in the wood stove was dead, and he was glad he had worn his insulated long underwear in his sleeping bag. He didn't think he could have stood the chilly air against his bare trunk and legs. He woke his friends, slid out of his bunk, and put on two pair of socks, one cotton, the other heavy wool. He stepped into his thick trousers, then slipped his feet into ankle-high L. L. Bean hunting boots.

Keats was out the front door before the others had disentangled themselves from their sleeping bags. He breathed in the air, reveling in the sharp crispness that stung his throat. He walked up the hill from the cabin to the outhouse, defecated quickly and efficiently, and walked back again, broke the ice in the basin that sat on the railing of the tiny porch, and splashed frigid water on his face. It made him even more wakeful than before.

Back inside, the men joked, ate donuts, and drank the coffee they had made the night before. Then they finished dressing, ending with the heavy coats of safety orange, put wads of toilet paper under their scope covers so the lenses wouldn't fog in the colder outside air, and stepped outside to hunt, and to be hunted.

It took Peter Keats a half hour of walking in near darkness to reach the spot he had chosen the day before, when they had helped each other erect their stands, the elevated platforms in which they would perch and wait for a deer to wander by. One of his friends was a half mile to the northwest, the other a mile south. Keats could easily hear their shots, and if he did he would hold still for five, ten minutes, waiting even more silently in case

FIRST KILL

of a miss or a wounding, in case the deer should run, limp, or drag itself past his stand.

By the time Peter Keats had climbed onto his perch, he could just make out streaks of rose through the ragged treetops to the east. He settled himself, his Remington pump .760 resting across his legs. His feet dangled over the edge of the stand, fifteen feet above above the ground. For comfort's sake, Keats had placed a small, flat pillow under the spot where his knees rested against the sharp edge of the stand.

Keats thought that it seemed colder than it had in years before. He rubbed his fingers against each other inside the heavy mittens, and wished that the orange of his jacket was as warm to the touch as it was to the eye. The deer must really be colorblind if that hue didn't startle them. He had heard other hunters say that it appeared white to the deer's eyes. Well, if it did it did. It didn't much matter, and besides, it was the law.

In his fifty years of deer hunting, Peter Keats had always obeyed the law. His father had taught him that when he had given him his first deer rifle at the age of fourteen. One deer a year, no more. No shooting one for your friend, and no shooting a doe in buck season. Keats had done none of those things, simply because he had never been tempted to. And he had never been tempted, because in his half century of what he called hunting, he had never shot, nor had he ever wanted to shoot, a deer.

The pattern was set the first year he went hunting with his father. Keats was positioned next to an oak tree, crouching among the acorns on which the deer loved to feed. His father was a half mile away, and Keats, his heart beating rapidly, waited, waited, feeling youthful erections of excitement come and go. An hour passed, during which Keats stood up several times, stretching his legs. He was standing when he heard the deer approach. He froze, felt the wind on his face from the direction of the sound of breaking leaves, snapping twigs, and saw a buck and two doe push through the brush less than fifty yards away.

He raised his rifle with what felt like the slowness of a watch's second hand, and by the time the buck had cleared the brush, Keats was looking at it through the notch of the open sight. Its smooth coat made it look carved of wood, its brown eyes stared into his like some spirit of the forest, and he felt, holding the deer's life in his fingertip, as though he was defying God, like a vandal in a cathedral. If he pulled the trigger he knew he would violate a far more solemn contract than the one forged between him and his father.

He lowered the gun, and never raised it to a deer again.

Still, he went hunting every year, and patiently bore his fellow hunters' good-natured teasing. He suspected that the old friends he was with now knew the truth, for he no longer even fired a shot or two to make them think he had tried but failed. He had had plenty of chances over the years, and his heart still pounded when he saw a buck approach, pass by him, pause, look up, startled, and run. But he did not lift his loaded rifle to his shoulder.

And it was loaded, always. Every year he went through the ritual of sighting in the rifle at the sportsman's club to which he belonged, cleaning it, taking out the same bullets from the cabinet, bullets that had turned green where lead met brass, and shooting at the targets on the range, until his offhand scores equaled those of men years his junior.

Keats loved the ritual, the preparations, the chance to be with his friends and by himself. His two companions with whom he had come to Potter County shared his love of the outdoors, but he seldom saw them outside of deer season, so that when they did get together there was much to catch up on.

But the solitude was the best part, the sense that there was no one but him in the world to see the sky grow brighter, feel the air become less bitterly cold, behold the dread miracle of winter. He sat and waited, and while he was alert to the sounds of the woods, he also escaped into himself, his past, his thoughts and memories of seasons before.

He thought of his wife, of when they had both been young, though no happier than they were now, of the job at the steel mill he had held for over thirty years before he had retired four years ago, of his church where he served on the budget committee, of his three grandchildren, of the oldest boy, who wanted to go hunting with him next year when he was old enough.

Peter Keats thought of many things as the morning brightened, until the sun slashed bright streaks through the latticework of branches, bathing his orange garb with fire, making him a perfect target.

The hunter saw the man in the tree stand just before 7:30. Ever since dawn he had been moving stealthily, stalking. It was estimated that fifty thousand people would be roaming through the quarter million acres of Potter County's state forests today. Since that averaged out to one hunter per five acres, it was only natural that they would come across each other now and again.

That was what calmed and excited and worried the hunter. It calmed him because no one would take a second look at another man dressed in orange; it excited him because the statistic made it certain that he would find game; and it worried him that the game might be *too* plentiful, tripping over one another in the haste for their own prey. A herd would do the hunter no good. He had to find a single animal, cut off from the rest.

That was when he saw the man in the tree. Thank God, he thought, for the orange. Its warm brightness protected him on the cold ground, marked his targets in the chilly air.

He stepped behind a thick-boled pine tree, and peered

out at the man in the tree stand seventy yards away. The man gave no indication that he had seen the hunter.

The hunter slipped the glove from his right hand, put it into his coat pocket, and wadded small bits of wax into his ears. Then he lifted his rifle, a Ruger Model 77, 7 mm. Magnum, and leaned against the tree. He placed his right cheek against the smooth walnut stock, and looked through the Weaver scope with his right eye.

The man in the stand did not fill the field of vision, but the hunter could make out certain details. The man was older, in his sixties, and had probably killed deer for many years. The hunter found a poetic justice in that fact. His hands were mittened, so the hunter could not tell if he wore a ring. Probably married, the hunter thought. He looked like a married man, happy to be alone in the woods. The man had a little gray mustache, and wore glasses with black frames. His booted feet dangled over the edge of the stand, and he swung them back and forth like a child, a movement that any deer would notice immediately. The man did not appear likely to bag a buck this year.

Still, he was hunting deer, so it was the hunter's obligation to hunt him. Maybe he was only a harmless old man who enjoyed sitting in a tree house holding a loaded rifle, but surely he had taken his toll over the years. Now it was payback time.

The hunter flicked off the safety, breathed in icy air, leaned against the tree so that his forehead rubbed roughly against the bark, moved his Ruger in a series of infinitesimal motions until the plain of blaze orange was settled directly under the scope's cross hair. Only then did he place his bare finger on the cold metal of the trigger, let out half his breath in a white puff, hold the rest, and begin, very gently, to squeeze. When he had exerted enough pressure, the firing pin descended, the powder ignited, the bullet left the barrel and flew across the seventy yards in the merest fraction of a second, meeting the man in the tree, expanding the instant it struck the orange jacket, widening as it tore through flesh and muscle and bone. The man flew backwards into a red cloud of himself, and fell from the tree, landing on the dry leaves below like a sack of lime.

The hunter held his pose for a moment, the sound of the explosion reverberating like a great gong. Then he operated the bolt and lowered the rifle so that he still looked through the scope at the man on the ground, ready to fire a second shot at the hint of motion.

There was none. It had been a clean, quick kill.

From the corner of his eye, he had seen the spent shell fly from the ejector, and it took him only a moment to find the gleaming brass amid the floor of dead pine needles. He dropped it into his pocket and walked to the tree stand, pulling the wax wads from his ears. Although he listened intently, he heard no other sounds, neither voices nor footsteps in dead leaves. No, no one would come. No one would leave their stands and jeopardize their own chances of making a kill. It would be safe to do the field dressing.

It was extraordinary, he thought, the damage a single, small projectile could do to a human body. The man had not moved since he had fallen, and the glassy stare told the hunter he was dead. Heart and lungs had been ripped through, and the blood must have ceased its pumping to the brain instantly. He hoped the man had felt little pain, only one, short, sharp, and savage, before he lost consciousness and his life.

The hunter stood for a long time, looking down at the first man he had ever killed, indeed ever even harmed. He thought he had readied himself for it, but no philosophy, no cause firmly and chokingly believed in, had prepared him for this moment. It had prepared him for the stalking, the sighting, even the pulling of the trigger, but not this. He struggled to stop shaking, told himself it was only the cold, that he could not be shaking from emotion because he had none. He was a machine that had functioned as it was supposed to, and would continue to do so.

Again he repeated his manifesto to himself, like a mantra of destruction, all the proper words about the purity of life, the reverence for nature, the abomination of hunting in a country where no one need do so to eat, the thousands of animals wounded and not found, dying slowly and painfully. He thought about the protests he had made with the others, the signs and speeches that had done nothing to slow the annual slaughter, thought about his decision to do more, administer true justice, turn the tables on the hunters, show them all too clearly just what they were doing to another species, going over it again and again in his mind, establishing his alibi, changing his appearance, going far, far from where he lived, to a place where no one knew him, a place rich with human game, where he could make his kill, and show that any species could be preyed upon.

And now he had killed, and now he must continue, be strong, finish the lesson, plant the seeds of legend and terror.

There. He was all right now, ready to do what had to be done.

He propped his Ruger against the tree that held the stand, put on both gloves, and knelt by the side of the dead man. He unsnapped the man's jacket, grasped his neck, hauled him to a sitting position, and removed the sodden mass of cotton shell and goose down. The hole in the man's back was greater than the hunter had imagined.

He let the body flop back onto the bloody leaves, and saw that some blood on the man's small mustache had frozen. It looked, thought the hunter, as though he had cut his lip shaving.

The hunter took a horn-handled knife with a five-inch blade from its sheath, and tried to forget that what lay

FIRST KILL 33

before him was a human being, tried to think of it only as a slaughtered animal, as the other hunters would think of the deer they had shot.

He cut open the dead man's sweater, shirt, and thermal undershirt, exposing the pallid flesh and the entrance wound to the freezing air. He yanked the upper clothing off the body, then removed the boots and socks, and sliced through the waistband of the trousers, tugging them off, along with the long underwear, until the corpse lay naked on the frozen bed of leaves. The hunter had read over and over about field dressing, and now he would recreate the procedure. It wouldn't be perfect, for the anatomies of deer and men were different. But they would see, and realize, and tell the tale, so that everyone would know there was an avenger in the forest.

A true field dressing would have begun with cutting the penis and scrotum free, then scoring around the anus, but the hunter wanted no hints of sexual psychosis to dilute the true purpose of his act. He left the genitals intact, and instead slipped the razor sharp knife beneath the skin of the lower abdomen. Blade up, he slid the knife through the flesh until it struck the breastbone, exposing a layer of yellow fat and muscle.

He had not reckoned on the fat. It looked greasy and slimy, and although he thought the presence of blood on his gloves would arouse no curiosity, the same could not be said for remnants of fat. So he took off the gloves and laid them next to the butt of his rifle. When he was finished, he would wipe his hands as best he could with the dead leaves.

The incision had drawn back the skin, and the warm, moist organs steamed in the cold air, like clouds rising from a valley. The hunter rolled up his right sleeve, made a few quick, short cuts, and lifted away the fat and the sheet of muscle beneath it. His cold hands nearly burned when he touched the hot, wet innards, and for a moment the steam rose from his hands and forearms. He then cut the diaphragm away from the rib cage, and reached up inside the chest until he found the esophagus and windpipe, both of which he severed, accidentally nicking the palm of his left hand in the confined space. He pulled both tubes back and out, and the lungs, now deflated sacks, followed. It was nearly as easy as the books had said.

A little more cutting of the membranes removed the diaphragm, and in another moment he was able to work the heart free and remove it. Then he reached in with both hands, as though he was embracing the carcass, and lifted most of the viscera out, except for the lower intestine, which was still attached to the anus. He dropped the innards on the leaves, where the smoking, multi-hued mound settled itself like a nest of lazy snakes in sunshine. Then he picked up the knife again, intending to sever the recalcitrant lower bowel, when he heard a crunch of leaves behind him, and a voice. The hunter turned his head and saw, twenty feet away, a man with a gray beard, dressed in blaze orange, holding a rifle pointed at the ground.

When Peter Keats had heard the single shot from the south, he had listened for more, for the signals that he and his friend there had established. If Keats heard one, he could assume it was a single killing shot. If two, a downing shot and a finishing shot. But if three, a miss. His friend's hands were arthritic, especially in the cold, and he could not begin to field-dress a deer. Keats had offered to do the gutting if necessary, and the single shot had told him it was.

It had taken Keats nearly fifteen minutes to walk the mile between the two stands, and when he had seen the figure bent over something red and white he had thought that his friend must have already begun. But he saw quickly that the kneeling man was smaller and narrower through the shoulders than his friend, and Keats walked more quietly, stepping on exposed rocks and patches of pine needles that offered no crisp, betraying resistance.

When he saw his friend, he could not believe it, and said, "God," and stepped on dry leaves. The kneeling man turned then, and looked at him over his right shoulder, and Keats could see his red and glistening hands and forearms.

"What—" Keats began to say, and the man twisted the other way, to his left, toward the tree against which his rifle leaned, stretched, his left hand sliding on the ground as he tried to grasp the rifle's grip with his wet, slippery right hand. He came around toward Keats, one knee on the ground, left leg extended, the barrel bobbing in his efforts to grasp the gun securely.

But before its dark eye could look at Keats, he had raised his Remington, flicked off the safety, and fired before his rifle stopped in motion. The sound of the shot hammered his unprotected ears, and he pressed his eyes shut, waiting to feel the man's bullet tear into him.

The answering shot assaulted his deafened ears, but he felt no pain, and when he opened his eyes he saw the man lying on the ground, still gripping his rifle, blood streaming from a hole in his torn neck like a parasitic serpent escaping its host.

Slowly he lowered his rifle and looked at the two dead men. Then, very softly, he began to cry. He cried for a long time, the hot tears quickly cooling on his stubbly cheeks in the winter air.

Peter Keats had made his first kill.

Colder Than Hell

by Edward Bryant

Ed Bryant is a perfectionist. You can always depend on him to deliver a finely wrought story. He's been in the writing business for more than twenty years, and has won two Nebula Awards (one of which was for "Gi-ants," an affectionate homage to Ed's favorite movie, Them*). In that two-decade span he's published four collections of short fiction:* Cinnabar, Wyoming Sun, Particle Theory, *and* Among the Dead; *a novel in collaboration with Harlan Ellison,* Phoenix Without Ashes; *and he has edited an anthology,* 2076: The American Tricentennial. *After spending the '70s as an up-and-coming science fiction writer, Ed abruptly changed gears and became a horror writer in the '80s. In fact, he's a finalist for the Horror Writers of America Bram Stoker Award as of this writing. Read this and you'll find out why.*

The Norwegian, Amundsen, had reached the South Pole on the fourteenth of December. For some reason, Logan McHenry found the lengthy newspaper account fascinating. He had reread it many times since purchasing the latest issue of the Laramie *Daily Boomerang* when Opal and he had picked up supplies in Medicine Bow. The date on the paper was now nearly three months out of currency. The crease along the edges of the folded newsprint had begun to split.

"Damned Scandehoovians," said Logan. "They

know cold up there, but they don't know *real* cold," he added vehemently.

He got up from the straight-back chair by the fire and walked stiffly over to the small kitchen window. With his thumbnail he scraped a silver cartwheel-sized patch free of ice. Logan could see nothing. Just the endless, blinding white of wind-whipped snow. "Don't look like it's gonna let up," he said.

"Hasn't looked like it was going to let up for six days now," his wife commented. She slowly and expertly carved the peel away from a fist-sized potato. Opal was thin, whip-tough, taller than her husband. He had never much liked that.

Logan continued staring out at the unvarying blizzard. "Maybe I better lay in some more wood." He gestured vaguely at the pile of quarter-splits piled against the wall to her side. "We got maybe enough to last until night."

"Mighty cold out there," said his wife.

"Ain't gonna get no warmer."

"How cold do you figure?"

Logan shrugged. "Last time I checked, it was somethin' like eighteen below. And then the wind cuts it pretty fierce."

"Want to take that out when you go?" Opal gestured at the full bucket of peels, scraps, and trash.

"No, I don't want." He wasn't sure why he said it. *Just to be contrary.* "All right," he contradicted himself. "I'll set it out. Wind'll blow it clean to Nebraska."

She stared at him a moment. "Thank you kindly," she said.

Logan pulled on his heavy cloth coat. He tugged the worn old Stetson down tight over his ears and wrapped the long woolen muffler over the crown, down under his chin, and then looped back around his neck. He slipped on the sheepskin-lined work gloves. "I'm ready," he said. "Help me with the door?"

Something tickled the inside of one nostril. He

couldn't help himself—Logan emitted an enormous sneeze. He winced. It was painful. The dry skin at the bottom of his nose was cracking.

"Company's coming," said Opal automatically. It was how she always answered when he sneezed. Logan's usual response to a sneeze—when he said anything at all—was the standard "Gesundheit." Opal's "Company's coming" was, she said, something her family had said for as long as she could remember.

It was strange—whenever Logan heard the phrase, he usually thought also of *his* mother's saying that one of those unexplainable, wracking shivers was because "Someone's walking over your grave." Different thing entirely, he knew, but somehow the situations seemed the same, at least on the surface. *Walking over your grave.*

He picked up the handle of the trash bucket. Logan could already feel the knives of the Wyoming wind jamming into his joints; piercing and then twisting with icy blades. But it was worse when he opened the door.

The cold sucked at him, tried to pull him bodily out of the house. Logan braced himself, his free hand locked on the jamb. Opal had the strong fingers of both slender hands wound around the doorknob. "Be back in five minutes," he shouted. He knew his wife could not hear him in the blizzard din.

Logan let loose of the jamb and let the wind pull him forward to the edge of the porch. Behind him he felt the heat vanish as Opal tugged the back door shut. He was alone with the wind and the snow. And the cold.

He staggered forward and wrapped his free arm around the corner post. Then he ran his hand down to waist level. Three ropes were tied to the post. The one angling off to the left led a hundred yards to the barn. The other end of the center rope was nailed to the door of the outhouse. The right-hand rope stretched tautly between porch and the root cellar, perhaps ten yards distant.

The man couldn't see any of the three destinations. In every case, the ropes fuzzed indistinctly and vanished a few feet into the snow. That same snow sawed past him like sand, moving nearly horizontally. He knew the drifts on the other side of the house must be right up to the eaves.

First things first. Logan shook out the contents of the bucket. They vanished instantly into the blizzard's maw. He would use the bucket to carry wood back from the barn. He'd need one hand to hold the rope.

Without the rope's guidance, he'd be confused in a foot, lost in a yard. Probably dead in the length of his own body. Maybe not immediately, but in short order. He was under no illusion how long he could last in this storm.

Before starting for the wood, he squinted at the thermometer nailed to the corner post. Getting colder. Thirty below. The gauge only went to forty. Logan shook his head.

According to his daddy's old railroad watch—he'd checked it before abandoning the shelter of the kitchen—it was high noon.

The snow.

It felt like thousands of tiny mouths, lined with needle teeth, all sucking the heat from his skin. He had to admit to himself that it was frightening, once he was away from the porch, to be surrounded completely by the blizzard. With the handle of the bucket still clutched firmly, he moved hand over hand toward the barn. For perhaps the hundredth time, he chewed himself out for not hauling in nearly enough wood when the first flakes of the storm had drifted down.

But who knew? Wyoming blizzards, even in the dead of winter in the middle of the Shirley Basin, usually blew themselves out in a day, two at the most. Logan had never seen anything like this storm. He'd heard stories of the big one in 1899—the tellers never tired of listing the stock that had died, and there had been plenty—but Opal and he had still been in Pennsylvania then.

The dark plank wall of the barn loomed out of the storm like a cliff. Logan staggered into the lee side and luxuriated for a moment at being given a respite from the wind. Then the wind's direction changed and the icy nails raked at his face.

Logan took hold of the peg that lifted the latching bar and opened the door. It was dark inside. That didn't matter; he knew exactly where the wood was stacked.

He heard a hoof stamping and an anxious whicker.

"You need some more hay?"

The horse whinnied.

"All right, boy. Hold your—" He laughed at himself and did not finish the line. Logan set down the pail, then picked up a few bats of powdery alfalfa and dropped them over the side of the stall. The big bay, Indian, brushed Logan's arm with his muzzle, then leaned down toward the hay. The man turned, bent, and broke off a chunk of crusted snow from the drift that extended from the door into the barn. Double-handed, he dropped it into Indian's water pan.

"Better than nothing, boy."

Logan found the wood in the dark, wedged as many splits as he could into the bucket, set another three pieces under his left arm, and shoved open the door against the wind. He slid his right hand along the rope to the house.

Three times, the wind almost broke his grip. Each time he recoiled against the blast, then hunched over the rope and kept pushing his way toward the porch. One of the sticks of firewood slipped out from beneath his free arm. He did not try to retrieve it. The wood disappeared into the snow as though it had never existed at all.

In this storm, Logan thought, *anything* could as easily vanish—a horse, a cow, a human being. A wife. Why had he thought that? he wondered.

And then he wondered that he wondered.

* * *

They had married when she was sixteen and he was twenty. That had been in the year this god-forsaken territory of Wyoming became the forty-fourth state of the Union. Neither of them had even dreamed they would find themselves here two decades later.

1890—a year of unbounded promise for all. Almost all, he amended the thought. There had been the killing of the hundreds of Sioux redmen at Wounded Knee. There had been stories of massacre in Dahomey, a far-off African kingdom. Other accounts in the newspapers of death in Madagascar, Angola, other distant places.

Logan had always been fond of reading the papers, although he wasn't all that enamored of regular books. When Opal and he had married, her mother had given them a copy of *Hedda Gabler*, a play by another of those Scandehoovians. It was brand spanking new, but he had never read it. He didn't even know where it was now.

The farmstead in Pennsylvania had failed and the bank had assumed control. At the end, the McHenrys had been given a generous three days to vacate. They had gone west.

Wyoming—and the Shirley Basin—had welcomed them in the spring. Summer had been moderate, the autumn bounty generous. Then winter had come.

Somehow they had stayed on for eight years. Both of them were stubborn.

They lived by themselves.

At first, it was not by choice. Logan blamed himself for their marriage being barren of progeny. He knew Opal blamed herself equally. So many days they stared at each other silently, accusations against self unvoiced. So many nights they lay silently in their narrow bed. Sometimes Logan would turn on his side and look at Opal. In the dim moonlight he would see her staring at the low ceiling. Opal would sense his look, then meet his eyes. At least he thought she was looking at him.

COLDER THAN HELL

With her deep-set eyes lying in shadow, it was difficult to tell.

The wind blew hard and constantly, and the cold lay upon the land. The springs seemed all too short, the summers increasingly parching. The autumns became as arid as their marriage bed.

The winters savaged them.

Of course I love her. Logan stared at the outside of the kitchen door until the wind nearly rocked him off balance. He clutched at the firewood and cradled it close to the warmth of his body. *Of course.*

He reached out with a stick of pine and tapped on the door, knocked harder, finally beat on the slab fiercely until the dark door became an oblong of light and heat. Opal stood in the doorway staring at him for what seemed a long time. Then she stepped back and beckoned him enter.

Logan could not feel his fingers or toes.

"Doesn't look good," said Opal.

Logan protested.

His wife sat him down in the ladder-back chair by the kitchen stove. She shoved two of the sticks he'd brought in with him into the stove, then put on a pan of water to heat. "Get them off, and right now," she mumbled, grabbing the boots in question, one at a time, and wrestling them off his feet. "How do they feel?" she said, peeling the socks loose. They stank.

"Can't rightly feel nothing at all."

"Fingers too?"

"Same thing," Logan said.

"Give them here." Opal took his right hand between her own two hands and rubbed. At first there was no sensation. Then Logan saw the gray flesh begin to grow pink, then glow a flushed red. Opal rubbed his left hand with the same result. Steam was beginning to rise from the pan on the stove. The woman set it down on the floor and put Logan's feet in the water. Sensation was slow in coming, but eventually it did arrive.

Finally, Opal stood from her ministrations and said, "You wait right here."

"Wasn't going nowhere." Logan didn't crack a smile. Needles of pain lanced through his fingers and toes.

His wife put on his coat, slipped on her own gloves. "Won't be gone but a few minutes," she said. She slipped out the kitchen door, seemingly opening it so narrowly that only a small amount of snow sheeted in. Opal was a skinny woman.

She told the truth. She was not gone long. When she returned, Opal dropped the large armload of cut wood on the floor by the stove, took a few deep breaths of warm air, then turned and headed out the door again. She brought back two more loads of firewood.

"That ought to be enough," said Logan after the third trip. "It will get us through tonight. You'd better stop, or pretty soon I'll be out looking for your frozen carcass in the blizzard."

Opal surveyed the pile of pine splits. Snow and ice had melted in a shallow puddle around the wood. "Reckon you're right." She turned toward him. "Ready for some coffee?"

Logan nodded. Opal slipped another piece of wood into the stove and slid the coffee pot over the hottest iron lid. It was still the breakfast brew. What she finally poured into her husband's cup was black as coal and smelled vile. Logan hunched over the coffee until it was cool enough to sip.

Opal scraped a patch of frost off the kitchen windowglass and stared out at the constant snow. "You know something," she said, "you lose your fingers or your feet, and you'll have the makings of a mighty poor dryland farmer."

"Rancher," he corrected automatically. "We're ranchers now."

COLDER THAN HELL

"Rancher," she said. "No matter. We'd do poorly."

"So?"

"Maybe," Opal continued slowly, "it's time we thought about moving on to the Wasatch Valley over there in Utah, or maybe even go clear on out to California." She paused. It was a long speech for her.

Howling, the wind whipped around the eaves of the small house.

"So you think we should go?" said Logan. "And save my hands, my toes?"

She stared back at him mutely.

"Or perhaps you feel if I lose those limbs, we'll *have* to leave the Shirley Basin."

"That's not what I said." Opal's eyes seemed for a moment to gleam the milky white of their namesake. Then they were blue again. The wind's howl rose in pitch and volume.

Logan felt suddenly obstinate. "If we don't live here," he said, "we will die here."

The wind screamed.

Logan didn't know from where the idea had come to him, or, indeed, *when* it had come. Maybe it had always been there. He listened as the wind keened wildly and the snow rattled against the walls, the shake roof, the frost-blinded windowpanes.

He had picked up a cold from his sojourn out to the barn and back. His nose ran continually now; the rag he used as a handkerchief had grown sodden. The wracking sneezes were the worst, though.

And every time, Opal smiled thinly, sympathetically, and said, "Company's coming."

If company was indeed coming, it would not be for a while yet. The storm had continued through the afternoon and into the evening. In the lantern light, his father's watch said that the time was past midnight. The wind did not abate. The shrieking was like the red-hot prickles he had felt earlier when his fingers and toes defrosted. The sound entered his head and stayed there, even when the wind varied its pitch.

He could not sleep.

Logan watched his wife slumber. Opal's gentle snores indicated she was able to ignore the blizzard and sleep.

Unless—The thought came to him and lodged in his head like a straw driven by a tornado. Unless she was pretending.

Why would Opal pretend such a thing?

Logan puzzled over that a long time, almost until his concentration on the problem had brought him close to uneasy sleep. But he was brought up short by the realization: Opal could not possibly be sleeping. The storm forbade that. She must be pretending in order to fool him, and she was fooling Logan so that he would not know what she truly felt and thought.

He watched her for the remainder of the long night. He stared at Opal, waiting for his wife to make the slightest mistake. He knew she would trip herself up sooner or later. All he had to do was to be patient.

His patience was inexhaustible as the hours ticked away and some distant dawn approached invisibly.

One mistake and he would have her.

The wind screamed triumphantly.

It happened after breakfast.

Opal had fixed a platter of flapjacks, with a plate of salted beef on the side. She had also brewed a fresh pot of coffee that tasted slightly better than yesterday's preparation.

The taste of the food almost allayed Logan's suspicions.

The knife-edges of wind in his head kept him from hearing most of Opal's slender pronouncements as the morning wore on with no apparent respite from the storm. This portion of Wyoming still reeled.

COLDER THAN HELL

After breakfast, Logan pushed back from the table and said, "I'll be getting some wood now."

Opal nodded, fixed him for a moment with her alien and intense look, and said, "Will you take that out?" She gestured toward the bucket of scraps and trash.

Logan remembered the previous day when he had had to manage both the empty bucket and the wood. He recalled what had happened to fingers and toes. He could walk today, and he could touch things.

He knew suddenly that what Opal really wanted was for him no longer to be able to do those things. With no fingers or toes, perhaps even without feet or hands, then they would have to move on. They would be obliged to move to a more temperate place, some foolish golden paradise as California was reputed to be, a heaven on earth where oranges and other fruit would be free for the plucking from the tree.

But at what cost to his soul?

The wind—

"All right," said Logan. "I will take it out."

And he did. He did it carefully and quietly and without argument, so that she would suspect nothing.

And then he brought back three loads of wood from the barn, one after another, the painful product of following the rope back and forth as ice crystals flayed the exposed flesh of his face.

"That's enough for now."

Opal smiled agreement. "I will get some more food stocks from the cellar." She put on her cold-weather clothing.

The wind—

Logan got the door for his wife. He braced his legs and held the back door open for her. A wind gust exposed the length of her to his sight; then the snow closed in and she was gone.

Her husband glanced at the thermometer. There was

no mercury in the gauge. The bulb had shattered. It could never be colder than now.

Logan didn't even think about what he was doing. He looked down at the three ropes fastened to the porch. It was far too cold to fiddle with the ice-encrusted knots. He took the clasp knife from his pocket and unfolded the blade. Then he sawed at the right-hand rope. He didn't hesitate when the final strands began to ravel. He sliced across them with the knife. Tension whipped the free end of the rope into the storm.

It was gone.

The man chopped at the center rope, the one that led to the outhouse. He could make do for the duration of the storm. It was what the bucket really was for. Cut through, this rope also vanished in the snow.

Logan hesitated, then sawed at the remaining rope that could guide him to the barn. The wood was there, and so was Indian, but the storm surely could not last another full day and night. He would not need the barn.

The third rope parted, strand by strand, and was abruptly gone.

The wind laughed as Logan retreated into the kitchen and shut the door. He paused a moment, then slid home the bolt that locked it.

Logan spent much of the day reading old issues of the Laramie *Daily Boomerang*. He discovered himself always returning to the issue detailing Roald Amundsen's arduous conquest of the Southern Pole. The entire account fascinated him.

But he was equally intrigued by the subsidiary story detailing other polar expeditions. Logan had long been fascinated by the Englishman, Robert Falcon Scott, who had led a successful scouting expedition to the ice pack in 1900, twelve years before. There had been speculation that Scott might become the first man to trek to the South

Pole. The Norwegian had apparently beaten him to that goal.

"At least Scott is a white man," muttered Logan. But then, it occurred to him, so was Amundsen.

Logan wondered how Scott might feel, finding out that he had been beaten out by a longtime rival. Would it be like death?

The light had begun to fail. Logan looked around him.

Was twilight falling, the storm abating? He turned up the wick of the lamp, but the dark continued to encroach.

Maybe he was just out of kerosene.

Logan shook his head. He had felt himself begin to drift, nodding, perhaps beginning to catch up to the sleep that had eluded him for so long.

Someone knocked at the back door.

Logan jerked awake.

He heard another knock. It was a solid rapping sound, easily discernible above the wind.

Logan got up from the chair and tentatively started to cross the kitchen. He didn't have to unbolt the door, after all. If that was Opal still out there . . . But it couldn't be. He had cut the ropes hours before.

He didn't have to unlock the door.

The door opened anyway.

Logan saw the hand appear through the snow blowing into the opening between the door and jamb. The fingers were slender and gray, curving around the door's edge. The wrist extended into the kitchen, the lower arm—

The man hit the door with his shoulder, slamming it shut with all the hysterical strength he could muster.

Shut.

Sheared off below the elbow, the wrist and hand tumbled to the plank floor. The fingers shattered with the sound of tinkling crystal. Bright shards of icy flesh scattered across the floor like broken glass.

Still hunched against the door, Logan stared down at

the floor. The lamplight still flickered, but he could see ruby fragments melting.

The ice-jewels became drops of blood.

The light on the bits of flesh and bone and blood transfixed him, he didn't know for how long.

And when Logan came back to himself, still wedged against the door, there was no blood on the floor. There was nothing.

And the door was still locked.

From outside, the wind said everything. But the wind was inside now too.

Dear Lord, he wanted to sleep.

Logan thought it was morning. He was not sure because the watch had stopped during the night. *At the time the door had been flung open and the hand thrust inside* . . . No, because he had forgotten to wind it.

He levered himself upright. He had been sitting on the floor beside the door. His muscles were cramped, his limbs stiff and sore.

The man realized the fire in the kitchen stove had gone out. He clumsily stuffed wood into the grate, picked up some of the shavings used for tinder, tried to light them with the sulfur match that lay on the table. The match went out without passing on its flame.

Logan couldn't find another match. There must be another one somewhere. There must be an entire box.

After a while he gave up looking and hauled a comforter from the bed across the room. He draped it around his shoulders and sat down in the ladder-back chair. He needed to think for a moment. The wind didn't allow him to do that.

Logan realized that the kerosene lamp was out, yet he could still see. A gray light filtered dimly through the window.

Was the blizzard over?

COLDER THAN HELL

He didn't feel any warmer with the realization. He didn't feel much of anything at all. His arms and legs felt much as they had upon completing that trip from the barn days before when he had gotten his frostbite. Had it been days?

Logan wasn't sure.

But he was increasingly certain that the storm was abating.

The wind still shrilled, but the sound of snow raking the side of the house was no longer there. Yes, the blizzard had dwindled.

That meant he was no longer trapped. That meant people could come to the house.

That meant—

Company's coming.

His nose tickled.

Logan tried to get up from the chair, could not, sank back resignedly.

"Opal—" he said. He could say no more.

He began to sneeze uncontrollably.

The Kikituk

by Michael Armstrong

Michael Armstrong's first novel, After the Zap, *has been described by no less an authority than Ed Bryant as "an incredibly manic after-the-bomb tale." His latest novel,* Agviq: Or, the Whale, *will be published in July of 1990 by Questar Books. Whitley Strieber calls* Agviq *"an extraordinary book... so deeply understood, so powerfully felt, that it left me staring off into frozen Arctic space, silenced by the immensity and terrible beauty of the concept." Michael has published several stories in* The Magazine of Fantasy and Science Fiction. *He writes periodically for the Anchorage* Daily News, *and the Alaska State Council on the Arts awarded him a $5,000 Individual Artist's Grant in 1987.*

An adjunct instructor at the University of Alaska, Michael has "taught such courses as English, Science Fiction, Creative Writing, and Dog Mushing." Before he found it possible to eke out a modest living as a writer and professor, he worked as a computer operator, silk screen printer, technical editor, and field archaeologist. Michael "still dabbles in archaeology and periodically disappears into the Alaskan bush to do survey and excavation, in the process discovering several ancient Eskimo sites." Clearly, these experiences have served him well in his writing... as you will see in the following story.

The north wind screamed across the pack ice and the tundra ponds, across the sandstone blocks jumbled along the hill's ridge. Blasting over the ridge, the wind scoured the snow off the spine—the sandstone boulders like the knobs of vertebrae—and swirled the snow into fine powder around the lee side, building up on the gently sloping terraces downwind. The snow seemed to pull him onto the ridge, Nick thought, sweeping him from the sky above and down onto the earth; the snow encircled him, shrouded him in its cold comfort.

A man walked the top of the ridge toward Nick, his arms jerking around the way a puppet's arms would, the movements of his legs hesitant, as if the man were not a man but some stop-action animated model in a cheap movie. Ragged tufts of fur rippled around the ruff of the man's hood. Hunks of crudely carved ivory, yellowed bone, and bleached fox and raven skulls hung on the man's parka, clattering in the storm. The snow whirled around the man, seeming to run away from him. It did not stick to the stiff hairs of his caribou skin parka, did not cling to his sealskin pants or boots.

The man twitched forward, his face hidden deep in the folds of his hood, behind the thick fur of the ruff. Frost from the man's breath collected on the inside of the hood, and every few seconds a puff of white vapor from the man's breathing escaped from the hood. Something glowed within the hood, two little red dots, perhaps the reflection of the setting sun—the brief Arctic day—on the man's eyes. The man came closer and closer to Nick, straight to him, climbing over the larger boulders, not going around them.

As the man came to Nick, he raised his right arm. The sleeve of the man's parka stuck out straight and stiff, a long tube empty at the end. Something wriggled inside the sleeve where the man's hand should be. Nick looked at the left arm of the man, saw no hand there, either, and assumed the man had pulled his hands up into the

THE KIKITUK

parka and out of the cold. The man stepped forward one more pace, stopped, and pushed his right arm up at Nick's face.

A thing shot out of the sleeve, the head of an animal on some long body. The creature screeched, its long jaws clacking up and down, thin needle teeth shining in the light of the orange sun. Two jet-black eyes glared at Nick, tracking him, the small red dots of the thing's pupils swinging back and forth. The jaws turned, the head twisted, screwing around like an auger, grinding toward Nick's nose and eyes, closer and closer. Its ears folded back, bat ears pointed and hairless, but small, the size of a dime hacked in half. More needle teeth rustled on the thing's long, thick neck, the teeth all pointing backward, the ends glistening with sticky dew.

A long tongue darted out from the thing's mouth, the way the thing had darted out from the man's sleeve, and as the tongue moved up to lick Nick's eyeball, Nick saw that the tongue had a man's skull at the end of it, and *that* skull opened its mouth and a twin of the thing shot out at Nick: thing, skull in its mouth, thing in the skull's mouth, all with clacking teeth and dripping slime on their teeth, grinding toward Nick, screeching and screeching . . .

Nick held his hands up before his face, sat up in bed, the red numbers of his alarm clock casting a ruddy light on the room: 1:31, the numbers read. Something warbled on the bedside table. Then a tiny red light on a box clicked on, and Nick heard his own voice speak.

"Hi, I'm probably here, but you never know, so what I want you to do is talk to the little machine so I can talk to you later."

Nick rubbed his eyes, shook his head, and groped for the stop button on the answering machine. He picked up the phone receiver, broke into his message. "I'm here, what the hell's up?"

"Nick?" a woman asked, her voice slightly husky. "*Nick*, it's me, Martha."

"Martha?" Through sleep-fogged consciousness the name rolled around in his head, like a steel marble pinging around in a pinball machine, buzzers clicking as the name triggered memories. *Martha*. Nick picked up his watch off the bedside table, checked the date. 2–15. "Martha—"

"You know Simeon's plane is late from Kotzebue, don't you?" Her voice teased, the lilt at the end of the sentence offering him an out. "I'm *sure* you called the airport and heard that the plane wouldn't be in until two."

"Uh, yeah. Yeah, right." Nick remembered the letter then, the note she'd sent him a week ago asking him to pick up Simeon at the airport, put him up while he was in Anchorage for the Fur Rendezvous. Damn. He'd gotten the dates mixed up, thought the early-morning plane would be coming in the next day. "He get on the plane all right?"

"He's on his way, Nick." Martha paused, and Nick could hear the hiss of the long-distance line, could imagine her calling all the way from Kotzebue, 500 miles distant. "Take care of him, okay? He's got a check from Red Dog you'll need to deposit. Okay?"

"Yeah. Okay, I'll watch him." Nick smiled, remembering Martha's persistence, remembering how she'd kept on him all the way through the custody hearings, never satisfied with a quick answer, demanding he investigate every last detail to make sure she had a solid case—that she could really get custody of Simeon from her sister. "I'll take care of him. He can stay here."

"Good. *Good*. And Nick?" He heard the pause again, knew she did that to get his attention.

"Yeah?"

"Whatever you do, don't let Simeon see his mother, don't let him even *try* to see his mother. She's in Anchorage, Nick, living on the Avenue. He wants to see her but don't let him. Okay?"

"Okay, Martha. *Okay*." Damn, she could be persistent, he thought. He smiled. "Miss you, Martha."

"I miss you, too. Thanks, Nick. Thanks."

The cold hugged the hard February night, low to the ground and filled with frost. As Nick drove west on Tudor Road toward the airport, he saw steam and smoke rising from hundreds of chimneys, the narrow plumes shooting up in nearly straight beams. A full moon lit the plumes, and where the cold, ground air met the warmer, higher air, the plumes spread and joined into broad bands of ribbons coursing across the flat plain of Anchorage. An occasional hill or knob rose up from the plain, catching a bit of smoke. Auto exhaust and smoke clung to the cold in a thin inversion layer, the air biting in the cold, acrid from the pollution.

Frost in the air channeled light from street lamps into tight beams rising up into infinite shimmery shafts, a million tubes pulling the streets into the sky. A wind earlier in the week had blown the last snowfall from the trees, and hoarfrost had replaced the snow, shrouding the branches in a crystalline coat, wrapping around the wires of chain-link fences so the frost almost filled the diamond gaps between links.

A cop car swung by Nick as he turned onto the airport road. The cop, a woman with short brown hair, glanced over at Nick as she passed him. He vaguely recognized her from when he'd been on the force, and she seemed to know him, too, nodding as she went by. He followed her taillights into the long curving drive up to the airport, past cars coated with snow and frost in the long-term lot, past taxicabs idling outside the baggage claim area, more plumes of exhaust rising into the cold air.

The 737 jet had just pulled into the gate as Nick worked his way through security. Through the glass partition separating the main terminal from the gates he could see friends and family of the arriving passengers milling around the waiting area. He had to loop around security, back down a hallway to the end gate, and got there just as the first passenger deplaned. Even if he hadn't known it was a Kotzebue flight, he could have guessed by the big white guys in brown duck coveralls with RED DOG MINE and COMINCO MINING COMPANY logos on them, or the Native guys with NANA native corporation caps.

Women in floral print-covered atigis or men in corduroy parkas trimmed with wolf walked out of the gangway, many of them clutching neatly tied brown boxes: the telltale signs of a bush flight. In the brown boxes would be wild foods, caribou or seal or beluga whale, to be shared with city family. When they returned to the village, they'd take other brown boxes, filled with fresh vegetables or liquor. A man in an ancient, ratty parka got off last, walking in a slight crouch, his toes pointed slightly in. The sleeves of the man's parka came down over his hands, inches longer than his arms, and the man held a cheap black plastic briefcase in his left hand.

At the sight of the parka, Nick sucked in his breath. *The parka*, the one from his dream. He felt something cold hit him in the groin, something that tightened up his scrotum. Made of spotted reindeer hide, the parka had the same swatches of fur sewn around the seams at the shoulder and along the arms and wrists, the same ivory figurines and little skulls dangling from it. The man in the parka turned, and Nick sighed, his muscles relaxing and warm blood flowing back into his crotch.

Simeon.

Simeon. Nick saw the boy—the young man, he had to correct himself—before Simeon saw him. In the strange parka, his back turned to Nick, a NANA cap low on his forehead and his hair hiding his face, for a moment Simeon looked almost normal, like any other Inupiaq Eskimo coming off the plane. But when Simeon turned

THE KIKITUK

to him, looking at him and not seeing him, Nick was reminded how different Simeon was, how different he always would be. Nick had hoped that the last five years had somehow changed him, that all the training and special education and growing up might have performed some miracle, but in the brief instant when Simeon looked right at him through his big glasses, Nick knew that could never be. He might have gained a few years, gone from his teens to his early twenties, but he hadn't *grown*.

Simeon could pass for a normal kid with the hat, the shaggy hair, even the thick glasses, but the lower face ... The face was smaller, the bridge of the nose low, the space between the tip of his nose and his lips wide. He had a thin upper lip, too many teeth for his mouth, and—most distinct of all—almost no vertical groove, no philtrum, between upper lip and nose.

"Simeon!"

He saw Nick then, smiled. In his odd, unsteady crouch, Simeon pushed an old lady out of the way, oblivious to her—the old woman fell back against a younger man—and brushed by another woman so close the fur on her parka rustled. He set the briefcase down, and hugged Nick, his thin arms barely going around him, the top of his head just reaching Nick's chin. Simeon patted him on the back, then stepped back, still touching Nick's parka.

"Hey," Simeon said, "that's the parka Mom made you."

Nick smiled, brushed a little lint off the blue corduroy, fiddled with the trim along the hem. Martha had made it for him when Nick had taken Simeon back to Northwest Alaska, up to Point Hope that summer five years before. "Yeah. Nice parky *you* got there, too."

Simeon grinned. "It's my grandpa's—you know, the one who was a shaman, an angatkok? Mom said I shouldn't wear it but I wanted to, so I did. I sent you a card with a picture of my grandpa in it. You get it?"

Card? Nick remembered getting a card with an old E. Curtis photograph, a sepia-tinted picture of a young man standing on the deck of a sailing ship. The man wore the same parka, a newer parka, of course, not as many amulets on it. It had the same spots though, same white triangles sewn on either side of the neck that looked like a walrus' tusks. "See you soon," someone had neatly printed inside the card, not signing it. A Kotzebue postmark on the envelope, no return address and no signature.

"*That* was your card? Nobody signed it. You can sign your name, Simeon."

Or maybe not, thought Nick. Simeon was an FAS child, fetal alcohol syndrome, learning impaired because his mother had drunk while pregnant with him. Simeon couldn't make change, couldn't think into the future, and might do something like forget to sign his name to a postcard. Hell, give the kid credit, Nick reminded himself. *I* could forget to sign a card.

"I didn't sign it? I forgot, Nick." Simeon shrugged. He scratched at his right sleeve, and through the cracked hide and worn hairs of the skin, something stiff stretched from the elbow of the sleeve to just above the wrist, like Simeon wore a brace or a splint on his forearm.

"You hurt yourself?" Nick asked, pointing at the sleeve.

"Unh-uh. It's just the . . . naw."

A Native man in a maroon parka came up from behind Simeon, put an arm on his shoulder, and whirled him around. Simeon stared at the man, smiled, and reached up to touch the guy's shoulder. He knocked Simeon's hand away.

"Hey—" Nick said, stepping toward the man.

"You knocked my *aaka* down," the man said. Taller than Simeon, he wore a KOBUK 200 sled dog race cap. The man smelled of whiskey, his eyes faintly red. "Don't you have any respect for your elders?"

THE KIKITUK

"He didn't see her—" Nick began, trying to explain. How could he, though? How could he tell this guy that it wasn't that Simeon didn't care, he just didn't *think* to care?

"*Fuck you*, honkey," the guy in the Kobuk cap said to Nick.

"Let's go, Simeon..." Nick took his elbow, tried to steer him away from the drunk man.

"No," Simeon said. "Grandpa said I should take care of myself. He said when I grew up I would have to take care of myself *his* way." He smiled at the guy. "I'm sorry."

"That's right, you're sorry," the guy said. He shoved Simeon with his fingertips, pushing against his chest. "You'll learn not to shove old ladies."

"Wally..." The old woman came up behind the drunk man.

"Okay," Simeon said. His voice had an edge to it that Nick hadn't heard before. "*Okay*." Wally had pushed him against a wall, and Simeon stood straight to the wall, straightened up from his usual stooped crouch. "*I'm sorry*," he tried again.

"Not good enough, asshole."

Wally pulled his left hand back, to slap or hit Simeon. Simeon raised up his right arm, as if he were doing a Nazi salute, the stiff arm blocking Wally's swing. Wally hit something in Simeon's sleeve, something hard, his blow stopping. Wally fell back a step, and Simeon pushed the right sleeve of his parka into the man's face. Something shot out of the parka, a snake or an ermine, it looked like, Nick couldn't tell. Something round and deep brown, the brown of old wood oiled by generations of hands. A flash of red eyes, a whirl of teeth, and a chittering like a cat on the pounce... The thing shot out of Simeon's parka in a flash, into Wally's face. Wally fell back, pulling his hands up to his face.

"You—" He looked down at his hands, at the blood

on his hands. Something had cut Wally on his left cheek, the shiny white bone gleaming through a quarter-sized circle of shredded flesh. "Sonofabitch." Wally backed away farther, turned to his grandma. The old lady stared at Simeon, at the end of his sleeve, at the blood dripping out the end of the parka.

Simeon turned to Nick, stooping again, his face blank. He grinned, not at what he had done, just his usual, placid grin. "I got a letter for you." He reached into his parka, and Nick winced as he saw Simeon's right hand come out of the sleeve. Simeon handed Nick an envelope, the incident moments before completely forgotten, dealt with.

Nick glanced at the envelope, at the bloody fingerprints Simeon had left on the white paper. He recognized Martha's handwriting. He looked over at Wally, hurrying away down the concourse, a white handkerchief spotted red held up to his face. Wally's grandmother still stared at Simeon.

"What the hell was that?" Nick asked.

Simeon shrugged. "A friend," he said, picking up his briefcase. Nick didn't know if he meant Wally or the beast inside his parka.

"The kikituk," the old lady said, pointing at Simeon. "The kikituk." She hurried off after her grandson.

Simeon sat quietly in the Toyota as they drove to Nick's house, staring out the frosted windows. The buildings and bright signs and old houses along Tudor Road were a blur to Nick, but Simeon pressed his nose to the window, looking at Anchorage as if it were all new and shiny, a snow-dusted Disneyland. Well, Nick realized, to a kid who hadn't been back to the city in two years, it probably was. As he stopped the car at a light at the intersection with the Old Seward highway, Nick thought again about Martha's letter, the one Simeon had given him in the airport. He thought about the letter and what

THE KIKITUK

Simeon had done in the airport to that drunk guy.

"Dearest Nick," the note had read, the closeness of the salutation hitting Nick hard. *Martha*. Yeah, well, he'd done a little more for Martha than investigate and watch Simeon—okay, he'd slept with her a few years back, for all the wrong reasons and a few right ones. "Take care of Simeon again," her note continued. *Take care of Simeon again.*

That was the problem with Simeon, Nick thought. Someone always had to take care of him, always watch him, always shove him in the right direction—give him directions—and make sure he lived in a pocket of safety, like an ignorant robot let loose in a warehouse full of dangerous machinery, a million simple ways he could die.

Nick sighed. He'd been taking care of Simeon off and on for fifteen years, ever since that day when he'd been a cop with the child-abuse unit and he had walked into Simeon's slimy apartment, his mom passed out in her own vomit and Simeon—still in diapers—tied with rags to his crib, shit smeared on his body and the mattress soaked with piss. He'd helped Martha get custody of Simeon from her sister, helped her get settled in Anchorage, and when that didn't work out, helped her get back out to Kotzebue. He'd helped her whenever she brought Simeon to town, or—when Simeon was old enough—when he came to town alone. He'd helped Simeon get through his vocational training, helped him get set up with a job at Red Dog.

In all those years, in all the dozens of embarrassing moments when Simeon would blunder or make some mistake anyone with an ounce of sense would have avoided, Nick had had to stick up for Simeon, explain, keep him from getting his face pounded in like Wally had been about to. "He's FAS," he could explain, once enough FAS kids had become obvious that most anyone knew what you meant. And whomever Simeon had offended would nod, and smile, and say, Yeah, I've got a nephew like that. With all the alcoholics in Alaska, with all the women who couldn't stop drinking, even when it meant poisoning their kid, it seemed like everyone had "a nephew like that." He'd always had to stand up for Simeon, always had to help him.

Until now. Until Wally and the thing that shot out of the sleeve. A kikituk, the old lady had called it. What the hell was that?

"Hey, Arctic Roadrunner," Simeon said, pointing down Old Seward. To the south, beyond a row of auto dealers, glowed the yellow and red sign of the burger joint. " 'Friendly Local Burgerman.' Can we go to the Roadrunner?"

"It's two-thirty in the morning, Simeon." Nick eased the clutch out as the stoplight began to change.

"Can we go?"

"*Two-thirty ay-em*. The Roadrunner isn't open."

"Oh." Simeon stared out the window again. "I got a coupon in my briefcase." He rooted around on the car's floor. "Will it be open at two?"

Nick sighed. "No, Simeon. It's past two."

"Two twos in a day, Nick," he said. "It open at the next two?"

"Yeah, uh—" Nick laughed. "That two, yeah, the afternoon two, but the morning two, it's past that . . ."

"So can we go to the Roadrunner now, Nick. At two in the afternoon?"

"*Shit*, Simeon, it's not—" He looked over at him, glared.

Time. The kid didn't know time, could hardly tell time. The future meant nothing to Simeon, money meant nothing to Simeon, abstract reasoning meant nothing. In her letter Martha had enclosed six single-space typed pages of lists, the routine Simeon had learned and that he was to follow in Anchorage. Martha had also enclosed Simeon's paycheck from Red Dog, forty-three hundred dollars and some change, for three weeks work as a bull cook up at the Red Dog lead and zinc mine near Kotzebue.

In neat, precise handwriting Simeon had endorsed the check to Nick. Simeon couldn't understand money, couldn't write checks, didn't understand the concept of value. He couldn't even make change. So Nick would be his bank, would deposit the check in the joint account Martha had set up for Simeon years ago—his "town account" that held Simeon's money but that only Nick or Martha could draw on.

"Let's go to the Arctic Roadrunner *now*, Nick."

"No. No, Simeon—*that's enough*." He put an edge into the words, said them hard so Simeon would understand. *That's enough*, like he'd yell at a dog, the words themselves not really having meaning, just the sound. Those had been the words Martha had yelled at Simeon when she couldn't stand him getting absurdly insistent, the words Nick had learned, the words that broke Simeon's monomania, that snapped him out of whatever loop his brain took him into. *That's enough*. Simeon looked down, fiddled with the latch of his seat belt, then turned to Nick, a blank grin on his face again.

"Okay."

Good, Nick thought. The words still worked. "You like Red Dog?" he asked.

"Red Dog's fine," Simeon said. He turned, looked in the backseat of the car for something, turned back to Nick. "It's nice. I wash dishes and chop up stuff and serve food there. Lots of guys from the old village there, lots of Tikeraq people—Point Hopers, you know? They got a satellite dish TV there on a big screen and lots of pop, you don't have to buy the pop. It's all free." Simeon leaned around, rooted around behind Nick's seat.

Free. It was the ideal system for Simeon—just take the food you want. "Sounds all right. They got the new part built yet?"

Nick remembered going up to Red Dog when it was under construction, doing a stint himself as a security guard in the construction camp when he'd been strapped for the cash. They had this long road from nowhere that ended at the mine, and the mine looked like a moonbase, a bunch of dome buildings and the dormitory on stilts with smooth edges. He'd flown in and it had been rolling hills and tundra and then this moonbase out of nowhere.

"Yeah. Moved in that time the bear got into the garbage." The light changed and they moved through the light, up to another stoplight a block east. "Hey, have you seen my briefcase?"

Nick was still trying to figure out the bear. Bear? Simeon did that, related past events to things that he remembered, no matter if someone else would know what he meant. He shook his head. "No, Simeon." Nick stopped the Toyota at the light, turned the dome light on to look in the back. "It's not in the car?" Simeon shook his head. "Then it's probably at the airport. We'll get it in the morning, I'm sure a janitor or someone picked it up."

"*No*," Simeon screamed. "No! I *need* my briefcase, I have to have my briefcase. It's got Ernie and Fozzie in it and all my important papers. Someone will take it or blow it up, like that kid's Ninja Turtles." Nick had told Simeon once about someone's lost luggage the airport police thought had a bomb; they'd blown it up and found nothing more harmful than a bunch of melted Teenage Mutant Ninja Turtle figurines.

"Simeon. . ."

"Please, Nick? Now?"

Nick glanced at his watch. It was only fifteen minutes to the airport. What did he care about time? What did Simeon? "Yeah. Yeah, okay." He took a right, on the frontage road toward International Airport Road.

* * *

THE KIKITUK

Nick parked the Land Cruiser in the pickup lane outside the airport baggage claim area and left his emergency flashers blinking. A few cabs picking up the Kotzebue passengers waited outside the terminal. One lone truck, its side dented in, sat parked by the door, an airport cop slipping a ticket under the windshield wipers.

"I'll run inside real quick," Nick said. He paused, mentally reviewing where Simeon had been in the building. "You use the bathroom?"

"Yeah," Simeon said. "Hey—maybe I left my briefcase there?"

"Maybe." He slipped his keys in his pocket. "*Wait here.*"

Nick quickly checked the Alaska Airlines claim area, down by the west end, but didn't see Simeon's briefcase. A baggage handler picked up stray luggage off the carousel and dragged it over to a bunch of bins against one wall. Wally's grandmother, the old lady, sat by the door, guarding a pile of luggage. Nick turned away, hoped she didn't recognize him. The old lady stared straight ahead, watching the door of the men's restroom in a short hallway down from the baggage carousel.

Nick followed her gaze, moved to the restroom. Just as he got there, a blond guy with a scraggly beard and a ponytail came out of the women's restroom, pushing a pail and mop. The janitor took down a sign that read RESTROOM CLOSED FOR CLEANING, glanced at Nick.

"I'll just be a second," he said.

"Yeah, right." The blond guy put the sign on the door.

Inside the doorway, Nick stepped in something wet and sticky. He pushed the second door in, had to shove harder to get it open—something blocked it from the other side. "Shit," Nick mumbled. Back when he'd been a beat cop, he used to run into blocked restroom doors all the time, usually because someone inside was smoking dope or getting a blow job. The inside door flung open.

Nick slipped on something wet on the floor, had to catch his balance on the door frame. He took another step, more carefully, looked down at his feet to be sure of his footing. He saw the red stuff first, the red fluid flowing along the white tiling, the liquid draining along the grout between the tiles: red-orange fluid, viscous like thin motor oil, sticky like sugar. Nick sniffed, smelled something else along with the rusty odor of the red stuff—the acrid smell of piss. He shivered with the recognition of the blood, of the smells.

A man lay face up in front of the sinks, one arm stretched toward a floor-height urinal, the arm lying in the urinal and a rivulet of blood swirling around in the flushing stream of water. Thick black hair hung down over the man's forehead, over his ears, clotted with blood. The left side of the man's face had been chewed into stringy flesh, the muscles shredded and spikes of white bone poking through or speckled among the hamburger of the guy's face. A cap lay on the floor, the word NANA embroidered on the front. Air bubbled out of the man's lips. The man's maroon parka had been zipped open, two buttons of his stiff, brand-new blue jeans still undone. A spray of blood speckled the ceiling, the mirror above the sinks, the walls. Underneath the paper-towel holder Simeon's cheap plastic briefcase leaned against the wall.

Wally—the man Simeon had hit upstairs, barely a half hour ago.

Nick grabbed the briefcase, sucked his breath in, turned away, and stumbled back out of the restroom. The janitor leapt back as Nick kicked the door open, pushing through. Nick paused, the soles of his shoes sticky, took a deep breath, another. The janitor looked at Nick, at his pale face, at his bloody footprints.

"Hey," he said. "*Hey*."

"Get a cop," Nick said. "Get a goddamn cop." The janitor nodded, started to go in the restroom. "*No!*" he screamed. "No, man, you *don't* want to go in there." Nick ran for the building exit. Simeon. Shit, *Simeon*.

"Hey!" the janitor yelled after him. "Where you going? Hey!"

Nick pushed into the cold air, the piercing air, idling taxicabs and air thick with hydrocarbons, he didn't care. Simeon. Wally. It had been a long time since he'd seen bloody bodies, a nice, long time. He gasped in the cold, breathing it in, deeper and deeper, the noxious fumes from the cars filling his lungs. The blood on his soles stuck to the cold concrete, freezing and the soles cracking as he moved toward the Land Cruiser. He switched the briefcase to his left hand as he yanked the passenger door open. *Simeon*.

The seat was empty.

"Sonofabitch!" Nick yelled as he flung the briefcase into the back seat. "Goddamn motherfucking sonofabitch!" The briefcase popped open, and a ragged Sesame Street Ernie doll fell out of it, limp, its arms dangling over the edge of the seat.

Crash lights whirled around and around outside the baggage claim area, their beams flashing through the glass doors and against the white walls. An airport cop stood by the door like a butler, opening it for cops and detectives, keeping out everyone else. The airport cop let in two men and a woman in dark blue jackets, CORONER stenciled on the jacket backs. They dragged a gurney with a big plastic box strapped on top. Another cop guarded the restroom door. A young native woman sat next to Wally's grandmother, an arm around her while a woman in a blue suit asked her questions. Nick recognized the woman, a rookie when he'd left the police force, now some kind of detective. The janitor stood next to Nick, and every time a cop or detective went in the restroom and came back out, tracking red footprints on the tile, the janitor grumbled.

"Fucking damn mess," he said. "A pissy mess."

Nick glanced at him, tried to smile. "When's your shift up?"

"An hour."

"Well, chill out, Harv," Nick said. The guy had said his name was Harv. "I know cops, they won't be through in there for at least two hours."

"No shit?"

"No shit. The next shift will have to clean it up. If he—"

"Jess."

"—if Jess's lucky, they'll seal the room off for another eight hours."

"Jess'll love that." Harv grinned. He lit a cigarette, offered one to Nick. He shook his head.

One of the plainclothes came over to Nick and the janitor, clapped his hand on Nick's shoulder. "Hey, which one of you turkeys saw the body?"

Nick looked up to a heavyset black guy with a thin mustache and graying hair. "*Franklin.*" He stood.

"Hughes." Franklin nodded, then smiled. "*Nick.* How's it going?" The detective shook Nick's hand.

"Okay." Franklin, he thought. He hadn't seen the guy for ten years, since he'd quit the police and gone into the more sane profession of security consulting. "Shit, *Franklin*. Yeah, yeah—I found the body."

"You see anyone in there?"

"No."

"*Anything* in there?"

"No, uh—"

"Nothing?" Franklin smiled, cocked his head.

Hell, Nick thought. Franklin might act dumb sometimes, but Nick knew him, remembered him as being able to hone in on the slightest verbal cue—an intonation, a word—and make a clue out of it. Simeon. It would be

THE KIKITUK 71

nice to keep the kid out of it, but Nick figured Wally's grandma had already told a cop about some weird kid in a strange shaman's parka. They'd check the flight lists, come up with Simeon's name, call Martha, she'd send them to Nick . . .

"Uh, a briefcase." Nick sighed. "A friend of mine left his briefcase in there, I went in to get it."

"A friend? Where'd he go?" Franklin looked around the lobby, mocking Nick. Other than the old lady and the janitor, the baggage claim area was full of nobody but cops.

"That's the problem." He shrugged. "Simeon's gone."

"Uh-huh." Franklin jerked a finger at the old lady, at a uniformed policeman standing in front of her. "Reporting patrolman said some man ID'ed the dead guy. That you?" He looked at the janitor.

"Hell no."

"Nick?" Franklin asked. Nick looked down. "You know the dead guy?"

"Not *personally*." Nick sighed. "Wally. That's what his grandma called him." Fuck, he thought. Damn Simeon. "This friend of mine hit the guy earlier." He told Franklin about the incident in the arrival area, told him about Simeon.

"So this friend of yours—Simeon?—he hit the guy—uh, hit this Wally?" Franklin asked.

Franklin looked at Nick, and Nick recognized the intense stare, the probing eyes. Damn. Cop smells a suspect and he can tidy the case up neat and easy.

"*Self-defense*. The guy swung first, was harassing Simeon."

"But Simeon cut him?"

"Ring or something. Simeon hit Wally, his ring must have nicked his cheek." He didn't want to tell Franklin that this strange thing hissed out of Simeon's sleeve and bit Wally on the face. Franklin would never believe it. Nick wasn't sure *he* believed it.

"Yeah, that'd be convenient, the way Wally's left face got chewed up." Franklin stared at Nick, then nodded. "This Simeon guy, you said he's gone?"

"I left him in the car, told him to stay there. I looked around the baggage area for his briefcase, went into the restroom, saw the dead guy, found the—"

"Found what, Hughes?"

"The briefcase." Fuck, he'd *told* him.

"Okay. You got the briefcase?"

Nick nodded. "In the car—come on."

They went back out to the Land Cruiser. Nick reached in, stuffed the papers and the Sesame Street dolls back in, handed it to Franklin. As he handed the case to the cop, he noticed a bloody handprint frozen in the textured plastic. Franklin did, too.

"Yours?"

Nick shook his head. "Never touched the body—oh, the door, might have been blood on that." He held his hand up to the print, measured it. The print was smaller.

"I guess not. This kid? Wally's?" Franklin asked.

"Maybe." Shit, but how could it be Simeon's? He'd left the briefcase in there *before* the guy had died.

"We'll see. It's late, Hughes," Franklin said. "You stick around, come down to headquarters tomorrow for a statement."

"Right. Don't leave town, check in, just a formality."

"You know the routine. Good. You sure you don't know where Simeon went to?"

"He wasn't in the car, Franklin. You find him, let me know, too, okay? He's an FAS kid, you know. You might remember him, real bad child abuse case fifteen years ago? Simeon's okay but he needs watching. He gets seizures, too, he's on medication. I don't think he has his drugs. I want you to find him, but he didn't off that guy, he couldn't have."

THE KIKITUK

"Right," Franklin said. "Get some rest."

"Yeah."

As Nick drove home, though, he kept seeing the bloody handprint, and remembered something odd about it: no lines were on the palm, the palmprint was smooth and bare—just like an FAS kid's hands. Just like Simeon's hands.

The snow fell in tiny flakes, more like windblown frost, a hard snow, a cold snow from fog, not heavy or warm or wet. Nick pulled his hat down tighter around his ears, watched his breath mist away in the westerly wind. He'd parked over by the downtown park strip, the old hunk of land on the south edge of the urban core that had been an old airfield. His footsteps squeaked in the snow, on the hard-pack pedestrians had pounded into the pavement.

A range of mountains blazed white to the east, bright above the waning fog hugging its lower slopes, bright from the reflecting fog and the deep snow, the clean snow that covered everything but the highest branches of the spruce forests. The afternoon sun rose above the fog bank, above the blowing hoarfrost starting to burn off. Ice in the air and ice in the sky, the sun cast sun dogs—parhelions—through the mist, little blips of the rainbow circling the sun at nine, twelve, and three o'clock. The fog and the Chugach Mountains hemmed in the city, kept it from spreading beyond the wall into the wilderness beyond.

On a ball field covered in two feet of snow, a snowshoe softball game was in progress, a runner stomping to first base on big wood-frame snowshoes, a red ball whizzing over the second baseman's head. Rondy, the Fur Rendezvous, the annual winter carnival.

Some musher had set up his dog team on another end of the park strip, lining out his team along the backstop of another softball field and giving dog rides. Japanese tourists in thin leather jackets snuggled under the wool blankets of the musher's freight sled, a friend snapping their picture—flight attendants on layover, Nick figured, the only Japanese crazy enough to visit Alaska in the winter. The dogs lay on the snow, licking their paws, bored. Nick had seen sled dogs frantic, jerking at the lines, but these had been round and round a field, bored silly.

Along Ninth Avenue, on the north side of the park strip, houses barely fifty years old nestled up against thirty-floor glass and steel skyscrapers. *Oil company* skyscrapers, Nick thought, remembering five years ago when the buildings had risen up almost in one summer, the big buildings blocking the summer light and casting the park strip in darkness hours before the night actually came. Well, at least the winter sun, the southern sun, favored the little houses, favored the park.

He came up to the Avenue, Fourth Avenue. An oldtimer had told him that before the war the west end of the Avenue had been the respectable part, the east end the red-light district, where all the sleazy bars and the hookers had been. Now almost all the bars had been torn down, what was left of them from the '64 earthquake, until only a small block remained of about three bars, a package liquor store, and a pawn shop. Nick walked from the respectable end, past a hideous luxury hotel, past the *Anchorage Times* newspaper building, past the Fourth Avenue Theatre, past the Woolworth's and the old city hall.

Snow fences lined the Avenue, and snow had been plowed back onto the street. Big dog trucks with double rows of doors, sled dog noses poking out of the airholes of the doors, were parked along the snow fencing. Nick recognized a couple of the mushers hanging out by their trucks: a woman with wavy blonde hair who'd won the Fur Rendezvous World Championship race the year before; a silver-haired Athapaskan with a stiff leg who had

THE KIKITUK

won the Rondy more than anyone else; a guy with a walrus mustache and a ponytail. The sled dog teams would go out one at a time, two minutes apart, down the Avenue, along the city bike trails, and out of town into a wild city park, and then back, twenty-five miles total. Up by the finish line TV technicians set up their cameras and microphones, and an announcer rattled out statistics on the mushers, the dogs, the racecourse, filling in time before the race, counting down to when the first musher went out: "Thirty minutes, thirty minutes to race time."

And then Nick passed the bars, the bars with the plate glass windows painted black, around the corner from the fur shops, the police substation, and a cheap art gallery that sold tacky tourist prints of growling grizzlies. The bars: Nick couldn't remember the names, the decor, but the flavor never changed, the clientele never changed, only the owners. Eskimos and Indians and Aleuts and a few white bush rats weaved up and down the sidewalk, slipping on the ice, bumping into the snow fences, drunk already at 1:30 in the afternoon. Nick knew intellectually that this was a thin slice of Native culture, that for every drunk on the Avenue were twenty clean and sober Natives. But this was the Native most white people saw. For every drunk woman Nick saw, he saw Simeon's mother, saw the damned curse alcohol inflicted on a good and decent people. Bad enough to destroy one life that could be healed, it was worse to destroy another life that could not—destroy a culture and a way of life, too.

Nick moved through the bars, asking for Simeon, asking if anyone had seen a strange kid in a weird shaman's parka. He asked for people from Point Hope, from Kotzebue, figuring they might know Simeon. Three Point Hope girls said they'd seen some guy who looked like that the night before—he had bought a bottle of Jim Beam at the package store—but they hadn't seen him that day. Maybe at Bean's? Yeah, Nick thought he might try Bean's Cafe, might try the city soup kitchen down in the warehouse district, off the Avenue. Maybe the tent city? But he kept cruising the bars, nursing cups of coffee, asking questions, buying drinks when he needed information.

Simeon. He had to find Simeon for Martha.

Nick thought of the last time he'd seen Martha and Simeon, up at Point Hope some summers back. Nick and Simeon had gone out caribou hunting with some of his relatives. He and the boy had gone for a walk, away from the others along a long ridge, more hiking than hunting, though they'd taken their rifles. Fog had moved in, fog from the coast, and they'd been heading across a brushy gully between two ridges, up and over a bank, when Simeon had stopped Nick suddenly, shoving him to the side.

Quiet Simeon, unassertive Simeon, gentle Simeon who never argued with anyone older or touched anyone harder than with a pat, *that* Simeon had grabbed Nick's shoulder and pushed him to the side. Out of the corner of his eye Nick had seen that the boy had raised his rifle, chambering a round in one quick motion, and just as Nick heard the shot and the bullet flying through the air, he saw the brown blur tumble toward them. A second later he heard the hard thud of the bullet hitting flesh and not wasting its energy on air, saw the brown blur roll, saw the grizzly bear fall head first and somersault back over head, rolling and rolling, and stop. One shot, an almost impossible shot right through the only thin spot on the skull—a half inch any other direction and the bullet would have bounced off the skull and the bear would have come right on Nick and ripped his throat out.

He had glanced at Simeon as he fired and in his face Nick saw Simeon *think*, deliberately think, concentrating on the shot and speculating ahead a brief second into the future, into the calamity to come. When the bear stopped, Simeon's face went slack again, into its perpetual vacant glare. Nick had to remind Simeon to eject the shell. But

THE KIKITUK

the kid had saved his life, saved their lives. Yeah, Nick thought, Martha could ask him to take care of Simeon, but she never, ever had to say it, demand it, insist upon it. Simeon had earned his care for the rest of his life.

And now he was missing, maybe dead. *Couldn't be*, Nick thought, but he nonetheless imagined horrid scenarios, created them as if by imagining the worst he could avoid the worst. Yeah, he thought, the boy had probably wandered off into the woods to die. Nick wanted to prepare himself for Simeon's possible death, didn't want to deny the possibility of it, because he'd done that once before. He had denied the possibility of a death and then the death itself, even through his father's funeral, and it had hurt that much harder when the discovery came.

Dead.

It wasn't even the thought of Simeon's dying that scared him, because in a way that would be a blessing, for the poor kid whose life never had a chance because his damn mother decided to get pregnant when she was a drunk, had no damn right to get pregnant and ruin someone's life. Hell, Simeon hardly seemed human, hardly seemed to be able to love, to abstract, to imagine, to think, to do all those things humans did which made them human. And yet he'd killed that bear, had loved Nick enough to save his life, had thought enough to realize that his life was in danger then, too. So that would be a shame, maybe the kid had something human after all.

Martha, Nick thought. That's what would hurt: telling Martha.

If Simeon turned up dead, Nick would have to tell Martha, have to be the one to give her the bad news. The boy she'd rescued from an abusive mother would be dead. The hopes and dreams she had for him would be gone, even the bare hope that Simeon could live a halfway normal life. Lost. He could face Simeon's death, but Martha—Nick would rather face that bear again than be the one to say her son had died.

Nick sipped his coffee, looked around the bar again—the Alaska Bar, he remembered it had been called, but now it was known as something else. No one had seen Simeon that morning, though Nick was damn sure he had to be on the Avenue, around the Avenue. It was the only place he knew to go. Even Martha had told him that, when he'd called to let her know Simeon was missing. Did she know where Simeon could have gone to, why he had left Nick's car at the airport and—Nick guessed—taken a cab somewhere?

"He's going to kill his mother," Martha had said. "All along he said he was going to go to Anchorage and find Angie and kill her. I thought he was kidding, but now . . . I think he meant it."

That had scared him more than anything—not that Simeon said he was going to kill his mother, but that Martha now believed Simeon when he said it. Martha knew Simeon better than anyone, she had figured out his moods and his temperament and how to get through to the distant mind lurking somewhere in his damaged head.

Simeon's mother . . . Nick finished his coffee, smiled. He'd been asking the wrong question. Simeon was new to the Avenue, and unless someone who knew him from his village had bumped into him, no one would notice another nameless Native. But Simeon's mom . . . she had probably been on the street long enough, had probably made a name for herself one way or another, and someone would know her. He looked around the bar again, saw the three women from Point Hope still in the corner, flirting with a big tall black man. As he walked toward them, Nick tried to remember what Simeon's mom looked like, who Angie was, where she would be.

Angie. Find Angie, and he'd find Simeon.

* * *

THE KIKITUK

Nick walked down a well-beaten path that led from behind the Alaska Native Hospital on Second Avenue to a clump of woods between the hospital and the warehouse district below. Thin puffs of smoke rose up from fires and wood stoves in the woods. A charred oil drum cut in half smoldered in a clearing just off the trail, cardboard boxes flattened around it, whiskey bottles neatly pushed into the snow, necks up, trophies from a night of drinking.

At the edge of the clearing, yellow holes had been drilled by piss down to the frozen ground, through the deep snow. Nick remembered pissing like that once himself, stepping off a ski trail in the mountains east of Anchorage and shakin' hands with the governor. His pee steamed in the cold air, the hot urine melting deeper and deeper, a narrow, funnel-shaped well hole. Frozen pee caked the trunk of a skinny black spruce tree. Dogs, he thought, dogs peed like that.

The first two fires Nick found were built outside clear plastic shacks, their inhabitants huddled around the fires. Nick stopped at one fire long enough to roll a drunk guy away from the fire, before he fell into the flames and burned up in his old sleeping bag. Long habit learned on the police force made Nick check the drunks' fingers for frostbite, their cheeks and noses for patches of white—their necks for pulses, even. No cold hands and face, no dead bodies... He moved on.

The third curl of smoke rose not from an open fire, but a neat wall tent in a clearing off the trail. A light layer of frost rimed the guy ropes leading from the tent, but heat from a stove inside had melted the frost off the walls and roof of the canvas. Inside a tinny radio played, twangy country-western music. You couldn't knock on canvas so Nick just hollered a hello.

"That you, boy?" a woman asked from inside. "Boy, come on in."

Inside, a woman lay on an aluminum cot, snuggled

up inside a sleeping bag. She had long black hair, a little greasy, but neatly braided in a tight plait fastened at the crown of her head with a beaded hair clip. Low light from the winter sun made the white walls of the canvas glow dull yellow. A scrap of old carpeting had been set on the floor, in front of a tin Yukon stove with a shiny galvanized pipe that poked through the roof of the tent. Hanging from a safety pin stuck in the tent wall was a dime-store picture of Jesus. There was a closed trunk on the ground and some clean pots, pans, and dishes on top of the trunk. When Nick came in she looked up and laid down a tattered Gideon Bible on the trunk, next to an open bottle of Jim Beam whiskey.

"Hey," she said, "you're not my boy. I know you?" She stared at Nick, not hostile but probing, and it took Nick a second to realize she was checking him out not only to see if she knew him, but to see if he was bringing her good news or bad news. "You got a bottle?" She pointed at the Jim Beam, a quarter full. "I'm about out an' it's gettin' cold, you know? My boy said he'd go get me a bottle."

"I don't have a bottle." Nick held up his hands.

"You a cop? I didn't do anything, railroad said I could camp here on their land."

"I'm not a cop." Nick looked at her, tried to see a resemblance between her and Simeon, couldn't find it. He tried to remember if this woman was the woman with ratty hair he'd found when he had investigated the report of an Eskimo kid tied to his crib. He couldn't tell.

This woman hadn't gone to fat like a lot of Eskimo women, hadn't gained the gradual weight years chewing seal meat and Eskimo doughnuts would give you. He could see a resemblance between Martha and Simeon in their eyes, but if this woman was Simeon's mom, her eyes were so yellowed it would be hard to tell.

"I'm looking for someone. You from Point Hope?" The woman nodded. "You got a kid named Simeon?"

THE KIKITUK

"Simeon?" The woman looked at Nick, looked through him as if she were staring past Nick through the open tent flap, beyond to the flat Arctic miles north of them. "Yeah, maybe. I had a boy once, but I didn't call him Simeon. That's my goddamn father's name, I wouldn't name my son after that bastard. I had a son but my *goddamn* sister took him away from me, some *cop* and a goddamn judge took him away. My only boy, they said I couldn't raise him, but my slut of a sister could."

"What's your name?" he asked. "I'm Nick."

"Angie."

Angie. Bingo, Nick thought. He grinned.

She sat up, took a swig from the bottle, waved it at Nick. He shook his head, and she took another sip. "So, Nick, what you want? Something about my boy?"

"I'm looking for him. He's in town, you know?"

"I know. He came to visit me. Last night."

Last night. Shit. "He hurt you? Did he touch you or threaten you?"

"Simeon? No way, man. Why would he do that? He's my boy. What have I ever done to hurt him? Why would he want to hurt me?"

Nick shook his head. She didn't know, he thought. Didn't realize what she had done. The damn tragedy of it all. She didn't know how she had ruined her son's life even before his life had begun—or she denied knowing. "Yeah, right. He say anything to you?"

"What you care? You think you're his momma?" Angie stared at him, cocked her head. "I don't know you, do I?"

"No," Nick said. "I just know your son. He do anything to you?"

"He just said hello. He said 'Momma, it's okay, I don't blame you,' what would he blame me for?" Nick shrugged. "And then he said, 'It's over with, now,' and he pointed his arm at me, raised the sleeve of my papa's ratty old parky at me, this thing popped out. This carved wooden thing, I remember it. My papa used to show us it, play this game with us—he'd be all dressed up in the parky. Papa gave it to Simeon, that thing. The kik... the kik-i-something."

"Kikituk."

"Yeah. That thing. He pointed it at me. Papa said you shouldn't point the kikituk at someone, it was like a gun and it might go off by accident. But Simeon did." She rubbed her stomach. "Kind of just *tapped* my tummy with it. Got me a little bellyache now. Funny, huh? You sure you don't got a bottle on you?"

"Go to Bean's," Nick said. The local soup kitchen. "Heard they got a road-kill moose last night. Get some stew, you're probably hungry."

"Yeah. Yeah." Angie took another swig.

"Simeon say where he was going?"

"Nah. Came in, said that stuff, pointed that stick at me, left me a bottle, and left." She squinted at Nick. "You *sure* I don't know you?"

"No."

"Okay. Simeon said he'd come back, said he'd get me another bottle this morning. Said he had lots of money and he'd get me a bottle, 'cuz I was his momma and I'd been good to him. You haven't seen him?"

"No."

"I'm right here, Momma."

Nick whirled around, came face-to-face with Simeon. He held a flap of the tent up, pushed Nick out of the way, over to the side of Angie's bed. Nick put a hand out to him, to touch him, but Simeon swept by, hardly noticing him.

"Simeon."

"I got you a bottle, Momma," Simeon said. "*Two* bottles. Three."

"*Simeon*," Nick said. "Where the hell have you been?"

Simeon turned to Nick, stared at him. He stood

THE KIKITUK

straight, like in the fight with Wally. He glared at Nick, looked straight through him, his eyes two dark hunks of glossy obsidian. "Nick." He said it flat, emotionless, the same tone of voice the time he'd hit Wally: in control, intelligent. "*Nick.*" His voice softened. "You should go."

"Can't go. Told Martha I had to find you. I can't lose you again, your momma told me she'd beat me to a pulp if I lost you again."

"*I'm* his momma, not that whore," Angie said.

"Sure you're my momma," Simeon said. He glared at Nick. "You *should* go."

"Sorry."

Simeon shrugged. Nick shivered. Simeon usually didn't shrug, didn't show much emotion, didn't know the subtleties of intonation, of body language. He was usually a lumbering doll, a robot.

The man in the shaman's parka took a bottle out of a paper bag, a quart bottle of clear liquid. He took out two more bottles, same brand, and then a plastic baby bottle. Simeon unscrewed the cap off one bottle, the tax seal snapping free, and tossed it away. With a paring knife Angie had left on the trunk next to a browned apple, he cut away the tip of the nipple on the baby bottle.

"Everclear?" Angie asked. "I tol' you to get Jim Beam."

"Everclear's better, Momma. Lots better."

"Simeon?" Nick asked. "What are you doing?"

"You like Everclear, Momma. That's what you gave me when I was a kid. Everclear in my baby bottle." Simeon unscrewed the top of the plastic bottle, filled it with grain alcohol, screwed the cap back on. "Drink it. Suck on it, Momma."

"No, Simeon. My liver, I can't—"

Simeon moved over to Angie, shoved her down on the cot, tilted her head back. He put the tip of the baby bottle between her teeth, squeezed the bottle, forcing the

Everclear down her gullet, holding her mouth closed and stroking her throat so she'd swallow. He refilled the bottle, squeezed more alcohol down her. Again. Again. He unsnapped another cap, kept refilling the baby bottle, forcing Angie to drink. Two quarts, three quarts, straight.

"Pretty good, huh?" Simeon asked. "Love that liquor, right?"

Angie lay back, pure grain alcohol drooling from her mouth, her eyes glassy. Come on, Nick thought. Puke it up. That much in her, she should just barf it up, save herself. Her eyes rolled back in her head, the whites showing, her mouth went slack and she drooled some more. Didn't throw up, though, didn't puke, didn't heave. Nick tried to go help her, but Simeon stood between him, glaring at him, the kid's eyes still hard and black, his back still straight. Not dumb, no, Nick thought. Not stupid, not placid. Not then.

Simeon turned to Nick. "Kikituk gets thirsty, Nick. Had to water it. Shouldn't be long now." Simeon extended his left hand out of the sleeve of his parka, read his watch. "A few more minutes, Nick."

Time, Nick thought. He knows the time.

The woman, Simeon's birth mother, the woman who brought him into the world, who cursed him with his disability—Angie arched her back. She sat up straight, pushing the sleeping bag off her, swinging her legs over the edge of the cot. Something moved in her stomach, her stomach swelled, contracted, ballooning in and out, like a womb expanding. Her shirt ripped away, exposing Angie's naked belly. A circle of raw flesh, slashes of red cuts around her belly button, oozed droplets of blood. Her stomach swelled once more, the circle of cuts spreading into a mouth, and then Angie's belly burst.

A brown snake burst forth, its ermine head whipping around, staring at Nick with its red eyes. The kikituk snapped its jaws, the teeth gleaming, its tongue darting out. The skull on the tip of the tongue opened its mouth,

THE KIKITUK

and Nick didn't have to look, he knew that on the tongue of the skull would be another kikituk. The kikituk crawled to Nick, chittering. It hissed, saw Simeon.

The little monster wriggled toward Simeon, dripping with blood. Blood splattered the floor, spattered the walls of the tent, splattered the dime-store picture of Jesus. The blood hissed on the stove, down through into the fire, and the alcohol from Angie's stomach flared up, tongues of flame flickering away from the stove toward a pool of blood on the tent floor.

The tent stank of Everclear, stank like the amniotic fluid of Simeon's birth stank. Martha had been there at his birth, had told Nick of it, how the birthing room reeked of alcohol, how Simeon reeked of alcohol, how Angie had drunk so much, had polluted her body and Simeon's body with so much ethanol that her womb's fluid stank up the room. "If you had lit a match," Martha had said, "you could have burned the place down."

Squirming through the flames, the kikituk sought its womb, sought its home. Simeon held out the sleeve of his parka, held it down to the kikituk, and it crawled to him, inside his sleeve. Nick backed away to the door, away from Simeon.

"I'm sorry, Nick," Simeon said. He held out his right arm to Nick. The kikituk slithered out, its jaws clacking, its tongue and the jaws of the skull on the tips of its tongue clacking.

"No, Simeon . . ." Nick took a deep breath. "Simeon, *that's enough*." The words flew at him, the harsh words, the bitter words. *That's enough*, he had said when Simeon stole money from Nick's wallet, because he didn't want to spend his own money. *That's enough*, he had said when Simeon would scream and rage when Nick tried to get him to take his medicine. *That's enough*, he had said when Nick wanted to go to the Arctic Roadrunner the night before. *That's enough, that's enough, that's enough*, he had repeated a hundred, a thousand times, the words that broke through the fog of Simeon's consciousness, that made him stop, that now made Simeon stop.

Simeon lowered his arm, hunched his shoulders, looked down at the burning blood on the floor, at the broken belly of his mother. "Momma . . ." he said.

"Dead," Nick said. The flames crawled up the tent wall, up the legs of Simeon's pants. "You killed her, Simeon. The kikituk killed her."

He turned to Nick, nodded. "I know, Nick." He smiled, his usual placid grin. "Momma's dead."

"Yes, Simeon. Your momma's dead. Let's go. Got to get out of here." Nick moved back another step to the open tent flap. Simeon followed him. "The parka, Simeon. Leave the parka." Simeon grinned, pulled the parka over his head, let it drop to the floor. "Good." Nick took his hand, pulled him from the tent, to the clearing beyond.

The flames roared up the side of the tent, the spruce poles swirling with flames. Through the open flame Nick saw the parka writhe around. Once, he had to step up to the tent, and beat at the kikituk with a stick until it crawled back in. The sleeping bag caught fire, Angie caught fire, and the tent became totally consumed.

Nick put an arm around Simeon, brushed little bits of curled, burnt hair out of his eyes. He put his coat around him, walked him along the path. Two railroad workers from the equipment yard down the hill ran down toward them, carrying fire extinguishers the size of scuba tanks.

"Anybody else down there?" they asked him.

"A woman . . . she was drunk, passed out. I think it's too late. I could only save the boy."

The railroad workers nodded, but went on to the burning tent. At the top of the hill, Nick looked down, saw only a charred frame of poles, the tin stove, and a lump of something hideous and burnt.

"Can we go to the Arctic Roadrunner now?" Simeon asked.

Nick pulled him close, put an arm around his shoulder. "Sure, Simeon. Sure."

The Christmas Escape
by Dean Wesley Smith

Dean Wesley Smith writes: "I've sold somewhere around forty stories to professional markets over the last six years, including Amazing Stories, The Magazine of Fantasy and Science Fiction, The Horror Show, Night Cry, Oui Magazine, Gambling Times Magazine *(a sf/ghost/gambling story),* Obsessions Anthology, The Clarion Awards Anthology *(edited by Damon Knight),* Modern Short Stories Magazine, Gem Magazine, *and four or five other anthologies.*

"My first novel (to appear) was called Laying the Music to Rest, *and was published by Warner Books. It is a sf/ghost story and is now on the final ballot of the Stoker Awards for best first novel. It got a lot of good reviews, too. Amazing...*

"I am also the owner and publisher of Pulphouse Publishing. Editor Kristine Kathryn Rusch and I put out eleven books last year and this year we will do about thirty. Last year, for our work on Pulphouse, Kris and I won the World Fantasy Award. Kristine Kathryn Rusch and I are also co-editing the 25th Anniversary Clarion Anthology. Busy, busy, busy."

The first things you notice when you move into a nursing home are the smells.

The choking, ugly smell of sickness. The crisp, biting smell of antiseptic. The thick aroma of death. Smells that make visitors nervous, in a hurry to leave. Smells that the nurses and aides can never seem to completely wash from their uniforms.

For me, after a week of days and a longer week of nights, I stopped noticing all the smells, except one. The sickening sweet smell of people waiting to die. That smell stuck to the surface of everything like oil on water. It coated every minute of every hour of every day. And for the ghost, not even dying let her escape the smell and the waiting.

I moved into the Hillside Nursing Home in August, two months after I learned I would never get out of the wheelchair, ten months after the fall that had put me in it, one month after my children, Donna and Steve, both said, "Mom, it's for your own good."

My room was E–71, right next to the nurse's station past where the ghost was supposed to walk. My room, like all the rooms, was small, with a single bed, a closet, a night stand with a lamp, and a small desk that held my old typewriter that I used to write letters to Donna and Steve, and occasionally to an old friend. The room was so small that for the first year or so I kept the door open to make me feel less imprisoned. Of course, that was only an illusion. Even with the door open, I was trapped in that room until I died.

And I knew it.

It was the day after Thanksgiving, at lunch in the cafeteria, that Gretchen, the woman who lived four doors down the hall from me, started telling me about the ghost. No reason that I can remember. One minute we were talking about the weather and the rain and the next she was telling me about a ghost.

Helen, my favorite of all the nurses, was sitting at the next table feeding Mr. James. All the way through Gretchen's story, Helen nodded. I asked her the next day when she brought me my pills if she had seen the Christmas ghost. She half laughed, but I could tell from the

THE CHRISTMAS ESCAPE 91

deep sadness in her brown eyes it was not a happy laugh. "Everyone who has been here more than a few years has seen her."

The story goes that a woman named Anne, about forty years ago, had decided to spend Christmas with her family instead of in the nursing home. Gretchen said she wasn't sure whether this Anne really did have a family or where they were on that Christmas Eve, but for some reason Anne decided to leave.

She put her cloth coat over her nightgown, took her brown purse, slipped on her shoes, and walked right down the hall past the nurse's station and out the side door into the snow and cold. No one saw her leave and they found her frozen body the next day beside the bridge embankment. It seems she had sat down to rest before crossing the old bridge and had frozen to death.

The next Christmas Eve an aide saw her walking down the hall, purse in hand, bent on leaving, and went to stop her, thinking she was a current resident. Only, the poor aide's hand went right through Anne's arm and the aide had to be taken to the hospital for shock.

Anne disappeared the moment her hand touched the door handle. Every year since, she has made her Christmas Eve walk from her room to the door.

My first Christmas Eve in the home I watched the entire walk. Both my children were too busy with their families to travel the long distance to visit, so I had nothing else to do. At ten-thirty I moved down the hall and joined ten other residents and three of the nurses beside the nurse's station. I could feel the tension from everyone and no one talked, except in hushed whispers as if we were in a big church.

At exactly eleven, Anne faded into being outside of the closed door to her old room, two doors farther down the hall than my room. Without so much as a look around, she turned and headed down the hall toward us, her brown cloth coat flapping slightly open as she walked, her large brown purse hanging from her left hand. Her shoes made no sound on the hall's tile floor.

She wore a scarf over her gray hair and her eyes had the look of desperate determination. She walked past us without so much as a look, turned left at the nurse's station and headed firmly for the door. When her hand reached for the door handle, she faded and disappeared.

My stomach clamped into a tight knot and no one around me said a word. I just sat there, dazed, staring at the door and that handle, lost in what I had seen. I think one of the aides finally wheeled me back to my room. I really don't remember.

As the next year went by and the smell of the waiting to die became more and more overwhelming, I became obsessed with Anne and her walk. I wanted to find out everything I could about her. I was allowed to search through the nursing home's old records from the time and discovered that she had had three children, none of whom lived in town at the time of her death. Her husband had died the year before she moved into the home and the night she died she still owned the old family estate, even though her son had put it up for sale. Maybe she was attempting to get there that night?

Through the newspapers I discovered she had been a popular figure around town. She and her husband had done numerous activities to help the poor. Yet she had been forgotten. The home's records show that in the three months before Christmas, only one person had come to visit her. And that was the pastor from her church, hoping to get her to donate to a charity event.

I knew how she must have felt. With Al, my husband, dead and Donna and Steve living so many hundreds of miles away, I very seldom had visitors either. Most of us here didn't.

The more I discovered about Anne, the more I think

THE CHRISTMAS ESCAPE

I would have liked her. I think I would have called her a friend if we had met. As the year went by and the time grew closer for Anne to make her walk, I became more and more determined to help her gain the freedom she had tried and failed to get on her own. I didn't know how, exactly. But I knew I had to try.

The weather on that Christmas Eve turned out to be much like the weather on the night that Anne died. A cold northern storm had hit the city and the streets were piled high with snow, with more falling every hour. I stationed myself in the hallway beside my door at ten and waited in the dim light for Anne to appear. By ten-thirty a dozen other residents and nurses were standing or sitting near the nurse's station, also waiting for the show to begin.

I had butterflies in my stomach and my hands were sweaty on the arms of my chair. I had tried over and over again to put myself in Anne's place, to understand what would be important to her. I had made ten different plans and decided against them all. I still wasn't exactly sure what I was going to do. I was just going to trust my instincts and hope for the best.

At eleven the air in front of the third door down the hall shimmered and Anne appeared, ready again for her walk. She turned and headed toward me, her eyes focused off ahead, her purse clutched tight in her hand.

Quickly, I wheeled my chair directly into her path, turned and sat facing her. As she neared I said in as solid yet friendly a voice as I could manage, "Anne. Anne. Please wait. Let me take you home."

At first I didn't think she heard me. She kept coming at me head-on and I figured she'd walk right through me as if I were so much air.

"Please, Anne. Let me drive you home. It's cold out tonight and I really don't mind."

I hadn't driven a car in years, but I hoped she didn't know that.

Anne stopped in front of me, blinked, and then glanced around the hall. I heard the gasp of surprise from the residents and nurses as Anne looked down at me.

"I'd love to help you get home," I said. "Won't you let me?"

She stared at me for a moment and then, as if seeing the hall for the first time, looked around, her gaze lingering for a moment on the group near the nurse's station.

"Will you let me help?"

She looked at me again, our gaze holding, her dark eyes studying me. Then, with a faint smile, she nodded.

Without a moment's hesitation, I turned my chair around and started down the hall in the direction she had been walking. Even though I couldn't hear her, I knew she was following me from the expressions on the faces of the nurses and residents.

At the nurse's station I turned left toward the door and Anne fell into step beside me. It was difficult for me to wheel my chair as fast as she walked, but I managed. I couldn't let her down now.

As we reached the door she moved to take hold of the handle.

"No," I said. "Let me."

She paused, then smiled. At that moment I knew I had been right. I would have called this woman a friend.

I pulled the door open, backing my chair out of the way as I did it. The cold storm air cut through my bathrobe as I held the heavy door open wide.

Anne looked out the door for a moment, then turned and nodded thank-you.

"Better get going," I said.

She smiled and, for the first time in forty years, stepped through the door and into the cold night air. She was gone before she left even a single footprint in the new snow.

THE CHRISTMAS ESCAPE

The sound of the wind cut through the silence in the hall. And the fresh air, for the moment, washed away the smell of the waiting and the death.

I took a deep breath and tried to plant the smell of freedom deep in my memory. Then, with one last look into the white snow, I rolled back into the hall and let go of the door.

As I watched it swing shut, locking into place with a solid thump, I wondered who was going to open it for me.

A Winter Memory
by Michael D. Toman

Born "one hundred years and a day after the death of Poe," Michael D. Toman grew up and lived in Lansing, Michigan, until he "moved to the Omega Coast (aka California) in 1980. Sold first story in 1972, attended the Clarion Workshop in 1973, and saw that first story published in 1974. Joined Borges, Casanova, the Brothers Grimm, and Andre Norton ('Hi, gang!') in the noble profession of Librarianship that same year." Michael has published short fiction in the United States, England, France, and Germany. Most recent story: "Why Tigers Hate Spiders" in Pulphouse Six. *He likes "to read more than write, which is not a recommended attitude for a flourishing career as a wordsmith. I haven't committed a first novel yet, and I love to read autobiographical notes but hate to write 'em."*

Along with Michael's submission to Cold Shocks *came a letter which, in part, stated: "Seems to me that the theme is a natural, considering all of the great horror and fantasy stories done on it already. Everybody remembers Blackwood's 'The Secret of the Snow' (for my money one of his creepiest Dr. John Silence stories, about the undead Priests of the Snow Cult) and Shirley Jackson's chilling novel about a haunted skating rink,* We Have Always Lived in the Ice Castle. *But I also remember with affection things like* The Tundra Books *by Rudyard Kipling, with the tale of 'Nayak the White Reindeer' and his fine story of Eskimo polar bear hunting and obsession 'Brother to the Bear.' Not to mention* The

Frost World, *Arthur Conan Doyle's adventure uniting Professor Challenger and Sherlock Holmes in the Himalayas. (But then I've always been a sucker for any story featuring Challenger, Holmes, or a woolly mammoth.)*

"But I have to confess my favorite story is Lovecraft's 'The Colour Out of the Wild,' in which Arthur P. Eden paddles his skin boat into a Yukon hell with his comical, faithful, heroic dog Buckfang. (Like a lot of kids, I saw the Disney movie before I read the book. I'm not ashamed to admit that my eyes still get scratchy and I get a lump in my throat at the part in the movie where it looks like that big shaggy old yeller-and-red wolf-dog has been killed by the Shoggoth!)

"Don't know if my story is up to those wonderful old standards, but I hope you like it."

I'm pleased to report that Michael Toman's story is of a very high standard indeed, though I believe it was composed in a slightly different continuum than the above classics.

They were talking about dreams and that of course meant nightmares.

"I don't know," Allan said. "I used to have nightmares about having library books overdue that I didn't know about or remember. Also used to wake up convinced that I had assignments due for German class a year or so after I quit taking German, probably because I hated doing the homework so much."

"I dreamed once that I broke both my legs and had to crawl along the curb while all sorts of cars kept coming at me . . ." she said.

He listened while he watched her right index finger trace a slow path from under her chin to the corner of her lip and back, watched with the pious attention of a small child observing dust in sunlight. He remembered her telling him once how she had decided to quit biting her fingernails to the quick, and had never done it again.

"Yeah," he said. "And I'm afraid of things getting in my eyes. I don't know if it's blindness or being blinded that I fear. I dreamt once that I was totally blind. No images or anything in this dream, I was just able to feel things like doors and walls." Like the car door handle in his back when he moved behind the steering wheel in order to face her.

Now her head moved in that slight tilt to the left that it always had whenever she was nodding toward him to show her interest.

"I even remember trying to type a paper that I knew was overdue, even though I couldn't see the paper and I couldn't even see the words in my mind. Just typing toward something in the darkness..."

"What's the thing you fear most?" Jane asked.

He pulled his eyes away from her eyes and looked out at the trees. He could never remember the color of her eyes when he wasn't with her, and when he was with her he somehow always forgot to look.

Fear? His greatest fear?

"I don't know, there are so many things, so many..."

What? What could he tell her?

The trouble was that he did not know what to do. Finding a place to be alone with her, where he could just sit and *talk* to her, was the least of it. He had even gotten it down to a routine once, one he had told her when he could still joke about it, before it had become something sharp cutting deep into the naked rock of his heart that made his mouth curl into a derisive mockery of a smile whenever he did *the bit*.

"You see, I missed all that stuff back in junior high. I got the health lectures with the live-action slides showing the radiant red *wounds* you got when you fooled around with diseased doorknobs. I even sat in the health classroom over the gym with all the other guys in the mandatory question-and-answer session, where you weren't allowed to leave unless you handed in a slip of paper with some dumb question on it like 'Why do some pictures make guys get all hot?' The gym teachers made everybody hand in a question because they *knew* there were questions and they *knew* that guys were just too shy to ask them. So everybody had to volunteer, right?

"But I missed the rest of it. You know, where to go after a date, what to do, all of that stuff. I figure they passed out the mimeoed instruction sheets one day when I was absent and the paperwork just never caught up with me."

She had laughed warmly. That had been on the first date, last October, when he had finally gotten up the courage to ask her for a date after having lunch with her in the school cafeteria. Now it was January. Tonight they had seen a movie and stopped at Scarfie's for a burger and a Coke and he had, once again, run out of things to say.

Not to tell, but to say.

What could he tell her? That he couldn't see how to kiss her?

He'd figured it and figured it too many times while shaving and appraising himself in the mirror, trying to keep his mustache even. The kissing itself he could visualize; it was how to get to the kissing that completely eluded him. Tonight in the car with her, kissing had somehow become confused with images of snow, of streetlights, of the wisp of hair distracting him as it danced upon her lips, moving with her breath as she spoke.

"Yes, but what are you *really* afraid of?"

Once he *had* been kissed by her. They had gotten into an involved conversation and he had told her some (not *all*, of course, never *all*) of the things that had been bothering him, about his grades, about not feeling as smart as everybody else seemed to think he was or should

A WINTER MEMORY

be, about what his future might be like. She had responded in kind with a dismaying enthusiasm and trust.

She had told him then that she needed someone to talk to, someone willing to just sit and listen, *with no strings attached*. Then, after he had taken her home and was standing at the door while waiting for her to find her keys and let herself in, she had suddenly thrown her arms around his neck and kissed him lightly and searingly upon the ear, whispering something so sincere, so heartfelt, that he could only stand there stunned and curse himself. He had not known what to say then, either, not after what she had told him that night, and it was only after a moment of complete and utter rout that he had been able to take her up in his delicate, clumsy hands, ever so gently, as if she were some sort of wild beast, and break the grip she had upon him, her breath still warm upon his throat.

Now he sat talking to her, slouched between the steering wheel and the car door. He couldn't tell her about that.

What *could* he tell her?

Then he remembered.

"Once," he said, his voice quickening as it all came back to him and he tried to repress a shiver born of cold and half-forgotten memory, "when I was just a kid, we got an afternoon off from fourth grade in order to see a play put on by a bunch of college students. It was sort of a musical fantasy, about this peasant boy who gets an enchanted staff from an old wizard after saving his life." Why was he telling her this? But he had started, and he couldn't seem to stop.

"Near the end, the hero was tricked into using his magic stick to gain riches and power for himself, something the old wizard had warned him never to do. Anyway, just as he raised his staff to use it, the stage went completely dark except for a single red spotlight on him, and a hand from the darkness grabbed the stick away.

Then there was a really horrible laugh from the demon king who had been trying to get the kid all the way through the play, and the kid was grabbed from behind by a bunch of bodiless hands and arms."

"Demon king..."

"However," Allan continued, "there was an out for the hero, if he could just say some special magic words. Something like '*Tchuree, Tchuree, Tchelkash—*' I can't remember all of it."

Jane was looking at him with a puzzled expression. Why couldn't he just shut up and leave well enough alone?

"So there I was, screaming and yelling at the guy on stage to remember the words, just like every other kid was doing in that auditorium, as he kept getting dragged farther and farther away from that red spotlight by those bodiless hands and arms, while that awful laughter kept getting louder and louder."

"Sounds frightening," Jane said. "Especially for kids."

He looked away from her briefly but couldn't see the stars from where they were parked. There was no moon that night.

"Well, it certainly was for me. I still knew, see, that it was all make-believe, just like I know what's coming when I go to see Disney's *Snow White* again, but I still get this creepy feeling when the queen transforms herself into the old witch. Part of me was *on* that stage trying to remember those stupid words!" He laughed, as if in apology for the story, but it went wrong somehow and his next words spilled out in even more of a rush.

"At the last moment, he shouted the first word: '*Tchuree!*' and the place became as quiet as it had been noisy before. And then the strange thing happened..." *As long as I'm in this, I might as well go all the way with it*, he thought. "Everything seemed to ... *stop*."

A WINTER MEMORY

On the last word he snapped his fingers loudly in a satisfyingly theatrical gesture.

"He said '*Tchuree!*' again and then looked blankly out at the audience as if he didn't know where he was. No one spoke. I'm sure that part wasn't in the script. The demon king on stage looked just as surprised in the illumination from that red spot as we were out in the audience. He had moved forward so that only his face, or the shape that had to be his face, could be seen in the shadows. I remember . . . I remember that he was dressed in a dark outfit of some kind, and that there was something funny, not a limp, exactly, about the way he walked."

Allan took a long breath.

"I don't know why he did it. Maybe he was just trying to cover for the guy who had blown his lines, I don't know. The magic words *were* rather complicated, or at least they seemed that way to me at the time. But he didn't just start laughing again, like he'd been doing before."

No, he hadn't done that.

"All he did was give out with this really scary low chuckle, the kind of thing you remember from old radio shows that always had a creaking door and howling wolves, only terribly *right* this time, as if he had been given an unexpected stroke of good fortune, which somehow seemed to me to be even more horrible than everything that had gone before, because I knew, knew sitting there and being up on that stage at the same time, that the hero *really couldn't remember the words!*

"That moment seemed to hang in the air forever, and then the guy playing the hero finally picked up his cue, and there were flashes of light and kids screaming as he got away from the demon king. *Or so they thought* . . ."

"So they thought . . ."

"So they thought. Because he didn't get away. It was

way too late for the words to have saved him. Too late..."

She shivered and hugged herself with her arms. "I don't think that I *like* that story."

Up the street toward his home the houses were all dark. They were parked behind the old power station at the end of his street, which continued a few feet past them until it turned into a gravel road that led to a gravel pit in a small wooded tract. The trees before them loomed shapeless in the night.

From the corner of his eye he regarded the streetlights. The Willis house a few yards up the street, the last house on the block before the woods began, had been the last house to go dark, and now he couldn't even see the cold glow of a television. There were just the streetlights and (he knew, although he couldn't see it) the small lamp on the television set at home that his parents always left on for him whenever he was going to be out late.

He felt no fear at being alone with her in the night. All the car doors were locked and windows were up. He felt even more secure in the knowledge that cop cars were supposed to prowl around down here every so often. All that the cops could do would be to tell him to move his father's Chevrolet. It certainly wasn't as if they were doing anything *wrong*.

He looked again for the stars and thought of the music to one of his favorite songs.

"My evening star, I wonder who you are,
Set up so high like a diamond in the sky . . ."

Suddenly solicitous, he asked her if she were cold. He could start the motor and run the heater again. No, that wasn't it, she just felt tired all of a sudden, and maybe he had better take her home since she did have that plane to catch to visit relatives back East tomorrow afternoon. He and Jane were still on an extended holiday break.

A WINTER MEMORY

All right, it was time to go back, and he turned the key where he'd left it in the ignition slot, started the engine, put it in gear, and started to back up.

And was stuck.

He put it in forward, he tried it in low, he tried backing up again.

And was stuck.

"Just a sec, okay?" He reached over her to the glove compartment and got out the spray can of special stuff that you put on your tires when it's slippery. Or something like that. He'd seen it on TV once.

And was stuck.

He got his pocket penlight out of his shirt and used it to look at the tires and then tried scooping snow away from them until he hit ground, his breath coming a little more quickly as he got behind the wheel again.

And was stuck.

"Let's try something else," he said to her, snow falling in clots of white from his clothing. "You'll have to drive. I'm going to try to bounce the wheel out sideways. What you'll have to do"—and here he paused to twist the knob on the radio, which until then had been playing all unnoticed—"is to back us out the same way I drove in here. Don't hit it too hard, if I'm going to get us out, it'll have to crawl." This time he didn't ask if things were okay. The smell of the tires was beginning to make him feel sick.

And was stuck.

"I'll try leaning on the trunk, to add my weight on the tires. When I tell you, go forward and then back so it'll rock." He got out again and went to the back of the car. The window by the driver's seat was open so that she could hear his instructions. Snow struck his face in discrete planes of wet particles. His hands were cold in his thin gloves but something burned behind his eyes.

And was stuck.

"All right," he said, sitting again behind the steering

wheel, his breath an aching in his chest, but he wasn't talking to her. He had done everything he could think of and now that he knew he couldn't get the car out, he was thinking of walking the two blocks home and taking the second car and driving her home, thinking out what to say to his old man if he were still up and wanted to know why Allan needed the second car. "All right," he said.

She said nothing, but he was saying enough, in his mind, for both of them.

He locked up the Chevy and walked with her in silence the two blocks back to his home. Leaving her seated in the Falcon parked in the garage, he slipped in through the back door and on the back of a page torn from the calendar block-printed a note, and left it under the light on the television set:

> MOM AND DAD:
>   HAVE BORROWED BOTH CARS.
>   THERE IS NO, REPEAT,
>   NO CAUSE FOR ALARM.
>   BACK SHORTLY.

He thought about signing the note, but rejected the idea as ridiculous. Almost as ridiculous as parking a car two blocks from home and then getting it stuck in the snow.

When he left the house he was careful to make sure that the door didn't close too loudly behind him and wake his parents up. He still had an idea of coming back after driving her home and somehow freeing the Chevy from the snow all by himself, even though he had failed to do it with her help. That way the only ones who would ever have to know about it would be Jane and the little voice in the back of his head that kept speaking to him in intimate, accusing words.

A WINTER MEMORY

He drove the Falcon in silence, and walked with her to her door, saying only: "Sorry."

Only the constant brushing back of his hair from his forehead betrayed him.

"*Don't* . . ." she said before she turned in, as if she had more to say.

At that moment he wished that he could be instantly rid of her. He needed to go back and be alone with the car. He had an appetite for darkness and silence. He wanted the snow and the wind, desired the cold embrace of the night, the trees whipped by the wind, the inquisitive cop with the spotlight, the sudden light glaring into his eyes, the cop asking him, "Why'd you park here, *boy*?" He wanted and needed all of these things.

He did not know what to do except go back and somehow make things the way they had been. But it was too far to walk, much less drive in the second car, overdue for a trade-in, the clunker, just like him.

"Yeah, sure," he said, and turned with an insanely military grace and walked back into the lightly falling snow.

A cry against the rising wind: "*Allan* . . ."

He made a half-turn and looked at her. She was inside the house now, with one glove on and the other in her hand, and he almost lost his balance, staggering a step backward. Now what?

She put a finger to her teeth and then dropped her hand to her side. "It's not your fault . . . you did everything you could."

At least she knew him well enough so that she didn't clutter it up by apologizing or asking him if it were okay. The snow blew in moiré patterns between them on the open porch.

He turned and took another step away.

"*Allan*." This time it was a challenge. He turned toward her again.

"I think you're wrong. I think he did remember in

time ... That's all. You're wrong. I ... let me know what happens."

He said something with his throat and his hands and stood there until she closed the door. Then he walked back to the Falcon.

He saw the dead rabbit as he was about to turn into the driveway. It was about eight feet in front of where he had to turn and for a minute he didn't know what it was. Then the wind blew some of the snow off its fur. It was sprawled near the side of the street across from his house. He parked the car on the left side of the garage, turning the headlights off until he passed his parents' bedroom on the side of the house, and got out.

Walking a little way up the driveway, he could make out a fresh set of tire tracks where a car had driven through and then backed up since he had taken Jane home. He could not have missed seeing the rabbit when he and Jane had walked up from the end of the street, and he was sure that he hadn't hit it while slowly backing the second car out of the garage.

Wait a minute. Backed up?

By the carcass he saw a beer can, and a broken glass bottle a couple of feet from it, obscured by the snow.

He looked quickly at the body. Backed up. The can and the bottle hadn't been enough. He hoped the bastards got a flat from the glass. Hoped, but doubted that it would happen. Things seldom worked out that neatly.

He walked back up the driveway and through the garage door he'd left open. It was easy to find the shovel he wanted in its rack without using a light. They only had two shovels. He took the big one with the rectangular pan. Then he walked back down the driveway and stood for a moment before moving into the street, alert for the sound of a car. Hearing nothing, he returned to the rabbit, powdered snow crunching under his light galoshes.

"Dammit."

It was nothing but glass and guts in the road, but when he slid the edge of the shovel under it, the rabbit twitched and he almost dropped the shovel in his surprise. It was still alive.

"Dammit to hell."

The wind nipped at his face and hands. He hadn't remembered to put his gloves back on after getting out of the car and his fingers were pink with exposure. He clutched at the shovel as if it were a weapon in his hands.

It *was* still alive, dammit. It had been hit by a beer can and a bottle and it had been run over but it was still alive, still in pain.

It moved again even though it had been irrevocably broken and hurt and Allan saw bright blood through the fur on its belly. It was trying to crawl broken-backed across shards of brown glass in the snow, trying to crawl up the curb and away from the light and the hurt and him.

Gently, he eased the edge of the pan from under the rabbit, not looking at the shovel but watching with a horrified fascination the movement of the animal dying before his eyes. Gently, but there was blood and glass and snow on the shovel, and a patch of freshly torn fur. Gently, gently, but the dented corner of the pan caught on something and the rabbit twitched suddenly and Allan jerked involuntarily and picked up the rabbit a couple of inches before dropping it. All, all in silence.

And it was still alive, with its nose moving and its eyes wide open and watching him, alive and dying as he looked at it.

"*Dammit*," he whispered, implored, his hands shaking so much that he almost dropped the shovel on it.

Wind sang through the trees and he stepped backward, his legs unsteady, the muscles in his right thigh twitching with the cold.

He looked up and down the street again and then at the streetlight overhead, the streetlight that shone into his bedroom on the second floor every night, its light visible even through the shades he usually kept drawn. He shuddered as the wind sharpened itself on his spine.

He raised the shovel and without looking at the rabbit, he brought it down upon the rabbit's head with all of his strength.

The rabbit screamed.

He hadn't looked and he hadn't done it right and now he had to strike it once more, strike while *looking at it*, the taste of sour oatmeal in his throat, and then it was over and it was still.

Then he did it again, and again, striking at the snowbank on the curb until he couldn't strike anymore, and then flinging himself away before he vomited over the carcass. He had a sudden horror of violating the body of the beast further after his two blows.

"Dammit, dammit, dammit, dammit..."

He dug a shallow hole in the snowbank farther down by the curb and buried it there under a light covering of snow. He would get the spade from the garage and take it down to where the car was by the woods in a moment and dig a proper hole for it there, but he couldn't just leave it in the street until he was ready for it.

It took him almost an hour to finish the grave. Under the trees the ground was frozen but he managed to dig deep enough to satisfy himself that dogs couldn't easily dig up the body. He found some small stones and a couple of larger rocks by the side of the road under the snow and arranged them as a crude cairn.

Now that it was all done he stood for a moment to catch his breath, looking up at the sharp stars in the sky overhead. It had stopped blowing snow again. Light snow had fallen off and on over the past hour and a half but now the night was quiet and clear. Since there was no moon he easily picked out first the Pleiades and then

A WINTER MEMORY

Orion close to Sirius, which was low on the horizon. He could also make out the Big Dipper.

He liked to look at the stars while standing in the snow. It reminded him of the scene from *War and Peace* when Pierre is looking up at the stars during the retreat after the burning of Moscow. He had read that book in the middle of summer and for the first time had thought favorably of the idea of winter. Before then, summer had always been the best season for him, despite the sneezing and red eyes from his hay fever.

"You think of books too much," she'd told him once, just after they had talked about their favorite books. "Don't you ever think of yourself as just *yourself*, and not like some character in a book?" He had pondered that for a long time and now it made him feel self-conscious.

Still, he felt as if the situation called for him to say or do something more for the rabbit, but he couldn't think of anything that seemed real enough.

"R.I.P. Unless there's better. I did what I could and I'm sorry."

"You really are a, Libran, looking for order and balance in everything," she'd said earlier that week, when she had visited him at his home. Then she'd laughed.

That had been after he had told her of his plan to listen to *all* of the records in the high school library (and the public library too) "in order to give myself a better musical background." He had played for her some of his favorite pieces of classical music: "Fantasia on a Theme by Tallis" by Ralph Vaughan Williams (taking care to display his sophistication by pronouncing his first name as "Rafe"), the Wolf's Glen scene from "Der Freischütz," and Stravinsky's music for "Pétrouchka," among others.

But he had never played for her the old song that now came unbidden to his thoughts.

*"When from out the shades of night
Come the stars ashining bright,
I spy the one I do love
I recognize my true love
Amid the tiny orbs of light.
Search the sky from East to West,
She's the brightest and the best,
But she's so far above me
I know she cannot love me.
Still I love her and more than all the rest."*

He'd found the song on a record of turn-of-the-century music and had proceeded to play it five times in a row because he liked it so much. It was "My Evening Star," with words by Robert B. Smith, music by John Stromberg. It was only after he'd listened to the song so many times that he had memorized the lyrics that he found the book in the library on American popular music that told what had happened to the composer. Beset by ill health, he had been found dead, a probable suicide, a copy of the lyrics and the just-completed music for the song in his pocket.

Allan would have been embarrassed for her to hear it.

*"My evening star, I wonder who you are,
Set up so high like a diamond in the sky.
No matter what I do
I can't go up to you,
So come down, my evening star.
Come down!
Come down!
Come down from there, my evening star!"*

He started walking up the street toward his home, the shovel in his right hand, the spade in his left.

There was hardly any sense of transition, of a feeling of displacement or movement. One moment he was walk-

A WINTER MEMORY

ing down the street, then there was a practically instantaneous sensation of vertigo, of night falling into him, and then he was facedown in a snowdrift. Sputtering in his surprise, he rolled over onto his back, dropping the spade next to him.

The shovel was gone. He must have dropped it in his fall.

It was a big drift, bigger than the drifts left after the big blizzard when he had been ten years old, when it had snowed steadily overnight, leaving seven inches on the streets and confusion in its wake.

Snowdrift? Snow was up his nose, down his collar, and in his shoes. But there had been no such drift on the street. Had he fallen asleep and walked into the side of the curb in a daze?

He got up, shocked into sudden wakefulness from the peaceful mood he had been in moments earlier. He must be getting really punchy to do something like that. He brushed snow off his coat collar and shook his pant legs out as much as he could in order to get rid of some of the snow up them. Snow was all over him, and inside his clothes, too, as if he had been buried in it. He wondered if he had ruined his shoes.

Pale light shone down from overhead. He picked up his father's spade with his right hand but still couldn't see the shovel. When he looked behind him he saw the moon.

Moonlight? But there *was* no moon tonight.

And all of the streetlights seemed to be out.

Now he took a closer look at the scene around him. The drifts stretched down the street as far as he could see.

He automatically glanced at his watch to see what time it was. Had he passed out or something in the snow? He felt confused. He must have, because that much snow doesn't appear magically from nowhere. He must have been mistaken about the moon.

And what had happened to the streetlights?

The watch read 2:17. It had stopped again. He peered at it and then tapped the crystal that still had the long scratch on it from when he had accidentally cracked it against the sink in the kitchen while taking it off to help his mother with the dishes. It wasn't unusual that it had stopped: he had the nervous habit of winding it. It was a bad habit, like biting his fingernails or pulling the hairs of his mustache with his teeth, and every time the watch stopped on him because it had been overwound, he thought about breaking all of the old habits, as if they were all a part of a chain that had to be dealt with at the same time.

Stop this. Stop this and think.

He heard what must be a dog baying in the distance but it sounded unlike any dog he had ever heard.

That was when he finally noticed the ruins of the Willis house a couple of yards across from him. The windows were gone and the place looked as if it had been gutted by fire.

He looked back the way he had come. His father's car, stuck in the snow, was gone. *Stuck in the snow and gone.*

The wind blew snow-devils across the tops of the drifts and past him down the street toward the woods.

It was only then that he really started to get scared, ribs spiking into his heart. In a panic, arms waving wildly even while he hung onto the spade, he galumphed his way through the snow toward home. His fear made him clumsy and he fell more than once on the way, fell and then picked himself up and kept thrashing his way through, as if he were drowning in an ocean of white. All around him was a suddenly unfamiliar neighborhood filled with houses that were ruined and deserted.

He stopped just as he reached his own house and took a deep, shuddering breath. What was wrong with the stars overhead? He forced himself to look down and saw

A WINTER MEMORY

that the living room windows in front were still intact. He couldn't see any light behind the curtains.

With the deliberation of nightmare he walked up the driveway to the back, his legs sinking deep into the snow that covered the neighborhood and his home, his breath rasping in his ears.

The garage was still there. Both doors were pulled down.

But the back door to the house was gone. The window into his parents' bedroom that faced the backyard was broken. There were just a couple of large daggers of glass left in the frame. He moved closer to the house.

The moon came out from behind a cloud and he saw the ghosts of his parents in the broken glass.

He couldn't scream. The sound had somehow caught in his throat. He made a harsh, guttural noise, a noise like he'd heard himself make once when he'd been having a nightmare and had been trying to scream and wake himself up because he *knew* that he was having a nightmare and it was out of control. Then the hurt in his throat had awakened him, not a scream because nobody else had heard it in the almost silent house, and he had lain awake in his room and listened to the sounds of his home at night and stared at the green glow-in-the-dark head of the *Tyrannosaurus rex* model that he had built and broken and now kept on top of his bookshelf, the darkness breathing with him until he realized that it had been just a nightmare after all and not something real, real and terrible, something the world had been trying to tell him since childhood, that there is something hidden in the dark.

An answering growl came from his parents' bedroom, a growl and the sound of something *moving* in there, something that didn't sound human.

As if in a nightmare, he knew that he couldn't run away, that he had to stand there as if rooted to the spot, that he must find out what was in there. Slowly, slowly, as the wind rose and the moon went behind another cloud, he fumbled at the buttons of his winter coat, the night air slashing at his exposed throat, and found the pocket penlight. His fingers found it, found it and then almost dropped it as he worked it out of his shirt pocket one-handed. His grip was uncertain in his light gloves. He still held the spade in his left hand.

Cold, so cold. There didn't seem to be any sensation in his toes anymore.

The moon came out again. He saw that the image in the glass was the reflection of his own face. Then he flicked the penlight on and caught the red eyes behind the glass, red eyes and snout in a bearlike head.

The thing in the bedroom growled again, growled and then seemed to lunge through the glass after him.

He dropped the penlight and weakly swatted left-handed at the thing with the spade, smashing the glass left in the frame.

And then he was running through the snow, running in his own tracks, back up the driveway to the street. Behind him he heard the sounds of the thing moving through the snow.

Suddenly he saw the huge red dog baying and running past him from the street. He threw himself to one side, tripped over his own feet, and fetched up sprawling against the base of the streetlight in front of his house, spade still clutched in his hand.

Not ten feet from him in the street he saw a dark figure dressed in furs pointing a rifle at him. Allan couldn't see his face since it was wrapped up against the cold. The man was wearing snowshoes.

Then the figure took three steps toward him and there was something funny, not a limp, exactly, about the way he walked.

The snow and the night surrounded Allan as he pressed back against the post of the broken streetlight. The sounds of the dog and the thing fighting behind him seemed closer. He turned and looked.

"SAMMAEL—CUT!"

Allan jumped in surprise at the voice, hitting his head on the post.

The rifle cracked three times. Snow seemed to explode around the thing, kicking it into the air, and then it jerked spasmodically for a couple of seconds and died.

Looking at it now, looking at the large feet, arched back, long hair and bushy tail, Allan recognized it finally as a wolverine. He shivered and looked back at the stranger.

The figure with the rifle, the shape out of his nightmares, was pointing the rifle directly at his head. From where he was standing he could not miss.

The strange red dog whined, making a tentative move toward Allan, and that unfamiliar command was given again.

Allan looked at the stranger, looked at the rifle that he could only identify as a rifle since he knew nothing about guns, and without raising the spade he still had in his left hand said: *"Tchuree!"*

The man kept the rifle pointed at him, his face shrouded, even the eyes, doing and saying nothing.

And then Allan heard him begin to laugh, a laugh unlike the laughter of the demon king from his memories and his nightmares, laughter like he had never heard before and never wanted to hear again, moving from a low to a high pitch, becoming fuller, louder, while the dog began to whine and then to howl, and then a sudden gust of wind slapped snow at Allan's eyes and the moon was gone and he was sprawled at the base of a lit streetlight before his home. Through the window curtains he could see the welcome glow of the night lamp on the television set.

He dropped the spade in his astonishment. Rubbing at his face with both gloved hands, he took a moment in an attempt to regain his bearings. And then, with a rolling, unsteady gait, he walked back up the driveway, the *clear* driveway, the driveway that he had just run down, dreading what he would find.

And went into the house, took off his coat and galoshes and shoes, and drew a cold drink of water from the tap in the kitchen, finding a glass in the light from the living room night lamp under which his note rested unread.

The water made him gasp at its coolness and he had trouble swallowing two tablets of aspirin.

His hands and feet and mind were numb, and it took him a couple more moments before he could bring himself to leave the light in the living room, *turn off* the light in the living room, and go upstairs to his room.

From their bedroom came the oddly disquieting sounds of his parents sleeping.

A dream? Nothing but a dream?

He walked catlike up the stairs as if a hole might open up in them and swallow him. He set his alarm clock for 6:00 A.M., so that in case he fell asleep he would still be sure to awaken before his parents so that he could tell his father about the car. Breathing shallowly, he took off all his clothes, soaked with sweat and snowmelt, and then put on fresh ones. He stretched out fully dressed on his bed, unable to look out the window at the street and look fully at the streetlight whose light pervaded the room.

The tiny dinosaur head glowed like a green beacon in the distance on his bookshelf.

He never found his penlight, but he did find the shovel a couple of feet from the car the next day while the guy from the gas station was using his power winch to extricate the car from the snow. The whole thing only took about fifteen minutes and ten dollars, and his father was able to use the car to go to work that morning and wasn't late at all. It was uncomfortable explaining how the car had gotten stuck but that was all it was.

A WINTER MEMORY

He never told anyone else about his strange experience, and the events of that night became like a half-remembered dream. While he thought of them occasionally, he tried not to think of them often, until that time, much later, when the memory of that night had become an obsession.

He had been roused from a restless, feverish sleep of memories by the barking of his dog. After so many winters of waiting and remembering, trying to recall exactly a momentary glimpse of strange star-patterns, it was only the mischance of a minor injury to his right leg a week earlier while tracking the *carcajou* that had been despoiling his traps that had delayed him from making his way farther south that winter. He had decided two days ago that his quest was in vain again this year, that he would have to wait until next year to resume his vigil.

Tracking and killing the *carcajou* was mere habit.

Then there was the figure in the snow, the recognition, the raising of his 30.06 rifle, the wolverine's attack, the memories of the things he had seen and done to get to this moment, this chance, the decision as he looked at the figure huddled in front of the streetlight, and then the uncontrollable laughter, his awful broken-backed laughter.

No, he was not to be like some rabbit condemned to neverness, not tonight, anyway. Snowsurf roared in his ears and he swayed where he stood with the rifle. He was too weak to be even a demon king. Then he started laughing again, laughing so hard that he felt as if he were falling, laughing and crying at the same time.

The wind writhed through the trees. A flurry of snow, cold, so cold, caught him full in the face, like cold ashes in his mouth, and then the apparition was gone.

A dream? Nothing but a dream?

Where was that dog of his? Had it caught another scent in the wind?

He listened like a beast, then called for his dog, looking down the street where he had grown up, or at least lived until he thought he had grown up. *The same street.* But that had been so long ago, back before the end, back before the beginning of the days of flame and the days of sickness, the wind-age and wolf-age, holofrost winter, before the world was wrecked.

What had been her name?

Jane; dead in the blast that got Boston.

The night around him seemed to move, whispering in a dream, the world like wind, and he couldn't make out his own tracks in the snowfall. Snow fell blameless in the night air.

How did the last verse go? *Remember, damn your eyes!*

> *"Love, I think, has made me mad*
> *'Cause when nights in clouds are clad,*
> *I want her more than ever*
> *Want her to leave me never*
> *And all around is sorrowful and sad.*
> *Then when comes the day's bright light*
> *And my star fades from my sight*
> *My love is unabating*
> *I grow impatient waiting*
> *To see again my love, my light, that night."*

He looked before him but could not see the body of the wolverine. Then he glanced upward in the direction of the stars he couldn't see.

Finally he moved down the street, away from his house and the woods, calling for his red dog, Sammael, the windsong in his head winding down finally like the music-box memories of his past.

The Sixth Man

by Graham Masterton

Graham Masterton is the best-selling author of many horror novels, as well as a number of historical novels. The Manitou *was made into a 1978 film starring Tony Curtis, Susan Strasberg, Stella Stevens, and Burgess Meredith, directed by William Girdler. Other books are* Revenge of the Manitou, Charnel House, Death Dream, Death Trance, The Djinn, Night Warriors, Picture of Evil, Mirror, *and* The Wells of Hell. *Graham has edited one anthology,* Scare Care, *which was quite well received; all profits went to abused children. He lives in Epsom Downs, Surrey.*

We were walking back to the house when Michael said, "I've discovered something rather strange. I don't quite know what to do about it."

It was a perfect English summer's day. There was a deep, sweet smell of meadow grass and clover, and above us the clouds lazed slowly over the Lyth like huge cream-colored comforters. Not far away, next to the split-rail fence, a small herd of Jersey cows stood thoughtfully chewing, and occasionally flicked their tails.

"Do you want to tell me what it is?" I asked. Michael was a petroleum geologist, a discoverer and an exploiter of oil fields in far-flung and undesirable places, and not exactly the sort of chap who ever thought anything was "strange," let alone worried himself about it.

"I've found a photograph," he said. "I've looked at

it again and again. I've even had it examined by the photo lab. No doubt about it, it's quite genuine; but it makes no sense at all; and I'm afraid a lot of people are going to be quite embarrassed and hurt about it."

We reached the edge of the meadow and climbed over the stile. I didn't push Michael any further. He was always careful and deliberate in his choice of words, and it was obvious that he was genuinely disturbed.

"I think I'd better show you," he said at last. "Come into the study. Would you like a beer? I think I've got a couple of cans of Ruddles in the fridge."

We made our way through the tangled dog roses at the end of his garden, past the overgrown sundial, and in through the old-fashioned kitchen. His young wife Tania was out, collecting their three-year-old son Tim from play school. Her apron lay across the back of the chair, and a freshly made apple pie stood in a circle of lightly dusted flour. I had known Tania long before I had known Michael; and in a funny way I still wished that she and I could have loved each other more. It was unsettling for me to see her carrying Michael's son in her arms.

Carrying frosted cans of beer, we climbed the uncarpeted stairs to Michael's study. There was a smell of warm days and dried-out horsehair plaster, and oak. Michael's house had been built in 1670, but his study had all the equipment that a petro-geologist needed: an IBM computer, a fax machine, seismic charts, maps and rows of immaculate files and books and atlases.

He took out a large black folder labeled *Falcon Petroleum: Ross Ice-Shelf*, laid it flat on his gray steel desk, and took out an envelope. Inside the envelope were several copies of old black-and-white photographs.

"Here," he said, and passed one over. As far as I could see, it was the famous photograph of Captain Scott and his ill-fated party at the South Pole: Wilson, Evans, Scott, Oates, and Bowers, frostbitten and making no

THE SIXTH MAN

pretense of being bitterly dejected. I turned it over, and on the back there was a typewritten label: *Captain Robert Scott and party, South Pole, January 17, 1912*.

"Well?" I asked Michael. "What of it?"

"There were *supposed* to be five of them," he said. "Actually, of course, there were originally only supposed to be four—but for some inexplicable reason Scott took Lieutenant Bowers along on the last leg to the Pole, even though they didn't have enough food."

"There *are* five of them," I told him.

"Yes, but who took the photograph?" Michael insisted.

I gave him the photograph back. "They operated the camera with a long thread, everybody knows that."

"Everybody *supposes* they used a thread. But if that's true . . . then who's this?"

He handed over another photograph. It showed Scott standing beside the small triangular tent left by the Norwegian explorer Roald Amundsen, who had beaten the British expedition in their race to the Pole by just over a month. There was Oates, bending over beside one of the guy-ropes; there were Evans and Bowers, standing close together, Bowers making notes in a notebook. But in the background, about fifty or sixty yards away, another figure was standing, in a long black coat, and a huge black hat, neither of which remotely resembled any of the coats or hats that the rest of the party were wearing.

Michael tapped the photograph with his finger. "Presumably, this picture was taken by Dr. Evans. It's not the kind of photograph you could take with a thread, anyway, not with the type of camera that Scott took with him to the Pole. Too far away, too difficult. But look at the caption . . . Dr. Evans hasn't attempted to give any special emphasis to this unknown sixth man; and none of the others seem to be concerned that he's there. Yet, he isn't mentioned in Scott's diary; and we know for a recorded fact that only five set off on the last leg across the polar plateau. So where did he come from? And who is he? And what happened to him, when all the rest of them died?"

I stared at the photograph for a long time. The mysterious sixth man was very tall, and his hat had a wide sweeping brim, like a coal-heaver's hat, so that his face was obscured by an impenetrable shadow. He could have been anybody. I looked at the back of the photograph, and read, *R. Amundsen's Tent At The Pole, January 17, 1912*. No mention at all of the man in black. A mystery, nearly eighty years old, but Michael was right about its sensitivity. At the time, the tragedy of Captain Scott's Antarctic expedition had moved a whole nation to tears; and there were many people in England, even today, who would find any revisionist explanations of their fate to be gravely offensive.

"Where did you find this?" I asked Michael.

"In the private papers of Herbert Ponting, the expedition's photographer. I was looking for pictures of the Ross Ice-Shelf and the Beardmore Glacier, the way they used to be."

"And you don't have any idea who this sixth man could be?"

Michael shook his head. "I went through Scott's diary with a fine-tooth comb. I checked Amundsen's account, too. Amundsen left nobody behind at the Pole; and he saw nobody else."

I held the photograph up to the window. "It's not a double exposure?"

"Absolutely not."

I shrugged, and handed the photograph back. "In that case, it's one of the great unexplained mysteries of all time."

Michael grinned, for the first time that afternoon. "Not if I can help it."

* * *

THE SIXTH MAN

The Chinook helicopter slowly circled and then landed on the ice, whirling up a white blizzard that sparkled and glittered in the sunlight. The cargo doors were opened up immediately, and the orange-jacketed engineers heaved out tools and ropes and crates of supplies. Michael wiped his spectacles with his thumb, and then tugged the hood of his parka tight around his chin. "You ready?" he asked me.

The Antarctic wind sliced into the open cargo doors like frozen knives. "I thought you said this was summer," I told him, following him along the fuselage, and then down the steps to the ice.

"It is," he grinned. "You should try visiting here in June."

Slowly the Chinook's rotor-blades flickered to a standstill. Michael led me across the hard-packed ice to the largest of the nine huts that made up Falcon Petroleum's Beardmore Research Station. It looked like rush hour. Sno-Cats bellowed from one side of the station to the other, dog teams panted past us, and dozens of riggers and engineers were working on aerials and scaffolding and two more half-finished huts.

The research station covered more than eleven acres, and the once-pristine Antarctic ice was strewn with discarded Caterpillar tracks, broken packing cases, and heaps of windblown rubbish.

"I thought it was going to be all peace and solitude," I shouted at Michael.

He shook his head. "Not a hope. These days, the Antarctic is busier than a Bank Holiday in Brighton."

We entered the hut and stamped the ice from our feet. Huge fan heaters made the inside of the hut roaringly hot, and it stank of stale cigarette-smoke and sweat and something else, something musty, a smell which will always remind me of the South Pole, for ever and ever. It was almost like the smell of something which has been dead and frozen for a very long time, but is at last beginning to thaw.

Michael said, "It's a pretty gruesome life, but you get used to it. We get a regular supply of Johnnie Walker and porno videos from the Falklands."

He led me along a gloomy sisal-carpeted corridor, and then opened one of the doors. "Here, you're lucky, you can have this room to yourself. Dr. Philips had to go back to London for six weeks. His wife got tired of him being away so long, and she's divorcing him."

I threw my suitcase onto the bed. The room was small, with a narrow steel-framed bed and a small desk and a packing case that did duty as a bookshelf. On the chipboard wall was a color photograph of a large mousy-haired woman in a pale blue cardigan, with washing pinned up behind her; and next to it, a pinup of a massively busty blonde with her legs stretched wide apart.

I thought of Tania. "What does Tania think about *you*, being away for so long?" I asked Michael.

"Oh, she doesn't like it, but she lumps it," he replied, rather evasively. He went to the window and peered out at the blindingly sunlit ice. "We all have to make sacrifices, don't we? That's what made Britain great—sacrifices."

I started to unzip my anorak, but Michael said, "Don't take it off yet. Rodney Jones can probably take us out to see the drilling site pretty well straight away. That's unless you're hungry."

I shook my head. "The chaps on the *Erebus* gave me steak and eggs and all the trimmings."

We went back along the corridor, and turned left. The first room we came to was marked SEISMIC STUDIES. It was large and untidy, crammed with desks and packing cases and all kinds of flickering computer screens and noisily zizzing fax machines. A handsome thirtyish man with a thick gingery beard was sitting with his thick oiled fishermen's socks propped up on one of the desks, reading a copy of *Woman's Weekly*.

"Hullo, Mike," he said, dropping the magazine on the desk. "I'm thinking of knitting myself a guernsey and matching scarf, what do you think?"

"You haven't finished my gloves yet," said Michael.

"I'm having trouble with the reindeer," Rodney retorted. "All those damned antlers."

Michael introduced me. "This is James McAlan, pathologist extraordinary, from Sussex University. He's come to look at our discovery."

Rodney stood up and shook hands. "Glad you could make it. *We* don't know what to do about it. I mean, *we're* only geologists. Is this your first time at the South Pole?"

"This is my first time at either pole," I told him. "Up until now, the furthest south I've ever been is Nice."

"Well, you'll hate it," said Rodney enthusiastically. He picked up his windcheater from the floor, and banged it with the flat of his hand to beat the dust off. "Borchgrevink said that the silence roars in one's ears. 'Centuries of heaped-up solitude,' that's what he called it. Borchgrevink was a Norwegian explorer, one of the first to spend the winter here. I've spent three winters here, which qualifies me as the stupidest bugger on the base."

He led us back out of the hut and across the rutted ice. Off to our left, a pack of huskies were yapping and jumping as they were fed. "Bloody dogs," Rodney remarked. "I don't care if I never see another dog again, not one, as long as I live."

It took us only six or seven minutes to reach the site of the excavation. It wasn't very impressive. A shallowish scour, surrounded by heaps of filthy broken-up ice, discarded equipment, and a half-completed tower for seismological soundings. In the bottom of the scour, a green tent had been erected, to shield their discovery from the Antarctic weather, and protect it from stray dogs.

Michael led the way down to the tent, and Rodney tugged free the frozen laces and opened up the flap. It was solid with ice, and it made a sharp cracking noise as he turned it back. "You'll have to crawl," Rodney told us.

We got down on hands and knees and edged our way into the tent. "I was out all night in a blizzard once," said Rodney, touching the roof of the tent with his gloved hand. "The snow piled up so heavy on top that the canvas was only an inch away from my nose. And to think I used to get claustrophobic in the tube."

We shuffled ourselves into a crouching position. By the darting, criss-crossing light of Michael's torch, I had already glimpsed something very grim. But now he concentrated the beam on the center of the tent, and there was what he had brought me three-quarters of the way around the world to see.

"Jesus," I said under my breath, and my breath froze against my chin.

Rodney sniffed. "You couldn't see it with the naked eye, but there was a deep crevasse just here. We discovered it when we started our sound survey. We dug down sixty feet or so . . . and this is what we found. We haven't touched either of them."

Tangled together in the snow lay the remains of two human beings. If there hadn't been two skulls, however, I wouldn't initially have guessed that there were two of them. There were only shoulders and ribs remaining, and ripped-open snow-jackets. But what made the sight so horrifying was that on some of the bones, there were still some fragments of flesh, tanned by age and extreme cold to the color of prosciutto. One of the skulls had been stripped almost completely bare of skin and flesh, but the other was practically intact—the mauvish, frozen face of a man dying in abject terror—his eyes empty, his mouth stretched wide, his lips thick with frost.

"Are you sure that it's them?" I asked Michael. Inside the confines of the tent, my voice sounded oddly flat and featureless.

Michael nodded. "Evans and Oates. No doubt about it." He inclined his head toward the frozen face—still locked in a scream that had been screamed nearly eighty years before. "There were papers, bits and pieces. Not much, but enough for us to be completely sure."

I couldn't take my eyes away from the gruesome, frost-encrusted remains. "I know that Evans collapsed and died around here, at the head of the Beardmore Glacier. But Oates didn't walk out into the blizzard until they were well down on the Ross Ice-Shelf, only twenty-nine miles away from One Ton Depot."

"That's right," said Michael. "So the question is . . . how did Oates get all the way back here? He couldn't have walked back. His feet were badly frostbitten, and the whole reason he walked out into the blizzard was because he couldn't drag himself any farther. Apart from that, even if he *could* have walked back, why on earth *would* he?"

I peered at the remains more closely. "I think I can probably answer that," I told him. "These bones have been gnawed. See there? and there? Definite teethmarks, although it's hard to guess *what* teethmarks. Eighty years ago, this crevasse could well have been the shelter for some predatory animal. It might have been following Scott and his party, the way jackals follow herds of antelope, just waiting for one to drop and die. Evans dropped, then Oates dropped. It dragged them both back here and used them for its winter food."

"James . . ." said Rodney. "I hate to be pedantic, but what kind of predatory animal could that have possibly been? There are plenty of walruses and seals and seabirds in the Antarctic, but there are no natural inland predators—no bears, no tigers, no snow leopards . . . nothing that could have used these men as a winter larder."

I turned to him seriously. "A starving man is a predatory animal."

Rodney looked dubious. "Scott wasn't the kind of man who would have condoned cannibalism, surely? He was reluctant even to eat his dogs. And there's not a single word in his notes that suggests it so much as crossed his mind."

"I'm aware of that," I told him. "But you asked me what happened to these men and I told you. The probability is that some predatory animal dragged them here and ate them. Now, whether that predatory animal was a rogue husky or a man who was prepared to eat anything and anyone in order to survive, I just don't know . . . not until I've made all the necessary tests."

Michael said, "You think it was Scott, don't you?"

I didn't reply. It was difficult, even now, to compromise one of the most glorious tragedies in British history.

But Michael persisted. "You think that Scott was lying, don't you . . . and that they might have killed and eaten Evans and Oates, just to keep going? All that stuff about Oates going out into the blizzard so that he wouldn't be a burden to the other three . . . you think that was so much guff . . . an inspired bit of heroic invention?"

Dry-mouthed, I said, "Yes. But I don't think you can blame anybody for what they did under extreme duress. Remember the Donner Party. Remember those schoolchildren when their aeroplane crashed in the Andes. You can't judge men who were starving to death in the middle of nowhere when you've just eaten steak and eggs on the good ship *Erebus*."

We hunched our way out of the tent, climbed out of the ice-scour, and walked slowly back to the hut.

"How long will it take you before you know for certain?" asked Michael.

"Twenty-four hours. Not longer."

THE SIXTH MAN 131

Michael said, "You remember that photograph I found? The one of Scott and all the rest of them at the Pole?"

"Of course. Did you ever find out who that mysterious sixth man was?"

Michael shook his head. "I decided in the end that it was probably Evans, in a different hat, and that he'd somehow managed to rig up a very long string to take it."

"You said you found papers, bits and pieces. Do you think I could see them?"

Back in the hut, Michael brewed up some hot coffee, laced with whiskey, while I poked through the few pathetic remnants that had been discovered with Oates and Evans in the crevasse. A comb; a pair of leather snow-goggles (unglazed, and very ineffective, since plastic had not yet been invented); a single fur glove, dried up like a mummified cat; and a small snow-blotched diary. Most of the diary's pages had stuck together, but at the back there was a single legible entry... not in Scott's handwriting, but presumably in Oates's.

It said, simply, *Jan 18, now for the run home but Despair will soon overtake us.*

I sat sipping my coffee and frowning at the diary for a long time. The entry seemed simple enough, but the phraseology was odd. Apart from the capital "D" for "Despair," why had he said that "Despair will soon overtake us"? Despair was an emotion that might certainly have overtaken anybody who found themselves at the South Pole, with 800 miles to walk to safety, and scarcely any hot food. But you didn't normally talk about it overtaking you until it actually did.

It was as odd as saying "Tomorrow, when we climb the mountain, we will be overtaken by fear." The chances are that you certainly *will* be overtaken by fear, but you just don't express it like that.

I said to Michael, "Can we go to the Pole, and then slowly fly back over Scott's route?"

"If you think it'll help. I was going to take you to the Pole anyway. Bit of a letdown to come all this way and not quite make it."

We left the research station at the head of the Beardmore Glacier at a little after seven o'clock the next morning. The Chinook lifted itself diagonally into the sunlight, and across the peaks of the Queen Alexandra Mountains, toward the polar plateau. The wind had been rising throughout the night, and when I looked down at the ice, I saw long horse's tails of snow waving across the ice.

"Unlucky for Scott he didn't have a helicopter," Michael shouted above the roar of the engines. He passed me a ham roll, wrapped up in plastic wrap. "Breakfast," he told me.

It was about 350 miles to the South Pole from the research station, and the flight took us low over the icy plateau. "Terrible terrain for man-hauling sledges," Michael pointed out. "Dragging a sledge across those ice crystals is like dragging it across sand. No friction at all."

We were only twenty minutes away from the Pole when the pilot turned back to us and remarked, "I'm getting some adverse blizzard reports, Michael. Looks like we won't have too long."

"That's all right, we just want a quick shufti," Michael told him. "Besides, it's tripe tonight, and I don't want to miss that."

As we circled around the Pole, however, the winds began to buffet the Chinook violently, and I heard the rotor-gears whining in protest.

"Are you sure it's going to be okay?" I asked Michael. "We can always come back when the weather's better."

"Don't worry, we're going to be fine," he reassured

me. "Here you are, Andy, put her down wherever you like."

"Is this really it?" I asked. "The actual South Pole?"

"Didn't expect to see a real pole, did you?" laughed Andy.

We were almost down. Michael had unbuckled his seat belt. Then abruptly the Chinook lurched and banged, and I heard metal screeching hideously against metal. I was hurled sideways, my shoulder colliding against the seat next to me. I heard somebody shout "Jesus!" and then the whole helicopter seemed to tear open all around me, like a theater curtain being parted, and I was dropped face-first into the shatteringly cold snow.

It was a long time before I realized what had happened. I thought I was dead; or at least that my back was broken. But gradually I was able to creep up onto my hands and knees, and then sit up, and look around.

A sudden gust must have caught the Chinook just on the point of landing—either that, or her rotor-gears had sheared, which had occasionally happened with Chinooks, and her two synchronized rotor-blades had enmeshed. Whatever it was, she was lying on her side, split apart, with her rotors sticking up into the Antarctic air like abandoned windmills. There was no sign of Michael, and no sign of Andy or his copilot. All I could hear was the rising wind.

I crept cautiously back into the wreckage, sniffing for aviation fuel, in case of fire. I found Andy and his copilot sitting side by side, both with their eyes open, both plastered with blood, as if they had emptied pots of red paint over their heads for a joke, both dead. Shaking, I retreated from the cockpit and climbed back outside. It was then that I saw Michael standing about thirty yards away, without his glasses, looking stunned.

"Are you all right?" I asked him.

He nodded. "Are they dead?" he whispered.

"Yes," I told him. "I'm afraid they are."

"Oh, hell," he said. It seemed to be the worst expletive he could think of.

In the first two hours, our moods swung dramatically from hysterical relief to deep, silent moodiness. It was only the shock, and it soon began to wear off. We climbed back into the helicopter, trying not to look too closely at Andy and his copilot, and attempted to get the radio working. But one of the rotors (apart from shearing off the lower half of Andy and his copilot) had cut right through the wiring, and it would have taken an honors graduate in popular mechanics to get it going again.

"Still, they'll come out looking for us pretty well immediately," said Michael. "And we always carry a tent and emergency rations and survival kit."

We manhandled the bright orange tent out of the helicopter and set it up. It wasn't easy, because the wind had risen to even greater ferocity, almost a blizzard, and neither of us were particularly brilliant at playing Boy Scouts. However, we managed to climb inside, and zip it up, and light the butane heater which was part of our survival kit. Michael managed to brew up two tin cups full of passable tea, with lots of sugar in it.

"I reckon it'll take them three hours to find us, at the outside," said Michael, checking his watch. "We should even be back in time for supper."

But outside the tent, the blizzard rose to a long and unearthly scream, and we felt snow lashing furiously against the fabric. I opened the vent just a couple of inches, and all we could see outside was howling white.

"Looks like we're getting a taste of Scott's expedition first hand," Michael remarked wryly.

We both assumed that, since it was summer, the blizzard would die away by morning. But it screamed all night, and when we woke up at eight o'clock the next day, the tent was dark, and it was still screaming. I tugged

THE SIXTH MAN

open the vent and a heavy lump of snow dropped in. During the night, the tent had been totally buried.

"This can't last much longer than twenty-four hours," Michael said confidently. "How about some morning tea?"

But throughout the long hours of the day, the wind and the snow never abated. It was well up to Force 8— "blizzing like blazes," as the ill-fated Bowers had described it. By six o'clock that evening, we were feeling tired and cold and depressed. What was more, our butane gas was running low.

"There's another two cylinders in the back of the stores locker," Michael told me. So I tightened the laces of my hood, and scooped my way out of the tent, and into the storm.

I had been in snowstorms before; in Aspen, and in the Swiss Alps. But I had never been in anything like this. The wind was screeching at me as if it were human, but insane. It actually had a *voice*. I was barely able to stand up, let alone walk, and all I could see of the crashed Chinook was a hunchbacked tomb of white snow and four twisted rotor-blades.

However, I managed to plant one boot in front of the other, and with curses and grunts I began to traverse the space between the tent and the helicopter.

I was less than halfway across it when I saw the sixth man.

I stopped, staggering in the ferocity of the blizzard. I was already cold; but now I was chilled with an extraordinary dread; a fear that I had never experienced before in my life.

He was standing so that he was just within view behind the whirling snow. Tall, with a black cloak that silently flapped, and a huge black hat. He said nothing, he didn't move. I stood and stared at him and didn't know whether to stagger back to the tent, or to shout out to him, or what.

Hallucination, I thought. *How could he possibly be real? Nobody could survive out in this weather . . . and besides, the last picture I saw of him had been taken eighty years ago. No doubt about it—he's an optical illusion. A snow ghost.*

Still, I kept a close eye on him as I battled my way to the helicopter and back. All the time he remained where he was, sometimes standing in plain sight, sometimes almost invisible behind the snow. I heaved myself back into the tent and zipped it up.

"What's the matter?" asked Michael. His lips looked blue and he was chafing his hands.

I shook my head. "Nothing. Nothing at all."

"You've seen something."

"Of course not," I told him. "There's nothing to see but snow."

He looked at me narrowly and wouldn't take his eyes away. "You've *seen* something."

The next day the blizzard was worse and we were almost out of butane. The temperature dropped and dropped, like a stone thrown down a bottomless well, and for the first time it began to occur to me that we might not be rescued—that the blizzard might go on for ever and ever, until we starved or froze, whichever came first.

Michael volunteered to go back to the Chinook to see if he could rummage any more food, and anything that we could burn for heat. I helped him to crawl out of the tent, and then lit the lamp and started to brew up some hot chocolate, to warm him when he came back.

But he was back almost at once, and his eyes were wide in their snow-rimed lashes. "He's there!" he croaked.

"Who? Who are you talking about?"

"You know damn well who's there! The sixth man! You must have seen him yourself!"

THE SIXTH MAN

He could see by the expression on my face that I had. He scrambled awkwardly back into the tent.

"Maybe he can help!" Michael suggested. "Maybe he can help us escape!"

"Michael, he can't be real. He's some kind of hallucination, that's all."

"How can you say he's not real? He's standing right outside!"

"Michael, he simply doesn't exist. He *can't* exist. He's in our minds, that's all."

But Michael was too excited. "The South Pole only exists in our minds, but it's still the South Pole."

I tried to argue with him, but both of us were hungry and numb with cold, and I didn't want to waste energy, or hope. I brewed up the chocolate on the last few beads of dwindling gas, and we sat close together and drank it. All the time Michael kept staring at the tent flap, as if he was gathering himself together to go out into the blizzard and meet the sixth man face-to-face.

The blizzard had been screaming relentlessly for nearly five days when Michael grasped me by the shoulder and shook me awake. His eyes glistened red-rimmed in the dim light of our failing flashlight.

"James, there's no hope, is there? We're going to die here."

"Come on, don't give up," I told him. "The blizzard can't go on for very much longer."

He smiled, and shook his head. "You know it's all up, just as well as I do. There's only one thing left."

"You're not going outside?"

He nodded. "I understand now, who he is, the sixth man. Oates understood, too. He's Despair. He's the total absence of human hope. The Eskimos always used to say that in some intensely cold places, extreme human emotions could take on human shape. So did the Kwakiutl Indians."

"Come on, Michael, you're losing your grip."

"No," he said. "No! When Scott got to the Pole and found that Amundsen had got here first, he despaired. He knew, too, that they probably couldn't get back alive. And that was the sixth man, Despair; and Despair tracked them down one by one; and you know what they say about Despair? Despair tears the very flesh, right off your bones."

Michael didn't look mad; but he made me feel mad. He kept smiling as if he had never been happier. *Despair will overtake us*, that's what Oates had written, and Michael was right. It did make some kind of inverted sense.

He hugged me tightly. "I want you to look after Tania. I know how much you care about her." Then he opened the tent flap, and crawled outside.

Slitting my eyes against the blisteringly cold wind, I saw him trudge away, in the direction of the helicopter. Scarcely visible in the snow, I saw the tall man in black waiting for him, unmoving, infinitely patient. *In some intensely cold places, extreme human emotions could take on human shape.*

Michael stood in front of the man like an obedient soldier reporting to his captain. Then the man raised both hands, and plunged them into the front of Michael's anorak, plunged them right through fabric and skin and living flesh. With a grisly cracking noise that I could hear even over the screaming blizzard, he literally ripped Michael inside out, in a storm-bloodied chaos of lungs and heart and wallowing stomach.

The blizzard blew even more fiercely then, and obscured them. Trembling, muttering with fright, I closed the tent flap and sat huddled in my anorak and my blankets, waiting for one kind of death or another.

I said the longest prayer that any man ever said, and hoped.

* * *

THE SIXTH MAN

The tent flap opened and I found myself sitting in a triangle of sunlight. There was no blizzard, no wind, only the distant whistling of helicopter rotors, and the sounds of men shouting.

It was Rodney. He said, "James! My God, you're still alive."

I sat with Tania on top of the Lyth, looking out over Selborne. It was one of those still, hot, timeless August evenings.

She said, "Mike used to love these summer days."

I nodded. Two house-martins swooped and dived just above us. Very faithful, house-martins, always return to the same house to build their nests, every year.

"Sometimes I get the feeling that he's still with us," she remarked.

"Yes," I said. "He probably is."

"He didn't suffer, though, did he?"

"No," I told her. "All three of them were killed instantly, no pain. They wouldn't even have felt the fire."

"You were lucky," she said, a little sadly.

"Come on," I coaxed her. "Let's get back."

I helped her up from the grass, and together we made our way down the hillside, between the gorse bushes and the brambles. At one point, Tania went on ahead; and I stopped for a moment and looked back, at the warm and fragrant woodland, and those peaceful summer slopes, and at my own shadow, tall and black and motionless, like a memory of something that has never been.

The Ice Downstream
by Melanie Tem

Melanie Tem has published short fiction in Isaac Asimov's Science Fiction Magazine, Women of Darkness I *and* II, Women of the West, Skin of Our Soul, *and a number of small and literary magazines; her new stories will soon appear in* Fantasy Tales, Whispers, *and* Final Shadows. *Her first novel,* Prodigal, *a dark fantasy, will be out from Dell in April 1991. Melanie lives in Denver with her husband, writer Steve Rasnic Tem, and their four children.*

If your editor's not mistaken, this may be the first time a husband and wife have published a noncollaborative story in the same anthology.

Downstream, the ice on French Creek was starting to break up. It rumbled and rasped all the way up past Torey's house. It shook the world.

"Ice breaking up downstream," her father warned, as if she didn't know.

Torey frowned and nodded, kicked restlessly at the rungs of her chair. She'd finished her supper a long time ago, but if she left her father at the table alone he'd forget to eat. She knew his food must already be cold.

The leafless grapevines on the arbor outside the kitchen window screeched across the glass, a cold sound that set her teeth on edge. "Ice breaking up," her father said again. He mumbled and was hard to understand these days, but she could see his breath in the chilly air of the kitchen, and she imagined that she could see his words and even his thoughts, no two of them alike and all of them about Ryan. "Sure sign of spring." His tone made spring this year sound dangerous, and Torey understood why.

Her father pushed his chair back stiffly and stood up, leaving most of the food on his plate untouched. Torey resented that, even though she cooked as much to get warm as to please him. She stood up, too, and scraped the leftovers into the pan. She would throw them out onto the snow for the birds, who couldn't possibly be finding enough to eat when this winter had gone on so long. Earlier, her father had objected to her doing that, saying the birds had better get used to winter weather. Now he didn't seem to notice.

"It's hot in here," he said, and turned the thermostat down even more. Torey heard the click of the furnace shutting off.

She wanted to yell at him but since Ryan had died she didn't dare. Instead she said, almost under her breath, "I'm freezing."

"We don't need the heat on so high at night," he said, and Torey was surprised that he'd heard her. "There are plenty of blankets."

She put more blankets on her bed and was, in fact, warm enough, but still she didn't sleep well. The ice kept waking her up, and her father's cries for Ryan. She wished the dreams would come to her instead. All she could dream about was the ice breaking up downstream, when she should have been dreaming about Ryan.

She'd expected him to haunt her. He must still be mad at her for that time last year when, just to bug him, she'd sneaked into his room and messed up his baseball card collection; Dad hadn't believed that somebody almost fifteen years old would do something so mean and childish to an eight-year-old, and so she never had been blamed, except by Ryan, who knew. He must still be mad at her for not having been the one to fall through the ice that morning, even though she'd yelled at him that it was stupid to go so far out so early in the winter. Her father was mad at her for that too, although he didn't say so. They must both still love her; she was still, after all, her brother's big sister and her father's daughter. They must both, she thought, have a lot left to say to her.

So she kept waiting for one of them to say her name again. She braced herself for Ryan to shove past her and race ahead up the long snowy road to the schoolbus stop on the highway. She searched for his little-boy ghost in the thin swirly frost that every morning had formed on her bedroom mirror. The frost would have been pretty if it hadn't been so cold; at first, Torey had traced designs in it with her fingertips or cleared away patches so she could see her reflection, but lately she hadn't wanted to get that close to the radiant closeness, and anyway, she hadn't wanted to see herself in the glass.

Ryan had been dead all winter now, and she'd seen no trace of him, not even in her dreams. He was gone. He really was dead. All she seemed able to dream about was the violent melting of the ice downstream, and then French Creek flowing full and fast and rich with life again. Because they were warm dreams, she didn't tell her father about them; they made her feel like a traitor.

Her father stood in the doorway now, looking out through the locked storm door. He hadn't been out of the house since they'd found Ryan's body under the ice. He didn't go to work anymore. He didn't shovel snow. He didn't build snowmen or slide down the hill; Torey was too old for such things, but she'd have done them with him if he'd asked. The cold sunshine lit up the edges of his silhouette, making the white tips of his hair look golden. He kept rubbing his hands, but not very vigorously, as if really he didn't care whether they warmed up or not. Beyond him, through the glass in the door, she could see that it was still snowing, even though the sun was out.

The ice on French Creek boomed, and her father said, maybe to her, "With the ice this thick, we'll have floods." He backed away, shut the heavy inside door that kept that much sunshine out of the house, and went to sit in his chair.

On Saturday mornings, her father used to read to them. Torey had been getting restless; she was too old to be read to, too old to do anything with her father and baby brother. The last few Saturdays, she'd sat sullenly on the hassock clear on the other side of the room, watching the fire in the fireplace, half listening, while Ryan still squeezed in beside their father in the big warm chair.

Now there was plenty of space on either side of her father, as if he'd shrunk from the cold, and the chair was coated with rime. Torey thought maybe she could fill in the space. Maybe—although she was shivering herself and the tip of her nose was numb—she could warm her father up.

The chair was still surrounded by stacks of books, dusty now and sticky with the cold. She hadn't seen her father read anything since Ryan had died, and certainly he never read to her anymore. She picked up a book at random, opened it at random, held it out to him. "Read to me, Dad?"

She had to say it twice before he gave any sign that he'd heard. His eyes were like snowpack in his gray-white face, and she was sure he didn't see her. It was as if she'd interrupted something, or asked for something outrageous. Finally, he rasped, "It's too cold."

"I'm cold, too."

"It's the dead of winter." His words changed shape after he'd spoken them and then froze in place, like icicles.

Cold radiated from him, and Torey didn't know

THE ICE DOWNSTREAM 145

whether to try to combat it with her own body heat or to stay as far away and keep herself as warm as possible. "But spring's coming," she insisted. "You said so yourself. The ice is starting to break up." She almost said, "Whether you like it or not," but stopped herself in time.

"It'll be cold for a long time yet," he said.

"Winter can't last forever," Torey said at once, stubbornly.

She saw for the first time that a paleness, like frost, had formed over her father's cheeks and chin and around the outline of his mouth, like a double beard. She imagined his throat freezing shut, and his diaphragm, and maybe his heart. "Floods," he managed to whisper. "There'll be terrible floods. We'll all drown."

"I miss Ryan," Torey heard herself say.

Her father gasped as if she'd struck him, and lowered his head.

A gritty film of ice lay like a shawl across his shoulders. Torey put her hands over her mouth, then forced herself to touch it. What little warmth there was left in her hands dislodged the ice from her father, caused it to melt enough that it peeled away in glittering shards and fell to the floor at her feet.

He didn't seem to realize that she'd saved him. He moaned, or maybe it was the miniature protest of his ice.

Over the next few days, the house got colder and colder, while Torey could tell from looking outside and listening to the ice that the weather was getting warmer. Her father sat in his chair all the time now. He slept there. He took his meals there, what little she could get him to eat. He wore his heavy winter jacket, fur cap with earflaps, boots, lined gloves, but ice crystals whitened his beard and coated the backs of his hands until Torey brushed them away. She was afraid to leave him. She was afraid to stay.

Defiantly, expecting him to object and rehearsing

what she'd say if he did ("I'm *tired* of being cold!"), Torey went to the thermostat on the kitchen wall and turned it up to eighty. There was no answering click of the furnace coming back on. She frowned and with her thumb turned the thermostat up as high as it would go. Nothing. "The furnace isn't working," she told her father without turning, though she suspected he knew. When he didn't say anything, she said flatly, "You disconnected something," and he didn't respond to that either.

Torey pushed past him to the fireplace at the far end of the living room. She crouched in front of it, struck match after match from the several books in her pockets and held them to the crumpled paper and kindling she'd surreptitiously laid in. The fire wouldn't start. She checked the flue, stirred the firebox with the poker, tried again. The tiny, brief, nearly heatless flame of each match went out before it could make any difference at all in the chilly air.

The fireplace was made of stones from French Creek, roundish stones and thick flat ones, gray and brown and almost pink. There hadn't been a fire in the fireplace since Ryan had died. Torey sat down in front of it and forced herself to remember: in the crawling and leaping flames, she and Ryan used to try to find creatures who had lived in the creek, creatures who had somehow been mortared into the fireplace and would come back to life if they could just get warmed up enough.

Except when French Creek froze during particularly hard winters—and this one had been the hardest; the creek had frozen solid—it was always full of life. When spring really came and even this thick ice melted, the creek would teem again with squishy brown mud puppies that you never saw until you stepped on them, hard-shelled flickering waterbugs and long-legged spiders, quick little snakes the same gray-brown as the water itself. Torey's father used to say that French Creek was

THE ICE DOWNSTREAM

so deep and wide and ran so fast that in northern Michigan where he came from they'd certainly have called it a river.

Torey's parents had built the fireplace themselves. When they first bought this little house for eighteen hundred dollars. When they were first married. Before Torey was born. Before Ryan was born. Before their mother left. Before Ryan died. Before this long cold winter. A lot of things had happened; thinking about that sometimes made Torey breathless. Things she had no idea about, things she knew about only because she'd been told, things she remembered only vaguely, things that were as clear and fast-running in her mind as French Creek when they hadn't frozen up. A lot more things would happen, too, come spring.

Her father shuddered as another muffled boom rattled the house. "Ice breaking up," he said again. At least, she thought that was what he said; his chapped lips moved so little when he spoke now that he was hard to understand. Torey imagined his lips and tongue as cold and hard as the creek stones in the unlit fireplace, as cold as ice. The ice groaned.

These years, when the winter had been cold enough to freeze the creek all the way across and when spring warmth came suddenly, the ice always started melting at a particular place about twenty miles downstream, where the creek widened and slowed past the town of Cochranton. Torey had often wished she lived in Cochranton, so she could be standing on the bank at the instant the first crack appeared, so she could understand melting. As it was, she woke up every night and every morning to the noise of the ice melting downstream.

When she lay in bed that night, the ice thundered, and she heard her father calling Ryan's name. She knew she should go to him, but she was curled up tightly under heavy layers of blankets and she was afraid to move. In the morning the frost on her mirror had started to melt in long strings, pooling onto her dresser. The sky through her window was hazy blue, and she thought she saw faint green-yellow tips on the long-dead branches of the trees along the road.

Fearfully, she went out into the living room. Still in his chair, her father was hugging himself and rocking. His clothes were wet, and water on the floor around him made his boots glisten. Tears ran freely down his cheeks and puddled inside his collar.

Torey held out her mittened hands. "Come for a walk with me. Let's go see if the ice up here by our place has started to melt yet."

She couldn't tell whether he'd heard her, whether he even knew she was there. He was sobbing. The twisting of his body in the chair sent flakes of ice and drops of water spraying, and all around him the faded upholstery was damp.

It would be kinder, she decided, and much easier just to leave him where he was, sitting in his cold damp chair that would freeze up again when the sun set or the weather changed, grieving the rest of his life for his lost son, grieving the rest of her life. She would inspect the ice herself. She turned away from him and started quickly toward the door.

He got up and came after her. The ease and fluidity with which he moved, after so much time immobile in one cold place, surprised her. They both left wet tracks across the carpet; Torey imagined the strings of frozen puddles that would form here later.

When she opened the door, her father winced at the inrush of warm air. Torey hesitated, then took off her mittens, scarf, and heavy jacket and left them in the hall. It had been a long time since she'd worn so few clothes, only a sweater over her sweatshirt and jeans; she felt both freed and exposed. Her father kept his coat and boots on, ears covered and gloved hands in his pockets,

THE ICE DOWNSTREAM 149

but she watched him leave all his blankets and quilts behind in a soggy heap.

They made their way across the rutted road and through knee-deep snow that crusted inside Torey's sneakers. Losing their balance and sliding—but without any of the whooping and laughing she remembered from sliding down this hill with Ryan—they climbed down to where she thought the edge of the creek was. Their tracks blended behind them into one long precipitous trail. Torey's hands and feet were wet and her jeans already soaked through, but she was only a little chilled; her father was panting, as if this first real spring day was too warm for him.

One continuous gray-white surface stretched from where they stood to the island in the middle of the creek, and picked up again on the other side. Torey couldn't tell for sure where land stopped and water or ice began; it was important to know, so that she and her father wouldn't fall through the ice themselves.

She considered taking the dark line of trees as evidence of the edge of the creek bank, but they were uneven and unpredictable. They leaned at odd angles, and their ridged trunks dripped with icicles that somehow made them look both larger and smaller than they were. Torey wondered if it was possible that their roots had broken off inside the frozen ground, so that when the spring thaw came in earnest they'd topple into French Creek, which would be flowing full-force by then and would carry them off.

The ice downstream boomed, and Torey saw movement, a softening and shifting, in the ice at her feet. She crouched, leaned far forward, rested her palms on the snow-covered ice, and put her weight on her hands. The surface was not quite solid, although it held; she could feel the water flowing underneath, and life stirring.

She sat down in the wet snow. She stretched her legs

out onto the frozen creek, then lay back and wriggled her whole body flat onto the ice. She was shaking with the pulsing current.

"I miss Ryan!" she shouted, and the ice downstream rumbled.

"Oh, God!" her father roared behind her. "Ryan!"

Suddenly, the ice under her split. Torey felt the crack grow in a split second from her groin to her throat, and she managed to roll away just as the whole cold, gray-white section broke apart. Icy water seeped, then poured out, drenching her, making the packed surfaces of the creek and the land glisten.

Torey rolled onto her hands and knees and looked for her father. He was farther away than he should have been and at a different angle, confusing her. Then she realized that she was now on an ice floe that was starting on its own separate journey downstream.

Her father didn't seem to notice that she was in any danger, or that she was drifting away. He crouched well up on the creek bank, poking at the edge of the ice with a long thick branch. She heard him sobbing, keening, above the bass growling of the ice breaking up right here, no longer downstream.

Knees and hands slipping out from under her again and again, Torey finally managed to scramble to her feet. Without thinking much about it and without taking aim because she couldn't tell where she was in relation to anything else, she leaped.

She landed in six-inch-deep bitter cold water; there was solid ground underneath. Her father was a hundred yards upstream, still crouching, still wailing, and up to his waist in the frigid water. All around them, the ice boomed, and overhead the sun shone warm and dangerous in the soft blue sky.

Torey sloshed toward her father, fighting the strong current, the slippery footing, and her own strong desire just to plunge headlong into the creek and become part

THE ICE DOWNSTREAM 151

of its traveling, teeming life. The water—still with heart-sized chunks of ice in it—was rising around her father.

They made it back to the house ahead of the flood, which was rising at an impossible pace. The moment she entered the cold house, Torey felt her wet clothes begin to stiffen, and she hurried into her room to change. When she came out her father was sitting in his chair, and through the picture window behind him she saw the floodwaters rising.

"You should change into dry clothes," she told him. "You'll catch your death."

He looked at her as if he didn't know her. "I don't want to be any warmer."

"Spring's coming, Dad. Spring's *here*, whether you like it or not." Suddenly angry, she went and stood in front of him, in his line of vision. He didn't turn his head away or close his eyes, but she still wasn't sure he saw her. "*I'm* here, whether you like it or not, and so are you."

"Ryan is—*dead*," he gasped.

"I know Ryan's dead!" she cried, and, daringly, leaned down to put her hands on her father's shoulders. The fabric of his jacket was starting to ice over again. "Daddy, don't do this! Ryan's dead, but you and I are alive!"

"I—can't—stand—it," he whispered. Torey backed away from the crystals of his breath in the air between them.

By noon, the water had risen above the foundation. By midafternoon it was almost to the bottom of the windowsills, and a film of ice as thick as her hand had formed. When Torey looked out any window toward French Creek, she saw layers: gray-white ice sparkling in the spring sunlight on its top surface and glimmering on its underside as the still-liquid water struggled to break free, then darker and darker gray layers filled with frantically swimming and swirling creatures, debris, ghosts, down to the frozen and saturated ground.

By evening, Torey was wearing every dry piece of clothing she could find in her closet and drawers, and she was still trembling so violently that it was hard to catch her breath. The water hadn't risen much higher, but the ice had descended, and in the thin spring twilight she could see almost no movement at all either inside or outside the house.

Her father sat in his chair. His clothes had frozen solid. His hair had stiffened into a glittering cowl, and the patches of ice that had formed over his mouth and eyes looked like silver coins.

Torey went to him. She was so cold that she could hardly walk, and her thoughts were sluggish. Everything was very quiet; the ice downstream was no longer breaking up, and even sound seemed frozen.

She bent over him. He seemed to be breathing, slow and shallow, but otherwise he didn't move. She kissed him, and her lips stuck to the cold skin of his cheek, hurting when she pulled them away. "I love you, Daddy," she said aloud; every word formed a cloud between them. "I love you, and I love Ryan, but it's too cold here for me."

At first she thought he wasn't going to respond at all. Then she saw and felt the frost spreading rapidly up over him. She backed away, turned, ran.

Ice was pressing against the door from the outside, and she couldn't get out. Frantically, she ducked inside the cold fireplace, reached up into the short chimney for footholds and handholds, and pulled herself out onto the roof of the house. It was a short drop to the rising ice.

Sliding, falling, struggling to her feet again, she hurried around to the picture window for one last look at her father. He was completely encased in a translucent and impenetrable drape of ice.

Trembling, afraid of the floods but far more afraid of the ice, Torey put her head down and fled.

Morning Light
by Barry N. Malzberg

Barry N. Malzberg writes that since he last communicated with your humble editor, he has "sold 10–15 new short stories and an essay (on J.G. Ballard) and Carroll & Graf have reprinted Galaxies *and* Beyond Apollo. *I'm slowly pulling myself together this year, have written more and at a higher level of ambition than at any time for a while and am trying to push on (the idea of writing my 83rd novel fills me however with terror). I think that Carl Nielsen & Ralph Vaughan Williams are dynamite symphonists (close to the absolute top) and badly need more concert hall performance and evaluation and I think that Marla Maples is too much of an optimist. These three latter facts probably comprise everything I've learned since* Tropical Chills' *publication." Rest assured that Mr. Malzberg still writes like an angel, as in the following gem.*

Sell She-Us: Dark my light and darker my desire. Roethke wrote that, I think. Theodore Roethke (1908–1963), mentor to a lot of slightly younger poets who did it to themselves by way of ovens, candlelight, bridges, walkways, or the more civilized spaces of furnished rooms and alcohol. For Ted it was a heart attack but who is to say, who is to calculate the etiology? But my desire is not dark, it is light, light as night, full as flight, plumes of breath drifting upward into the cold and preservative spaces as slowly, slowly I enter into the quiescent, embalmed spaces of my beloved. Live and learn. Look and listen.

At the heart's stubborn zero, on the bed where all connection is borne. Think of it, Frances, think what it could have been like, the two of us on those mild and quiescent shores of passage, the two of us locked and linked to the essentialities of the spirit. Of course, you had other ideas, Frances, which is what has led to these more difficult and sullen choices. Enraptured, enthralled, I nonetheless roll and roll toward that stubborn zero on these frozen sheets, looking for the still heart of desire. A generation of sunken poets would have approved. Desolate, those inner spaces of yours and yet, five miles from desolation in the Vegas desert is the dazzling sun of the Strip itself. One must counsel patience then in any direction.

Centigrade: "Excuse me," Randall Jarrell says. His eyes twinkle with introspection, with secrets which could stop a world were he only to divulge them. Some years later he will take that stroll down the highway and make fast calculations as headlights reach toward those secret-laden eyes. "What do you think you're doing? Shouldn't you put on the heat? It's awful in this room, at least you should have a blanket. And look at your partner. She's absolutely blue."

"Blue is true," I agree. "She's cooperating now, though. There's something about real cold that brings them around, haven't you noticed?"

Randall Jarrell shrugs. Carrying original sin and the lost forests of childhood within him, considering this history (and the barren aspect of grown-up life) leaves him little room for dialogue, for the rigors of eschatology. "I wouldn't know," he says, "I wouldn't know what brings any of them around." He removes his coat, tosses it. "Here," he says, "place it on the lady, if you won't protect yourself, at least be a gentleman. Even a bear cares."

"Don't tell me what to do," I say. Nonetheless, I hold the cloak at arm's length, then toss it atop Frances. The folds conform to her limbs, she looks both smaller and more sufficient on the bed. A small arc of steam seems to come from beneath the coat, clouds the space above. "Well, thanks anyway," I say, "thanks a lot."

"Fifty-one American poets," Randall Jarrell says. He seems almost happy, now that Frances has been cloaked. "Fifty-two disasters. I am talking of a generation here. But don't let it bother you, it's not your destiny. It's the ball-turret gunner we must fear." He dematerializes, glides through a wall. "See you," he says, "in just a little while. Down the highways and byways of life." His stride is heavy, resonant in the new emptiness, I imagine that I can see his little bearded form speeding toward resolution. But that of course is surely not mine to say.

"We had plans, didn't we, Frances?" I say. "Big plans, large outcome." As usual, she says nothing. She has said nothing for a long time. Sometimes I feel culpability, other times sorrow, now and then the perverse need to enter her even in this diminished state and place the crystals of my being deep within her but more or less, more and more I try to control myself, keeping the example of my mentors and possessors before me.

Absolute Zero: Sylvia Plath is shivering. Upstairs her children sleep on and on, wrapped in their midday doze, unavailing, unrepresentative of her condition, but in the kitchen. Sylvia grasps herself, hugs herself, gasps. "I'll never get warm," she says. She bites her lips until little premonitory flecks of blood appear. "Oh Daddy," she says, "oh Daddy you bastard." Her gaze sweeps the room, she looks at me with interest. "It's not you," she says, "you're not Daddy."

"No I'm not."

"Who are you?"

"I'm an observer," I say, "a watcher in the glade of life. Fifty-one dead American poets keep me busy with their adumbrations. Are you very cold?"

"So cold unto death," Sylvia says. She looks longingly at the oven. "In there I can get warm," she says. "I'll just put it on, have a spot of tea."

"You must consider this carefully," I say. "Absolute zero is no foundation, it is only a possibility."

"Why fifty-one?" Sylvia says. She turns a switch, we listen to the ooze of released gases. "Why not forty-nine or fifty-four? Why are you so precise?"

"I was accused of that," I say. "Precision is all that stands between me and the void. You too. Most of us. Rigor, circumstance, ritualized versions of ourselves. You'll never get warm, not even there. Just a falling, a falling and then a cold you cannot conceive. I know."

"How do you know?"

"Don't ask," I say. I think of telling her about Frances, but it is a superfluity. Sylvia has enough on her mind; all of her compassion is reserved for herself. Not even the kiddies upstairs can distract her. She opens the grate of the oven, kneels. "I know it's different in there."

"Not necessarily."

"I'm looking for a way out," she says. She leans forward, puts her head inside, sniffs. "Yes," she says, "it's warm." She inhales deeply. "Aah," she says, "this is warmth." Her respiration levels, keens, I hear the sound of her panting. "Ariel," she says, "*a-real, a-real.*"

It is time to take my leave. Rounds are necessary, perhaps, call it a survey course, but they are also depressing. So much disaster! So many dead poets, damned poets, dying poets, self-loathing poets, self-mocking poets. So much copulation, fornication, inebriation, alcoholism, imbibition. So much adultery, fondle and putter in the small groves of academia, uptilted breasts like chalices, small groans as if from the vestry of self, distinguished heads leaning over the cusp of toilet bowls in their soon-enough remorse. It is more than one can bear, for penance or research.

Sylvia takes one shuddering breath and is still as I pad out of the English countryside, as deft and invisible at this moment as Jarrell. "Frances," I say, "it is unfortunate that you have driven me to this." I reach out, find myself on the accustomed bed, place her splendid and icy fingers on the back of my neck. Now at last the momentary soothing of embrace. I huddle with her under the blanket which Randall has so wisely suggested to us and ponder all of the circumstances of this difficult odyssey.

In the Ice House: Full fathom five Delmore Schwartz lies, crumpled in the corridor of the Times Square hotel where, so recently, he has incurred a fatal attack. His blood cools toward the risible, his eyes are already frozen in contemplation of that constancy he has for so long sought. "Genesis," I say, as if the sound of his own work will speed him toward a milder fate. "The world is a wedding of successful love." Delmore has no response to this; unlike the chatty Randall or the chilled Sylvia, he has taken a determined step toward the next phase of his career.

Considering him, considering the detritus within Delmore's room, the shambles of which I can clearly see through the open door, I think of the strange and shared fate of these postwar poets, some of whose work will even discuss the pity of their situation. If I were to look carefully enough, use the periscope of accommodation, I would—it seems to me—probably find underneath the orange rinds and incoherent handwritten manuscripts, the unreadable poems and the whiskey bottles heaped on the bed, the perfect and molded form of Frances, still hiding out in yet another poet's room, waiting for the line that will vault her into some kind of understanding of her life (and therefore mine) but I dare not look. Frances got around, Frances had a real understanding of modern poetry but only by proxy. In the sheets I would quote and sometimes lecture, promise her further insights but I would not escort her to the world. Humping toward the flower of her being, immersed in the cold and arching speech of the poets the century had bestowed upon me, I committed a rigorous and insistent research.

Falling to the Abscissa: On the high cliff, Berryman waves to me, measures himself for the leap. "What say, Henry?" he calls. "Are you ready for that great jump, are you ready for the dark? Soon there will be none of us, once there are two." He waves again. "It's cold in the river," he says, "and my bones are steaming. The river will put out the fire."

"Don't do it!" I say. The intensity of this confrontation, so soon after the dialogue with Sylvia, the vision of Delmore, has quite undone me. "Always the eternal cold, past the fire. You'll never warm again, the river will sink your bones."

"I hope so," Berryman says, "I've had enough, Henry, I've had enough." His grip is perilous, he sways, his glasses flash in the spectrum and tumble from his face. The arc of his lunge seems foreshadowed by desperate swaying. "Join me, Henry," he says, "we'll find the ice together."

"No!" I say. Unwillingly, desperately, I scramble on the rocks, reach out, assault the blank space of the wall with hopeless tread. "Suffer the warmth, stay with us, stay with us—"

"I think not," John Berryman says, "the late century condition is going to be even more hideous, the millennium is unattainable." So saying, he lets go, waves jauntily, falls like a shot tern into the river. There is nothing to be done, I scramble on the pebbles and watch him hit the stones, fall away. It is, as John undoubtedly planned, an unanswerable, in fact an insuperable, statement.

The Ice Age: "You see what I mean, then?" Robert Lowell says. He leans hugely over Frances and myself, his New England features rocklike and magnified by their accusation. "There's no way out, not at all." He touches my shoulder, that connection huge in the room, then withdraws. "Absolute silence is absolute darkness," he says, "but you'll have to find your own way in the canon."

There is much more to say, there seems to be much more to say, but clutching my absent beloved in the congealed spaces of that blanket, trying to avoid that gaze which freezes like that of John Procter, it is impossible to find the proper response. Perhaps there is no response. "Your problem," Robert Lowell says, adjusting his tie and coat for the walk to the flight to the taxi in which he will die, "is that you took modern poetry all too seriously. You confused anguish with answers. But then again, perhaps they are synonymous." And so on and so forth, he has a lot more to say and had I the patience I would record all of his magnificent if somewhat patronizing speech but Frances, insistent now in the absolute fury of dead zero, is drawing me in, drawing me in, taking me like a fragile candle flame into the center of her own necessity and nothing to do but follow. The snow rises and falls atop us. We become enormous, timeless, rigid in history, the snows of the century coming around us then to shelter us from the millenial fires. "Oh, Delmore," she seems to whisper in my ear, "oh Robert, oh Randall, oh John and Ted, oh rack and roc." But this must be illusory. I am, as the poet says, beyond words.

Bring Me the Head of Timothy Leary

by Nancy Holder

This remarkably stylish story surely has the most unusual title in this anthology. Its author is Nancy Holder, who writes that she is a "native Californian and I've lived in Japan and Germany, where I moved to study ballet. Eventually I graduated from the University of California, San Diego, with a degree in communications. I put this degree to good use by working as a sales clerk at Sea World. After a string of equally fulfilling jobs, I became a writer. I started out selling romances, some of them for the junior high market. I was on the Waldenbook Romance Bestseller list seven times and I won a couple of awards. My romances have been translated in sixteen languages, including German, Korean, and Serbo-Croation (!). I also wrote mainstream women's fiction novels, the most recent being Rough Cut, *out from Warner in May of 1990.*

"Horror was always my first love, though, and about a year ago I switched to it full time. I've sold short stories to: Shadows 8,9, *and* 10, Best of Shadows, *and* Final Shadows, Noctulpa #5 (Guignol); Borderlands; Obsessions; Women of Darkness; Pulphouse; Greystone Bay 2,3, *and* 4 *(if there is a 4) and* Women of the West. *I've also written essays on writers and writing for* Writers West, The Horror Show, *and for a book on Charles L. Grant, to be published by Starmont House.*

"I live in San Diego with my husband, Wayne, who

is president of FTL games, and I write the prologue/ scenarios for his computer games. These have been translated into German, French, and Japanese. We are owned by two border collies, Ron and Nan, who have retired from public life—as performing dogs at the Wild Animal Park and Knott's Berry Farm.

"I'm working on my first horror novel and writing more short stories." Whew.

Floating on a stinging sea of ice cubes. Ice floes coursing through hard, constricted veins. Some say the world will end in a purple haze of pain. A numbing cloud of goose bumps and stiffened limbs.

Some say the world will end in fire. And that was true, wasn't it? Isn't that what had happened?

For a long time, Tom shook and remembered a fireball. He recalled the seat in front of him igniting like a torch, the blistering heat. But now he lay somewhere else, floating frigid and shivering, and then he dozed.

His eyes opened. Closed. He drifted along, wondering where the hell he was, and why he was so cold.

Eyes opened. Closed. He shook. Shock? Was he in shock? Had he had so much to drink he'd passed out?

Floating inside a refrigerator with tiny, glittering bottles of gin—so many jewels in the field of his life. No, dear God, he was in a coffin! But he was alive! He was only drunk!

He remembered a woman's voice purring, "Gee, maybe. Do you have a, um, card?" A plastic cup filled with ice and a Beefeater's mini. Oh, yes, his third; he was celebrating his coup—yes, Dr. Leary had agreed to appear in the documentary!—and the stewardess was flirting with him, bending over to stow his luggage . . . yeah, honey-buns, stow that briefcase. Heft those overnight bins.

She was impressed, because he wasn't bad-looking for

an older guy (older, jeez) and there were agreements from Dennis Hopper and Timothy Leary and he was on his way to talk to Mick's people in New York. She was impressed, because he'd been there for the first acid, Dr. Leary's acid, and she and he got to talking about what they had been like, those crazy days. She was young, very young, and beautiful. And he wanted her, through the haze of gin and ice, very, very much.

When the explosion ripped through the cabin, the cup shot straight up and the ice showered down on his head, pelting him. He screamed his surprise—everyone was screaming—and she aged before him, ripping off his glasses and pushing his face into the seat of the man in front of him, shouting, "Assume the position. *Now*! Assume the position!"

Noise. Terrible roaring. Thunder and lightning. Needles.

Ice cubes. Sleet.

Fire.

He opened his eyes.

A shape hovered in the blackness, very close.

"Mr. McWilliams? Tom?" the shape said. Yes, yes, it was the stewardess. Her voice shook. "Are you ... oh, God."

Something brushed the crust of his cheek. He couldn't feel it exactly, only sensed the pressure. He heard a gasp.

"*Tom?*"

Her name. Her name, her name. "Sssh ... Sheila." His voice croaked and quavered like an old man's. He tried again. "Sssh ... sssh."

"Oh, God." The shape moved, and the pressure grew.

Eyes opened, closed. Dozing. Shaking.

"Tom!"

"We crashed," Tom said. "Jesus."

"Yes. But you're all right. You're just ... bleeding a little. But you're fine."

He swallowed. "I can't see. I can't move."

"It's dark. We were flung away from the craft. You're just cold. It's been snowing."

"You . . . ?"

She hesitated. "I think I'm okay. But I can't really tell."

Eyes closed.

Nothing.

"Tom?"

Assume the position. She had taken his business card with a lovely, young hand. Long nails, polished red. Such a kid; he'd been ashamed of himself for putting the make on her. Maybe that's why he'd drunk so much on the plane. At the lunch meeting, there'd been only mineral water. These were not the days of drugs and roses.

These were not the days at all. The sixties are over; long live the big chill that crept through everyone's fiery veins these days, iced their radical, raging hearts.

"Tom?"

Her voice was weak. She was crying.

"Yeah," he managed. "Yeah, baby."

"Oh, God, I thought you were . . ." She inhaled noisily. "We're the only ones. I located them all. I accounted for them." Through her tears, she spoke in a monotone, as if reciting from a manual. A checklist, engraved on her brain during her training. Locate the passengers. Determine the extent of their injuries. Something like that.

A light flashed in his eyes, bounced past his ear. "I found this," she said, brightening a little.

He saw her face in the halo of the flashlight beam. The same blonde hair, the same big blue eyes, peering out from a field of red. Her face was covered with blood. She looked like a demon.

"Aah," he moaned. "Aaah."

Eyes closed.

* * *

"... and I was pretty sure I'd call your hotel," she was saying when he woke. Her head was nestled under his chin. She smelled of blood and perfume.

Cold. So very cold.

"Please turn on the flashlight," he pleaded.

A click, and there she was, the blood wiped away; red gashes, now, on a blanket she had draped over the two of them. She had worn a little hair thing, he remembered, with a bow cocked jauntily to one side. Navy and red, like her uniform. Now a scarlet smear zigzagged across the place where the headband had been. She was cut, badly. Crystalline white flecked over it like shredded coconut. The white sparkled and danced in the flashlight beam.

Her lower lip quivered. She looked eighteen. When he was eighteen, he'd been tuning in, turning on, and tripping day and night.

"I said, I was going to go to your room," she murmured, and kissed his forehead. Blood and perfume, a slight pressure, nothing else but tears that welled into his eyes and a shearing, overwhelming panic.

"Will they come?" he asked, straining to raise his hand, touch her wrist, cling to her. "Will they get us?"

She cupped her hand over the crown of his head, his cheek. "There's a black box. Like you've seen on TV? It's sending out signals."

"How long will it take?" He was whimpering. He heard it, was ashamed. Couldn't help it. If only he could move. Goddamn it, he should be able to do something.

"It could be just a little while." She shifted. "I should turn off the flashlight. We should conserve the batteries."

"Don't you people have special flashlights?" he demanded. "Don't you have first-aid kits and ... and emergency things?"

"My legs won't work anymore," she said, and there was an anger in her eyes that made him more ashamed. She was terrified. She was doing the best she could.

He said, "I'm sorry."

"And besides, I couldn't crawl over them again. The ... others."

Closing his eyes tightly, he rasped, "I am sorry."

Floating on a sea of gin and ice. He was going to Manhattan to talk to Mick's people about his film. How Mick felt about drugs these days. Wow, man, look how far little Tommy McWilliams had come.

Yeah, five miles down, brother. With his soul on ice, for real.

Fire. Fire was the answer, to burn off the chill and give the power to the people and the Bank of America had to go; just give me some heat, sisters and brothers, and I'll use it. I'm a man on fire, baby, a young, hot man, and I'll . . . I'll . . .

Tom sank down and down, beneath a sea of icebergs, into the ocean of snow. Bobbed along below the surface, unable to breathe because his arms were frozen and his legs were frozen, and his lungs were packed with hail and it hurt too much to suck it in.

". . . Timothy Leary?" she asked him.

Up a bit, toward the warm surface, the fire dancing above the icy crust.

"I'm sorry? What?"

A ringing slap against his cheek. He heard it, did not feel it.

"Stop sleeping! You'll die if you sleep!" she shrieked at him, her voice shot through with hysteria. The needles. The needles had been bits of the fuselage, piercing him; or perhaps the ice-rain that froze the wings. He had worried about that during the stop in Denver. Had even asked her, while the new passengers got on, Is it okay to fly? Is it safe? Oh, yes. Oh, fer shure, like, it's fine. We have all the latest modern equipment. We wouldn't let you go if it wasn't safe.

"After all," she'd said airily, "I don't have a death wish."

Yeah, baby, she was just starting down the runway. Assuming the position.

Yessssss. Steam on ice. Fire from the jet engines, shooting into the blackness. Had he heard that? Had he seen that?

Such an insane way to travel, huddled in a bullet five miles above the world. Crouching in a metal box, getting liquored up so you wouldn't panic and start screaming, like poor old William Shatner in that *Twilight Zone* episode. Seeing monsters on the wings, gremlins in the fuse boxes. A bad, heavy trip all the way. Gotta drink, chase the boogies away.

Black box. Black box, come and find us. Come and save us.

Such crazy way to die, stone-drunk and frozen.

"Are you listening to me?" she accused.

"Uh. Uh huh," he assured her. He was being unfair to her, making her do everything, even the talking. Well, it was her job, wasn't it? She'd been trained to deal with things like this. Didn't she have a manual that told her what to do?

If they got out of this, he would never be able to face her. Assume the position, what a joke. Not with him. He was too old for her, anyway. Damn, how had he gotten too old for anyone? He was a young radical, fuck the pigs and set the world ablaze! Now he was lying in a snowbank in a three-piece suit.

For a long time, she said nothing. He wondered if she had dozed off. Then she asked, "Did you go to Woodstock?"

His mind was nothing but ice-cold panic, white-hot fear. Woodstock, had he gone to Woodstock or had he only seen the movie? He could think of nothing but radio signals, beacons, men in sheriff's hats and flashlights tromping through the snow. Flashlights tromping through the snow. Here they are! Hot coffee. Blankets! And a medal for Sheila the wundergirl, who talked the old dude through, kept him warm beneath the blotter-thin blanket with her overhead luggage. Oh, God.

His teeth chattered and he tried again. "No, but I went to San Francisco when I was seventeen. Lived in the Haight."

"That's where you met Timothy Leary," she said. "And dropped acid."

He found it within himself to chuckle. It was an alien sound. He thought he saw it undulate out of his mouth and pirouette slowly in the air before it dissipated, and then he remembered the flashlight was off. Maybe freezing to death was like being on acid.

"Yes. He's an amazing man. He was really crapped on. Now he's doing computer stuff. All that intellect. The Establishment..." He listened to himself. "Circumstances wounded him. All those plans..."

"Yes. Yes, you told me all about him," she said, and her voice was drowsy. Alarm roused him. As she said, they had to stay awake. What if someone called to them? What if they didn't answer?

Despite his fear, he was suddenly very tired; defeated, he closed his eyes.

Assume the position. They ran through the cabin, Sheila and the other stewardesses, telling the passengers to brace themselves. Gin flying toward the ceiling as the plane nose-dived; the man in front of him screaming like a woman—

—Tom and some chick, cuddling naked in the redwood tub at someone's house in Berkeley, stoned out of their minds. The middle of winter, and they had been tripping, and the hot tub was such a groovy idea. Everything was intense, heavy; steam swirled around them and beyond, the fields of whitefire, of redfire and white, of blood and fog—

Sheila was straddling him, pointing the flashlight directly into his eyes. He flinched, but couldn't turn his head.

"Please," he rasped, and she flicked her wrists, sending the light into the sky. He could see nothing but a ball of yellow and he blinked while she said in an undervoice, "Wake up, wake up."

His eyes adjusted. Her navy-blue sleeves were covered with freeze-dried blood. The front of her jacket was a layer of blood and snow, and something else. Bits of . . . bits of things.

His eyes closed. "I can't," he apologized. "I'm sorry, Sheila. I just can't."

Rain. Ice cube rain. Acid cube rain. He heard it, but he didn't feel it.

Murmuring. Chanting. He couldn't understand what she was saying.

"Timothy Leary," he muttered. He forced his eyes open and swore they creaked like rusty hinges. She sat on top of him with the flashlight beneath her chin, painting her face with shadows the way they used to do when they were tripping, to freak themselves out. Death on your face, baby. Death creeping up through your veins, chilling you out, man. She looked like Omar Sharif in *Doctor Zhivago*. Blue with cold, eyes ringed with black suffering. Blue skin, blue eyes, purple lips, black, black eyes.

"I was going to be fired," she said. "They made me pee in a cup this morning and I knew what they'd find."

His lips parted. She nodded dully. "Surprise drug test," she said. "I, um, I did something yesterday. Off duty."

Double standard. In the news these days. *Wall Street Journal* article. What could the yupsters tell their kids? I got stoned and had a lot of fun. But you live in a different world, Megan/Brooke/Jason/Joshua. Dr. Leary and me, we had a different scene. But you've got ice and crack and sweet little girls like this are getting their wings clipped because we dicked around with sugar cubes in a lab, and we came up with Lucy in the sky. Lucky in the sky. And the plane came tumbling down.

She pulled the blanket around herself and stuttered through chittering teeth. "I dreamed of being a flight attendant all my life. In my training class? Half the students failed. I was number one. I gave a speech." Her eyes filled with tears.

"Waste," he said. Jesus, wasn't it all a waste? All the things he'd done, or thought about, were they all going to stop now, because of a stupid plane accident? Was this it? Then why the hell did everybody try so damn hard?

"Dr. Leary," he said. "Why do we bother?"

She shook her head and started weeping, steadily and hard.

"I'm sorry," she whispered. "If only we'd met sooner."

"Mmm." He dozed.

Why try? We only die. Wasn't that what everyone said these days? And why did we try? Why did we try?

"Dr. Leary's going to have his head cut off and f-frozen," he told Sheila, and heard his voice crapping out. He was freezing here himself, the whole thing, not just his head. "Head c-cut off. And frozen. That's what he's g-going to do."

"Say what?"

"He believes his m-mind will survive. His thoughts. His . . . sssself."

She said nothing. In the darkness, he wasn't sure he was speaking aloud. Maybe he only thought he was talking. Maybe he was asleep.

"His head?"

"Just his h-head. So the thoughts will freeze. The blood will n-nourish the grey cells." He chuckled grimly. "Feed his head, like the old song."

"You mean, the blood keeps him alive?"

"Something like that. Since there's not as much... stuff to ah, f-feed, I guess. I don't really understand it. But he's very serious about it."

She was quiet for a long time. He thought she'd fallen asleep, then realized he was the one who'd passed out. He didn't feel her pressure on him, didn't see her shape.

"Sheila?" he asked querulously. "Shhhh?"

Nothing for a moment, and then something on his shoulder. Something bending over him.

"Sorry," she moaned. "Sorry."

He wished he could hold her, put his arms around her. He couldn't tell where his backside ended and the snow began. Hell, he was on his own personal cryogenics program.

"This was, this was my last flight anyway. Because they were going to find what they were looking for. They just needed an excuse. They said, they said I had problems—"

She flicked on the flashlight. Her eyes were glazed, ice-blue, black as a bruise. She looked completely out of it. She looked the way he used to look when he was on something. A deepfreeze chill sliced subzero down the center of his heart. Had she lost it? How was he going to take care of her? Ease her through this bad trip?"

"Ssshei... ssh."

She put her hand on his cheek. "Hush, Tom."

As she leaned over him, he felt the pressure on his lips. Harder. He fell into the blackness, swam up. Perfume and blood. And the pressure.

"After we were airborne, and I met you, I was sorry," she said against his mouth. "They shouldn't have let me go without checking. They waved me through the crew room. They didn't check." She sat up.

The pressure. Something ripped away.

"Won't they come now?" he whispered, because he could no longer talk. His mouth felt funny, smaller. There was something pink stuck to Sheila's lower lip. Confused, he added, "Because of the box?"

"Do you know we carry an axe on board?" she asked. "So the officers can escape, if terrorists . . ." She muffled tears as she tucked in her chin, shook, then raised her face.

Through his rusty, filmy eyes, Tom saw her eyes, ringed with suffering of long duration, something she had brought with her. An excess baggage of pain, packed to overflowing with fire. He knew about that fire. But his had melted. When that plane had dropped, he was halfway to freezing anyway. The documentary? A freeze-dried chronicle of dead hopes and dead dreams.

In one hand she held the flashlight. "Maybe the blood *would* feed your head," she said.

Puzzled, he managed a chuckle. "Oh, I don't think so," he whispered. His mouth wobbled. "I think that's just his way of—"

In her other hand, she held an axe.

"It's worth a try. It's the least I can do."

His eyes widened.

"It won't hurt," she promised, as the axe wavered in her blue fist. "We're going to freeze anyway. But if all your blood goes to your mind, you might . . ." she smiled grimly ". . . you might see Dr. Leary again."

She couldn't be serious. She couldn't mean . . .

She lifted the axe. The head glistened with chunky red; something was frozen to it—

—Christ, it was a *finger*. Oh, God. Oh, Jesus, God.

He screamed. His voice tore out of his throat and caromed off shapes in the darkness.

"Don't be scared." The axe dipped forward, backward, hacking an arc.

"Help! God, help me!"

BRING ME THE HEAD 175

"Hello! Hello!" a voice called.

Someone was coming! He heard the crash through the underbrush. Looked up, past the flashlight glare, into the sky—lights! Lights, flashing on the axe head. Helicopter! Flashing blue, flashing red—

down and down, blue and red, blue and red, ice-blue bloodred—

Blackness. Nothingness. Silence, but for his screams.

He blinked. Where were they? Where the hell were they? Where was the crash? Where was the helicopter?

Tears streamed down her face, hardened into frozen tracks. "T-Tom, it's okay. Don't be frightened. You're just having a bad trip."

Wildly, he searched the sky, closed his eyes to listen. Fireballs. Men on fire. Young men on fire.

He opened his eyes. A flash of metal, blue light (not flashlight, not, but blue, blue like from a helicopter, damn it) gleaming off the gore.

"Stop!" he screamed.

"Good luck," she murmured.

Down and down, a pressure he did not feel as something ripped away

Help me, Dr. Leary, he'd cried out on his first trip. *Help me*—

(Dr. Leary wouldn't let you go if it wasn't safe)

—down harder, down deeper, a pressure

that fed (perhaps)

his head.

The Bus

by Gregory Frost

Gregory Frost is the author of three fantasy novels and dozens of short stories of horror, fantasy, and science fiction. He lives in Philadelphia, a city where, he says, "homelessness and poverty are growing monsters that the city has thus far attempted to beat into submission with sticks of surplus Reagan-era butter." He claims to have touched the statue of Rocky.

The doors opened.

Driskel awoke on his back inside a cloud of hot steam. A stretch limo was pulled up at the curb beside his vent, one window cracked slightly. Music poured out of the window, and its bass beat pounded through the pavement, punching at his spine.

The light turned green. The limo thumped on into the night, but Driskel, the derelict, knew he could not go back to sleep.

He didn't stir or try to sit up on his soggy cardboard pallet but lay there passively, blinking like a lizard. The residue of numerous siphoned cheap wines still floated his brain, and he could not think clearly enough to piece together his surroundings right away. Off in the distance, there was a different music than the thunder from the limo. Then came a sharp hiss, and the music stopped. None of this made the slightest impression upon Driskel. He was an unpunched ticket, a steaming heap of rags.

He heard footsteps approaching and slowly, instinctively glanced in their direction. He glimpsed a face—a woman's eyes beneath a hat, a fleeting sideways glance. Disgust and fear stared down at him, but he was inured to such looks. He pawed loosely at the crust on his eyelids while the footsteps moved away.

The stoplight changed again, from green to red, drawing his attention. He saw the woman. Her back to him, she had crossed the street and was walking straight along the sidewalk toward—he lowered his hand from in front of his face—toward a big bus. Its orange running lights, low and wide apart, glowed like two predatory eyes, but the interior through the windshield appeared to be dark. Further back, a few cars whizzed by on the Franklin Parkway, meaning as little to him as had the limo and the woman; he'd mislaid the memory of the last time he had been in a car.

Driskel snerked deeply at the back of his nose, then raised his head and spat at the street. His head weighed a ton. He lay back down, rolled off his side, facedown. His blood moved like clotted oil through a rustbucket pickup truck. His blankets and coat had kept him warm while he slept, but the vent really made all the difference, heating the cardboard beneath him enough to keep him toasty. He guessed that he probably stank, since he couldn't recall his last appearance before a sink, but it was an acridness he could not say he noticed. It was the smell of humanity without their tubs and soaps, and it had been around longer than toilet paper.

His fingers had gone numb. He tried first flexing them inside his raggedy gloves and then hanging them out past the edge of cardboard, where the steam could heat them.

He recalled that he had been dreaming about a lost tooth. Somebody—the specific memory was gone—had told him once that dreams about teeth were actually sexual in nature. Driskel had never really understood that; besides, he knew without any doubt that his dream about the tooth was about a tooth. He'd lost three in the past month. He was going to lose the rest. His gums were all inflamed. *Periodontal*—the word came unbidden out of the miasma of his brain, some word his dentist had once used. His dentist. One memory had a way of triggering another, releasing buried treasure. He thought about that for awhile, then about suits and ties and razor cuts blotted with dots of tissue on his neck. For a second he could smell the tang of witch hazel upon the breeze.

The bus hissed. Driskel looked its way.

A line of light cut across the sidewalk, up the side of the building beside the bus. The door had opened and, as he watched, two people climbed aboard. A black woman and her little boy—he could see them brightly detailed. For a moment, he watched their shadows moving, blocking most of the light; then the door hissed again and swung shut.

Driskel yawned. Some poor fucking woman, he thought, dragging her kid with her to Atlantic City so she could play the slots. She would come home tired, broke, and nasty, beat the kid for making her lose, and then have to borrow from somebody to buy food, and maybe fuck the landlord in order not to have to make the rent right away. Jesus, how many of them just like her had he encountered in the shelters? Used to be it was mostly men like him who lined up for soup and beds; nowadays it was whole damn families, broken pieces of families. Whole fucking world in the soup kitchen. "Vote Republican," he croaked, then began to cough. He spat again and had to sit up. His lungs ached when he inhaled. They were wet from the steam, full of fluid; but so long as he could stay full of fluid himself, that'd be okay. What he needed was to get some booze. He looked the other way down the sidewalk, past the St. George Restaurant, but nobody was on the street tonight. The cold had driven them all away while he slept. Everybody had gone to a shelter except him. Driskel felt a distant pang of emptiness at being closed out of even this withered society. In truth he chose his solitude, but sometimes he wished he was like the others.

Behind him, the bus hissed again, and he twisted around to see a short guy standing in the strip of light. The short guy was wearing an old pea coat and a watch cap; he barked a couple of words and gestured at the air once before lurching up into the bus. The door closed.

Driskel knew the guy vaguely—had encountered him in the shelters once or twice. His name was Eddie and he was a schizo, one of the ones the city of Philadelphia had released on their own recognizance some years back. Trying to cut costs by shutting down asylums. Driskel chuckled, and coughed again. Even he was smart enough to know that if you put crazy people on the street they only got crazier and soon couldn't recall when to come in or when to take their medicine. The junkies had beat Eddie up a few times when they knew he had his medicine on him; they never hurt him much because they wanted him to get more medicine. Driskel had seen it happen a couple of times. Poor bastard Eddie lying in the alley outside St. Anthony's Hospice, spitting up blood and shouting his stupid, disconnected swear words at anyone who approached him.

Driskel stared hard at the bus. What the fuck was a guy like Eddie doing getting on a bus to the casinos? He expected to see the door roll back and Eddie emerge in a bum's-rush skid across the walk, but it didn't happen, and he couldn't figure out how.

Another figure came weaving along the sidewalk. Somebody in a nice heavy coat. Somebody with money. Driskel waited as the figure passed the bus and crossed the street, then he said as clearly as he could, "Sir, pardon me, but can you help me get something to eat? I'm freezing here."

Most of the time it didn't work, but every now and then, as in this instance, the mark didn't immediately dismiss him. Close up, the man in the coat was nicely dressed, with a gray scarf and earmuffs. His mustache was crusted with ice, and his cheeks were deeply flushed. But his eyes didn't focus so well, and Driskel realized enviously that he was drunk.

"Shit," the mark said. "Freeze your nuts off tonight, buddy. Here." He had dug under his coat and come up with a five-dollar bill; for a second he looked as if he hadn't planned to produce that much money and might take it back. Then he resigned himself to the act and laid the bill across Driskel's hand. "Get some soup, hey." He straightened unsteadily and plunged on along the sidewalk.

"God bless you, sir, thank you!" Driskel called to him. He kissed the five-spot, crumpled it in his dirty hand. He dragged the blankets off his legs, then spent a moment scratching at his ankles. Under the old wool socks, they were scabby. He dragged his fingers through his hair. Then came the hard part—getting to his feet. His knees were stiff and needed coaxing. He knelt for a time, while he coughed and wheezed and spat out more clog from his lungs. He needed badly to piss. There was an alley on the way to the St. George that would serve, and Driskel got to his feet, proud in the knowledge that he was formulating a plan with rare clarity and foresight, all the actions coming together. With one glance back at the bus, he headed away.

The counter girls at the restaurant knew him. He never made trouble for them, behaving with what passed for civility in his realm. He stayed away from the other customers, too—the late-night diners, the teenagers munching pizzas—because he knew they would complain about him and get him tossed out. But this time he had money. He went to the cooler and took out two beers. He'd have preferred his wine but the liquor store was too far away and probably closed. He was afraid to stray very far from his vent for fear that somebody mean would settle there in his absence. Sally, the sweet black woman behind the counter, sold him the beers, then stuffed a pepper-cheesesteak into the bag with them for his five dollars. She told him, "Go get your ass warm someplace. You gonna *die* on that street." He thanked her, promised he'd obey. A final glance up at the clock told him it was after eleven. No liquor store tonight; no more money, anyway. He went back out.

A few minutes in the warmth of the restaurant made the return outside a shock as powerful as diving into a pond. He shook uncontrollably, humming beneath his breath as his fingers fumbled with the foil around the steak. Steam rose out of the bag like out of his vent.

Driskel bit off a huge chunk of meat and bread, and chewed, savoring the sweetness of the peppers and the solid taste of beef. He'd plodded all the way down the block before his stomach rebelled and he doubled over and threw up. Cheesesteak and gray wine mixed with blood from his gums. A dozen knives stabbed him in the belly and he had to lean on a railing in front of a row-house to keep from falling on his face. He spat to clear his mouth, and slid down on the house steps while he tremblingly opened one of the beers and drank it. He gasped between gulps, his system pumped up, his body clammy. The cold brick step stung his ass, and he wriggled his coat down under him. Once the beer was empty he took a chance and tried some more of the sandwich, just a little bread and meat. A minute passed and, when the first bite did not threaten to come back up, he ate some more, then started on the second beer. Looking around he saw, on the far side of the bus, light knife across the darkness, detailing the stone face of a building. A shadow moved across the light, climbing aboard, blotting it out.

Driskel took a half-smoked cigarette from his shirt pocket and lit it up. The first inhalation made him cough

THE BUS

again till his sides hurt. He spat into the darkness, then leaned back and took another drag.

Complacently, he started wondering about the bus. How was it that he couldn't see lights through the windows? And what was a casino bus doing picking people up after eleven o'clock in the P.M.? It ought to have been in Atlantic City hours ago.

Driskel took the second beer and hung it into his coat pocket, forgetting that the pocket was torn through. He got up off the stoop. The can dropped to the sidewalk, spraying a jet of foam across his feet.

He yelped. By instinct, he swooped down, snatched up the can and held it over his mouth while he sucked lovingly at the foam. He shuffled on in some haste, leaving the trash from his meal on the steps.

By the time he had reached the corner, the beer can was empty. He tossed it aside as he belched in deep satisfaction.

Through the cloud of steam, the bus glistened in the streetlights. The strip of four "Michigan" lights on top of it winked on and off as if signaling to him.

Driskel waited but nobody else approached. The winter cold was keeping people home. His stomach rumbled and he knew he would need to find a toilet of some kind soon. On the bus they would have a toilet. Maybe they would let him use it. If they let Eddie on, why not him, too?

He nudged his blankets into a heap with his foot to make it look like he was still sleeping there on top of the cardboard, then crossed the street and started toward the bus. Drawing closer, he noticed that the sidewalk practically vibrated under his feet—the bus engine was running.

The window glass was smoked all around, but the driver's windshield—a clear square embedded in the larger smoked panel—revealed darkness, too. He could just make out the steering wheel and the line of the single seat. No light. Above, no destination sign. This bus wasn't going to Atlantic City. Driskel scratched his ass and began his circuit around, streetside. The lights from the parkway burned balls of halogen fire in the dark windows. Beneath them, a swirled insignia read simply *Worldwide* all the way to the rear. There, exhaust smoke fanned lazily out, drawing his attention.

He wandered around to the back and looked it up and down. He saw himself reflected, a shadow in the metal. There was no rear window. The bus exhaust stank worse than he did, and he got back up on the sidewalk.

For a while he leaned upon a parking meter and tried to sort through what he had discovered. A taxi buzzed past.

With a slow, confused shake of his head, he headed back toward the front of the bus. Approaching the door, he slowed up, watchful. The bus continued to thrum its subterranean power, down into the depths beneath the sidewalk and rising up into him, binding him to the spot. Transfixed, he became aware of his fingertips beginning to smart from the cold. Down the block, the insubstantial steam promised immediate warmth and security. Driskel wrestled against the pull of two gravities. He took a faltering step toward his vent.

The door of the bus opened.

A stream of bright light flooded over him, and more than light, for it seemed that the light contained particles of warmth; an envelope of heated air enclosed him as if he were standing before an oil-drum fire. Inevitably, he edged over to peer up the stairs; he had to hold up his hand to see clearly. There was noise, some kind of celebration going on, further inside. The driver's area was curtained off from the rest of the bus, but light was shining through a crack in the curtain and into the driver's mirror, which had been twisted to reflect out the door. Nobody sat in the seat to watch the dashboard lights.

Driskel put one foot on the stairs. A strong smell

poured forth—of cooked meat and good cigars and all kinds of perfumery; there was food inside there, where Eddie and the others had gone. The smell tempted him like a woman's polished fingers stroking his chin, drawing him up one step and then another and finally up a third. The door panels closed smoothly together behind him without a sound, like the blades of a flytrap.

He lingered in the ruddy dimness at the top of the steps. He peered through the narrow slit in the curtain, which showed him movement, glimpses of well-dressed bodies, bottles and glasses of cut crystal. The noise seemed to swell as he stood there. He heard music that he could not quite pin down—some kind of foxtrot, maybe—more voices, cheering and crazy laughter. He finally extended one grubby hand and peeled back the edge of the curtain.

A man in a tuxedo bent straight at him. The grinning face filled up the opening. "Well, all right, another one! How do you do? Come in, the water is *fine*." The man took hold of his hand and dragged Driskel out of the darkness. The nearer celebrants turned, smiling warmly; the noise damped for a second. Driskel's eyes were watering from the light.

The front ranks of people surrounded him. They handed him a drink, slapped him on the back and on the shoulder. One woman kissed his hairy cheek, and he knew she'd left lipstick there. As though parched, he drank his drink, and the glass was taken from him. A Japanese man offered him a cigarette and he accepted it—a straight, foreign, gold-labeled cigarette, unsmoked. The luxury of it awed him.

Driskel let a woman light the cigarette. She was wearing a black sequined gown, very low cut. She snapped the lighter shut and gave him a brief sultry look before turning away. "Are you hungry?" asked a handsome blond gentleman in a white tux, and he nodded. He let himself be led forward into the throng.

Somebody said, "Here, let me take that," and grabbed hold of his coat from behind, dragging it from his shoulders. He let it go. The interior of the bus was so warm it made him sleepy. Another person offered him a tuxedo jacket in place of the coat, and he put it on over his stained flannel. The jacket was much too large for him but no one seemed to notice. Then the crowd—all of whom said hello to him as he passed—opened up, and Driskel found himself confronting a wide table covered in food. Cuts of meat, cheeses, bread surrounded a row of silver tureens and warm chafing dishes. "Help yourself, old man," said his guide. "The bar's back there." Driskel glanced around to see a carved mahogany bar beyond the crowd. He had circled the bus and knew its exterior was nowhere near as large, but the proximity of food and drink blotted out his doubts entirely.

He snatched a piece of bread and began to construct a sandwich of skyscraper proportions (everything looked too good to pass up), until a slinky woman with the most heady perfume leaned against him and said, "You don't have to do that, you know, my dear. There's no limit. You can always make another."

Driskel stared into her smiling black eyes, and all at once he found himself weeping. Disquieted, the woman drew back and his guide stepped in again. "Here, fella"—handing him a glass of port—"you look like you could use this. Be good for you."

Driskel slurped it, then blubbed, "What's going on? Why are you doing this?"

"Why, it's a celebration. You've moved up in society tonight. Up from the depths, straight to the heights."

"And Eddie—"

"Who might Eddie be?"

"I saw him get on before me."

"Ah"—the man in white grinned—"yes, well, you're not the only one ascending around here. It's a *big* bus, now, isn't it?"

"I suppose."

"Well, you just eat and drink your fill, mingle all you want. I'll keep an eye on you."

"Bathroom, I need—"

"Right there, the far side of the bar." The guide patted him.

"Thank you."

"Nothing of the kind. It's us thanking *you*." And he merged gracefully back into the crowd. Snuffling, Driskel bit into his sandwich, half of which spilled out onto the table. His mouth full, he set the rest of the sandwich down on a sterling silver tray and stabbed out his cigarette. He kept the half-smoked butt for later. From the table, he wove his way to the bar and from there made a beeline to the men's room.

It was deserted except for him. The facilities included a corner shower stall. Driskel looked at himself in the circular mirror. The squalid image had little impact, more as if he were peering through a window at someone in the next room. He could hardly recall what he had looked like, back when he could con people into believing he was a poor working stiff who'd lost his wallet and needed just a few bucks to get home. Then it had been easy to accumulate enough money to get lost; back then he could still get into washrooms in office buildings and hotels to clean up. For a few weeks, maybe months, he had maintained a false veneer of dignity. It had been a long, liquid journey from that place to the steam vent.

The water in the shower was almost scaldingly hot. It swirled into the drain as a grimy soup. There were white towels on a rack and, even though he had washed well, he still left a dirty smear on them. He slicked back his hair once he had dressed, and emerged out of the bathroom, a new man. The change in his appearance had no effect on the crowd; they treated him as the same old friend as before.

He'd left his drink in the bathroom. He took a bourbon

from the bartender and mingled again. Now, pausing beside different clusters of people, he tried to insert himself into the conversations, even when he didn't know what they were talking about. A new play someone was backing or a hostile corporate takeover, the outrageous tuition at Yale being offset by the tax exemption their congressman had written into law for them, the price of a really fine Armagnac—he learned that he had nothing to say on their favorite topics. He wandered on. The crowd subtly manipulated him away from the bar, away from the front and further into the depths of the party. Voices seemed to be screaming around him now in a dozen languages, the laughter grew positively maniacal.

He noticed booths ahead and to either side. The crowd here at the back was more congested than ever; he just managed to percolate through. The booths presented an even stranger reality than the party itself. In them, Driskel discovered people copulating openly; a man pouring champagne between a woman's legs and then burying his face in her; a table where a woman wearing only a long string of pearls danced above a group of cigar-chomping CEOs; another where two naked men in neckties were doing things to each other on the cushions before a sinister woman in leather garb. Driskel just gaped. Nobody else seemed remotely interested that this was going on nearby. They continued to chatter away like a horde of enraged baboons, as though they had witnessed these perversions a thousand times. Their faces were all round and red, baby-fat cheeks and thinning, pasted hair. Food dribbled from the corners of mouths, cigars and cigarettes jounced as they spoke. Their shirt fronts were stained with spills of food and drink. He sensed an increasing madness about their eyes, the way they looked at him.

The air had a stench upon it much like he had upon him. He was sweating heavily now as if drawing close to a fire.

THE BUS

He downed the last of the bourbon but it couldn't begin to quench his thirst. Another one was needed, maybe two or three to steady his nerves. There was a reason he shied away from shelters these days; they were like this, packed tight like this. He turned to go back, but the crowd had closed in after him. He couldn't even spot the bar.

"Well, I see you've come through," shouted a voice behind him, and he turned around to find his guide there, a white island of unruffled compassion. "Did you have a good journey? Get all you wanted to eat and drink?"

"I could use another. It's hot, you know? Like a vent in here."

"A vent? All right, if you say so. It's only natural it would be hot this close to the engine." He led Driskel on, ever the reassuring guide. The crowd, suddenly, had thinned to a bare handful, and these few moved aside as the two men approached.

They were nearing what looked like a steel freezer unit beneath the dark rear wall of the bus. There still weren't any seats like in a normal bus, but the width of the compartment had returned to something like the right size.

"Now it's time for you to bid us farewell," said the guide.

"It is?" Driskel realized that he had expected no less. It had all been too impossibly good to last, just a bunch of rich people having their big joke with the bum. "Look, I took a shower."

"Yes. You're fairly presentable." He gingerly tugged the tuxedo jacket off Driskel, helping him extract his arms from the sleeves. "But by itself it isn't enough, really, is it? Besides, we can't have that." Someone produced a small silver container out of which he scooped a black paste. With the tenderness of a mother washing her child, he smeared the paste over Driskel's face, obscuring his freshly scrubbed features.

"I'll need my coat back," Driskel complained while this was going on. "It's cold outside."

"Yes, but you aren't going back outside." Two of the revelers turned toward him and took hold of Driskel's arms. They stared straight ahead, not at him. There was no mistaking their firm grip. The top of the steel unit opened up quietly and Driskel was propelled toward it, his guide just behind him. "I told you before, it's a big bus, and big buses have to run on something if we are to stay warm and happy and safe. You can see that."

The two who had hold of him lifted Driskel off his feet. He struggled helplessly, then wedged his feet against the side of the steel "freezer" out of which searing heat emerged. He had strong legs and he held his position while the two of them pushed and bent him back. Upside down he glimpsed the crowd behind him, packed together as far as he could see. On the fringe a few glanced his way with something like rapture on their faces. The naked men in the last booth were standing up like prairie dogs on the cushions to watch, while the dominatrix whipped them from behind. His guide leaned close beside him. "You belonged on this bus once, didn't you? I could tell. You understand how things work in the real world." He squeezed Driskel's shoulder, benign as a priest, a father confessor. "Don't give us a hard time. You're at our disposal, all of you."

His captors held him steady until Driskel stopped resisting. He lowered his feet from the side of the box.

They lifted him over the opening. Below was a chute, a gullet, into whirling cylindrical gears. Eddie the schizo's watch cap lay snagged in the chute. It had a big button pinned on it: *Don't worry. Be happy*. Driskel looked back one final time upon the respectable crowd.

They let him drop as though through a gallows trap. He landed atop the cap, dragging it with him down into the shredder. He bit into it to take the pain; the agony was sharp and brief. Any noise he made was drowned out by the wild celebratory shrieks of the crowd above.

His guide, the man in white, handed the shed tuxedo jacket to someone else in exchange for a handkerchief on which to clean his blackened fingers. He turned and plunged back through the melee as the steel lid clamped down again.

The motor hum picked up, and the lights on the walls burned briefly brighter. At the far end, behind the tantalizingly not-quite-drawn curtain, the entrance doors hissed open again.

Adleparmeun

by Steve Rasnic Tem

Steve Rasnic Tem has stories coming up in Fantasy Tales, Greystone Bay 3 & 4, *and Robert Bloch's* Psycho Paths. *His novel* Excavation *was recently published by Avon. He has been a finalist for the World Fantasy Award and has won the British Fantasy Award for Best Short Story. In 1991 England's Haunted Library will be publishing a limited edition chapbook of his traditional ghost stories—*Absences: Charlie Goode's Ghosts. *Steve is married to Melanie Tem, who also has a story in this book, and is without a doubt one of the finest stylists working in the field of horror fiction today.*

Once upon a time, a very long while before the white men came to Alaska . . . That was the way his grandfather had always begun his stories. He'd come to believe that was the true beginning of his own story as well.

He knew there could be no light brighter than sun reflected off snow. That was his last image of the village: after weeks of overcast, the sky filling with light, the white ground reflecting it so perfectly there seemed no difference between sky and ground. Six years old, the last one alive, he'd decided he must be dead—no one could live once the village died. Now he was in heaven, in the wonderful land of Koodleparmiug his grandfather always talked about, where everybody is happy and the ice and snow are swallowed up by the light so that all the Innuit could sing and play all the time, wanting for nothing.

But even at six years he knew this was wrong. The entire village was dead. He could remember their faces: Ekaluk, Kiana, Ootoyuke, Akla. He could remember his mother's body: great white hills of ice. He could remember the smell of the fish, the breath of the dogs against his face. He could remember every story his grandfather ever told him, and those last days alone he watched as the people from the stories ran and played in the endless white. He could remember the taboos he had been taught, and it worried him that there were so many taboos he would never know about, that he would violate without knowing, because there was no one left to teach him.

But he could not remember his own name. His soul had gone walking, a darkness on the snow with fire eyes, and it never came back.

Denver was having its mildest winter in over a hundred years. There had been a few snowfalls, but the snow melted within hours of touching the ground. A few weeks ago the sun came out late in the day even as the snow was falling, filling the air with a mist that made the sun look red. Examining this vision from his office window, Joseph thought, *Some taboo has been broken*, and then felt like a fool, no more clear-headed than one of his drunken or schizophrenic clients. The altered sun behind the drifting flakes had stirred a memory, but he'd been unable to bring it into focus.

Today was bright and clear, the sun returned to normal, and on a day like this Denver was very much like his grandfather's idea of heaven. Once the sun fell things would be different, though; with no cloud cover to hold the heat they were already predicting one of the coldest nights of the year. Joseph was not looking forward to it—with each passing year he became more sensitive to the cold. When he retired, in less than a week, he might not even leave his house during the winter months. The cold brought painful memories. And when he tried to imagine his future, he had a vision of his body lying stiff and blue beneath the snow, like an old fox caught out in a storm. He had never married; there were no children. The village would die with him.

Denver's weather was as suddenly changeable as a dream, or as the weather in one of his grandfather's stories: storms exploding into being and just as suddenly subsiding, high winds dropping out of the sky as if in ambush, temperatures falling twenty degrees in an hour. His grandfather would have called it weather for evil spirits, tonraks and shape-changers, weather fit for a shaman. Or the grandson of a shaman.

Joseph had gotten rid of his last client a half hour ago—a Ute referred to him by another social worker. Those who knew him sent all the Indian clients his way. The rest seemed to figure he was either Chinese or Hispanic; one fellow down in the adoption unit insisted on calling him "that old Hawaiian." He wasn't sure which presumption irritated him the most.

He remembered the people in their bulky fur jackets and hoods, like animals swollen with shadow. He remembered women cutting meat, lighting cooking fires, men dragging home the seals. He remembered drying racks hung with fish. Counting the meat with his mother *uttoe-seek . . . aypok . . . pinayoke . . .* So much had to be stored away before kill-cach tutt-cat, white hawk's moon, when the beautiful days would suddenly betray them, turning into a blizzard of howling winds that sucked at their breath. He remembered that day long ago when the shadow left his small body, escaping across the glittering plain of snow, not turning its bright eyes back even when he'd screamed.

If he were to be frank with his colleagues he would admit to them that he was probably less effective with the Indian clients than anyone else in the agency. He was an orphan in more ways than one—he'd been away from the village too long, and the problems with insanity and alcoholism filled him with guilt and an anxious shame. With each new case he was torn between screaming at them for their weaknesses and excusing them wholesale. They were as orphaned as he in their way, and his grandfather had told him that the souls of orphans often went walking. The orphan had to hunt and conquer his own soul, just as he would a seal or caribou. Alcohol and madness filled them with spirit to replace the spirit they had lost.

His grandfather said there were two kinds of madness, the madness that might make you a shaman, a medicine man for your people, and the madness that made you a danger to the tribe—where you had to kill yourself or permit someone else to eliminate you. If they had lived in his village, many of Joseph's clients would not have survived, although some of them would have become medicine men. Joseph stared at the Rockies, at the white mist drifting rapidly eastward. By nightfall the Denver sky would be white and endless as the ice fields of northern Alaska.

Those early years appeared to him in a world consumed by white. After a long melt when the snow came again it was as if the sky and the ground traded places. The snow became a magic powder that spread its way through everything. It was light as air, and yet it supported the world. Sometimes the world became as blank and brilliant as a sheet of paper—although he had seen little clean paper back then. It dared you to put your mark on it. People never seemed to fit into such a spare landscape. They became like smudges or doodles.

Below, in the street, the aging Ute was panhandling his way to the liquor store. Joseph looked back at the white mist—it suddenly seemed miles closer now, its front edge boiling with a multitude of shapes. As the light failed Joseph could see his reflection in the window, his eyes shining, his face shadowed, almost unrecognizable to him. He saw as many visions as the most desperate of his clients.

"You ever going home, Joe?" Walter Johnson from the next office stood in his doorway.

For a second Joseph didn't quite know how to answer. "Sometime," he finally said.

"Looks like a storm coming up. Don't go getting lost, now." Walter chuckled. It was a running joke in the office, his Indian blood apparently increasing the irony. Joseph had lived in the city for almost twenty years, but still got lost an average of once a week. Cops were always pulling him over—as a driver he was easily distracted. Walter finished putting on his coat, waved, and shut Joseph's office door behind him. Joseph could feel the pressure of the cold building steadily on the other side of the window.

He had a vague memory of a similar cold pressure in the hours before they had found him. Joseph's adoptive parents had been relief workers, among the first group to arrive in the village after the long illness and the starvation had run its devastating course. How they found him had become family legend, the story repeated hundreds of times over the years.

They hadn't stored enough meat. Their best hunters had been lost at sea. A shadow fell over the village. Nothing his grandfather tried could save them. It was the failure that finally killed him—Grandfather had always required little food. A medicine man might kill himself a hundred times over merely to make some point to his people. But the final death was one he would choose.

Over the years his parents had explained to him all the reasons the village had failed. They did this with a great deal of respect and reverence for his people, and with a great deal of love—but it seemed to him they had explained why he had become an orphan as if it were a natural thing, an unavoidable disaster. And yet his grandfather had taught him that there were rules about the way things happened. That there were taboos that might be broken, souls that might go walking.

The climactic moment of their stories was always the discovery of the orphaned Eskimo child with no name. "... and there he was, dark and tiny in a great snow-filled white world."

In his teenage years Joseph had been filled with rage toward his people for having been so stupid, so helpless as to lose their lives in such a way. His parents had understood, and yet they made it clear he needed to be proud of what he came from.

If he had stayed there he would have become a hunter of seal, fish, and caribou. And perhaps later the medicine man, the shaman like his grandfather. Here he was a mediocre social worker for people who would not dream if it were not for the drugs and liquor.

Shadows filled the street, making their way home. Joseph looked for the one shadow with no human body attached.

"You have to *want* to change," he always told his clients. "Take a good look into your soul." He felt like a hypocrite, saying that. He'd been hunting his own soul since childhood.

Out on the streets the shadows disappeared into buildings and cars. Most didn't appear to notice the tall building he was in, towering over them. He might have been a spirit high in the sky. He watched carefully for the odd movement, the misplaced shadow which made no sense. He watched for eyes of shining ice and a tonrak's razor teeth. Once he'd retired he might hide away in his house. His soul might never find him.

By the time he'd completed the day's paperwork the sky had turned deep blue with a drumhead moon, then white again with snow clouds tainted silver by the city lights. As the low clouds rubbed against the tall buildings, misty pieces flaked off and drifted toward the ground.

He left the agency about six that evening, in the dark. The light snow and a quick melt had left the streets glistening with ice, white with the reflections of the streetlights. Joseph always drove carefully at such times, with what he thought must be a neurotic anxiety over the black ice which could not be seen. The name itself had a science fictional sort of quality—black ice as in black hole, a *negative* sort of ice that might suck him and his car down into an unreal, hellish world under the slick pavement.

A large woman in a white coat stood on a nearby street corner. She appeared to be waving for a taxi. As he passed she turned to face him: a great white bear with coals for eyes.

Joseph slowed the car.

The bear bellowed at the oncoming traffic and lumbered across the street to the vague median of trees beyond. Joseph switched lanes and turned onto a side street in that direction. Tires squealed and horns bellowed like hunted seal. Between the trees he could see the moving bulk of white fur, then the woman's face as the huge furry head turned to look at him, tease him into following her. The snow was falling again, thicker; he turned on the wipers and heard the massive beat of the animal's laboring heart.

The snow continued to fall as he tracked her through the alleys and abandoned streets of lower downtown, to the railroad tracks and the old warehouses. He caught glimpses of her infrequently, just long enough to gauge her direction. Her coat was spotted with blood. Once he thought he glimpsed a spear wedged into her side. The winter snow fell more slowly, heavier, the flakes as large as birds. White birds suddenly filled the sky. Somewhere he could hear his grandmother chanting her singsong through the long dark winter. They ate walrus in the winter. They hunted all the time. Without the fish, the seals, the many white birds, they would starve. They wore the seals and lived inside the seals. But he could not remember his name.

In the falling snow that filled the sky and filled the world he suddenly saw the dark shadow, the shining teeth. The car leapt forward into the bear and his eyes filled with red. When he opened them again the car was dead, the front wedged into a doorway. The snow fell nervously and completely, like sleep.

Someone had given the dogs some meat. Redness pooled around their legs. They fought, spreading the redness through the snow. His grandfather thrust a spear into the snow and the hole filled with blood. Later they dragged a seal up through this hole. Two men huddled together eating chunks of hard frozen fish.

Joseph opened his eyes. Calm had settled in. The sky was a dark blue. He was surrounded by the snow and a complete silence, except for an occasional sigh from the wind. It was December, the Moon With No Sun. *Siqinrilyaq tatqiq*. He wanted to stay awake; he knew that people sleeping in their cars during snowstorms often died. He searched the glove compartment for his knife. If necessary, he would murder his sleep.

He slept a long time in his car. He knew he was sleeping because every few hours he would wake up again and see the bear woman outside his car. He would struggle to stay awake, but sleep always won. He could sense the shadows stalking him, creeping closer to feed, but sleep wouldn't let him do anything. Days walked by. Nights walked by. The snow continued its burial of the world. Shivering and in pain, feeling his bones had fled during his sleep, he knew that his soul was out wandering somewhere in the snow. His soul was *cold*, and in great fear of the tonraks walking the land, hunting his soul as if it were a seal, or a small child wearing a mask. But his soul had teeth, and in its rage stalked him, the one who had abandoned it.

In the land of his childhood the twilight lasted day after day, the sun waning in the fall and waxing in the spring. The day did not start over every day, but continued on at the same pitch, the same rhythm. Only now was he beginning to understand the days of half-sleep he so vividly remembered, the familiar sensation of never quite waking, of walking through a dream. Even now he hated the darkness.

If he had stayed he would have been the hunter. He would have been the medicine man, the shaman. He would have had the visions. Driftwood masks painted with red ochre. Hunched figures waiting at a seal hole. A tupilak with an enormous, quarter-moon head. A spirit doll.

The rounded figures swollen with shadow—man or bear or seal. He suspected that in fact it made no difference. Women were bears. Men were bears. They hunted and struggled all their lives on the ice.

He could have been like the great medicine men in his grandfather's stories. Pynaytok the Fire Man and his son Nayatok who discovered the villages in the sky and brought mild weather and fish to their people.

The snow piled up without end, driven by the screaming wind. The sun had lost its heat, reduced to a cool waxy bulb in the sky.

Neshmuk, the miracle man of Hooper Bay, sat upon a great fire he'd had his people build, until he'd burned down to a fine white ash, white as fresh powder snow. When the people gathered in the kashim to discuss this demonstration, Neshmuk walked in unharmed.

Outside the car it was dark and cold, even though Joseph thought it must be morning. He'd been trapped inside his car all night. He moved himself stiffly across the seat and stretched out his cramped legs. He unlocked the door but the door would not open. Jerking on the handle he heard the door unlatch, but could creak it open only a quarter-inch or so. He imagined himself the medicine man, the escape artist forever young, and kicked at the door. It made a scraping noise, then snapped open. Handsful of white powder drifted in onto the seat.

The light was so full and brilliant it was like breath. He pushed out of the narrow alley half-filled with snow to where he thought a parking lot should be. Beside him the buildings were split and veined with white. Dark holes into another world gaped in their sides.

Tall ice ridges reflected the purple and amber dawn. A hard cold had fallen over the world. A light breeze scattered glittering snowflakes over the packed surface. Joseph walked a mile or more over the vast parking lot of ice, seeking the edge of the park where he had first seen the bear woman. From there it was only a short distance to his office where he could call for a tow. Behind him the ice crunched. Snow whispered around his feet.

A glacier ten feet high had crept over half the park. He skirted its edge. Beyond, ice caves pockmarked a downtown skyline of ice cliffs, towering serac, floating shelves and ice falls, many of the surfaces thickly crevassed, some collapsing into a series of roughly rectangular blocks. He walked around the edge of where the park should be until he found a relatively flat area with little snow. Where the cold had moved on he found large sections where ice had warped the ground and fields of talus where frost had shattered the rock.

Where his office was supposed to be an ice cliff towered. Joseph saw himself in the ice's reflection, a tonrak, blue with cold. He walked on through gulleys made by high winds through mountains of snow. Even his shadow on the snow was blue. At the end of the gulley was an abandoned car. Joseph climbed inside in search of warmth.

ADLEPARMEUN

The car's interior had been lined with furs and sealskin. The backseat had been removed and the carpet torn away: white ash spread across the metal frame, here and there a charred bit of wood or a bone. Joseph gazed out the back window, to where his grandfather labored in the empty white constructing an animal out of the snow.

His grandfather applied the finishing touches to a snow bear. A spirit entered it and the snow bear reached for the car. Bits of it, flakes and clumps, trailed to the ground. Thick muscles of snow rippled beneath the icy hide. It was not fair—dead people had so much power. It was a bad thing, causing evil to happen to others. His grandfather must know this. His grandfather turned to speak to him, but Joseph no longer knew the language. Noun, adjective, and verb telescoped into one word, his grandfather angrily trying to get it all said at once.

Joseph shook under the force of the deep bear voice filled with snow. He threw himself out of the car and ran down another snow gulley, onto a pure white slope that rose steadily toward the blinding sun. He turned and turned, screaming, a dog howling at his own shadow.

A snow-covered car crouched, then moved forward on four bear paws, finally standing up as a man in a heavy-lined parka and hood. Another car rolled over off the road, a seal in its death throes.

A giant tonrak raised itself up and pushed its hands into the sides of several buildings, pushing them over.

Upturned slabs of ice. A hollow at the base of a huge hummock showed the remains of a house inside, as if half digested by the moving expanse of white.

Pounding gales. Clouds of blown snow. The winds moved and crushed the pack ice, trapping the people in their homes. The sun vanished for months at a time.

The ice was magic. Ice filled the houses and killed people.

His grandfather had always told him that in the hell of Adleparmeun, which lay just below the surface of the tundra, it was always dark, no sun, with nothing but pain and trouble for all who tried to live there. Snow flew all the time, terrible storms, so very cold, so much towering ice. Once you went there, you could never return. You had to sit there with your head bowed in dejection, unable to raise yourself against such wind, occasionally snapping at the butterflies which were your only food. Adleparmeun was the Alaska of Joseph's dreams.

His grandfather had always told him that orphans had special powers. They saw elves, dwarves, fairies, and all manner of visions which other people and children could not see. The orphan was always the poor, brave boy who triumphed while remaining kind and honest.

In the distant white a shadow leapt in pursuit of something Joseph could not see. He started running, his feet finding firmer purchase in the drifting snow the faster he moved. A spear filled his hand and the shadow turned its head, flashing its teeth in invitation. Joseph filled his lungs with cold and knew he was the great hunter, that he could catch this thing. But he had to be careful, for bragging brought a hunter bad luck.

The shadow hid among the sharp towers of ice and the scattered boulders. But each time Joseph flushed it out. It was hard to placate an animal soul. Life's largest danger lay in the fact that man's food consisted entirely of souls. White men had ignored this—surely it must be to their eventual peril. Joseph had forgotten it, too. But not now. Now Joseph remembered everything his grandfather had ever told him. All the lessons. All the taboos.

The shadow snapped its teeth. Joseph thrust with the spear and pierced the shadow's side. "Give me my name!" he shouted, and the shadow howled.

Adleparmeun hell. The home of the Anti-Christ, the domain of Gog and Magog. Joseph had become the shaman who could walk under the sea and not get wet, who could be consumed by fire and yet be unharmed. Joseph, too, would be able to change the direction of the wind and soften the weather. He would walk through rock and walk under the sea.

The shadow reached up and clawed at Joseph's face. The shadow laughed and howled and it was his grandfather's laughter, his mother's howls as she died. The shadow screamed and it was the screams of the villagers raised together as they passed over to the islands beyond.

Joseph reached down to choke his name out of his soul. But his soul had longer arms, and used them to grab the sky and pull it down to the world.

The sky came down on him. It was blue and impenetrable and like a ceiling it came down to meet him. Joseph tried to stand up above this low sky to see if he could find heaven there: flowers in bloom and trees laden with fruit where he could climb up and stay forever.

But his soul had teeth, and, having let him see, would not permit him to climb.

Once upon a time, a very long while before the white men came to Alaska, a child with no name was left alone to die on the snow.

Close to the Earth

by Gregory Nicoll

Gregory Nicoll is a Southern writer whose disturbing fiction has been published in anthologies such as Ripper!, All the Devils are Here, *and* There Will Be War. *His acclaimed novelette "Dead Air" was selected for* The Year's Best Horror Stories Series XVII, *edited by Karl Edward Wagner. He has written nonfiction pieces for* Fangoria, Cinefantastique, Rod Serling's Twilight Zone Magazine, *and* The Penguin Encyclopedia of Horror and the Supernatural. *Greg has also dabbled in movie work, providing publicity and uncredited additional dialogue for the feature horror film* Blood Salvage. *His present project is a novel set in north Georgia, where he resides. Greg is the "proud proprietor of one of the world's foremost collections of rock 'n' roll records, imported beer bottles, chili recipes, and high-mileage Volkswagens." Perhaps he was driving one of those same VWs when he was struck with the idea for the twisted tale that follows.*

The early evening cold sliced at Tacker's neck like a frozen knife blade. Cursing the imperfect manufacturing which kept his Oldsmobile's window-glass from fitting precisely into the doorframe, Tacker groped for the controls on the car's heater. They were already set on maximum.

God, it's cold, he thought. *A Georgia boy can't take too much more of this.*

Billboards hyping small hotels loomed invitingly along the roadside, promising shelter, comfort, and warmth at budget prices.
SLEEP CHEAP.
HEATED POOL.
FREE BREAKFAST.
MOVIES.
SPEND A NIGHT, NOT A FORTUNE.
The signs gleamed in the twilight and then whisked past like shooting stars. Tacker kept driving. *Another hour*, he thought. *At least another coupla hours. Gotta make it as far as Harrisburg tonight.*

He reached up with his curling, nearly numb fingers and tried to pull the zipper of his much-too-thin cotton jacket up higher. His fingers couldn't close on the metal tab tightly enough to pull it. *Must be twenty degrees out there. A Georgia boy just can't take this . . .*

The radio in the dashboard sprayed snowy static. He'd already lost the only good North Carolina station over an hour ago, its dim signal breaking up in explosive crackles as Tacker drove out of range.

Antenna's probably broken, he grumbled.

He kept the radio switched on—the static had a soft sound, a small comfort to him in the unfriendly evening chill.

The car smelled of cold plastic and frosted vinyl. The once-inviting aroma of coffee was gone now, another victim of the freezing air slipping through the cracks in the Oldsmobile's door. A tiny reservoir of the muddy brown liquid still splashed around the bottom of the jumbo Styrofoam cup he'd bought three hours ago at the truck stop, where he'd topped off the fuel tank with a few gallons of overpriced diesel, grabbed the coffee for his head and a couple of Eskimo pies for his stomach, charging the whole mess on the company's credit card. It was against policy to buy food with one of XCCD's

CLOSE TO THE EARTH 209

fuel cards, but Tacker was past the point of caring about policy.

It's "policy" that we site inspectors get a company car with a heater that works and an antenna in one piece, he reasoned. *Anybody fusses, I'll tell 'em to cuss out the joes down in motor pool. Lousy maintenance. Probably the fuse or something....*

His personal disgust with company policy was mixed with professional annoyance. Heavy on his mind was the spill at the new site east of Memphis. Heavier on his mind was the "spill" that had leaked around Evelyn's birth control device six months ago, an accident of a far more personal nature. The long, lonely quiet drive had given him plenty of time to worry about both, and he was hungry for a distraction. *Preferably a warm distraction*, he mused.

Another sign loomed in the graying twilight.

MARYSWOOD DINER—COFFEE, EATS, BREAKFAST ANYTIME.

Coffee. I should stop and get s'more coffee, he thought. *Maryswood... How far's that?*

He fumbled with the auto-club map of Virginia, its thin rectangular pages fanning out from the tiny binder ring like dead white fingers on the car seat.

Four miles. No problem.

Yeah—a little coffee—that's what I need. Maybe make a quick call home to Evelyn and hope she's got something else to talk about besides the usual complaints.

Then maybe find me a waitress or a cashier who still knows how to really warm up a man...

As Tacker drove on, the clouds overhead converged to blot out what remained of the daylight. Yet the ground on either side of the highway retained a strange luster. It was several minutes before Tacker realized what he was seeing.

Snow! It must've snowed here recently. Well, I'll be... The minor novelty of a snowfall—Tacker had only seen enough snow to cover the ground a half dozen times in all his thirty-nine years—was mitigated by the agonizing extra degrees the temperature fell as the Oldsmobile crawled nearer to Maryswood. Tacker shivered. He eyed the dirty, patchy snow—mixed in the muddy soil like grits and gravy—with a combination of wonder and helplessness.

Despite the fall of night, no lights burned in the windows or parking lots of the scattered warehouses and smaller buildings Tacker saw from the highway. The rolling fields, where corn and tobacco plants would grow in warmer seasons, now lay dark with unlit farmhouses rising like lonely tombstones in the middle of their empty, lifeless acres.

The diner's probably closed, too, he thought. *Still, it's worth a chance . . .*

Sure hope the coffee's hot . . .

Tacker could remember stopping in Maryswood before, but couldn't recall when. *Sometime last year . . . maybe the year before . . .*

The exit loomed on the roadside up ahead. Just beyond the big, green metal sign put up by the highway department was a smaller one, made of cracked boards painted blue. Faded orange letters spelled out:

WELCOME TO MARYSWOOD.

Below the town's name was a row of small symbols— a ball of cotton, a peanut, a tobacco leaf, an ear of corn— and a tiny inscription in gold.

Tacker glimpsed it briefly as he drove down the ramp:

A COMMUNITY CLOSE TO THE EARTH.

Locating the Maryswood diner was relatively easy— it was the only building at the small, rural crossroads with its lights still burning. The hardware store, the International Harvester dealership, the dry goods shop, and a few others nestled beside them seemed to be closed for the night. The gas station on the south corner looked like it had been shut down much longer, if the shockingly

CLOSE TO THE EARTH 211

low price-per-gallon displayed on its rusting sign was any indication. Tacker swung the Oldsmobile into the diner's empty seven-car parking lot and switched off the engine. The big diesel shook with a death rattle and went silent.

Wind whistled, then howled, outside the car.

Tacker sighed as he slumped back in his seat. For the first time it occurred to him that perhaps the diner was closed, too—that its lights had been left on by mistake. After all, there were no other cars in the lot. He surveyed the building carefully through the mist of his own condensing breath.

It was a classic '50s diner—a long streetcar-shaped building of bare, gleaming metal with wide windows from end to end. A single amber lamp lit the metal-railed rampway up to the door and blue-green light glowed from inside. Tacker noticed that a powerful spotlight had been mounted on a pole behind the diner, illuminating a huge open lot out back. *Must be for the employees' parking*, he mused, *or maybe to light the way to the dumpster*. Tacker sighed. *With all those lights on, somebody's got to be on duty inside the place...*

Clenching his teeth to brace against the chill, Tacker pushed open the Oldsmobile's door and climbed out. His toes went numb before his shoes even touched the icy pavement. It was all he could do to shove the car door closed and stagger up to the frosted glass entrance door to the diner. He fell against the restaurant's metal door handle and with a tremendous rush of relief felt it swing inward on its hinges. An instant later he stood inside, sweet warm air soothing around him like a heavy blanket. He took a deep breath of it.

Tacker was alone in the place. The turquoise-colored pads of its counter stools stood uniformly empty, menus and napkin holders arranged neatly on the gleaming surfaces. The air smelled faintly of eggs and bacon. A coffee pot steamed on a warming station near the cash register.

"Hello?" he called out tentatively. "Is anybody there?"

There was no answer.

Tacker took a tentative step forward, then climbed onto a padded stool near the cash register and began to defrost his curled fingers over the steam rising from the coffeepot beside it. The earthy, dark-roasted fragrance was bracing. He looked around hopefully for a mug but didn't see one anywhere. He remembered the Styrofoam cup still propped up in the Oldsmobile and considered going back for it.

Maybe after I've warmed up a bit more, he thought, looking out at the car through the diner's windows.

"Can I get ya something?" asked a voice from behind him.

Tacker whirled around on his stool.

"Coffee, mister?"

She was relatively young—about twenty-nine or thirty, Tacker figured—with wide, dull gray eyes darkened by circles from lack of sleep and edged by slight wrinkles. Her hair was long and straight, frizzed with split ends, and badly in need of a comb and cut. She wore a tan fur-collared bomber jacket, hanging open to reveal a creased blue uniform blouse with *Marie* stitched in red letters over the right breast pocket. A thin trail of slush—part mud, part melting snow—on the tile floor behind her suggested she'd recently been outside. Tacker tried not to stare too intently at her, yet since reaching puberty he had developed the habit of evaluating each new female as a potential sex partner. *Give her some rest and a trim, and I bet she'd clean up nice.*

"Coffee," he said, diverting his eyes to the pot. "Yeah—some coffee would really hit the spot right now. Bring it on." She reached beneath the counter and produced a white ceramic mug with the casual grace of a stage magician. "You want cream or sugar with that?" she asked as she poured.

"Black'll be fine," Tacker answered. He accepted the steaming mug gratefully. As he hefted it from her grasp, he noticed something odd about the shape and size of the fingers on her left hand—but caught only a quick glimpse. *Did she have five . . . or more?* He sipped the coffee. It was good. And *hot*.

The woman shrugged off her jacket and hung it on a peg near a small doorway marked EMPLOYEES ONLY. She quickly slipped a cooking mitt over her left hand.

"Cold out there," Tacker observed.

She nodded. "I was out back checking on something. Didn't hear you come in. Sorry. Been waiting long?"

"No, not at all."

"That's good. You want some food?"

Tacker looked up at a row of small posters displayed overhead—laboriously hand-lettered with felt-tip marker on sheets of pastel paper, they advertised various special dinner combos and breakfast platters. He chose one at random. "I'll have the two-eggs-with-corn-fritters, please."

She hung her head as though ashamed. "Our corn crop was bad again this year," she said, speaking almost in a whisper. She looked up purposefully at him, forcing her eyes to meet his. "I should be able to find a few good eggs, though. Would you mind waffles or pancakes instead of corn fritters?"

He smiled, sipped his coffee—its warmth was nectar of the gods to his frozen body—and hunched his shoulders. "Waffles'll do fine. Long as they're hot."

She nodded and turned her back to him, removing a carton of eggs and a container of waffle mix from a tiny refrigerator on the cooking console. She began to pour the waffle mix into a large electric waffle iron.

Tacker took another revitalizing sip of the coffee, feeling its warmth spread through his system, breathing its earthy aroma. He watched the woman working, admiring the curve of her fanny as she bent over the stove. "Local corn crop went bad, hunh?" he said, just to make conversation.

She moved her head in response—Tacker couldn't tell exactly if it was a nod.

"Don't you ever bring corn in from other places?" he asked.

She closed the waffle iron and turned a switch. A tiny red light came on. "Sometimes we do," she answered quietly, "if we have to. But the folks in these parts usually take a lot of pride in using our own. We're close to the earth here. Take only what God sees fit to let grow in our own soil. Don't usually bring much in from other parts."

"I see," said Tacker. He finished his coffee in one final, searing swallow. He smiled. "Another cup of that brown joe might let me see even clearer."

She turned, glanced down at his empty mug, and distractedly refilled it.

"Thanks," said Tacker. "It's *good* coffee." He sipped it again.

"It's Colombian," she muttered unpleasantly, turning back to the cooking console. "The coffee's one thing we *always* have to get from someplace else." She moved the egg tray under the warming lamp and began to examine the eggs. Picking one up with her mitt-covered left hand, she prodded it and turned it over, studying the egg with the professional attention of a diamond cutter.

Tacker was fascinated. *What's she doing?* he wondered. He tried to remember what she'd said when he first placed his order. *Something about being able to find a few good eggs...*

Finally she cracked the egg on the griddle. It hissed like a viper as it oozed across the searing hot metal surface, its gooey translucence slowly clouding to a chalky white.

The sweet, delicious aroma of sizzling egg—sunny-side up, of course—made Tacker's mouth water. His stomach growled with impatience. It occurred to him that he hadn't told her his name. "My name's Tacker," he offered. "Jim Tacker."

The woman glanced back at him and smiled briefly as she reached for a second egg. "Call me Marie," she answered. She cracked the egg and spread it hissing across the griddle.

As Tacker admired her smile—*No sir*, he thought, *I definitely wouldn't kick her outa bed*—he sensed that something was suddenly, terribly wrong.

It started with the smell—a thick, pungent stink that seemed to come from everywhere at once, as though the air itself had gone instantly sour. Then came a fierce crackling, as if a string of firecrackers had been tossed on the sizzling griddle. At last there was smoke—an eerie blend of dark colors which swirled menacingly from the cooking surface like a tiny tornado.

Tacker nearly dropped his coffee mug. "What the—?"

"It's okay," she said loudly, to be heard over the crackling. "I know what to do with it."

The second egg was arching up in its center as foul smoke sprayed from its edges. It looked like a little snow-hill, as though a miniature snowman were struggling to stand up on the cooking surface.

Marie quickly rolled a small metal cart over to the cooking console. In its center was a large metal bucket half filled with some dark, oily liquid. Beside it lay what looked like a set of fireplace tools—poker, tongs, and a small, long-handled shovel.

Tacker was on his feet backing slowly toward the door, his coffee cup abandoned on the counter. *Christ Almighty*, he thought, *what the screaming hell is going on here?!*

Marie had the little shovel in one hand, the tongs in the other. She scooped the shovel blade under the pulsating, amorphous white glob and clamped the tongs around it. The thing quivered, changing shape as she hoisted it off the griddle, and Marie struggled to control it. Finally she swiveled in place and dropped the writhing, smoldering thing into the bucket. It dissolved in a cloud of gray vapor as soon as it hit the solution sloshing inside.

Tacker stood frozen in place, watching the final wisps of smoke drift from the bucket. Marie also watched purposefully, the long-handled tools still clenched tightly in her fists. She did not move.

With a surprisingly cheerful metallic *ding*, the waffle iron announced its contents were fully cooked. The little sound reverberated like a rifle shot through the otherwise silent restaurant.

The bell snapped Marie from her trance. She set the tools down on the cart and peeked over the rim of the bucket.

Tacker took a step backward toward the exit. His bare hands wrapped around the frosty door handle, stinging at the touch. He pushed and the door opened slightly. Piercing, freezing cold air rushed in, attacking his bare neck.

"Everything's all right," Marie called. "The acid ate it right up. You can come back now."

Tacker let the door swing closed. He didn't want to go back—but neither did he want to face the winter weather outside without a hot meal first.

Oh yeah, he remembered, *and I didn't call Evelyn yet* . . . He eyed the pay phone with a tiny pang of guilt.

Marie opened the waffle iron and busied herself brushing butter across the waffle, sprinkling cinnamon on it, and preparing the plate for her customer with casual dedication, as though the alarming incident with the weird white glob had never taken place.

The warm, inviting aroma of the toasty waffle—and the one good egg still hissing on the griddle—drew Tacker back to his seat at the counter. He watched Marie expertly fit the egg onto a plate, then select another and examine it carefully as she prepared it. She ignored him, avoiding his gaze and saying nothing until his meal platter was fully prepared. Within minutes it was set before him, steam rising from two perfect sunnyside-up eggs, a pat of butter melting slowly into an inch-thick brown waffle. There was even a garnish of parsley and a side dish of toast cut into perfect triangles.

Tacker accepted the plate happily and began to eat, but found he couldn't keep his mind off the scene Marie had made with the peculiar egg. He devoured the waffle and the toast, washing it down with more hot coffee, but couldn't bring himself to touch the eggs.

They watched him from the plate, two bulging yellow eyes.

Marie refilled his cup and began to prepare a fresh pot. "Can't blame ya for passing on those eggs," she said as she poured water into the coffee maker. "Guess I owe ya some sort of explanation."

Tacker sipped at his coffee and pushed the plate away.

The eggs continued to watch him.

He covered them with his napkin.

Marie switched the coffee maker on. It gurgled like a drowning man. She walked a few steps away and looked out the window, her back turned to Tacker.

"So tell me," Tacker said quietly, "what's going on around here?"

Marie continued to stare out the frosted glass. "It started back in the 1950s," she answered, her voice weak and nervous, "but nobody really noticed it until about twelve, maybe fifteen years later. Took that long to put all the pieces together."

"Pieces?"

She nodded. "Stories in the news about Love Canal, Three Mile Island—places like that—were what finally convinced *everybody*. Some of us, though, got wise to it all a whole lot earlier."

Tacker swallowed hard. "You mean, uh, radiation?"

"That's part of it. The chemical waste was the main thing. Ever heard of XCCD?"

Tacker set down his cup. "Sure. Xavier Commercial Chemical Development. Big Company. Everybody's heard of it. But you know, I think some of those news stories are a little farfetched. I've been around chemicals all my life and *I've* never had a problem."

The napkin had soaked into the eggs on his platter. The two yellow eyes stared through their paper blindfold.

"Well, I guess you're one of the lucky ones, then," Marie continued. "XCCD's got one of those processing plants a short ways up the interstate from here. Lots of folks from around these parts got jobs in it when it first opened back in '55, though most just ignored it. Maryswood's been a farming community for hundreds of years. We're close to the earth here."

"So you've told me," Tacker responded, trying to avoid looking at the eggs, to ignore their unblinking stare.

"It was almost 1960 before the first babies were born *different*," said Marie. "Most of 'em died stillborn or else they came premature and didn't last long. But some lived all right, even though they were different." She stroked her left hand, still completely covered by the cooking mitten. "I came along in '63 myself."

Tacker looked down at his coffee mug. It was empty. "When did it start affecting your crops?"

"Slowly," she said. "It was even slower getting to the livestock. It always got the people first."

She turned to face him, leaning on the cool, smooth surface of the counter. "When I was growing up, there was a tanker truck that always came from the XCCD plant twice a week. It rumbled up and down the dirt roads of our neighborhood, pouring something thick and purple from a spout in its back end. Supposed to keep the dust down, they told us. Filled up the gutter on one side of the road, then the other. We kids used to ride behind the truck, splashing in the stuff, yelling like wild

Indians. Later, when we went home, it was our mothers' turn to yell—we tracked it into the house all the time. It was all over our shoes."

She paused, thinking. "I remember Pokey Johnson, the little girl next door, sitting on the curb all covered over in the stuff and laughing, laughing, laughing. We had so much *fun* with it—it looked like runny grape marmalade and stuck to things even better than the paste we used in art class in school. Sure did keep the dust down, too, just like they said it would."

Tacker smiled weakly. He fidgeted with the empty cup, turning it in circles on the counter as though it were the gear in a machine.

"Pokey died when she was twenty-two," said Marie. "They told us it was cancer." She looked at her right hand, stroking it slowly through the concealing kitchen mitten as she spoke. "She didn't have a chance ... all messed up inside. Children don't ever stand much of a chance in Maryswood. I know it for a fact. None of us born since the early '60s have been altogether right. Even my ... my son."

Tacker cleared his throat. "Ahh, you have a little boy, hunh? My wife's expecting our first in the spring. What's your boy's name?"

Marie ignored the question. "I don't know who the father was," she continued quietly. "Coupla years ago I was drinking a lot. Don't remember much from those days. I—I was *with* a lot of men. You know, strangers passing through. Maybe even you."

The coffee gurgled in Tacker's gut. He shuffled slightly on his stool and glanced back at the cash register, wanting very much to get back on the road. Marie had begun to look a bit familiar to him, but he could not quite be sure. *There've been so many ...*

"Come take a look," she said. "He's out back."

"Oh, that's okay—I need to get going again." Tacker eased himself off the barstool and stood up. He reached for his wallet. "How much do I owe you?"

She looked at him pleadingly, her eyes wide—almost desperate. The purplish semicircles under their sockets seemed to darken. Marie seemed a fantastic figure, at once pathetic and menacing. "Please," she said. "He's right out back. Come see him."

She gestured at the small door marked EMPLOYEES ONLY.

Tacker took a deep breath. *Guess she's bound and determined to make me look at this kid of hers*, he thought. *Oh, hell, I'd better do it just to pacify her.* He feigned a smile. "Okay, sure."

He glanced one last time at the two eggs under the napkin. A thin line of moisture had seeped through on one side, creating the illusion of a tear running from one of the yellow eyes.

He followed Marie through the restricted door, passing into a strange, dimly lit storage room where stacks of wooden crates and pallets of cardboard boxes rose like crooked towers. A skull and crossbones leered from a gray metal canister near the back door. The chilly room smelled of flour, sawdust, and corrosive chemicals. Marie put her fur-collared jacket back on and zipped it up tightly. She left the oven mitt on her hand.

Out behind the diner, the huge spotlight lit an eerie circle of dirty, snowy ground.

Tacker shuddered as the night chill attacked his joints and muscles through his thin cotton windbreaker. His breath puffed out in cones of frost. He crossed his arms, tucking his bare hands into the pits.

"There," said Marie.

Tacker squinted. He didn't see anything at all resembling a child—just a black, cold wall of night, with a filthy carpet of earth spread in front of it. "Where?" he asked, shivering. "I don't see him."

Marie pointed solemnly to the east. "*There.*"

He saw it now—a simple wooden stake pounded into

CLOSE TO THE EARTH 221

the snowy dirt, a tiny pyramid of accumulated snowfall crowning its flat upper surface. There was a band of fluorescent orange ribbon tied around it. The loose end of the ribbon fluttered in the icy breeze, gesturing weakly.

Tacker looked at Marie, who stared hypnotically in the direction of the stake. "Is that where he's buried?" Tacker asked.

"*There*," she answered. "There he is right now."

Tacker glanced back just in time to see something small and brown begin to quiver in the ground near the stake.

A tiny head emerged from the nearly frozen muck. Thick fur grew on one side of it, and a black, toadlike eye peered from the other. The thing whined feebly once through its single nostril, then burrowed its way back down below.

"He likes it best here," Marie said quietly, her breath thick and white as smoke in the air. "He's close to the earth."

The dark empty highway spread before him, a tunnel through the night.

Tacker's freezing fingers clutched the steering wheel painfully as he drove. *Just a few more miles*, he thought. *Just a few more and then I'll stop. Sleep. Rest...*

He had a lot to think about; and tonight, he knew, he would suffer from troubling dreams—dreams of the child he had seen, and another child he might see three months from now when Evelyn gave birth.

When the sun returned the next day, he would meet as scheduled at the main plant with the XCCD board. They would have much to discuss; and, Tacker told himself grimly, he might lose his job before the meeting ended. Probably so.

He drove on, thinking. Wondering. Fearing.

Through many lonely nights, out on the road, Tacker had awakened in unfamiliar motel rooms with his arms around equally unfamiliar women and wondered to himself that the world could be such a cold, dark place. But tonight it had never seemed colder.

Or darker.

Snowbanks

by Tim Sullivan

Tim Sullivan has written eight novels and edited a previous anthology, Tropical Chills, *to which the present volume might be considered a companion of sorts. (It has been suggested that after* Cold Shocks, *only* Tepid Terrors *or* Wet Willies *will do as future titles for anthologies.) Sullivan has published many short stories, and has won the Daedalus Award for short fiction. He has been a finalist for the Nebula Award, and his work has been published in Donald Wolheim's 1983 Annual World's Best SF. Sullivan has been a fairly regular contributor to the horror field recently, with a series of short stories and novelettes. Born in Bangor, Maine, today he lives in Los Angeles, where he recently sold a screenplay,* Without a Thought, *in preproduction as of this writing.*

Jerry Witham knew that the other kids would never find him in the snowbank. He had scooped out a cubbyhole with his mittened hands and crawled inside, covering the entrance with a big, white chunk of packed snow. It pleased him that more snow was falling outside all the time. He was alone inside his snug blue-white tunnel, and that suited him.

Hiding was something Jerry liked a lot. Hearing people talk when they didn't think anybody could hear, seeing them do things they wouldn't do if they knew anybody was around, watching from up in the oak tree while the Vitellis went about their business in their backyard next door to his house. It was fun, but it was a game that had to be played alone. He liked being alone; it was okay sometimes to have other people around, like his buddy Hughie Burke, but most of the time he was happy all by himself. He'd started to feel that way right after the funeral last summer.

Jerry adjusted his mittens, and dug deeper into the snowbank. The blizzard had lasted for three whole days now, and school had been called off for the past two. Some people said it was the worst snowstorm ever to hit Connecticut. It sure was the worst one Jerry had ever seen. He thought it was cool the way you hardly had to bother with anybody when the weather was like this. And even if you did see people they didn't look human— ponderous creatures all bundled up and leaning into the wind.

This storm had followed another severe blizzard by two days, and there had been another one less than a week before that. Jerry loved it; not just because he didn't have to go to school, but also because the cold, enveloping whiteness was so different from the way things were the rest of the time . . . until the rock salt was thrown down and the tire chains spewed up brown muck to change the world back to the same old dull, busy place and ruin everything.

As he dug, Jerry began to see that he didn't have anyplace to toss the snow now that he had closed himself in. He would have to make an opening to get rid of it, if he wanted to go any deeper into the snowbank. The muffled sound of an automobile whooshing by gave him an idea. If he threw the snow out on the roadside, his friends weren't likely to see it. They might not figure out where he was at all if he just poked a hole here and there, dropped a little snow out every few feet, and covered up the hole as he tunneled further in. It was worth a try.

Jerry punched the far side of his tunnel, but he didn't

see any light coming through. He punched again, this time burying his arm up to the elbow. Leaning forward, he peered into the tiny tunnel within a tunnel, but it was really dark in there.

"Okay," Jerry said. "I really mean it this time." He drew back and thrust his arm all the way in, up to his shoulder. His bunched fist didn't come out into the air. If anything, it seemed that, where his fist made an impact, the snow was even more densely packed.

Jerry slowly withdrew his arm and looked thoughtfully at the snow flecks on his mitten. Maybe he was going in the wrong direction. The sound of the car might not have been coming from where he'd thought. He could easily have got turned around here in the dark.

Not that it was completely dark, but the shadows seemed a little deeper than a few minutes ago. Jerry guessed that it was because he had gone farther into the snowbank. Or maybe it was just getting dark outside. After all, how far could he have gone in such a short time?

He laughed a little, remembering an old, black-and-white movie he'd seen on TV, *The Mole People*, where John Agar and the guy who played Beaver Cleaver's dad fell into Himalayan caves and found a subterranean world with monsters and albinos who performed human sacrifices. It was pretty hokey, but Jerry loved it, just the same.

Still, he didn't want to be lost. That would spoil the game. He only wanted to hide, to be by himself. It was going to be dinner time soon, anyhow. He would just back out of the tunnel, and end up where he'd started. Nothing to it.

Right now, though, he wanted to go a little farther. Just dig in a little deeper, away from the world of boring chores, school, and big kids who pushed you around whenever they felt like it.

Even better, he wouldn't have to hear his Mom say

things like, "What did I ever do to deserve this?" when he'd done something wrong. He wouldn't have to put up with grouchiness when Dad came home from a tough day at work, either. And best of all, he wouldn't have to look at their faces, their blank eyes that didn't even notice him most of the time. Not down here inside the snowbank, he wouldn't.

Still, there was this problem of where to put the snow as he continued to excavate. Maybe he'd better go back home and think about it for awhile. He was starting to shiver, anyway, the chilly, wet snow seeping through his pants at the knees.

Just for a moment, Jerry sat still. He leaned back against the tunnel wall and listened to himself breathing. It was the only sound he could hear. The only thing in the world.

But he was shivering more and more. Time to go out and get warm.

Jerry backed down the tunnel until he found the irregular patch where he'd filled in the hole when he first crawled inside the snowbank. Giving it a little push with his rubber boot, he winced as the cold light blazed into his tunnel.

In a moment he was standing outside amid the drifting snowflakes. Brightness hurt his eyes for a long time, but gradually his vision returned to normal. He didn't see any of the other kids, not even Hughie, so he covered the tunnel entrance carefully and smoothed it over, trusting the snowfall to take care of the rest.

He'd work on the tunnel some more tomorrow, after Dad went to work. Noting a telephone pole a yard beyond the tunnel as a marker, he walked stiffly back to his house, stamping his feet on the rubber mat outside and brushing the snow off of himself as he went inside.

He smelled something good as soon as he walked in. He hung his wet coat on the newel post, laid his mittens on the radiator to dry them out, and sat on the bottom

SNOWBANKS

step of the staircase to pull off his green pack boots.

"That you, Jer?" Mom called from the kitchen.

"Yup." Jerry rubbed his toes through his thick wool socks. Tomorrow he would have to wear two pair, he decided—and an extra pair of long johns, too. That way he could stay inside the snowbank a lot longer.

"Come and have some of this stew," Mom shouted. "It'll warm you up in a hurry."

Jerry got up and padded toward the kitchen. Mom met him halfway, at the closet off the living room. She was getting out her coat.

"I've got to get to work," she said, "but your father'll be home in an hour or so. Keep the stew on a low heat for him, okay, hon?"

"Yeah, sure." He was glad she was going out.

"You don't even have to touch the stove. Just leave it the way it is. I've already fixed your plate. 'Bye."

She was gone a second later, leaving Jerry to watch the snowflakes melt on the rug in the foyer. He sighed and went into the kitchen, realizing for the first time just how hungry he was.

He'd only eaten a few spoonfuls of stew when the phone rang.

"Hey, man." It was Hughie Burke. "Where'd you disappear to?"

"No place, Burkie."

"No place? I looked all over the neighborhood for you."

"Well, I guess you found me, huh, dude?"

"Yeah, I guess so. What are you doing?"

"Eating supper."

Hughie said nothing.

After a long pause on the other end, Jerry sighed and gave in. "You want some beef stew, come on over."

"Sounds cool. My mom left me some crap I can't even stand the smell of."

As soon as Hughie hung up, Jerry went back to the

table. He chewed the chunks of beef and potatoes carefully as he mulled over the difficulties of extending his hidden tunnel. The problem of his knees getting wet could be solved by laying a flattened-out cardboard box on the tunnel floor. He could simply move it ahead a foot or two at a time as he made progress.

He was considering where to toss the snow when the doorbell sounded. Jerry got up and walked through the house to let Hughie in.

"Still snowing?" Jerry asked, even though he could see that it was.

"Harder than ever," Hughie said, following Jerry into the house without removing his boots. Bits of snow fell onto the hardwood floor and on the rugs as they passed through the living room and went on into the kitchen. Sometimes Jerry wondered why he liked Hughie, especially when the kid did things like this. Jerry could tell him to take off the boots, but Hughie would just give him a lot of bullshit, and he didn't feel like arguing right now.

"So, where were you, man?" Hughie demanded, helping himself to some stew.

"Around." Jerry noticed how much stew his friend was taking. "Hey, save some of that for my dad, okay?"

"Sure." Hughie didn't put any back in the pot, but he didn't take any more, either. He set his bowl down and pulled back a chair.

"Cool, man," he said as he sat down and scraped his chair closer to the table. "We don't even have to say grace."

"We never say grace at my house," Jerry said.

Hughie gaped, his spoon arrested halfway to his mouth. "No shit! Next you'll tell me you don't go to church."

"Not very often."

"Wow! You're folks must be like atheists or something." Hughie shoved the spoon into his mouth as he

SNOWBANKS

pondered Jerry's godlessness. Chewing, he asked, "You ever been baptized?"

"Nope."

"Aren't you worried that you might go to hell?" Hughie asked.

"Not really."

"Don't you believe in God?"

Jerry shrugged. "Guess not. I don't know."

Hughie dropped his spoon into the stew with a soft splat, as he considered the risky wonder of his buddy's unadulterated spiritual freedom.

"There's bread and butter if you want some," Jerry said, pointing to an opened loaf of bread and a half stick of margarine resting on a saucer. "Maybe it'll get you to heaven."

"You're weird, Witham," Hughie said, sticking his dirty hands into the brown, plastic sleeve to grasp a slice of bread. He slathered margarine on it and devoured it greedily. His words were slurred as he chewed meat and bread. "You're *really* weird."

"Takes one to know one," Jerry replied automatically, not really interested in fighting with his friend anymore . . . and he suddenly realized that this had been true only since Billy's funeral.

The phone rang. Jerry set his spoon down and got up to answer it.

"Hi, Jer." It was his Dad.

"Hi, Dad."

"What are you doing?" his Dad said.

"Just eating. Hughie's over here."

"Your mom gone to work?"

"Yeah. She told me to save you some stew."

"Don't bother, kid. I'm gonna be working late, so I'll get something next door. The snow's really backed things up down here. I might not be home till ten, eleven o'clock."

"Oh, yeah?" Jerry suspected that his Dad could have

come home now if he'd really wanted to, but this was okay.

"You lock up good after Burkie leaves, okay? I'll see you in the morning."

"Okay, Dad."

"Bye, son."

"Bye, Dad."

Jerry hung up.

"What's going on?" Hughie asked.

"Well, my dad..." Jerry was about to tell him that his Dad wouldn't be in for hours, but he hesitated. With both his parents gone for the evening, he could go back to his tunnel. But first he would have to get rid of Hughie.

"My dad said he'd be home in a little while. I gotta do my chores before he gets here."

"Shit."

"Course, if you help me..."

"Uh, there's some things I gotta do myself," Hughie said.

"Oh, yeah?" Jerry asked. "Like what?"

"You know—clean my room, stuff like that."

"Yeah, right." Burkie hadn't cleaned his room since last spring. The one-two punch—the threat of unrewarded labor coupled with Jerry's skepticism—hurried him along. He was out the door in ten minutes. Looking out the window, Jerry watched him trudge through the pelting snow until he was out of sight. He thought about the time a few weeks ago when Mom had said that Hughie was like a brother to him, and then she suddenly had started crying.

"See you later, Burkie," Jerry whispered. He looked up and down the street, seeing the halogen streetlamps flicker on over the peaked gables of his neighbors' houses. There was no one in sight.

He went down to the cellar and found a good-sized box in the pile next to the furnace. Tearing it up, he salvaged five big, cardboard rectangles from the remains and tossed the useless flaps from the box top into the trash. He would line the floor of his tunnel with these.

He carried the dog-eared, cardboard strips upstairs and set them down on the rug while he rummaged through the closet. He found an old pair of gloves that he could wear under his mittens, and put on an extra pair of socks as well as extra long johns. He wore a hooded sweatshirt over his flannel shirt and sweater, and his hooded parka over that. He'd be plenty warm enough with all these clothes on.

Before he put his boots and mittens on, he went into the study, pulled up the tambour on the captain's desk, and grabbed the flashlight Dad kept there. There was a little drawer inside the desk where the front door key was kept, but Jerry couldn't get it open with his gloves on. He tugged at the fingers of the right glove until it slipped off his hand, pulled off the left glove, and got out the key. Tucking it into an inside pocket of his coat, he put his gloves back on and went to the foyer to pull on his boots. He picked up his mittens and went to the front door.

Tying the string of his parka hood tight around his scarf-covered chin, Jerry opened the front door and the storm door. He stood at the threshold for a moment, an explorer into the icy wastes of the night. Then he went outside into the driving snow, shutting the front door, with the storm door propped against his hip.

He turned and fished the key out of his pocket. He could work it with his gloves on, and in a moment the door was locked. He stepped out from the partial shelter of the storm door and felt the snowflakes cling to his eyelids. Not much of his face was showing—his scarf covered his nose and the parka covered most of his forehead. A tiny triangle of pink skin peeked out from his layers of heavy clothing.

The snow, several inches deep now, even though he had shoveled it away before starting his tunnel three hours ago, crunched satisfyingly under his bootheels. He pulled on his mittens as he walked, slipping a little here and there but keeping his footing pretty well most of the time.

He saw the telephone pole up ahead. A yard before he reached it, he bent down and began to burrow into the snowbank with both hands. As soon as the tunnel mouth was large enough, he stood up and looked around. A dog was crossing the street fifty or sixty yards down Larkin Street Hill. Other than that, there was no movement at all.

It was almost the exact spot where his brother Billy had been run over by a blue car on a bright morning seven months ago. Jerry's eyes were stung by snow and memory as he watched the dog make his way through the swirling snow.

Headlight beams lanced through the falling snow, silhouetting the dog, who hurried out of the way of the oncoming car. It might be one of the neighbors. Feeling an adventurous thrill, Jerry tossed the cardboard inside the tunnel and crawled in after it before the driver could see him.

He laid the cardboard flat for as far as the tunnel extended, and hurriedly covered the entrance. He was finished in a moment, except for a tiny hole just big enough for him to look out with one eye.

He was delighted to see that the snowfall was coming down harder than ever, feathery yellow flakes in the streetlamp's glow. Plugging up the last of the hole with a fistful of snow, he snapped on the flashlight and surveyed his frozen, underground world.

He had two or three hours to dig. The way he saw it, he could go all the way to the end of the Vitellis' property, at least as far as their driveway. The Vitellis had left for Florida earlier this week, so the snowbank ran all the way in front of their yard, completely untouched. It must have been twenty-five or thirty feet long. Jerry figured

SNOWBANKS

he'd better get started if he wanted to come out the other side tonight.

He smiled, thinking about how cool it would be to emerge in the driveway of his neighbors' deserted house. Once he'd covered the exit with snow and gone home, he could go to bed and dream about the huge tunnel he would have to hide in tomorrow. He could stay in there all day if he wanted to, and nobody would bother him the whole time.

Setting the flashlight down on the cardboard behind him, he adjusted it until its pale ray lit the virginal wall of snow ahead of him. Then he started to dig, carefully piling up snow until he was ready to dispose of it. But after awhile he forgot about that, and forged ahead as fast as he could. He was so intent upon what he was doing that he forgot about the cardboard. His knees were buried in snow when he finally remembered. He began to crawl backwards, since the passage was too narrow to turn around in, and discovered that he was moving upward. That meant that he'd been digging downhill for awhile. He didn't remember any dip in the street in front of the Vitellis' place. Funny he hadn't uncovered the strip of dead grass between the sidewalk and the curb.

He slid the corrugated cardboard pieces down the passageway and crawled in on top of them. Snow crystals gleamed on the thick, brown paper as he readjusted the flashlight's beam. Brushing off his pants, he delved deeper into the frangible snow in front of him.

"John Henry was a snow-drivin' man," he sang softly, his steam-engine breath puffing in the dim light. He had to be quiet, though, in case anybody passed by in the darkness outside. If an adult heard him, he'd be found out and there might be trouble when his dad got home.

So he stopped singing, and continued mining snow. There was no sound in the world like the sound of snow being scooped out. As his mittens pushed into it, it condensed into a tightly packed hunk and made a unique rubbing noise. Soft as it was, the sound filled the narrow space; it was the only sound there was in here except for his breathing. Nobody outside could hear it, Jerry was sure of that. The walls of his tunnel would muffle his digging and keep his secret from the world. It made him feel warm inside to think about how this place was all his. He didn't want to let anybody find out about it just because he was making too much noise.

The flashlight beam flickered once or twice, but Jerry didn't pay much attention to it. The batteries would probably last another hour or so, he figured. Even if they didn't, he could feel his way in the dark. If worse came to worst, he could just dig his way out through the side of the snowbank.

But he wouldn't have to do that. No, he'd be all right.

It was strange, but he still seemed to be going downhill. The grade wasn't steep, but he could feel himself pitching forward, all the same. Of course, that made digging easier. He was really tunneling in deep now, the discarded snow lying in little, haphazard heaps on the cardboard behind him. Working harder than ever, he was simply tossing the snow over his shoulder now, instead of piling it up in an orderly way.

The flashlight ray blinked again. Its light seemed yellower, dimmer than before. Maybe the batteries wouldn't last as long as he'd hoped.

Jerry dug faster. His red mittens were a blur as he thrashed away at the snow. He couldn't work all that much longer, he realized. He didn't have a watch, and he couldn't risk staying out until his dad got home. If that happened, he'd spend tomorrow in his room, and probably the day after that, too. He might even have to stay in until he went back to school. He'd be by himself in his room, but he wouldn't be free to dig his tunnel.

He kept burrowing in deeper and deeper, curious as to how far downward this incline would go. Maybe he was already at the Vitellis' driveway? That might account for the dip. But how could the snow have piled so high in their driveway?

The only answer was that the plow had come along and kicked up a sizeable ridge. He must be inside the guts of that newly created, sinuous hump now. It was as though he had been swallowed by a giant, white python ... Who knew how far the ridge extended? Maybe he could keep going for blocks, miles even. He kept digging as the light faltered for another fraction of a second.

But this was impossible, wasn't it? He had to come to a shoveled-out driveway once he passed the Vitelli property. The Sargents' house, next door to the Vitellis', would be as far as he could go tonight.

But if it kept on snowing, he'd—

The light went out. At first he thought the batteries had expired, but the snow falling on the backs of his calves made him realize that there was a cave-in. His heart swelled up and beat wildly as he swung around in the pitch blackness, trying to find the flashlight. He only succeeded in knocking loose more snow, which hissed down on top of him, engulfing him. He felt the cascading snow creep into the opening between his gloves and his sleeves, biting the skin of his wrists with its frigidity.

Lying flat, he let the weight of the snow press down on him from above. He didn't move a muscle, fearing that the tunnel would collapse completely. There was no glow from the streetlamps, so the snowbank must still be standing. He was afraid that it would all come down if he stirred even a tiny bit; still, he couldn't just lie here like this forever.

The first thing he had to do was find the flashlight. His dad would kill him if he lost it. And if it got wet, it would probably be ruined.

Slowly, he pushed himself up. There was a glow coming from somewhere, he thought as the snow avalanched off his back. He glanced around. The light was coming from his groin! Laughing, he reached down and groped in the snow under him until he felt something hard. He jerked the flashlight out of its premature grave and brushed it off.

"Good as new," he said. His voice sounded oddly muffled, as if it had been swallowed up by the snow.

The cold was penetrating all the layers of his clothing, and it must have been getting pretty late. His shoulders ached from all the digging, and his knees were sore, too. Maybe it was time to go home.

He was pretty sure that he was facing the way he'd come in. At least he thought so . . . but he could have turned around more than once in his panic. Well, if he dug through a couple of yards, he ought to find the tunnel again. If he didn't find it, that meant he was going the wrong way, and he'd just turn around and go back.

Unless, of course, the entire tunnel had filled up with snow while he was flailing around in the dark. He might have messed up everything.

He might have trapped himself.

"No." That was ridiculous. He could punch his way out the side of the snowbank in a minute or two. It couldn't have snowed so much that he was stuck in here, could it? Nothing, not even the plow, could have buried him alive. He wasn't going to suffocate in here . . . was he?

He was breathing hard, even though he hadn't moved for a while. The air must be running out. Which way should he go? He had to get out of here.

"Cool it," he said in a voice that trembled more than he wanted it to. It was time to get hold of himself, like his dad always said. When the going gets tough, the tough get going. Which way, though? Which way should he get going toward?

Straight ahead. He took the flashlight up and started to chip away with it at the packed snow in front of him.

The snow gave way pretty easily, and he kept at it for awhile.

But he didn't find the tunnel behind the falling curtains of snow. Fifteen or twenty minutes must have gone by, and he kept finding more packed snow instead of the dark passageway he had cut into the snowbank earlier tonight.

So he must have been facing the wrong direction again. The thing to do was turn around and dig through the other way. But he was really having trouble breathing now, and the flashlight was faltering badly. The batteries weren't going to last much longer.

"I don't need it," he gasped, his voice seeming to come from far away. But he *did* need oxygen. It was time to bust out of here, once and for all.

He lay on his side and started to carve away the snow to his right. He *had* to come out either on the sidewalk or in the street. Either way, he'd be *outta here*. He could figure out where the hell he was once he was standing up outside.

Soon he had to bend at the waist to get into the new hole he'd gashed in the snow. A few minutes after that, his whole body was in there and he was still going at it.

"Can't be much farther," he grunted, winded from the effort. "Maybe a couple more feet."

Several minutes passed. Jerry didn't find anything but more snow. He wriggled deeper into the narrow antechamber he'd fashioned and flailed away with the flashlight.

Panting, he finally stopped, realizing that he had made a mistake. He must have been turned sideways after the light went out, and then he must have dug parallel to the main tunnel, more or less.

The thing to do was back out and see. He did so, loosening the snow around him. It took longer to get out than he expected, but finally he was at the point where he'd branched out. He felt around gingerly, trying not to start another cave-in.

Well, dark as it was, it seemed as if the branch was pretty much at a right angle to the main tunnel. The only thing he could figure was that he had veered off to one side or the other while he was in there.

He had to admit to himself that he was scared. It was getting harder and harder to breath, he was tired, and he was really getting cold, although his skin was itchy and clammy underneath all his winter clothes.

There was still one way he hadn't tried. He kicked at the opposing wall, starting a new tunnel there. The sidewalk had to be just a few feet away. He wasn't going to stop until he saw the light of a streetlamp. He would run all the way home and get out of these damp, freezing clothes, and take a hot, steaming shower. He just hoped that Dad wasn't home yet.

The opening grew larger as he lay on his back and kicked with first his left foot, and then his right, faster and faster. He pushed himself forward and kicked savagely at the snow until all the strength in his thighs was gone. His breathing was so labored now that he knew he was going to pass out soon.

He drew his knee back almost to his chin and kicked one last, futile time.

The snow poured down and revealed a ragged, glowing hole. Jerry could feel cold air swelling his lungs.

"All right!" he gasped.

Using his elbows, Jerry propelled himself forward on his back. Snow cascaded around him as he exultantly glided through the hole. Breathing heavily, he slid out and downward, somehow landing on his feet.

"Hey!" This wasn't Larkin Street.

In fact, this wasn't anyplace Jerry had ever seen before.

He was in a big cave, all lit up from inside its icy walls. Could this be the sewer? Had he come to an open manhole? No, he would have fallen straight down if that had happened. Besides, the manhole was on the other side of the street, over by the Teitelbaums' house.

"And whoever heard of a sewer with lights?" he said aloud. His voice echoed pleasantly through the glittering cavern.

At least he wasn't having trouble breathing anymore. Not only that, but it seemed a lot warmer here than in his tunnel. Even so, it was all ice and snow everywhere he looked.

Maybe he'd discovered something new. He walked around, examining the ice helictites and wondering how such a place could have existed underneath Larkin Street. He turned around to see where he had come through into the cave from the snowbank. The hole was clearly visible from where he was standing. It was pretty high up, but he could probably reach it, even if he had to pile up a lot of ice to get to it.

Reassured, he moved deeper into the cave, noticing that stalactites and stalagmites were meeting now in hourglass shapes. Beyond these were mysterious, gleaming columns that looked almost like statues. Jerry didn't want to move too far away from the hole, but he was so curious that he kept going in deeper. The columns were closer together the further in he went, and they looked more and more like people all the time.

At first they just had vaguely human forms, but now the outlines of shoulders and bellies, knees and thighs, and even eyes and noses were clearly visible.

"This is strange," Jerry whispered. It reminded him of going to the museum, looking at the mummy sarcophagi. He didn't know why, but he felt that these were only casings for something else. But what?

Jerry thought about going back, but he loved the solitude of this place. Besides, the army of ice statues was irresistible. Who had sculpted them? How could they have done it without anybody knowing? What if the person—or people—who made the statues caught him here? What would happen then?

"Relax," he said. There was nobody in the cavern but him, Jerry Witham. These statues could have been here for awhile, since November or December, without melting. Funny, though, because it seemed pretty warm in here, warm enough for him to loosen his hood and take off his mittens.

As he continued to move through the forest of crystalline figures, he began to realize that there were hundreds of them, maybe even thousands. And the deeper in he went, the more detailed, the more *complete* the figures were. They weren't just representations of men and women, either. There were more and more people of all ages as he got further in. Even kids.

"This is impossible," Jerry said. Nobody could have sculpted all these ice statues in a couple of months. Not even in a couple of years.

Did this mean he was dreaming? Had he fallen asleep in the snowbank? They said that was what happened when you froze to death. Could he be dead?

Jerry turned around to look at the hole he had fallen through. He couldn't see it from where he was standing.

"Maybe I better go back." He took a tentative step, and then stopped in confusion. He had threaded such a convoluted path through the statues that he wasn't sure how to get back the way he'd come.

"This is getting to be a habit," Jerry said, turning around. He could feel and hear the snow crunching under his bootheels, and his breath was a white vapor in front of his face. Well, he'd never heard of a dead person who could do that. But a lost person could, and a person who was lost long enough might soon end up dead.

"Gotta keep my head and get outta here." Jerry looked up at the cavern roof. It vaulted way, way up there, over his head. How could he have come down so far underground? Had he been walking on an incline again, without realizing it? He didn't see how he could have done it without noticing, but here he was. Somewhere, far above him, was Larkin Street and his house. Was his dad home yet? Jerry almost didn't care if he caught hell, if he could just get out of here and get back home.

But each time he thought he was nearing the hole, he was disappointed. He couldn't seem to find the walls of the cavern at all now. It was as if the place went on forever and ever.

He looked up again and studied the curve of the ceiling. If he went toward where the curve descended, he should come to some sort of wall. And if he followed that around long enough, he had to reach the hole sooner or later.

It seemed logical enough. But as he worked his way through the statues, he got lost again. When he looked up at the ceiling, the curve seemed all wrong. Maybe he wasn't going the right way after all. Maybe there *wasn't* any right way, he thought as panic constricted his chest. Maybe he was trapped in this cavern for the rest of his life.

"Which won't be long."

Would he freeze and become one of these statues? No, they couldn't really be frozen people. They were just ice sculptures. And the stalactites and stalagmites were simply statues that had melted a little. Yes, that was it. These statues had been down here for years, never completely melting. It was like his mom said when she put things in the freezer. The more you crowded in there, the quicker things froze. In old fashioned ice houses the ice had lasted all summer long, even before they had electricity. The statues on the perimeter would melt more quickly than those all massed together on the inside . . . it only stood to reason.

But that didn't explain how the statues got here, or who had sculpted them. Jerry wandered through the clusters of sparkling human figures, searching for a clue to their mysterious origins.

He went deeper inside the ice gallery, and saw that the sculptures became more and more lifelike. They were old people and kids, twenty-year-olds and fifty-year-olds. Fat people, skinny people, tall people, short people. He stopped and considered a man in a wheelchair, the ice lending a realistic sheen to the chair's chrome finish. Jerry could see in the man's grim expression that he wasn't happy. Maybe he didn't want to live any longer.

"It's only a hunk of ice!" Jerry shouted, annoyed with himself to think anything different. How could a statue be happy or unhappy? Was he going crazy?

"Yeah, you must be," he said. "Going crazy."

That was really the only thing that made sense. He had lost his mind. Maybe he was in shock or something. This was all wrong. It was like a dream.

But it wasn't a dream. No, this was really happening. He knew it, down in his guts. He really had dug into a snowbank just a few yards from his front door and somehow ended up here, deep inside the earth in a gallery of ice sculptures.

He kept walking, careful not to touch any of the statues. Now he noticed a definite pattern emerging. Most of the more detailed figures were of older people; not all of them, maybe, but a sizeable majority. What did it mean?

For some reason, Jerry thought he knew. It gave him the creeps, but he was certain that these were statues of people who were going to die soon.

Maybe they were already dead. He had to go a little farther and find out. As he walked on, the light from the cavern walls became dimmer, making it more difficult to perceive the statues clearly. That was probably why they didn't look transparent anymore.

But he soon saw that something entirely unexpected was happening. Color was creeping into the features of the still figures. They weren't just blue and green any-

SNOWBANKS

more—flesh tones were showing here and there on the faces and hands.

Jerry had to go on. He couldn't have stopped now if the world ended.

Maybe it already had. Maybe he was *really* alone now, the way he'd wanted to be for more than half a year. He moved faster and faster into the frozen jungle of human forms, toward the center. The statues became more detailed, more finished, all the time. The color became evermore vivid, and Jerry began to fear what he would find when he reached the frigid heart of this place.

But something froze him as still as the figures around him. It was a small statue, nearly two heads shorter than most of those around it . . . not even half grown yet.

It was Billy. His brother Billy—who had been fatally struck down by a car last summer—was standing there, dressed in a Ninja Turtle T-shirt and jeans, his straw hair glistening in the cold.

But Jerry could only see Billy clearly for a few seconds. His vision was blurred by tears. He turned around to escape the sight of his brother—his little brother whom he had not saved from the blue car, whom he had let play out in the street even though Mom had told him to watch out for him, and who had not been quite eight years old when he died. It wasn't fair. Jerry was just a kid himself. Why did he have to be the one responsible for Billy's death?

Jerry wanted to run, but he almost bumped into another statue. And this one shocked him even more than Billy's.

Hughie Burke was standing there, looking up as if he heard something coming from above. Except it wasn't really Hughie. It was a big piece of colored ice that looked just like him. Right down to the blue eyes and freckles.

"No," Jerry sniffed. His best friend had a double made of ice underground. Did this mean that Hughie was going to die? Or had he already died? A jet of bile rushed up from Jerry's throat, tasting of partly digested beef stew.

Jerry had a vision of his buddy sneaking out of the house and searching for him in the snow, getting lost and freezing to death. Or maybe Hughie would just slip and fall on the ice and split his head open. It was impossible to tell from his statue. In fact, now that he looked more closely, Hughie's statue didn't seem finished, not like Billy's.

For a long time, Jerry stood and stared at it. As he watched, Hughie became more and more real. It was a slow process, almost imperceptible, like the minute hand moving on a grandfather clock, but it was happening. Definitely.

The reddish brown hair on Hughie's head began to separate into individual strands. The lines around his frowning mouth slowly deepened, and a tiny speck grew into the mole on his right cheek.

"He's still alive," Jerry said, wiping away the tears. "My friend is still alive."

But not for long, if Jerry's assessment of the situation was correct. When this statue was complete, Hughie would be dead. Maybe it would really *be* Hughie then. Maybe it was his soul or something. But whatever it was, it was soon going to be just like Billy's statue—and Billy was dead.

How could Jerry prevent his friend's death? He wasn't God. He didn't even *believe* in that religious stuff. It was Hughie who believed in God, not him. Look what it had gotten Hughie.

But that wasn't fair. All he had to do was look around at the endless ice sculptures to know that. He had thought there were thousands, but now he saw that there were many more than that. Millions. Billions, even. It was endless, this cavern, and its ice statues were infinite in number.

"Not like you thought, Hughie," he said softly. "Is it?"

Hughie, of course, didn't answer. He had not only been taught that there was a God, but an afterlife, another world, as well. Well, here it was, and it was pretty peculiar. But how could anybody know what it was like until they'd been here?

"Jeez." This might have meant that Jerry himself really was *dead*, as he had feared all along. If so, being dead wasn't all it was cracked up to be. For one thing, he was a lot more active here than he would have guessed. For another... well, it wasn't that bad. There was no pain, nobody to bother him here, even though all these ... souls, or whatever they were, surrounded him.

The only real problem was what to do about Hughie. Maybe if he did *something*, he could save his buddy from dying. Hughie would have said that it wasn't part of God's plan, but what did God have to do with this particular afterlife?

It occurred to Jerry that this might be *his*, Jerry Witham's afterlife. Maybe everybody had one that was a little different from everybody else's.

"Then I can make my own rules..." But that was only true if he was right. And there was no guarantee that he was. It would make him kind of like a god, and that didn't seem right. On the other hand, he wasn't alive, and he wasn't dead, as far as he could figure. So where did that leave him?

He could see the blue veins forming on the backs of Hughie's hands, cuticles defining the curve of his nails where they grew out from under the skin on his fingertips. Soon Hughie would be complete, and then he would be dead.

"I gotta do something," Jerry said, his voice rising in panic. Perhaps he could melt the ice. But how? There was nothing in this cavern to make a fire with; nothing but snow and ice. Still, there was one way he could melt it.

He stepped forward and put his arms around the freezing sculpture.

His cheek stuck fast to the statue's, and he tried to dislodge it. He felt the skin on the side of his face stretching painfully, so he gave up. His body heat would melt the ice, and then he could move away.

"I don't know how long it's gonna take," he said, his words gusting out in a vapor cloud. "But you're my friend, and I can't let you die. I didn't know what it was like when people died, until Billy got hit by the car. You start to think about all these things you could have done while he was alive, things that nobody wants to hear about. A lot of kids wouldn't hang around with me because of that, but you're still my friend, Hughie, and I won't let you die."

Jerry wondered if it would work, and, if it did, if Hughie and his parents would think God had pulled the kid through. And what would Jerry's own mom and dad think? Would they miss him? Not a whole lot, he suspected. Once he was gone, they could do all kinds of things they couldn't do now. They would be together . . . and he would be alone. Completely alone. He began to shiver for the first time since he had slid down into the cavern, as much from the certainty that he would soon be forgotten as from the cold. Still, the prospect of solitude would have been inviting, if it wasn't for the problem of what to do about Hughie.

"Even if I'm dead, I don't want *you* to be dead, Hughie. It wouldn't be right, both of us dying on the same night."

He wondered if his dad had come home and found out that he wasn't there. Maybe Dad thought he'd gone to bed, and nobody would know he was missing until morning, when Mom came in from her night job. Maybe that had happened by now. It could be tomorrow already, the overcast sky brightened by the sun behind the clouds and the drifting snow. How could he tell? Maybe the storm had ended. Maybe days had passed; weeks, even. He would never know. For all he could tell, nobody even remembered his existence.

Once he had overheard his mom saying that she wished she'd never had any children. She and Dad had hardly known he was alive after Billy died, anyway. It was as if they blamed him. Well, maybe it was his fault. Maybe he could have jumped out into the street and pushed Billy out of the way and yelled at him, and even smacked him for being stupid enough to play in traffic. Instead, he had just stood there watching Billy fly through the air and land like a flapjack on the Sargents' asphalt driveway.

But now Billy was here, standing right behind him, looking exactly as he did just before the car hit him.

He felt the ice melting a little on Hughie's face. His own cheek had made an indentation, and cold drops were trickling down onto the zippered front of his parka.

"It's working," he said, exhaling a warm cloud. "You won't die, Hughie, see? I won't let you."

He clutched at the statue's hands. But he was still wearing his gloves, and not enough heat escaped from them. He stripped them off and stuffed them into his pockets, and then grabbed Hughie's hands of ice.

They were *so* cold. It hurt to hold on to them, but he had to melt as much of the statue as he could. Otherwise he would lose his friend forever.

Or would he? Maybe Hughie would join him down here after death. Maybe they could haunt the ice cavern together. They might never get old. They would never have to worry about growing up, and finding jobs, and getting married, and having kids. They could just stay down here and play in the snow forever.

"Nah." Jerry had to face up to it. Hughie wasn't coming down here. He'd live his life and die, and probably go to some heaven with God and angels and all that bullshit. He'd get to share his afterlife with billions of other people, but it really wouldn't be *his* afterlife at all.

"At least this place is mine," Jerry said.

So if he was the creator of this place, he could have it his own way, couldn't he? But he could feel Hughie's chill coursing through him glacially, stealing the warmth of his blood. Was it killing him? Or was he killing himself? How could he be killed, if he was already dead?

"I guess I can't be." He pressed himself deeper into the statue, and it dripped more and more onto his clothing and boots, forming icicles that clung to him like Christmas tree ornaments. He stopped shivering, feeling his blood flowing as slowly as sap through his arteries.

The ice gradually melted over him, blanketing him in its comforting coldness as it froze once again, numbing his senses even as his mind raced with a trillion thoughts. He comforted himself by thinking that he wouldn't have to go back to school anymore.

"No more classes, no more books," he sang lightly, "no more teachers' dirty looks."

And he wouldn't have to worry about his parents not caring about him. They didn't love him anymore, and he knew it. They didn't have any love in them, not since Billy had been killed. But *he* was with Billy now, not them. They would be here someday, too, though. He knew it. He just had to wait. All he would have to think about from now on was ... what? What did a piece of ice think about?

And then it hit him. He wouldn't be a piece of ice, and this wasn't the end. Once he was frozen in place, things would just be getting started. From here, he would watch the world above him, and nobody would ever see him. He wouldn't be physically active maybe, but some new part of him would, would ... kick in. Some part he'd never thought of before. Some part nobody on Earth

SNOWBANKS

really knew anything about, even the ministers, priests, and rabbis.

"Especially them," he said.

Those were the last words he spoke. Soon, Hughie's statue was gone, and Jerry was covered with ice, his blood no longer moving at all, for his circulation had become as still as the crystallized marrow of his bones. Every cell in his body had gone rigid. Oddly, he felt a warmth growing within him, from the inside out. His eyes, turned to vitric spheres, gazed out at the endless gallery of humankind before him, and he felt that same warmth emanating from every one of the unmoving figures in the cavern . . . even from Billy.

Best of all, he knew that Billy didn't blame him for his death. Even if Jerry *had* failed to save his brother's life, it didn't matter anymore. It had happened, and now he was someplace else, just like Billy. Funny. They were together, and yet they were each still alone. It was that simple.

Jerry would always be by himself from now on, just like Billy and the other dead people in the cavern. Each in their solitude, the statues welcomed him in some way that he did not yet fully grasp. But he sensed that he would come to understand, sooner or later. All he had to do was think it through until he knew the truth. His face was frozen fast in a beatific smile.

Hughie was alive, and Jerry was dead, turned to solid ice like his little brother. How it had happened remained a mystery, but he sensed that there was another, even greater mystery ahead. That new mystery would go on forever—for time, too, was frozen solid in this endless cavern. Jerry would be alone for all eternity.

That suited him just fine.

St. Jackaclaws

by A.R. Morlan

A.R. Morlan was born on January 3, 1958, in Chicago, and save for an eight-year period when she and her family lived in California, she has lived the rest of her life in the Midwest. She received her B.S. in English from Mount Senario College in Ladysmith, Wisconsin, where she graduated magna cum laude.

Her first professional sale (nonfiction) was to Twilight Zone Magazine in 1983. By 1985, she sold the first of nine stories to Night Cry, and followed that sale with fiction and nonfiction sales to Twilight Zone, The Horror Show, Grue, Weird Tales, Eldritch Tales, The Scream Factory, Doppelganger, 2 AM Magazine, The Blood Review, New Blood, Prisoners of the Night, Dark Regions, Writer's Nook News, Cemetery Dance, Pulphouse, Scavenger's Newsletter, Bone-Chilling Tales, *and the anthologies* Women of the West *and* Obsessions. *She has sold two novels to Bantam,* The Amulet *and* Dark Summer.

When Ms. Morlan isn't writing, she enjoys reading, drawing, and working on miniature dollhouse furniture. She is also "mother" to a houseful of cats, many of whom have made guest appearances in her stories and novels.

Her fiction is a unique contribution to the horror field, as witness the following dark, disturbing piece.

Winter in the Upper Peninsula hasn't changed very much in the last twenty-five years; come mid-October or so, the first staying snows come, tiny bright slanting flakes, like slivers piercing the frigid air-skin, and when the snow flies past your face come dusk (just as the streetlamps wink into life), you can almost see the jet trail of each flake lingering for a moment or two after each snowflake's passing. *Those* times, when the night sky was crossed and recrossed with snowflake trails, were the magic times, or at least they were when I was seven-going-on-eight.

And the old corner is still there, where Eighth and Green Avenue meet, and so is the flat silvery-grey painted streetlamp pole where we all huddled after supper, and the snow still glistens in almost horizontal paths under the strangely cold yellow light, but it just isn't *quite* the same anymore. Not without Kent.

Not that Kent himself was the magical part, no, Kent wasn't much different than the rest of us—me, Nancy, Debbie, and Steve—but, somehow, he was just more *attuned* to the magic around us. After all, he was the first one to notice the signs of St. Jackaclaws...considering what happened later, Kent's noticing *had* to have been magical in itself...

"Didja ever *notice*?" Kent began, like he always did when he'd made one of those improbable observations of his. Kent was standing on the raised base of our streetlamp, so that his gaze carried a little bit further than that of the rest of us, and he could see just a little more of the dim streets beyond than we could.

"Wha'd we ever notice?" Nancy asked from the depths of her zippered and hooded wooly coat, her breath misting out before her lips, the words cloud-carried down Green Avenue to the south. By unspoken agreement, it had been her turn to ask the rote question; we all took our turn. If memory serves, the next person to do the

ST. JACKACLAWS

asking—after Kent *noticed* something again—was to have been me.

Kent stepped down onto the snow marbled sidewalk, his Keds making delicate *squeedging* noises, before he shoved both hands into his dad's made-over pea coat pockets and said, "If you took some guy and plopped him down in the middle of town right about *now*, he wouldn't know when it *was*, whether it was Halloween or Christmas or—"

"He'd *know*," Debbie started to argue, but Kent just shook his head (the flakes dusting his woolen cap twinkled like the glitter on a fancy Hallmark Christmas card), adding, "Well, *first* you'd have to knock the guy out, take him from some place *warm*," as if we all should have just *known* that that was what he meant. And knowing Kent, I suppose we should have.

Kent then pointed at old lady Juchemich's house over on Eighth. "See her windows, her door? Now look at the house over there. In the big window. And on the roof *there*. *See*? And in Mr. Polskin's kitchen window. *Now* doya see?" Lecture over, he stuffed his reddened hand back in his pocket.

Funny, how we'd all seen things, but hadn't *seen* them, our perceptions blurred by familiarity. In every window, in every door, and on the roof of the big blue house with the bay window, was a different reminder of a different holiday, all winter holidays, all special days when nights were long enough to cut into daytime, and mica-dust snow blanketed the dead grass and damp leaf-covered soil. Here was a frost-withered jack-o'-lantern, there a sun-faded paper cut-out of Santa Claus, and over *there*, in that little corner window whose shade was never raised, was a tattered construction paper Valentine's heart. Some houses had the seasons mixed up—old lady Juchemich had a snowman cutout in her kitchen window, while a back-arched black cat decorated her front door, and the big blue house had a plastic chimney Santa smiling down on a lawn dotted with cut and uncut pumpkins. And too many houses, more than we could count, just left their Christmas lights strung around their garage roofs or peaked front-door stoops, because it was too much trouble to crawl up on a ladder to get them down come the too-short summertime.

Steve whistled, then said, "Sure is a lot of lazy people around here," but Kent corrected him, " 'Are,' dummy. 'Sides, lazy's got nothing to *do* with it," he added with that smug, satisfied tone that signaled something special to our little clique, the streetlamp-standers-after-supper. Before, Kent had revealed other mysteries to us—simple things, really, just the kind of things a fairly smart kid with a lot of free time (his mom and dad shooed him out of the house after breakfast and supper, often yelling as he ran across their bumpy lawn, "And don'tcha come home till after Walter Cronkite!") and a group of just slightly younger friends would take the time to observe and reflect on: How an orange isn't just a bunch of segments in a peel, but lots of *little* sacs with*in* each segment. How, if you scrunched up your eyes and peeked out through the slits you could see your own eyelashes looking as big and bright as a Capri shell windchime. How snowflakes looked like slivers in the sky if the light hit them just right. Insignificant things, mostly, but in that murky not-light-not-dark time when the sky was darkening or flat out dark, and the streetlamps made the trees and houses light, like the world was a photographic negative with dark and light switched around, Kent's little observations were special, near-magical things, the kind of stuff that somehow *stayed* with you, long after the really important stuff (school, presents under the tree, your first bike ride) sort of fuzzed out and faded.

And when you're seven-going-on-eight, and your classmates talk about last night's "Munsters" or "Addams Family" episode on the playground, and Mom and Dad shoo you out the door so you won't see too much of the war footage on the news, the little things that are *yours* are important. And near-magical is almost as good as real-magical . . . so good, it's sometimes hard to find the line of demarcation between them . . .

"If lazy isn't why they keep them up, why *do* they?" I asked, before one of the *girls* could beat me to it. Kent hunkered down until he was sitting on the heels of his worn Keds, and we all had to hunker down around him before he'd go on. When we were all knee to knee, faces so close our breath formed a single cloud, Kent said, "It's to honor St. Jacka*claws*," with a hard emphasis on the *claws* part, just so we'd know he didn't mean *claus*.

"St. *Jack*aclaws?" Nancy asked, half rising as she spoke, but Steve tugged on her coat until she was back in the circle. This wasn't anything like the tiny segments inside the bigger pieces of an orange, or snow slivers . . . Kent was clearly *on* to something, there was no doubt about it. Like, maybe he'd *seen* something the rest of us hadn't while we were trick-or-treating two weeks before (white Casper the Friendly Ghost outfits blending in with the snow-clotted lawns, witches starkly outlined, like ink on paper, and the occasional tumble on a patch of sidewalk ice), or his big brother Kurt had told him about some teenage thing—*doubting* Kent just didn't come into the picture. Not when we were seven-going-on-eight, and Kent was almost *nine*.

"Sure, St. Jackaclaws," Kent assured Nancy and the rest of us, "he's what all the holidays just split *up*. On 'count of the stores, and how they sell stuff." Which was true; Kent's mom worked in a department store (one of the few moms around who had to work, even though Kent's dad worked the iron mines), and we'd all noticed (after Kent told us) how every year Christmas stuff was placed out earlier and earlier, like in late *October*, and that was after the Halloween stuff was put out at the end of September.

"See, St. Jackaclaws is all the winter holidays blended together, which is what they are anyhow, 'cause the snow's here for all the holidays anyhow. They just split apart the parts of him and use them for different holidays. So they can sell more cutouts and lawn decorations." Kent was making sense, to us at least, so we huddled in closer, lips gaping. Our world was mostly a cold, snowy one; we never considered the prospect of a brown or even *green* fall and winter, so the notion of a St. Jackaclaws just seemed *natural*.

"But before there was cutouts and stuff, before there were *stores* even, there was St. Jackaclaws. He's just been *around* forever, before there were houses, before there were trees. Back when this all was just the bottom of a big *lake*—"

(That part, crazy as it sounded, was really true—the eastern part of the UP *was* an ancient lake bed—so if people could live on what had been a lake, St. Jackaclaws wasn't *that* much of an improbable being, if you thought about it.)

"—and he flew across the water all day. He's got wings," Kent added, before Debbie could start asking, "little white ones, with overlapping soft feathers, like in a pillow. Only St. Jackaclaws isn't little, like the cupid they gave his wings to. St. Jackaclaws is *big* . . . his body's round, so he don't get too cold in the winter, and he wears a red furry coat and hat, for when the wind is blowing, only it isn't *really* a coat and hat. It's *him* . . . his *pelt*."

The girls moaned a little at that, no doubt thinking about trapped things in metal jaws, or the deer some people hung on their front lawn trees come late November.

"But he hasn't got fur on his lower part, 'cause his feet are like a chicken, or a turkey maybe, 'cept the claws are big, and wide, like lawn rakes, with lots of hooked-down toes. Sometimes, nowadays, he rakes people's lawns when he walks across them. 'Cause his wings are tired.'' That made sense. Didn't birds all descend upon a lake or lawn come fall, to save up strength for the trip south?

"*But*—it's his head that's the best part," Kent whispered, so that we'd all lean in closer, forming a single merged shadow under the streetlamp's glow, " 'cause it lights up. From inside. That's where the fireflies go come winter, into his head. They fly into the holes where his eyes and mouth are, 'cause he needs a head that doesn't weigh a lot, so it don't tip him over when he flies. And the fireflies inside help, too." We all nodded; didn't birds have small heads?

"His head's got ridges which go this way"—Kent sliced the cold air vertically with his chapped hand—"and since his head is a real dark yellowy color, it just *looks* like a pumpkin. Least that's what people used to make his head when they split him up into different holidays. They pretended that they skinned him, to give his coat and scalp to Santa Claus. I seen pictures of *old* Santa Clauses . . . they wore just plain coats, in blue and green. Yellow, even. My great-grandma's got this box, in the shape of a Santa, from candy, and *his* coat is yellow."

Steve said, "I seen his great-gramma's yellow Santa, when our class made cookies for the old people in town. She had it near the front door—"

"On the little table," Kent finished for Steve, then went on, "see, it was when the *stores* got into the act that things *changed*. When they started *stealing* from St. Jackaclaws."

We didn't need to ask Kent why he blamed the stores for the division of his newly revealed saint; everyone in the neighborhood knew how his mom worked almost from the time Kent was born, something she hadn't had to do when Kurt was little, or so our moms and dads used to say over beers and poker, or little *Woman's Day* recipe-section tarts and bridge. His mom working was why Kent was out here in the first place, because his folks wanted a few hours almost-alone after suppertime, when they didn't want to be bothered with the imaginative observations and musings of a bright but unplanned-for second son. (Our moms and dads mentioned *that* last fact, too.)

Then, as if his words weren't as colorful as usual, Kent crab-scuttered to the nearest white lawn, and began to draw the outline of St. Jackaclaws in the snow with his finger. By the time he was finished, being careful not to step on his patron saint, Kent's forefinger was bloody red colored, the nail a half-oval of mottled pink-white, like a piece of Valentine's Day candy, the chalky kind with little red messages on each piece.

It was hard to see St. Jackaclaws unless you stood a few feet away from him and then went on tiptoes . . . but once Debbie and Nancy did that, they both stared at the figure (his outline fuzzy from freed blades of stubbly grass), then stared at each other, and then ran off for home, their thin screams trailing after them like ribbons of white smoke. Steve and I couldn't run off like *girls*, not with Kent standing there so expectantly near St. Jackaclaws's bloated head . . . but I know that I wanted to.

Hearing about him wasn't anything like *seeing* him; when Kent had spoken, we'd filled in his parts with images borrowed from school room cutouts and plastic lawn decorations. Nice, bright-colored things, with gentle curves and pretty lithographed surfaces, only cobbed together in a fanciful manner . . . not like what *Kent* had had in mind at all.

St. Jackaclaws was . . . *ugly*. His stubby wings were angular, threatening in the way they jutted out like spikes from his shoulders. And his jack-o'-lantern-like face was *mean*, sort of like the way Kent's dad's face looked when he came home after a bad day in the mines, with the dark lines and pores painting his rough skin. And his

ST. JACKACLAWS 259

feet, his *claws* . . . they reached close to where Steve and I stood, close to where we both reflexively inched away from those cruel lines drawn in the sparkling hard snow. But I think the worst part was that St. Jackaclaws didn't have any arms . . . just those wicked, long-toed claws, like a turkey who's realized just in time what's going to happen to him, and decides to fight back with everything he's got. The arms had been important to me when I was just imagining Kent's creature, since I'd thought of St. Jackaclaws in terms of his carrying a sack full of . . . something, what it didn't matter. Arms would've made St. Jackaclaws more *human*, more like something that thought like me and the rest of the gang. But there was nothing human about St. Jackaclaws, save for his hateful grin.

"I gotta go . . . 'Munsters' will be on soon," Steve mumbled at last, before running off to the happy make-believe of Herman and Lily and nice old Grandpa, whose fangs were harmless.

I mumbled something about the 'Munsters', too, even though I hated to leave Kent alone with St. Jackaclaws. I was tempted to run across the huge outline figure, but I didn't. Not because I was afraid of hurting Kent's feelings; it was starting to snow anyhow, and by dawn St. Jackaclaws would've been gone. But my running feet would have bisected that armless, swelling torso . . . and Kent hadn't said what St. Jackaclaws *ate* in order to get that big, and stay that way.

And I knew I shouldn't have asked, but Kent being *Kent*, I just had to . . . even if it was only to find out how much he *truly* believed in his discovery, his creation.

"What's he eat?" I asked, rubbing my booted toe along the indentation between the slabs of the sidewalk. Kent didn't look up from the outline, didn't look at me . . . but his voice was smug, as sure and certain as it had been when he told us about the little sacs inside an orange segment, something we'd all found to be *true*.

"Mean people," he replied, admiring the figure's big head. "Just mean people, who don't care."

That was when I sort of waved to him and ran off, not caring if he noticed my good-bye gesture or not. I had to run around an extra block, but it was worth it, just not to have to run through that figure, that . . . monster.

I never told any of the other kids in the gang about what St. Jackaclaws ate; none of us talked about him, but we couldn't help but *see* him all over, or parts of him at least. Making take-home paper ornaments was painful that winter, I remember that. None of us did Santas, that I'm sure of. And come Valentine's Day, hearts-only was the unspoken rule when it came to giving Valentine's cards.

And even Kent avoided mentioning the oddly formed creature when he led the beneath-the-lamp dusk meetings . . . but he never said "Didja ever notice?" again, either, as if he'd noticed all there was to notice in the world. By the time we were all eight-going-on-nine, and Kent was ten (and his brother was out of the house, at the university on a scholarship), no one stood by the corner at dusk watching the snow slivers cut the air; Barbies and Kens occupied Debbie and Nancy's evenings, and Steve and I were deemed "old enough" to watch the real-life G.I. Joe show on the evening news. And Kent? Who knew? Now, looking back as I stand beneath the old flaked streetlamp post, under the huge blind eye of the yellow lamp, I wonder, suppose the rest of us hadn't shied away from Kent (oh, not all at once, ours was a gradual fade into polite distance and ultimate desertion), and instead asked him more and more about St. Jackaclaws? Would he have gotten it out of his system, talked out his creation until his anger or loneliness or whatever it *was* that made St. Jackaclaws come into his mind was spent? Would it . . . would it have helped if I had told the others what it was that St. Jackaclaws *ate*?

ST. JACKACLAWS

It happened ten years later. During that time when, if you took some guy and bonked him on the head and then dropped him down in the middle of our UP neighborhood, he wouldn't have known which month it was, the time of year when lit-from-behind windows and doors illuminated the cutout silhouettes of hearts, witches, and snowmen . . . as well as the outlines of the stolen bits of St. Jackaclaws.

Unlike Kurt, Kent had won no scholarship; his school record was a little too filled with comments like "daydreamer," and "obsessed with unusual figures—see attached sheet," as well as the ever-improved drawings of St. Jackaclaws he'd produce during art classes, for Kent to be awarded any sort of scholarship, even the one the mine his dad worked for gave out to the child of a miner each summer. Kent worked in the mines, like his Dad, *with* his Dad. The rest of us, Debbie, Nancy, Steve, and I, we went on to school, or got married (like Steve and Nancy did), or went down state to look for better jobs, and we didn't see Kent for over a year after graduation.

We'd even forgot about St. Jackaclaws, until what Kent did made that snow-slivered night come back to each of us, made us put down the newspapers we'd been reading, or get up from the TV news show we'd been watching, whatever, and dial each other, flipping frantically through old phone books or through address books, and when we'd get through, ask, "Do you remember that night when Kent drew that—"

You saw it in the papers, too, or saw it on the tube . . . who could have missed it, especially when the story made its way into those sleazy detective and "true crime" magazines, or the tabloids got their hands on it months later . . . once someone greased the right palms and got only slightly censored pictures from the local cop-shop.

It happened in between holidays, after Halloween and Thanksgiving, before Christmas and St. Valentine's Day.

They caught Kent right away; he hadn't bothered to wash off the blood or change clothes, or even (God help him) brush the blood out of his teeth . . . no, you didn't read *that* part, not even in the tabloids. I only found it out from one of the cops who found Kent. After the cop had had a few in one of the innumerable bars here in town.

The mailman found them, noticed that the previous day's mail hadn't been picked up, and saw that the car was still in the garage, and hadn't been moved since the snowfall the night before, so he gave the door a little push and found that it hadn't been locked. They let the mailman take an early retirement, either that or explain to the world how bad the guy took it, how he was in a looney bin for a month. They didn't want the guy's family to be shamed like that.

The tabloids, they had to put little rectangles of black over the worst sections of the pictures, and the photos in the crime mags were grainy to the point of visual mush, but for me at least, the words the drunken cop used the other night in that bar were more vivid than the best color film in the most expensive camera:

"Their faces . . . I mean, how'd he *do* that? Leaving just the bone . . . and their *guts* . . . my woman, she knows better'n to serve tripe, lemme tell ya . . . an' I summered at my uncle's farm in Wis'*con*sin, too, but I never sawed the likes . . . worse'n what old man Gein did in Wis'*con*sin . . . musta been fricken *nuts*, y'know?"

Not nuts, I told myself, as I poured out the rest of my beer into my glass, *just a hurt little boy who couldn't come inside the house until after Walter Cronkite was off the air, and whose mother worked in one of the stores that ripped off his patron saint.*

"St. Jackel-somethin'-or-other," the cop said, fingering his stubbled cheek. "Punk said somethin' 'bout some *saint* making him do it, ain't that a new one? Wound up the same as all the other nuts, in the padded room—"

ST. JACKACLAWS

That much I'd already known; Kent was safely hidden from the world in the state hospital. For the criminally insane, natch. None of us had ever tried to visit him, none of us tried to write, even though Steve had heard that Kent was supposedly making some improvement, or so Kurt had told Steve's cousin, who told Steve.

I left the cop to his beers, and walked out into the icy night. Slivers of snow whizzed by me, some caught my exposed skin, stinging there. Kent's parents have been dead fifteen years, which makes Kent thirty-four now. Steve and Nancy's son is nine, same age as Kent was when he revealed St. Jackaclaws to the world... and thinking of Steve and Nancy's boy, after I'd stepped out of the bar, made me remember something, *notice* something, actually, that subtly changed *everything* about what happened to Kent's parents.

The picture was in the checkout rags as well as the crime 'zines; you've probably seen it; in it's day, it was as infamous as that mortuary shot of Ted Bundy on the slab that that one tabloid printed a year or so ago. I'm talking about the picture of the hallway where Kent's mom was stretched out, the one with her legs-up-to-the-knees showing on the left of the shot, and his Dad's outflung right arm in the lower right corner of the photo. With the blood marbling the floorboards. What made me think of the picture again was something Steve said to me, about Nancy not letting their boy go on an overnight visit to one of his friends, on account of its being close to the anniversary of What Kent Did.

Sleep-overs. Steve and I slept over at Kent's house once. I couldn't sleep right, on account of there being one of those big foam pillows under my head. I was used to squishy feather pillows, but there were none in Kent's house, because his mom and brother were allergic to the regular kind of pillow.

And... and if you take a close look at that picture of Kent's folks, you'll see them. Between his Mom's legs, and near his Dad's hand. Maybe you'd have to use a magnifying glass to be as sure of it as I am, but if you do, you'll see them.

Feathers. Little white ones, like the ones that worm their way out of pillow ticking. In a house where there were no feather pillows.

As if someone were waiting for the opportunity to ask, "Didja ever *notice*?"

The Pavilion Of Frozen Women

by S.P. Somtow

S.P. Somtow is a man of many talents. Not only is he a novelist and short story writer of some note, but he is also a highly regarded post-serialist composer. Born in Thailand in 1952, Somtow has lived in Japan, Holland, and England, and today makes his home in Los Angeles, having recently become an American citizen. He has directed, produced, scored, and played a role (as the villainous doctor Um-Tzec) in a feature film, The Laughing Dead. *Somtow has won the Campbell and Daedalus Awards for his science fiction, and has been a finalist for the Bram Stoker Award for his horror. He has been called one of the "fathers" of splatterpunk by critic Philip Nutman in* Twilight Zone *magazine. He is the author of two impressive, massive horror novels,* Vampire Junction *and* Moon Dance. *He is currently at work on a horror novel entitled* Valentine, *while simultaneously attempting to raise the financing for a new movie,* The Glass Pagoda. *Somehow, he found time to write this shocking, bizarre, and moving novella for* Cold Shocks.

1

"Alles Vergängliche
Ist nur ein Gleichnis...."
—Faust

She was draped against the veined boulder that jutted up from the snow and gravel in the rock garden of Dr.

Mayuzumi's estate. One hand had been placed demurely over her pubes—the Japanese have a horror of pubic hair that has caused it to become the last taboo of their pornography—the other was flung against her forehead. A trickle of blood ran from the side of her lip down her slender neck, past one breast, to a puddle beside her left thigh.

When I got there with my notebook and my camera, they were milling around in the cloister that ran all the way around the rectangular rock garden. Their breath hung in the still cold air, and no one had touched the body yet, not even the police.

I hadn't come to Sapporo to cover a slasher; I'd come there for the Snow Festival. I'd only been in town for a couple of hours. I'd only just started unpacking when I got the phone call from the Tokyo office and had to grab a taxi to this estate just outside town. I didn't even have time to put on a coat.

To say that it was cold doesn't begin to describe it. But I'd been feeling this cold since I was just a *winchinchala* back at the Pine Ridge Reservation in South Dakota. I stood there in my Benetton sweatshirt and my Reeboks and looked out of place. I ignored the cold.

A police officer was addressing the press. They weren't like stateside reporters; there was a pecking order—the Yomiuri and Asahi Shimbun people got the best places, the tabloids hunched down low in the back and spoke only when spoken to—gravely, taking turns, scribbling solemnly in notebooks. They all wore dark suits.

I'd had Japanese at Berkeley, but I couldn't follow much, so I just stood there staring at the corpse. There wasn't a strand of that stringy blond hair that was out of place. It was the work of an artist.

It was the hair that jolted me into remembering who she was. So this wasn't just another newspaper story after all.

The snow was beginning to obliterate the artist's handiwork—powdering down her hair, whitening away her freckles. She'd been laughing all the way from San Francisco to Narita Airport. I still had her card in my purse.

I snapped a picture. When the flash went off they all froze and turned toward me all at once, like a many-headed monster. It's uncanny the way they can do that. Then they all smiled that strained, belittling smile that I'd been experiencing ever since I'd arrived in Japan a week before.

"Look," I said at last, "I'm with the Oakland *Tribune*." Suddenly I realized that there wasn't a single woman among all those ranked reporters. In fact, there were no other women there at all. I felt even more self-conscious. No one spoke to me at all. It didn't matter that what I was wearing stood out against the black-white-and-gray like a peacock in a hen coop. I was a woman; I was a *gaijin*; I wasn't there.

Presently the police officer murmured something. They all laughed in unison and turned back to their notetaking. One reporter, perhaps taking pity on me, said, "American consulate will be here soon. You talk to *them*."

"Yeah, right," I said. I wasn't in the mood for bullshit. "Listen, folks, I *know* this woman. I can *i-den-ti-fy* her, *wakarimashita?*"

The many-headed monster swiveled around again. There was consternation behind the soldered-on smiles. I had the distinct impression they didn't feel it was my place to say anything at all.

At that moment, the people from the consulate arrived. There was a self-important bald man with a briefcase and a slender black woman. A few flashbulbs went off. The woman, like me, hadn't planned on a visit to the Mayuzumi estate on a snowy afternoon. She was dressed to the gills, probably about to hit one of those diplomatic receptions.

"I'm Esmeralda O'Neil," she said to the police of-

ficer. "I understand that an American citizen's been—"
She stopped when she saw the corpse.

The policeman spoke directly to the bald man. The bald man deferred to the black woman. The policeman couldn't seem to grasp that Esmeralda O'Neil was the bald man's boss.

"Look here—" I said. "I can tell you who she is."

This time I got more attention. More flashes went off. Esmeralda turned to me. "You're Marie, aren't you? Marie Wounded Bird. They told us you were coming, and to take care of you," she said. "I was hoping to meet you at the reception tonight."

"I didn't get invited," I said testily.

"Who is she?" she said. She was a woman who recovered quickly—a real diplomat, I decided.

"Her name's Molly Danzig. She's a dancer. She sat next to me on the flight from San Francisco. She works—worked—at a karaoke bar here in Sapporo—the rooftop lounge at the Otani Prince Towers."

"You know anything else about her, darlin'?"

"Not really."

She looked at the corpse again. "Jesus fucking Christ." She turned to the police officer and began talking to him in rapid Japanese. Then she turned back to me. "Look, hon," she said, "all hell's gonna break loose in no time flat; CNN's already on their way. Why don't you come to the reception with us?" Then, taking me by the arm so that her aide couldn't hear her, she added, "You don't know what it's like here, hon. Machismo up the wazoo. I'd give anything for an hour of plain old down-home girl talk. So—reception?"

"I'm not sure . . . I'd feel a bit like trespassing."

"Why darlin', you've already gone and done *that*! This is the Mayuzumi estate we're standing in now . . . and the reception is Dr. Mayuzumi's bash to welcome the foreign dignitaries to the Snow Festival." I had heard of this Mayazumi vaguely. Textiles, beer, personal computers. Finger in every pie.

The Japanese reporters were already starting to leave. They filed out in rows, starting with the upscale newspapers and ending with the tabloids. It was only then that I noticed the man with the sketch pad.

At first I thought he must be an American. Even from the other side of the rock garden I could see that he had the most piercing blue eyes. He was kneeling by the railing of the cloister. In spite of the cold he was just wearing jeans and a T-shirt. He had long black hair and a thick beard. He was hairy . . . bearlike, almost. Asians are hardly ever hairy.

The policeman barked an order at him. He backed off. But there was something in his body language, something simultaneously deferential and defiant, something that identified him as a member of a conquered people, a kind of hopelessness. It was so achingly familiar it made me lose my cool and just gape at him. That was how my mother always behaved when the social worker came around. Or the priest from the St. Francis Mission. Or whenever they'd come around to haul my dad off to jail for the weekend because he'd guzzled down too much *mniwakan* and made himself a nuisance. All my aunts and uncles acted that way toward white people. The only one who never did was Grandpa Mahtowashté. And that was because he was too busy communicating with the bears to pay any attention to the real world.

My grandfather had taken me to my first communion. Nobody else came. He knelt beside me and shouted out loud: "These damned priests don't know what this ritual really means." They made him wait outside the church.

God I hated my childhood. I hated South Dakota.

The man stared back at me with naked interest. I hadn't seen that here before either. People never looked you in the eye here. I had become an invisible woman. It occurred to me then that we were invisible together, he and I.

I stopped listening to Esmeralda, who was babbling on about the social life of the city of Sapporo—explaining that it wasn't all beer, that the shiny-modern office buildings and squeaky-clean avenues were no more than a veneer—and just stared at the man. Although he was looking straight at me, he never stopped sketching.

"Anyway, hon, I'll give you my card... and... here's where the reception's going to be... the Otani Prince Towers... rooftop, with a mind-boggling view of the snow sculptures being finished up." Esmeralda made to leave, and I said something perfunctory about seeing her again soon.

Then I added, "Do you know who that man is?"

"That's Ishii, the snow sculptor. Aren't you here to interview him?"

It showed how confused I'd become after seeing my fellow traveler lying dead in the snow. Aki Ishii was one of the grand masters on my list of people to see; I had his photograph in my files. It had been black and white, though. I couldn't have expected those eyes.

And he was already walking toward me, taking the long way around the cloister.

He said to me: "Transience and beauty..." He was a softspoken man. "Transience and beauty are the cornerstones of my art. It was Goethe, I think, who said that all transient things are only metaphors... should we seize this moment, Miss Wounded Bird? Or is the time not yet ripe for an interview?"

"You know me?" I said. I had suddenly, unaccountably, become afraid. Perhaps it was because there were only the two of us now... even the corpse had been carried off, and the Americans had tramped away down the cloister.

The temperature fell even more. At last I started to shiver.

"I know you, Miss Wounded Bird—perhaps you will let me call you 'Marie'—because the *Tribune* was kind enough to send me a letter. I knew who you were at once. Something about your body language, your sense of displacement; you were that way even with your fellow countrymen. I understand that, you see, because I am Ainu."

The Ainu ... it began to make sense. The Ainu were the aboriginal inhabitants of this island—blue-eyed neolithic nomads pushed into the cold by the manifest destiny of the Japanese conquerors. There were only 15,000 pure-blooded Ainu left. They were like the Lakota—like my people. We were both strangers in our own land.

It occurred to me that I was on the trail of a great story, an important story. Oh, covering the festival would have been interesting enough—there's nothing quite like the Sapporo Snow Festival in all the world, acres and acres of snow being built up into vast edifices that dissolve at the first thaw. It's all some Zen-like affirmation of beauty and transience, I had been told ... and now I was hearing the grand master himself utter those words over the site of a sex murder ... hearing them applied with equal aptness to both art and reality.

"Perhaps I could escort you to the reception, Marie?" he said. Behind his Japanese accent there was a hint of some other language, perhaps German. I seemed to remember from his dossier that he had, in his youth, studied in Heidelberg under a scholarship from the Goethe-Institut. It was quaint but kind of attractive. I started to like him.

We left the rock garden together. He had an American car—a Mustang—parked by the gate. "I know the steering wheel is on the wrong side," he said apologetically, "but I'll drive carefully, I promise."

He didn't. The thirty kilometers back into downtown Sapporo were terrifying. We lurched, we hydroplaned, we skidded, past tiny temples enveloped in snow, past ugly postmodernist apartments, past row houses with walls of rice paper crammed along alleyways. Snow bent the branches of the trees to breaking. The sunset glittered on roofs of glossy tile, orange-green or cobalt blue. I was glad he was driving with such abandon. It made me think less of Molly Danzig, laughing over how she'd been fleecing the rubes at the karaoke bar, trading raunchy stories about men she had known, wolfing down airline food in between giggles... Molly Danzig, who in death had become part of an ordered elegance she had never evinced in the twelve hours I had sat beside her on the plane from San Francisco.

The reception was, of course, a massive spectacle. These people really knew how to lay on a spread. The top floor of the hotel had been converted into a Styrofoam and plastic replica of the winter wonderland outside. Three chefs worked like maniacs behind an eighty-foot sushi bar. Elsewhere, cooks in silly pseudo-French uniforms sliced patisseries, carved roasts, and ladled soup out of swan-shaped tureens. Chandeliers sparkled. Plastic snowflakes rained down from a device in the ceiling. You could have financed a feature film by hocking the clothes on these people's backs—Guccis, Armanis, Diors—a few of those $5,000 kimonos. Although Aki had thrown on a stylish black leather duster, I found myself hopelessly underdressed for this shindig. It didn't help that everyone was studiously ignoring us. Aki and I seemed to be walking around in a private bubble of indifference.

One wall was all glass. You could see down into Odori Park, on the other side of Sapporo's three-hundred-feet-wide main drag. The snow sculptures were taking shape. Once the festival started they would be floodlit. Now they were ghostly hulks haunching up toward the moon. This year's theme was "Ancient Times" there was a half-formed Parthenon at one end of the park, a Colosseum in the foreground, an Egyptian temple complete with Sphinx, a Babylonian ziggurat... all snow.

A huge proscenium filled one end of the lounge, and on it stood a corpulent man who was crooning drunkenly into a microphone. The song appeared to be a disco version of "Strangers in the Night." There was no band.

"Jesus!" I said. "They should shoot the singer."

"That would hardly be wise," Aki said. "That man is Dr. Mayuzumi himself."

"Karaoke?" I said. There's only one karaoke bar in Oakland and I'd never been to it. This fit the description all right. As Dr. Mayuzumi left the stage to desultory applause, someone else was pushed up onto the stage amid gales of laughter. It turned out to be Esmeralda O'Neil. She began singing a Japanese pop song, complete with ersatz Motown gestures and dance steps.

"Oh," Aki said, "but this is the club where your... friend... used to work. Miss... Danzig." He pronounced her name *Danjigu*.

"Let's get a stiff drink," I said at last.

We went and sat at the sushi bar. We had some hot sake, and then Aki ordered food. The chef pulled a pair of live jumbo shrimp out of a tank, made a few lightning passes with his knife, and placed two headless shrimp on the plate. Their tails wiggled.

"It's called *odori*." Aki said, "dancing shrimp... hard to find in the States."

I watched the shrimp tails pulsing. Surely they could not feel pain. Surely it was just a reflex. A lizard's tail goes on jerking after you pull it off the lizard.

Aki murmured something.

"What did you say?"

"I'm apologizing to the shrimp for taking its life," he said. He looked around shiftily as he said it. "It's an Ainu thing. The Japs wouldn't understand." It was the kind of thing my grandfather did.

"Eat it," Aki said. His eyes sparkled. He was irresistible.

I picked up one of them with my chopsticks, swished it through the soy sauce dish, popped it in my mouth.

"What do you feel?" he said.

"It's hard to describe." It had squirmed as it went down my throat. But the way all the tastes exploded at once, the soy sauce, the horseradish, the undead shrimp with its toothpastelike texture and its exquisite flavor... there'd been something almost synaesthetic about it... something joyous... something obscene.

It's a peculiarly Japanese thing," said the Ainu snow sculptor, "this almost erotic need to suck out a creature's life force... I have been studying it, Marie. Not being Japanese, I cannot intuit it; I can only listen in the shadows, pick up their leavings as I slink past them with downcast eyes. But you, Marie, you I can look full in the face."

And he did. The way he said my name held the promise of dark intimacy. I couldn't look away. Once again this man's body language evoked something out of my childhood. It was my father, reaching for me in the winter night, in the bedroom with the broken window, with his liquor breath hanging in the moonlit air. And me with my eyes squeezed tight, calling on the Great Mystery. Jesus, I hated my father. Although I hadn't thought of him in ten years, he was the only man in my life. I felt resentful, vulnerable, and violated, all at once. And still I couldn't look away. Then Esmeralda breezed over and came to my rescue.

"You never stop working for a moment, do you, hon?" she said, and ordered a couple of *odori* for herself.

I said, "What about Molly Danzig? Any word about—"

"Darlin', that girl's just vanished from the universe as far as anyone can see. The press aren't talking. Nothing on TV. Even CNN's been put on hold for a few days.

Total blackout... even the consulate's being asked to wait on informing the next of kin... it's that festival, you know. It's a question of face."

"Doesn't it make you mad?"

"Hell no! I'm a career diplomat, darlin'; this girl doesn't rock any boats." She bit down on the wriggling crustacean with relish. "Mm-mm, good." No squeamishness, no regret.

I looked around. The partygoers were still giving us a wide berth, but now and then I thought I could see stares and hear titters. Was I paranoid? "Everyone knows about it, don't they?" I said.

"It?" said Esmeralda ingenuously.

"It! The murder that no one can talk about! That's why they're all avoiding me like yesterday's fish; they know that I knew her. I stink of that girl's death."

"It's nothing, hon." She took a slug of sake.

Aki tugged at my elbow. "I can see you're getting uncomfortable here," he whispered. "Would you care to blow this joint—I believe that's how you Americans call it?"

I could see where this was leading. I was attracted to him. I was afraid of him. I had a story to write and I knew that a good story sometimes demands a piece of your soul. How big a piece? I didn't want to give in yet, so I said, "I'd love to see the snow sculptures. Now, when the park's deserted, in the middle of the night."

"Your wish is my command," he said, but somehow I felt that it was I who had been commanded. Like a vampire, Aki had to be invited before he could strike.

In the moonlight, we walked past the Clock Tower, the only Russian building left on Hokkaido, toward the TV tower which dominated the east end of Odori-Koen. The park was long and narrow. Mountains of snow were piled along the walkways.

They had brought in extra snow by the truckload.

There were a few men working overtime shoveling paths and patting down banks of snow. A man on a ladder was shaping the entablature of a Corinthian column with his hands. Fog roiled and tendriled about our feet. I didn't ask Aki why the park and the zombie shrimp had the same name; I had a feeling the answer would unnerve me too much.

We walked slowly up the mile-long park toward the tableau that was Aki's personal creation—I knew from my notes that this was to be the centerpiece of the festival, a classical representation of the Judgment of Paris.

"What do you think of Sapporo?" Aki asked me abruptly.

"It's—"

"You don't have to tell me. It's an ugly town. It's all clean and shopping-mall-ridden and polished till it shines, but still it's a brand-new city desperately looking for something to call a soul."

"Well, the Snow Festival—"

"Founded in 1950. Instant ancient culture. A Disneyland of the Japanese sensibility."

It was not what I'd come to hear. I'd had the article half written before I'd even boarded the plane. I'd wanted to talk about tradition, the old reflected in the new. We walked on.

People go to bed early in Japan. You could hardly hear any traffic. A long line of trucks piled high with snow stretched the length of the park and turned north at the Sosei River end. It took three hundred truckloads of snow for the average snow sculpture. The snow came from the mountains.

Most of the sculptures had been cordoned off. Now and then we passed artisans who would turn from their work, bow smartly, and bark out the word *sensei*. Aki walked ahead. We did not touch. Public displays between the sexes are frowned on here. I had been relieved to learn that.

"It was a shame about that Danjigu girl," Aki said. "I have seen her many times, at the karaoke club; Mayuzumi rather liked her, I think."

Molly had said something about fat rich businessmen. I wished he would change the subject. I said, "Tell me something about your art, Aki."

"Is this the interview?" Our footsteps echoed. Ice tinkled on the trees. "But I have already talked about beauty and transience."

"Is that why you were sketching Molly's corpse? I thought it was kind of . . . macabre."

He smiled. No one was watching us. His hand brushed against mine for a fleeting second. It burned me. I walked ahead a few steps.

"So what are you looking for in your art, Mr. Ishii?" I asked him in my best girl-reporter voice.

"Redemption," he said. "Aren't you?"

I did not want to think about what I was looking for.

"I feel a bit like Faust sometimes," he said, "snatching a few momentary fragments of beauty out of the void, and in return giving up . . . everything."

"Your soul for beauty?" I said. "Kind of romantic."

"Oh, it's all those damned Germans, Goethe, Schiller: death, transfiguration, redemption, weltschmerz—going to school there can really fill you with Teutonic portentousness."

I had to laugh. "But what about being Ainu?" I said. "Doesn't that contribute to your artistic vision too?"

"I don't want to talk about that."

So we were alike, always running away from who we were. He strode purposefully ahead now, his shadow huge and wavery in the light of the full moon.

A wall of snow towered ahead of us. Here and there I could see carved steps. "I'll help you up," he said. He was already climbing the embankment. My Reeboks dug into the snow steps. "Don't worry," he said, "my students will smooth them out in the morning. Come."

The steps were steep. Once or twice he had to pull me up. "There will be a ramp," he said, "so the spectators can cluster around the other side."

We were standing on a ledge of snow now, looking down onto the tableau he had created. Here, at the highest point in the park, there was a bitter breeze. It had stopped snowing and the air was clear, but the sky was too bright from the city lights to see many stars. The artificial mountain wrapped around us on three sides; the fourth was the half-built viewer's ramp; the area formed a kind of open-air pavilion.

Aki said, "Look around you. It's 1200 B.C. We're on the slopes of Mt. Ida, in the mythological dawn. Look—over there—past the edge of the park—the topless towers of Ilium." It was the Otani Prince Towers, glittering with neon, peering up through twin peaks. It was an optical illusion—the embankment no more than thirty feet high, a weird forced perspective, the moonlight, the fog swirling—that somehow drew the whole city into the fantasy world. "Come on," he said, taking my hand as we descended into the valley. A ruined rotunda rose out of a mound of rubble. A satyr played the panpipe and a centaur lay sleeping against a broken wall. It was hard to believe it was all made of snow. On the wall, sculpted in bas-relief, was the famous judgment: Paris, a teenaged version of Rodin's *Thinker*, leaning forward as he sat on a boulder; the three goddesses preening; the golden apple in the boy's hand.

"Now look behind the wall," Aki said.

I saw a cave hollowed out of the side of the embankment. At its entrance, sitting in the same attitude as the bas-relief, was a three-dimensional Paris; beyond, inside the cave, you could make out three figures, their faces turned away.

"But—" I said. "You can't see the tableau from the spectator's ramp! At best, you'd see the back of Paris's head, the crook of Athena's arm. You can only see the relief on the ruined wall."

"But that is what this sculpture is all about, Marie," Aki said. He was talking faster now, gesticulating. "I hold the mirror up to nature and within the mirror there's another mirror that mirrors the mirrored nature I've created... reflections within reflections... art within art ... the truth only agonizingly, momentarily glimpsed... and that which is most beautiful is that which remains unseen. Come on, Marie. You will get to see my hidden world. Come. Come."

He seized my hand. I climbed down beside him. A system of planks, concealed by snowy ridges, led to the grotto. Like a boy with an ant farm, Aki became more intense, more nervous as we neared the center of his universe. When he reached the sculpture of Paris, he became fidgety. He disregarded me completely and went up to the statue, reshaping a wrinkle in the boy's cloak, fussing with his hair. Paris had no face yet.

Curious to see how the grand master had visualized the three beautiful goddesses, I turned away from him toward the interior of the cave. The chill deepened as I stepped away from the entrance. The tunnel appeared to descend into an infinite darkness; another illusion perhaps, a bend, a false perspective... unless there was really an opening into some labyrinthine underworld.

The goddesses were not finished yet. Two had no faces. The third—Hera, goddess of marital fidelity and orthodoxy—had the face of Molly Danzig.

I thought it must be some trick of the moonlight or my frazzled nerves. But it was unmistakable. I went up close. The likeness was uncanny. If the snow had started to breathe I would not have been more startled. And the eyes... what were they?... some kind of polished gemstone embedded in the snow... snow-moistened eyes that seemed to weep... I could feel my heart pounding.

I backed away. Into Aki's arms. "Jesus," I said, "this is sick, this is morbid—"

"But I have already explained to you about beauty and transience," Aki said softly. "I have been watching this girl ever since she started at the karaoke club; her death by violence is, how would you say it, synchronicity. Perhaps a sacrifice for giving my art the breath of life."

Molly Danzig shook her head. I think. Her eyes shone. Or maybe caught the moonlight. She breathed. Or maybe the wind breathed into her. Or my fear. I was too scared to move for a moment and then—

"Kiss me," he whispered. "Don't you understand that we are both bear people? You are the first I have met."

"No!" I twisted free from him and ran. Down the icy pathway, with the moist wind whipping at my face, past the Parthenon and the Colosseum and the Sphinx. Past the piled-up snow. Snow seeping into my sneakers and running down my neck. It was snowing again. I crossed the street. I was shivering. It was from terror, not from cold.

Jesus, I'm getting spooked by illusions, I told myself when I reached the façade of the Otani. I took a deep breath. Objectivity. Objectivity. I looked around. There was no one in sight. I stood on the steps for a moment, wondering where to get a taxi at one in the morning.

At that moment, Esmeralda and her portly aide swept through the revolving doors and glided down the steps. She was wearing a fur stole, the kind where you'd be mugged by conservationists if you tried to wear it on the street in California. She saw me and called out, "Marie, darlin', you need a ride to your hotel?"

I nodded dumbly. A limousine pulled up. We piled in.

As we started to move down the street, I saw him again. Standing at the edge of the park. Staring intently at us. Sketching. Sketching.

2

*"Das Unzulängliche
Hier wird's Ereignis."*
— Faust

Bear people—

When I was a child I saw my grandfather speaking to bears.

The hotel I was staying at was a second-class *ryokan*, a traditional-style hotel, because I wanted to get the real flavor of the Japanese way of life. The smell of tatami. The masochistic voyeurism of communal bathing. I tossed and turned on the futon and wished for a water bed in San Mateo. And the roar of the distant surf. But my dreams were not of California.

In my dream I was a *winchinchala* again. In my dream was my father's shack. Midnight and the chill wind whining through the broken pane. I'm twisting on the pee-stained mattress on the floor. Maybe there's a baby crying somewhere. A damp hand covers my mouth.

"Gotta see to the baby, *até*." I'm whispering.

"*Igmu yelo*," says my father. *It's only a cat*. The baby's shrieking at the top of his lungs. Dad crushes me between his thighs. Even his sweat is turning to ice. I ooze through his fingers. I run down stairs that lead down down down down caverns down down to—

"*Don't!*"

From the dirt road that runs alongside the frozen creek next to the outhouse you can see a twisted mountain just past the edge of the Badlands. The top is sheared off. I wish myself up to the ledge where I'm going to stand naked in the wind and I'm going to see visions and know everything that's to come and I'm going to stand and become a frozen woman like the other women who have stood there and dreamed until they dreamed themselves into pillars of red and yellow stone.

"*Tunkashila!*" I'm screaming. "Grandpa!"

I'm running from the wind that's my dad's breath reeking of *mniwakan*.

Suddenly I know that the man who's chasing me is a bear. I don't look back but I can feel his shadow pressing down on me, on the snow. I'm running to my grandfather because I know I'll be safe with him, he'll draw a circle in the ground and inside everything will be warm and far from danger and he'll put down his pipe inside the sacred circle and say to the bear: *Be still, my son, be still.*

I'm running from the cold but I might as well run from myself. I'm going to be frozen right into the mountain like all the other women from now back to the beginning of the universe, women dancing in a slow circle around the dying fire. I'm running through the tunnel that becomes—

The tunnel beneath the sea. I'm riding the bullet train, crossing to Hokkaido island, to the Japan no one knows, the Japan of wide open spaces and desolate snowy peaks and spanking-new cities that have no souls. I'm staring out as the train shrieks, staring at the concrete cavern. I see Molly Danzig's eyes and I wonder if they're real, I wonder if Aki has plucked them from the corpse and buried them in the snow woman's face.

The frozen woman shakes her head. Her eyes are deep circles drawn in blood. "No, *até*, no, *até*," I whisper.

Be still, my son, my grandfather says to the bear who rears up over the pavilion of frozen women. My grandfather gives me honey from a wooden spoon. He puts his pipe back in his mouth and blows smoke rings at the bear, who growls a little and then slinks, cowed, back into the snowy forest.

Circles. Circles. I'm running in circles. There's no

way out. The tunnel has twisted back on itself. I will turn to snow.

Molly Danzig's card: an apartment building a few blocks west of the Sapporo Brewery. It was about a fifteen-minute ride on the subway from my *ryokan*. The air was permeated with the smell of hops. Snow piled against a Coke machine with those slender Japanese Coke cans. At the corner, a robocop directed traffic. Its metal arms were heaped with snow. The first time I'd seen one of those things I'd thought it must be a joke; my Tokyo guide told me, self-importantly, that they'd had them for twenty years.

The afternoon was gray. The sky and the apartment building were the same dead shade, gray gray gray.

I took the elevator to the tenth floor. I don't know what I expected to find. I told myself, Hey, sister, you're a reporter, maybe there *is* a gag order on this story now but it won't last out the week. I had my little Sure Shot in my purse just in case.

The hall: shag carpet, dull modern art by the elevator. This apartment building could be anywhere. The color scheme was nouveau "Miami Vice." I followed the apartment numbers down the corridor. Hers, 17A, should be at the end. There it was with the door ajar. An old man in overalls was painting the door.

Painting out the apartment number. Painting out Molly's name. A brushstroke could obliterate a life.

I pushed my way past him into the apartment. I'd had a notion of what Molly's place would look like. Molly was always laughing so I imagined there'd be outrageous posters or funky furniture. She loved to talk about men— I don't—so I imagined some huge and blatant phallic statue standing in the middle of the room. It wasn't like that at all. It was utterly still.

The windows were wide open. It was chillier here than outside. A wind was sighing through the living room and the tatami floor was peppered with snow. No furniture. No Chippendales pinups on the walls. The wind picked up a little. Snowflakes flecked my face.

The kitchen: two bowls of cold tea on the counter. The stove was still lit. I turned it off. A half-eaten piece of sushi lay in a blue-and-white plate. I took a few snapshots. I wondered if the police had come by to dust the tea bowls for prints.

I heard a sound. At first I thought it must be the wind. The wind blew harder now and behind the sighing I could hear someone humming. A woman.

I stepped into the living room. Snow seeped through my sneakers. I was shivering. It was a contralto voice, eerie, erotic. I could hear water dripping, too. It came from behind a *shoji* screen door. A bedroom, I supposed.

I knew I was going to have to go in. I steeled myself and slid the *shoji* open.

Snowflakes whirled. The wind was really howling here. Through a picture window I could see the Sapporo Brewery and the grid of the city, regular as graph paper, and snowy mountains far beyond it. I smelled stale beer on the snow that settled on my cheeks.

The humming grew louder. A bathroom door was ajar. Water dripped.

"Molly?"

I could feel my heart pounding. I flung the bathroom door wide open.

"Why—Marie darlin'—I sure wasn't expecting *you*." Esmeralda looked up at me from the bathtub, soaping herself lazily.

"You knew who she was the whole time," I said.

"It's my business to know that, hon," she said. "Not too many American citizens in Sapporo, as you might have noticed, but I keep tabs on 'em all. Hand me that washcloth? Pretty please?"

I did so numbly. Why had she asked me who the dead woman was if she already knew her? "You tricked me!"

THE PAVILION OF FROZEN WOMEN 285

"In diplomacy school, Marie, they teach you to let the other person do all the talking. Oftentimes they end up digging their own grave that way."

"But what are you doing here?"

"This is my apartment. Molly Danzig used to sublet. "I've got a suite in the consulate I usually end up crashing out at, but the hot water in our building never works right."

She reached for a towel and slid out of the tub. She steamed; she was firm and magnificent and had a way of looking fully clothed even when she was naked; I guessed it was her diplomatic comportment. The Lakota are a modest people. I was embarrassed.

"Believe me, this ain't St. Louis. I mean, girl," she said, reaching for the hair dryer, "here's me, on a GS salary with perks up the wazoo, housing allowance, no mouths to feed . . . but if it weren't for all those receptions with all that free food, I'd be lining up at a fucking soup kitchen. Let's forget this and just go shopping somewhere, Marie."

"All right." I couldn't see where I could go with the story at this point. I had three or four pieces, but they didn't seem to fit together—maybe they didn't even belong in the same puzzle. Perhaps I just needed to spend a mindless afternoon buying souvenirs.

Esmeralda drove me to the Tanuki-koji arcade, a labyrinthine underground mall that starts somewhere in the middle of town and snakes over and under, taking in the train station and the basement of the Otani Prince. She parked in a loading zone ("*Gaimusho* tags, darlin'— they're not going to tow any of us diplomats, no way!") and although it was afternoon, we descended into a world of neon night.

When you're confused and pushed to the limits of your endurance and you think you're going to crack up, sometimes shopping is the only cure. I never went shopping when I was a kid. Yes, sometimes we'd take the pickup and lurch toward Belvidere or Wall, where at least you could watch the mechanical jackalopes for 25¢ or gaze at the eighty-foot fake dinosaur as it reared up from the knee-high snow. Shopping was a vice I learned from JAPs and WASPs in Berkeley. But I had learned well. I could shop with passion. So could Esmeralda. It was an hour or two before I realized that, for her as well as me, the ability to shop effusively was little more than a defense mechanism. As we warmed to each other a little, I could see that she spoke two different languages, with separate lexicons of gesture and facial expression; they were as different as English and Lakota were for my parents, except they were both English, and she could slide back and forth between them with ease.

We moved from corridor to corridor, past little noodle stands with their glass cases of plastic food in front, past *I Love Kitty* emporia and kimono rental stores and toy stores guarded by mechanical Godzillas, past vending machines that dispensed slender cans of Sapporo beer and iced coffee. People shuffled purposefully by. The concrete alleyways were slick with mush from above ground. Glaring neons blended into chiaroscuro.

By six or so we were laden down with shopping bags. Junk mostly—fans, hapi coats, orientalia for my apartment in Oakland, postcards showing the Ainu in their native costume, with ritual tattoos and fur and beads—not that there were any to be seen in the antiseptic environs of Sapporo.

"What do you know about the Ainu?" I asked Esmeralda.

"They're wild people. Snow people, kind of like Eskimos maybe—they worship bears, have shamanistic rituals—only for tourists—the Japanese forced them all to take Japanese names and they can't speak Ainu anymore."

It was a story I knew well. My grandfather Mahtowashté had told me the same story. "I can speak to bears," he said, "because once, when I was a boy, a bear came to me in a dream and gave me my name." And he'd give me a piece of bread dipped in honey and I'd say, "*Tunkashila*, make it so I can get out of here ... make it all go away."

"There're more Ainu around than you might think. A lot of them have interbred with the Japanese. They don't *look* Ainu anymore, but ... people still feel prejudiced. They don't advertise, unlike our friend Aki. Most of them just try to blend in. They'd lose their social standing, their credit rating, their influence ..."

I knew all about that. I'd spent my whole life escaping, blending.

"Come on," Esmeralda said, "time for coffee."

We stopped at a coffee shop and squeezed ourselves into tiny armchairs and we each ordered a cup of Blue Mountain at ¥750 a pop. Tiny cups of coffee and tall glasses of spring water.

"Help me, Esmeralda," I said. "Jesus, I'm lost."

"This isn't the place you thought it would be." A neon blue-and-pink reproduction of Hokusai's "Wave" flashed on and off in the window. The alley beyond was in shadow. You could hear the whoosh of the subway trains above the New Age muzak and the murmur of conversation. I wondered whether the sun had already set in the world above. "You're thinking dainty little geishas, tea ceremonies, samurai swords ... cute gadgets ... crowds. And you're on Hokkaido, which isn't really Japan at all, which looks more like Idaho in January, where the cities are new and the people are searching for new souls ..."

"You sound like that sculptor sometimes, Esmeralda."

"Oh, Aki. Did you fuck him yet, honey? He's a good lay."

"I'm not easy," I said testily. Actually, in a way, I was a virgin.

Oh God, I remembered the two of us in the cavern, I remembered the eyes of Molly Danzig, I remembered how he'd stared straight into my eyes, as though he were stalking me. A hairy beast of a man. Lumbering. A grizzly bear tracking me through the snow.

"Marie? Are you all right?" She sipped her coffee. "They don't give refills either—five bucks and no fucking refill." She drained it. "But you know, you should get to know him. You know how hard it is for a red-blooded American girl to get laid here? These people don't even know you're there—oh, they're polite and all, but they know we're not human. Blacks, Indians, whites, Ainu, we all look alike to them . . . we *all* niggers together. Besides, everyone here *knows* that all Americans have AIDS."

"AIDS?" I said.

"Stick around here, hon, and you'll know how a Haitian feels back home. Hey, I screwed Mayuzumi once— but I might as well have been one of those inflatable dolls." She laughed, a bit too loudly. A schoolgirl at the next table tittered and covered her mouth with her hand. "Molly Danzig now . . . he liked her a lot . . . actually he was paying her rent, you know. He liked to have her around whenever he needed to indulge his secret vice . . . I guess he thought it was kind of like bestiality."

"Molly was—"

"Shit, darlin', we all whores, one way or another!" she added. I felt I was being backed into a corner.

"Aki frightens me."

"Don't he! But he's the only man in this whole godforsaken country who has the common decency not to roll over and fall asleep right after they come."

The neon wave flashed on and off. Suddenly *he* was there. In the window. The blue-and-pink light playing over his animal features. "It's him!" I whispered.

Aki's eyes sparkled. He had his sketch pad. His hand was constantly moving in tiny meticulous strokes.

"What does he want?" I said. "Let's get out of here before—"

"What do you mean, hon? I told him to meet us here." Aki was closing his sketch pad and moving into the coffee shop. A waitress hopped to attention and bowed and rapped out a ceremonial greeting like a robot. His gaze had not once left my face.

"But—he *knew* her, don't you see? He knows you—he knows me—and she's *dead* and one of the three goddesses in his sculpture has her face . . . and the other two are blank . . ."

Esmeralda laughed. It was the first time I had ever voiced this suspicion . . . or even admitted to myself that I *had* a suspicion. I realized how preposterous it must sound.

I felt ashamed. I looked away. Stared into the brown circle of my coffee cup as though I could hypnotize myself into the phantom zone. I could hear his footsteps, though. Careful, stalking footsteps.

He stood above me. I could feel his breath. It smelled of honey and cigarettes. He said, "I understand, Marie. It's spooky there in the moonlight. You are in the middle of a city of a million people, yet inside my snow pavilion you are also inside my art, a sculpted creation. It's frightening." He touched my neck. Its warmth shot through me. I tingled.

"It was nothing to do with you," I found myself saying. "It's something else—out of my past—that I thought I'd forgotten."

"Ah," he said. Instead of moving his hand, he began to caress my neck in a slow, circular motion. I had a momentary vision of him snapping off my head. I wanted to panic but instead I found myself relaxing under his gentle pressure . . . sinking into a well of dark eroticism . . . I was trembling all over.

"Culture tonight!" Aki said. "A special performance of a new *bunraku* play, *Sarome-sama*, put on by the Mayuzumi foundation for the edification of the . . . foreign dignitaries."

"*Bunraku?*" The last thing I wanted was to go to a puppet show with him and Esmeralda. I had heard of *bunraku* in my Japanese culture class at Berkeley—it was all yodeling and twanging and wooden figures in expensive costumes strutting across the stage with excruciating elegance.

But she wouldn't hear of it. "Darlin', *everyone* will be there. And this is a really *weird* new show . . . it's the traditional puppet theater, sure, but the script's adapted from Oscar Wilde's *Salome*—translated into a medieval Japanese setting—oh, honey, you'll never see anything like it."

"But my clothes—" I said. I felt like a puppet myself.

"And what," she said, putting her hands on her hips, "are credit cards for, girl?"

Weird did not begin to describe the performance we witnessed at the Bunka Kaikan cultural center. The weirdness began with the opening speeches, one by Dr. Mayuzumi, the other by a cultural attaché of the German Embassy, which belabored endlessly the concept of cultural syncretism and the union of East and West. What more fitting place than Hokkaido, an island so rich in cross-cultural resonances, whose population was in equal parts influenced by the primitive culture of the enigmatic Ainu, by Japan, by Russia, and—in this modern world—by—ah—the "Makudonarudo Hambaga" chain . . .

Polite laughter; I had a vision of Ronald McDonald prancing around with a samurai sword.

I thought the preamble would end soon; it turned out to be interminable. But they had promised a vast buffet afterwards at the expense of the Mayuzumi Foundation. I saw Mayuzumi himself, sitting alone in a box on the upper tier, like royalty. Esmeralda and I were near the front, next to the aisle, with Aki between us. We were both wearing Hanae Mori gowns that we'd splurged on at the underground arcade.

The lights dimmed. The twang of a *shamisen* rent the air; then a spotlight illumined an ancient man in black who narrated, chanted, and uttered all the characters' lines in a wheezing singsong. We were in for cultural syncretism indeed; the set—Herod's palace in Judaea—had been transformed into a seventeenth-century Japanese castle, King Herod and his manipulative wife into a shogun and a geisha, and Salome into a princess with hair down to the floor. John the Baptist, for whom, in Oscar Wilde's revisionist text, Salome was to conceive an illicit and finally necrophiliac passion, was a Jesuit missionary. The centerpiece of the stage was the massive cistern in which John lay imprisoned. It was such a fascinating interpretation that it was hard to remember that I was sitting next to a man whom I suspected of murder.

In *bunraku*, the puppeteers are dressed in black and make no attempt to conceal themselves as they operate their characters. There were three operators to each of the principals. It took only minutes for the puppeteers to fade into the background . . . it made you think there *was* something to this ninja art of invisibility. The characters flitted about the stage, their eyelids fluttering, craning their necks and arching the palms of their hands, shrieking in paroxysms of emotion.

An American audience wouldn't be this silent, I thought.

The eerie rhythms entranced me. The rasp of the *shamisen*, the shrill, sustained wailing of the flute, the hollow *tock-tock-tock* of the woodblock did not meld into a soothing, homophonous texture as in Western music. Each sound was an individual strand, stubbornly dissonant. The narrator sang, or sometimes spoke in a lisping falsetto. In one scene, as Salome, his voice crescendoed to a passionate shriek that seemed the very essence of a woman's desire, a woman's frustration. He knows me, I thought . . . he has seen me running from my father, bursting with terror and love. I could hardly believe that a man could portray such feelings. At the back of the auditorium, aficionados burst into uproarious cheering. From the context I guessed it was the moment when Salome demands to kiss John's mouth and he rebuffs her, and idea of demanding his severed head first germinates in her mind . . . for the Salome puppet threw herself across the floor of the stage, the three operators manipulating wildly as she flailed about in savage mimicry of a woman's despair.

Jesus, I thought. I've been there.

I looked at Aki and found that he was looking behind us, up at Mayuzumi's box. As applause continued, Mayuzumi made a little gesture with his right index finger. Aki whispered in Esmeralda's ear. She said, "Gotta go, darlin'—be right back." The two of them slipped into the aisle.

Was there some kinky triangle ménage between them? I could see Aki and Esmeralda in leather and Mayuzumi all tied up—the slave master playing at being the slave . . . Esmeralda wasn't inhibited like me. Maybe they had become so aroused they'd slipped away to one of those notorious coffee shops, the ones with the private booths.

I didn't want to think about it too much, and after a while I became thoroughly engrossed in the play. I couldn't follow the Japanese—it was all archaic—but I knew the original play, and the whole thing was in such a slow-motion style that you had plenty of time to figure things out.

There was the dance of the seven veils—not the Moroccan restaurant variety, but a sinuous ballet accompanied by drum and flute, and a faster section with jerky movements of the head and eyebrows and the arms obscenely caressing the air . . . the seven veils were seven bridal kimonos of embroidered brocade . . . the demand for the saint's severed head with which to satiate Sarome-sama's lust . . . the executioner, his katana glittering in the arclight, descending into the cistern . . . I gulped . . . how could they be wood and cloth when I could feel their naked emotions tearing loose from them? A drum began to pound, step by pounding step as the headsman disappeared into the oubliette.

The drums crescendoed . . . the flute shrilled . . . the shamisen snarled . . . I heard screaming. It was my own.

A head was sailing out of the cistern, shooting up toward the stage flies . . . a human head . . . Esmeralda's head.

For a split second I saw her torso pop from the cistern. Blood came spurting up. The puppets' kimonos were soaking. The torso thrashed and sprayed the front seats with blood. The claque began to applaud.

O Jesus Jesus it's real—

The head thudded onto the stage. Its lifeless eyes stared up into mine. I was the only one screaming. Wildly I looked about me. People turned away from me. It was as if I were somehow to blame because I had screamed. An announcement started coming over a loudspeaker. There was no panic. The audience was filing slowly out by row number, moving with purposeful precision, like ants. No panic, no shrieks, no nervous laughter. It was numbing. Jesus, I thought, they're aliens, they're incapable of feeling anything. Only the foreign guests seemed distraught. They stood in little huddles, blocking the traffic as the rest of them politely oozed around them. The stagehands were scurrying across the stage, moving props about. The Salome puppet flopped against the castle walls with its doll-neck wrung into an impossible angle.

I stared up at Mayuzumi's box. Mayuzumi was gone.

Esmeralda's head was gone. They were mopping up

the blood. I could hear a police siren in the distance.

Then, up the center aisle, framed in the doorway between two columns of departing theatergoers, I saw Aki Ishii appear as if in a puff of smoke.

Sketching.

Sketching *me*.

Jesus Christ—maybe he'd lured her away to kill her! I couldn't control my rage. I started elbowing my way toward him. The audience backed away. Oh yes. We *gaijin* all have AIDS. Aki backed slowly toward the theater entrance. There was a shopping bag on his arm. The doors were flung wide and the snow was streaming down behind him and I was shivering in my Hanae Mori designer dress that wasn't designed for snow or serial killers.

He backed into the street. The crowd parted. Men with stretchers trotted into the theater and a police siren screeched. I started to pummel him with my fists.

"Am I next?" I screamed. "Is that it? Are you sucking out our souls one by one to feed your art that's going to turn to mush by Friday?"

He held his hands up. "It's not like that at all," he said.

The wind howled. I was hysterical by now. Fuck these people and their propriety. I shouted at a passing policeman, "Here's your goddamn sex murderer!" He ignored me. "That shopping bag! The head's in the shopping bag!" I tried to wrest it from him. I could feel something squishy inside it. There was blood on everything.

"How could you be so wrong?" Aki said. "How could you fail to understand me? I told you the truth. It's not me—it's—it's—" His eyes glowed. That odor of honey and tobacco again . . . startled, I remembered where I'd smelled it before . . . on my grandfather's breath. I kept on hitting him with my fists but my blows were weak, dampened by snow and by my own bewilderment.

THE PAVILION OF FROZEN WOMEN 295

You've got no right, I was thinking, no right to bring me those bad dreams . . . no right to remind me . . .

He grabbed my wrists. I struggled. His sketch pad flew into the snow. The wind flipped the pages and I saw face after face . . . beautiful women . . . beautiful and desolate . . . my own face. "My art," Aki said. There was despair in his voice. "You knocked my art out of my—" He let go abruptly. Scurried after the sketch pad, his black duster flailing in the wind like a Dracula cape. He found it at last. He cried to me across the shrieking wind: "We're both bear people. You should have understood." And he ran off into the darkness. He vanished almost instantly, like one of those puppeteers with their ninja arts.

It was only then that I realized that my dress was dripping with blood. It was caking against my arms, my neck. The wind and the sirens were screaming all at once.

No one's going to ignore *this* killing, I thought. A consular officer . . . a public place . . . a well-known artist hanging around near the scene of both crimes . . .

But as I watched the audience leaving in orderly rows, as I watched the policemen solemnly discoursing in hushed tones, I realized that they might well ignore what had happened.

I was going to have to go to someone important. Someone powerful. Power was all these people understood.

3

*"Das Unbeschreibliche,
Hier ist's getan . . ."*
     Faust

Midnight and the snow went on piling. I walked. Snow smeared against the blood on my clothes. I walked. I had some notion of finding my way back to the *ryokan*, making a phone call to the Tokyo office, maybe even to

Oakland. I could barely see where I was going.

Bear people . . .

No one in the streets. The wind whistled. Sushi pennants flapped against restaurant entrances. I breathed bitter liquid cold. At last I saw headlights . . . a taxi.

By two in the morning I was outside the Mayuzumi estate. There were wrought-iron gates. The gates had been left open and the driveway had been recently shoveled. He let me off in front of the mansion.

A servant woman let me in, rubbing her eyes, showed me where to leave my shoes, and fetched clean slippers. She swabbed at my bloodstains with a hot towel. Then she handed me a clean *yukata* and watched while I tried to slip it on over my ruined gown.

It was clear that I—or someone—was expected. Perhaps there was a local geisha club that made house calls.

"*Mayuzumi-san wa doko—?*" I began.

"*Ano . . . o-furo ni desu.*"

She led me up the steps to the tatami-covered foyer. She slid aside a *shoji* screen, then another and another. We walked down a succession of corridors—I walked, rather, and the maid shuffled, with tiny muffled steps, pausing here to fuss with a flower arrangement, there to incline her head toward a statue of the Amida Buddha. Beyond the Buddha image was a screen of lacquered wood on which were painted erotic designs. She yanked the screen aside and then I was face-to-face with Dr. Mayuzumi . . . naked, sitting in a giant bath, being methodically massaged by a young girl who sang as she kneaded.

He was a huge man. He was, I could see now, remarkably hirsute, like Aki Ishii; his eyes were beady and set closely together; he squinted when he looked at me, like a bear eyeing a beehive.

Behind Dr. Mayuzumi, the shoji screens had been drawn aside. The bathroom overlooked the rock garden where Molly's body had been. Snow gusted behind him and clouds of steam tendriled between us.

"Ah," he said, "Marie Wounded Bird, is it not? The reporter. I had thought we might meet in less ... informal surroundings, but I am glad you are here. Tomichan! Food for our guest! You will join me for a light supper," he said to me. It was an order.

"You have to help me, Dr. Mayuzumi," I said. "I know who the killer is."

He raised an eyebrow. With a gesture, he indicated that I should join him in the bath. I knew that the Japanese do not find mixed bathing lewd, but I had never done it before; I balked. Two maids came and began to disrobe me. They were politely insistent, and the hot water seemed more and more enticing, and I found myself being scrubbed with pumice stone and led down the tiled steps ... the water was so hot it hurt to move. I let it soak into my pores. I watched the snowflakes dance around the stone lantern in the cloister at the edge of the rock garden.

"No one will do anything," I said. "But there's a pattern. The victims are white and black ... people who don't belong to the Yamato race ... maybe that's why none of you people think it's important. The victims are all subhuman ... like me ... and I think I'm next, don't you see? The three goddesses ... the Judgment of Paris ... and the killer is subhuman too ... an Ainu."

"What are you trying to say?" Mayuzumi said. "You would not be attempting to pin the blame on Aki Ishii, the grand master of snow sculpting?"

I gasped. "You knew all along. And you knew that I would come here."

Just as the heat was becoming unbearable, one of the serving maids fetched a basket of snow from outside. She knelt down at the edge of the bath and began to sprinkle it over my face, my neck. I shuddered with agony and delight. Another maid held out a lacquerware tray in front of me and began to feed me with chopsticks.

It was a lobster salad—that is, the lobster was still alive, its spine broken, the meat scooped out of its tail, diced with cucumbers and a delicate *shoyu* and vinegar dressing, and replaced in the splayed tail-shell with such artistry that the lobster continued to wriggle, its claws clattering feebly against the porcelain, its antennae writhing, its stalk-eyes glaring. I had already started to chew the first mouthful before I saw that my food was not quite dead. But it was too delicious to stop. And knowing I was draining the creature's life force only heightened the frisson. "I'm sorry," I whispered.

"Ah," Dr. Mayuzumi said, "you're apologizing to the lobster for—"

"Taking its life," I said. Wasn't that what Aki had said about the shrimp?

"How well you understand us." I was conscious of a terrible sadness in him. There was more to him that just being a millionaire with a finger in every pie. "I, too, am sorry, Marie Wounded Bird." He ordered the maid to remove the lacquer trays. "Yet you did not come to dine, but to accuse."

"Yes."

"You have proof, I hope; a man of Mr. Ishii's standing is not indicted lightly. His reputation . . . indeed, the reputation of the Snow Festival itself . . . would be at stake. You can understand why I sought to discourage the press from . . . ah . . . untimely revelations."

"But he's *killing* people!" I said.

"Mr. Ishii is a great artist. He is very precious to us. His foibles—"

I recoiled. "How can you—"

"In the grand scheme, in the great circle of birth and rebirth, what can a few lives matter?" he said. "But Mr. Ishii's art . . . does matter. And now you are here, blowing across our fragile world like *kamikaze*, the wind of the gods, irresistible and unstoppable. You would melt us down, just as the spring sun will soon melt the exquisite snow sculptures which 1.6 million tourists are about to see."

I couldn't believe this. It was the most familiar line of bullshit in the world. I was soaking in 110°, in the nude, eating live animals and listening to the Mayor of Amity shtick right out of *Jaws I*. My own life was on the line, for God's sake! I remembered Aki's eyes . . . the way he had run his fingers along the nape of my neck . . . his long dark hair flecked with snow . . . the quiet intensity with which he spoke of beauty and transience and voiced his resentment of the conquering Japanese. Could he really be one of those Henry Lee Lucas types? I knew he had had sex with Molly and Esmeralda. I knew he had been tracking me. Sketching. Sketching. Smelling of tobacco and honey, like my grandfather.

God I wanted him and I hated myself for wanting him. For a moment, standing in the snow amid his creation, listening to him—Jesus, I think I *loved* him.

"Goddammit, I can prove it," I said. "I'll show you fucking body parts. I'll show you eyeballs buried in snow and skeletons under the ice."

I was doomed to betray him.

"All right," said Dr. Mayuzumi. "I feared it would come to this."

The limousine moved rapidly toward downtown Sapporo. We sat in the backseat each hunched into an opposite corner. It was still snowing. We didn't speak until we were within a few blocks of Odori Park.

At last, Dr. Mayuzumi said, "Why?"

I said, "I don't know, really, Dr. Mayuzumi. Maybe he's sending a message to the Japanese people . . . about discrimination, about the way you treat minorities." I didn't want to think of Aki just as an ordinary mad slasher. We had too much in common for that. But there was just too much evidence linking him to Molly and Esmeralda . . . and me. Four minorities. Lepers in a land that prized homogeneity above all things. I had a desperate need to see the killings as some political act . . . it might not justify them, but I could understand such killings. Like the Battle of Little Big Horn . . . like the second siege at Wounded Knee. "Politics," I said bitterly.

"Perhaps." He did not look into my eyes.

The chauffeur parked at the edge of the park.

We began walking toward the "Judgment of Paris" tableau. Dr. Mayuzumi strode swiftly through the slush, his breath clouding about his face. I struggled to keep up. I became angrier as we walked. I had come to see him with information and now it seemed he had known all along, that his coming with me now was merely the working out of some preordained drama.

The full moon lengthened our shadows. Even the snow-shoveling workmen were gone; the empty trucks were parked in neat rows along the Odori.

Dr. Mayuzumi strode past the snow Sphinx and the Pyramids of Gizeh; I trudged after him, awkward in the short coat that one of the servants had lent me. I was determined not to let him take the lead. I brushed by him. I was furious now. It seemed that this whole town had been built on lies. Snow gusted and flurried. Ice-shards lanced my face. I walked. Snow metropolises rose and fell around me. I didn't look at them. I tried to quell the cold with sheer anger.

We passed the columns of the Temple of Poseidon at Sounion, the icy steps of a Babylonian ziggurat, a Mexican pyramid atop which sat a gargoyle god ripping the heart out of a hapless child. Moonlight fringed the ice with spectral colors. Had the buildings grown taller somehow? Were the sculptures pressing in, narrowing the pathway, threatening to crash down over me? A skull-shaped mountain grinned down. Trick of the light, I told myself. I stared ahead. My shoes were waterlogged.

At length we came to Mt. Ida. I marched uphill. They

could fix the footprints later. Dr. Mayuzumi followed. We crossed the terrace with its classical friezes, its nymphs and shepherds gesturing with Poussin-like languor.

In a moment we stood inside Ishii's secret kingdom, the cave that the audience could not see. The mirror of mirrored mirrors.

There had been more tunneling. The walls were lit by reflected moonlight and the cave seemed to stretch forever into blackness, though I knew it was an illusion. Like Wile E. Coyote, we are easily fooled by misdirecting signposts . . . a highway median that leads to the edge of a cliff . . . a tunnel painted onto the side of a sandstone mountain. It seemed we stood at the entry to an infinite labyrinth.

Dr. Mayuzumi took out a flashlight and shined it on the interior of the cave.

There were the three statues. Molly Danzig stood with her arms outstretched. It was her—but dead she was more beautiful somehow, more perfect . . . the statue of Athena had the face of Esmeralda O'Neil. She glowered; she was anger personified. It was just as I had imagined. The third goddess had no face yet . . . and neither did the boy Paris who was to choose between them.

I could be beautiful too, I thought. Cold and beautiful. I was tempted. I told myself: I hate the cold. I hate my childhood. That's why I went away to California.

Dr. Mayuzumi said, "Look at their eyes . . . as though they were still alive . . . look at them."

Molly's eyes: a glint of blue in the gloom. They stared straight into mine. Esmeralda's looked out beyond the entrance. The Athena statue held a spear and a gorgon-faced shield. God, they were beautiful. But I knew the deadly secret of their verisimilitude.

"How long can the cold preserve a human organ, an eye, for example?" I said. "Doesn't this snow-clad beauty hide death? Tell me there are no human bones beneath . . ."

"You would destroy this masterwork?"

It was too late. Before he could stop me I had plunged my fingers into Molly's face. I wanted to pull the jellied eyeballs out of the skull, to thrust them in Dr. Mayuzumi's face.

The face caved in. There was nothing in my fists but snow, flaking, crumbling, melting against the warmth of my hands. And then, when the snow had melted, two globes of glass and plastic. Two marbles.

I looked at Dr. Mayuzumi. His look of indignation turned to mocking laughter. All my resentment exploded inside me. I smashed my fists against the statues of my two friends. Snow drenched me. The statues shattered. There were no bones beneath, no squishy organs. Only snow. Tears came to my eyes and melted the snow that had clung to my cheeks.

"A *gaijin* philistine with a stupid theory," said Mayuzumi.

I beat my arms against the empty snow, I buried myself elbow deep. I wept. I had understood nothing at all. The marbles slipped from my fingers and skated over a stretch of ice.

I felt Dr. Mayuzumi's hand on my shoulder. He pulled me from the slush. There was so much sadness in him. "And I thought you understood us . . ."

He gripped me and would not let go. His hands held no comfort. His fingernails dug into my flesh . . . like claws.

"I thought you understood us!" he rasped. His teeth glinted in reflected moonlight . . . glistened with drool . . . his eyes narrowed . . . his mouth smelled of honey and tobacco.

I thought you understood us . . . what did that mean?

And all at once I knew. When he had greeted me in the bath, when I mumbled *I'm sorry* at the writhing

THE PAVILION OF FROZEN WOMEN

lobster, had he not said *How well you understand us?* I had completely missed it before... "You're an Ainu too, one who's been able to pass for a Yamato," I said. "You've blended with the Japanese... you've climbed up to a position of power by hiding from yourself... and it's driven you mad!"

"I'm sorry... oh, I'm sorry," he said. His voice was barely human. Still he would not let go. In the dark I could not see his face.

"Why are you apologizing?" I said softly.

"I need your soul."

Then I realized that he was going to kill me.

The flashlight illuminated him for a moment. His face was caving in on itself. Dark hair was sprouting up through the skin. I felt bristles push up from his palms and prick my shoulders. I was bleeding. I struggled. His nose was collapsing into a snout...

"Bear people!" I whispered.

He could not speak. Only an animal growl escaped his throat. He had become my father. I was caught inside the nightmare that had haunted me since I was *winchin-chala*. I kicked and screamed. He roared. As his body wrenched into a new shape, I slipped from his grasp. The cavern shook and rumbled. Snow crashed over the entrance. I could hear more snow piling up. The cave was contracting like a womb. We were sealed in. The whine of the wind subsided.

The flashlight slid across the snow. I dived after it. I waved it in the air like a light saber. Its beam was the only illumination. It moved across the eyes... the teeth ... I could smell the fetid breath of a carnivore. I was choking on it. "What are you?" I screamed.

He roared and the walls shook and I knew he no longer had the power of human speech. He began to lumber toward me. There was no way to escape. Except by stepping backwards... backwards into the optical illusion that suggested caves within caves, worlds within worlds...

I backed into the wall. The wall pulsated. It seemed alive. The very snow was living, breathing. The wall turned into a fine mist like Alice's mirror... I could hear the tempest raging, but it was infinitely far away.

I was at the edge of an icy incline that extended downward to darkness.

The bear-creature that had been Dr. Mayuzumi fell down on all fours. He pounced. I tripped over something ... a plastic bag... its contents spilled onto my face. In the torchlight I saw that it was Esmeralda's head. The severed trachea snaked into the snow. There were no eyes. I bit down on human hair. I retched. There was blood in my throat. The bear-creature reared up. I screamed, and then I was rolling down the slope, downward, downward—

And then I was in a huge cavern running away from the were-bear my father with his rancid breath and the wind whistling through the broken windowpane and—

Darkness. I paused. Strained to listen. The bear paused, too. I could hear him breathing, a savage purr deep as the threshold of human hearing, making the very air vibrate.

I swung the flashlight in an arc and saw—

The fangs, the knife-sharp claws poised to strike and—

There was music. The dull thud of a drum. The shriek of the bamboo flute and the twang of the *shamisen*, and—

The bear sprang! The claws ripped my cheeks. I was choking on my own blood. I fell and fell and fell and my mouth was stopped with snow and I was numb all over from the cold and I was sliding down an embankment with the bear toying with me like a cat with a mouse and I screamed over and over, screamed and tasted blood and snow and—

I heard a voice: *Be still, my son.* The voice of my grandfather.

I was slipping away from the bear's grasp.

Into a circle of cold blue light.

In the circle stood Aki Ishii. He was naked. His body was completely covered in tattoos: strange concentric designs like Neolithic pottery. His long black hair streamed in a wind that seemed to emanate from his lips and circle around him; I felt no wind. Smoke rose from a brazier, fragrant with tobacco and honey.

"*Tunkashila* . . ." I murmured. I crawled toward him. Clutched at his feet in supplication.

The bear reared up at the edge of the circle. In the pale light I saw him whole for the first time. His face still betrayed something of Mayuzumi; his body still contained the portly outline of the magnate; but his eyes burned with that pure unconscionable anger that comes only in dreams.

"Be still," said Aki Ishii. "You may not enter the circle. It is I who am the shaman of the bear people. You cannot gain true power by taking men's souls; you must give in equal measure of your own."

And then I saw, reflected in the wall of ice behind us, miragelike images of Molly Danzig and Esmeralda O'Neil. They were half human, half cave painting. They too were naked and covered with tattoos. They had become Ainu, but I saw that they were also *my* people . . . they were also the Greek goddesses . . . Molly, who had fled from her home and herself and sought solace in the arms of strangers, had been incarnated as domesticity itself; Esmeralda, whose diplomatic career belied her bellicose nature, had become the goddess of war. What was I then? There was only one goddess left: the goddess of love.

But I was incapable of love, because of what my father

had done. I hated him, but he was the only man I had ever loved.

Three musical instruments materialized in the smoke of the incense burner. Molly plucked the *shamisen* of domestic tranquility out of the air; Esmeralda seized the war drum. One instrument remained: the phallic bamboo flute of desire. I took it and held it to my lips. Of its own accord it began to play, a melody of haunting and erotic sweetness. And the drum pounded and the *shamisen* sounded . . . three private musics that could not blend . . . until we faced the bear together.

"My son," said Aki Ishii softly, "you must now reap the fruits of your own rage."

The bear exploded. His head split down the middle and the mingled brains and blood gushed up like lava from a volcano. His belly burst open and his entrails writhed like snakes. The drumbeats were syncopated with the cracking of the bear's spine. Shards of tibia shredded the flesh of his legs. Blood spattered the ceiling. The walls ran red. Blood rained down on us. Each piece of the bear ate away at itself, as though dissolving in acid. The smoke from the brazier turned into a blood-tinged mist. And all the while Aki Ishii stood, immobile, his face a mask of tragedy and regret.

I didn't stop playing until the last rag of blood-drenched fur had been consumed. Small puddles of blood were siphoning into the snow. The images of my dead friends were swirling into the mist that was the honey-tinged breath of Aki Ishii, shaman of the bear people. Only the eyes remained, resting side by side on an altar of snow. Aki nodded. I put down the flute and watched it disappear into the air. I knelt down and picked up the eyes. They were hard as crystal. The cold had marbled them.

"I'm sorry," Aki said. The light was dimming.

"Are you going to kill me?" I whispered, knowing that was what an apology presaged.

"I'm not going to take anything from you that you will not give willingly," said the snow sculptor. He took me by the hand. "The war between the dark and the light is an eternal conflict. Dr. Mayuzumi wanted what I wanted... but his magic is a magic of deceit. He was content with the illusion of power. But for that illusion, he had to feed on real human lives. This is not really the way of bear people."

"The dead women—"

"Yes. I planted a piece of those women into the snow sculptures. We made love. I captured a fragment of their joy and breathed it into the snow. Dr. Mayuzumi devoured them. They were women from three races the Japanese find inferior, but each race had done what the Ainu have not done—they have fought back—the blacks and the reds against the white men, the whites against the Japanese themselves. That was what made him angry. Our people have had their souls stolen from them. By stealing a piece of each of the three women's souls, tearing them violently from their bodies in the moment of death, he sought to give himself a soul. But a soul cannot be wrested from another person; it is a gift."

He took my other hand. And now I saw what it was that I had feared so much. I thought I had locked it up and thrown away the key, but it was still there... my need to be loved, my need to become myself.

"Now," said Aki Ishii to me, "you must free yourself, and me."

I held out the bear's two marble eyes. He took one from me. We each swallowed an eye in a single gulp. It had no taste. It was like communion. And then he kissed me.

We made love as the light faded from the cavern, and when we emerged from the wall of ice, the statues were whole again, and the goddess of love had my face; but the face of Paris was still blank.

4

> *"Das Ewig-weibliche*
> *Zieht uns hinan!"*
> —Faust

It was a beautiful festival. By night, thousands upon thousands of paper lanterns lit the way for the million and a half tourists who poured into the city for the first week of February. The deaths of two foreign women were soon forgotten. Dr. Mayuzumi's bizarre suicide aroused much sympathy when his Ainu origins were revealed; it was only natural that a man in his position would be unable to cope with his own roots.

The death of grand master Ishii was mourned by some; but others agreed that it was only fitting for an artist to die after creating his masterpiece. He was found in the cavern, nude, gazing at the statues of the three goddesses; he had replaced the image of Paris with himself. It was agreed that he had sacrificed his life to achieve some fleeting epiphany comprehensible only to other artists, or, perhaps, other Ainu.

I can't say I understood it at all. I had stood at the brink of some great and timeless truth, but in the end it eluded me.

It was a beautiful festival, but to me it no longer seemed to have meaning. I was there in a plastic city of right-angled boulevards, a city that had robbed the land of its soul; a city that stood over the bones of the Ainu, that mocked the dead with its games of beauty and impermanence. Like Rapid City with its concrete dinosaurs . . . like Deadwood with its mechanical cowboys and Indians battling for 25¢ and all eternity . . . like Mount Rushmore, forever mocking the beauty of our Black Hills by its beatification of our conquerors.

You can't understand about being oppressed unless

you're born with it. It is something you have to carry around all the time, like soiled underwear that's been soldered to your skin.

I know now that I'm not one of you. You own my body, but my soul belongs to the mountains, to the air, to the streams, the trees, the snow.

I think I will go back to Pine Ridge one day. Perhaps my grandfather will teach me, before he dies, the language of the bears.

I think I will even see my father. Perhaps I can be the angel of his redemption, as I think I was for Aki Ishii.

Perhaps I will even forgive him.

Avon Books presents your worst nightmares—

...haunted houses

ADDISON HOUSE   75587-4/$4.50 US/$5.95 Can
Clare McNally

THE ARCHITECTURE OF FEAR
                      70553-2/$3.95 US/$4.95 Can
edited by Kathryn Cramer & Peter D. Pautz

...unspeakable evil

HAUNTING WOMEN   89881-0/$3.95 US/$4.95 Can
edited by Alan Ryan

TROPICAL CHILLS   75500-9/$3.95 US/$4.95 Can
edited by Tim Sullivan

...blood lust

THE HUNGER   70441-2/$4.50 US/$5.95 Can
THE WOLFEN   70440-4/$4.50 US/$5.95 Can
Whitley Strieber

Buy these books at your local bookstore or use this coupon for ordering:

Mail to: Avon Books, Dept BP, Box 767, Rte 2, Dresden, TN 38225
Please send me the book(s) I have checked above.
☐ My check or money order—no cash or CODs please—for $_____ is enclosed
(please add $1.00 to cover postage and handling for each book ordered to a maximum of three dollars—Canadian residents add 7% GST).
☐ Charge my VISA/MC Acct# _____ Exp Date _____
Phone No _____ I am ordering a minimum of two books (please add postage and handling charge of $2.00 plus 50 cents per title after the first two books to a maximum of six dollars—Canadian residents add 7% GST). For faster service, call 1-800-762-0779. Residents of Tennessee, please call 1-800-633-1607. Prices and numbers are subject to change without notice. Please allow six to eight weeks for delivery.

Name _____
Address _____
City _____ State/Zip _____

WHITLEY STRIEBER

The world will never be the same...
TRANSFORMATION
70535-4/$4.95 US/$5.95 Can

THE #1 BESTSELLER
COMMUNION
70388-2/$4.95 US/$5.95 Can

A NOVEL OF TERROR BEYOND YOUR IMAGINING
THE WOLFEN
70440-4/$4.50 US/$5.95 Can

THE ULTIMATE NOVEL OF EROTIC HORROR
THE HUNGER
70441-2/$4.50 US/$5.95 Can

Buy these books at your local bookstore or use this coupon for ordering:

Mail to: Avon Books, Dept BP, Box 767, Rte 2, Dresden, TN 38225
Please send me the book(s) I have checked above.
☐ My check or money order—no cash or CODs please—for $_____ is enclosed (please add $1.00 to cover postage and handling for each book ordered to a maximum of three dollars—Canadian residents add 7% GST).
☐ Charge my VISA/MC Acct# _____ Exp Date _____
Phone No _____ I am ordering a minimum of two books (please add postage and handling charge of $2.00 plus 50 cents per title after the first two books to a maximum of six dollars—Canadian residents add 7% GST). For faster service, call 1-800-762-0779. Residents of Tennessee, please call 1-800-633-1607. Prices and numbers are subject to change without notice. Please allow six to eight weeks for delivery.

Name _____
Address _____
City _____ State/Zip _____

STR 0589